CW00689174

Coup de Grâce

A novel by

PAUL L. CENTENO

Copyright © 2022 by Paul L. Centeno
All rights reserved
Indies United Publishing, LLC

This is a work of fiction. All characters, regions and events were created by the author's imagination. Any similarity to something outside of this novel is merely coincidental.

Illustrations by Paul Pederson
Interior Book Design by TeaBerryCreative.com

ISBN: 978-1-64456-505-6 (Hardback)
ISBN: 978-1-64456-506-3 (Paperback)
ISBN: 978-1-64456-507-0 (MOBI)
ISBN: 978-1-64456-508-7 (ePub)
Library of Congress Control Number: 2022942423

P.O. BOX 3071 • QUINCY, IL 62305-3071

For my family and all those who
have encouraged me to never give up
and make my dreams a reality.

Mystwal

Enbertum

Cogbarrow

Pavebaro

Quradale

Vel-Qatal

Vinestead

Bogdar

Sunken
of Kanis

Callopeak

Canyons of Rezekus

Faraheyde

Icdarus

GATTERSTANZ
TAYLE
DUNES OF YUL'FAQUAS
WELKIN
RENENGARDE
MOUNT WINDOM
Tomb of
Ma'vak Zaar
JYU'BAKYI
KAAL'AL
MULA'NANDIS
N

CHRONICLE I:

Industrial Era

PROLOGUE

Aether Awakening

In the beginning was the wordless. Formlessness defied nothingness. The shapeless took form akin to magic, heralding an essence that became known as the aether. Empty of birth and death, the incorporeal aether emerged beyond time unbound. Intangible like air, it flowed as a stream of consciousness through the amorphous cosmos. Like a plethora of decoctions, tinctures, and metals fusing into a divine elixir, the infinite constituents gave way to an elemental paradigm for immortality. The aether's transmigration reformed into an unfathomable entity, defying ephemerality. The wordless became the word. Formlessness took form. No different from a black hole that arises and consumes all in its path, the parasitical amalgamation manifested to devour life itself.

—Alchemic Origins 48:17

CHAPTER ONE

Transfusion Machine

I
The Optometrist

A burning sensation crackled in Kaimo de Morté's chest. Ill at ease from an eerie vibration, he raised his grimy face and, through the refracting lenses of his spyglass, fixed on a mysterious happening. An unnatural phenomenon stirred above, swathed in steam and drifting in the haze over his ramshackle town. Anxiety roiled. What would manifest itself next? An inkling of what was to come added restlessness to his apprehension.

Shrouded in smog, the spectacle lingered above the world of Zykard. But the strange occurrence was not a natural element. Rather, hidden within the murk was a mechanical invention that certain denizens would consider divine. The majestic heavens shifted, as if a piece of the polluted sky had detached and moved—no doubt an optical illusion, thought Kaimo, while he adjusted the focus knob of his monocular. Most onlookers, however, did not have access to a telescope to see its details. Limited to the naked eye, all but Kaimo tended to their business, oblivious.

As a miner, Kaimo lived and worked in the dusty backwater town of Icdarus, nestled in the southernmost mountains of Quradale. Renowned for its abundance of mineral deposits, the empire, embroiled in a civil war, demanded a surplus of supplies be shipped out every week to arm its steamships and automatons against insurgents. A poor but otherwise accomplished young man in optics and crafting lenses, Kaimo remained stranded in Icdarus, dreaming of a medical residency in a grand city that would lead him to becoming an optical surgeon for veterans.

"De Morté!" a man dressed in a three-piece suit and bowler hat yelled, his raspy voice evincing irritation. "We don't offer coffee breaks here. Get back to work!"

"My apologies, Lord Beaumont," Kaimo said.

Grabbing his tool, he sprinted down a grit path. Courtesy of the twin suns, the canyon's mellow glow radiated. Precious gemstones, waiting to be unearthed, sparkled throughout the excavation site. All the miners, however, focused on deposits of kogal—a rare, amorphous crystalline granite capable of immense alchemical power.

Entering an illuminated cavern with artificial lights strung along the serrated ceiling, the grimy miner returned to his mandated position. His colleagues beside him hacked the sharp walls in between grunts and groans, chiseling into the mountain in search of kogal or any valuable metals, rocks, and jewels.

"I said to find out what's causing those bloody tremors, not travel halfway across the world," said one of the older miners, perspiration glistening on his wrinkled forehead. "Where in tarnation did you go off to?"

Kaimo blinked, awkwardness plastered on his face. "There's no other way to put it, but, truth be told, I saw Welkin."

Miners within earshot scoffed at his pronouncement.

The old man, however, nearly lost his footing. "You saw the emperor's abode with your own eyes?"

"I didn't *literally* see it," he replied, lifting his pick-axe and striking the jagged wall. "It was engulfed in smog and steam, camouflaged in the clouds. But it was there, Liam. I know it. Strange, though. No one bothered to look. It's as if they couldn't see it."

"Says the half-assed doctor who doesn't even have a clinic," said a muscular worker, striking the same knobby wall.

"We *all* struggle with poverty here," Kaimo retorted, internally battling his shame. It was difficult enough for him to earn respect from a community that regarded an optometrist as a pseudo doctor, much like a psychologist, but the true crux was his lack of financial stability to open an optical shop. "At least I have aspirations instead of wasting my life. One of these days, I'll earn enough qauras to open an optometric emporium."

The brawny miner tossed him a look of scorn. "With *this* job? You were probably better off working in one of those lens tower thingamajigs."

"I didn't become a doctor to send optical telegraphs at a semaphore pylon," Kaimo protested, an expression of disdain etched on his face. "Besides, the imperium monopolizes the business and I'll have no part in politics or war."

"The qauras we get here is a joke," a middle-aged miner said. "Face it, kid, you're gonna wear those filthy rags for the rest of your life."

Many of the workers laughed at his remark as they continued chiseling into the rocks.

"Cut the doc some slack," Liam put in, wiping beads of sweat off his forehead. "He saw an optical illusion. Simple as that."

"Kaimo's always delusional," said another miner. "It's one thing to see an airship, but a flying city? More so—"

"Enough bantering, you lazy lot!" Lord Beaumont interjected, emerging from behind an ore-filled cart. "No one gets paid to talk. When your shift ends, you can scuttle to the bloody tavern and gossip like a bunch of women 'til you're drunk. Get to work!"

The miners wiped away their smirks, resentment etched on their faces. Kaimo paid no mind to them as he struck granite. He knew what he'd seen; he was not delusional. As for Liam, he squinted at him, suspicion in his jaundiced eyes. Then, like all the others, he focused on the wall in front of him, extracting more resources.

II
Downtown

Once they had finished working for the day, the miners left the excavation site and returned to town. Kaimo, like the others, relied on a steam-powered trolley. Its engine screeched, exhaust fumes spewing from rusty pipes. Holding onto a handrail while leaning out from one of the carriages, he gazed at the sky swollen with charcoal clouds.

The oversized tram passed brick homes constructed of wattle and daub. It reached an outdoor market where old-world boutiques boasted gothic façades with stained-glass windows. Kaimo hopped off the platform and joined the milling crowd. He strolled through the bustling town's broad mix of trades, ranging from antiques at an emporium, potions and herbs at an apothecary, swords at a smithy, to outdoor stalls with vendors selling food.

Kaimo's eyes wandered until he reached a particular stall laden with fruits and vegetables. He gawked at the produce, unintentionally ignoring the blonde vendor who wore a ruffled skirt and buckled spats. The girl waved at him, catching his attention. Pulling out a pouch of coins, he tossed a couple her way.

"The usual?" she asked, catching them.

"Yeah," he said simply. "Thanks, Clara."

Clara Laurent gave him a sharp smile and avoided the mottled produce. "So, how's the new job? Did you get fired yet?"

"Everyone has jokes today," he grumbled. "No. Just yelled at. But better than working with my old man." He watched her pick the ripest fruits and continued, "The war made him a tad loony."

"Don't say that about your father," she said. "Gabriel just works better tinkering with stuff alone, is all."

"He'll never admit that."

"Of course not. He loves you too damn much to say such a thing. Go easy on him." She paused for a moment, wrapping his food in a bag and handing it to him. "I'm glad you're following your heart."

"It's a start. My old man said I'm free to do whatever I want when I'm of age, and that's now. Even though I'm already an optometrist, I want to study medicine. Only need a little more money and I'll take up a residency at Krenanstein."

"Ambitious as always. Just don't go forgetting your heritage."

Kaimo gave her a long look. "Not like I'm royalty. Just the son of a militaristic gunsmith who's gone batty."

She chuckled but stopped short as she noticed a line forming. "You're too idealistic, but to each their own. Now get out of here before someone hears you."

"Have a good night, Clara."

"You do the same," she said, curtsying.

He offered a mock salute and walked away, returning to the main boulevard. A street musician played an accordion nearby. Merchants hollered at passersby while other onlookers smoked in alleyways; a couple of them eyed Kaimo. Farther ahead, a brigade of armored imperial soldiers admired the craftsmanship of the world's newest rifle, forged with a small scope, two gauges, and a blade directly beneath its barrel.

The soldiers' mechanical gas masks always unnerved Kaimo. Unable to see their faces, he considered them empty husks, or clockwork machines, because of the obscure breathing apparatuses, valves, and cogs sculpted on their helmets. As he drew closer, one of them gazed at him. He dared not make eye contact. Avoiding his home's attached workshop, he entered his house from the back instead.

"Freaks," he mumbled to himself.

Kaimo placed his coppola on a coat rack and brushed back his wavy, disheveled hair. He went into the kitchen and put down his bag. An old man with a mechanized arm and prosthetic leg emerged, grunting. He peered through bifocal spectacles, and his coarse face revealed a scraggly, gray beard with discolored teeth.

"There you are," Gabriel said. "I was starting to wonder if you'd got lost in those underground tunnels."

"It's better than making something that takes away my humanity."

"Mind your words, son," the old man barked. "These inventions put a roof over your head and provide food on the table."

"Looks like I'm the one providing now," he said smugly, revealing his bag.

Gabriel scoffed, barely able to contain his sarcasm. "Fruit and vegetables? Sustenance for pets. I understand you're naïve and haven't lost your faith in the gods yet, otherwise you'd be a competent gunsmith like me. But if you think you're a self-made man, then why don't you pack up and leave as your mother did?"

"What the hell is wrong with you? Shouldn't you be outside selling your inhuman crap to those imperialists?"

"My protégée is handling that, thanks to you quitting the family business."

"I have other aspirations. I'll have an optics emporium one day and intend to help people. Not kill them."

"I'm tempted to smack that uncensored, high-and-mighty mouth of yours."

Kaimo took a step forward and raised his face, taunting him. "Go ahead. Do what you're best at."

"I'm a damn war hero, sonny boy. I fought for the empire so we'd have a chance of *real* peace, here and now. In fact, the only reason why you might get a proper education is because of veterans like me. Oh yeah, and it's also thanks to me that you're familiar with optics, given the family business revolves around guns with scopes, *Mr. Optometrist*."

"Guess what? The war hasn't ended. All that killing was for nothing. And now you make guns for soldiers. This business is soaked with blood."

Veins bulging, Gabriel let out a roar as he slapped his son hard.

"I don't have time for your abuse today," Kaimo said, shoving his father out of the way.

"Unappreciative is what you are! An optometrist isn't even a real doctor! You haven't gone to medical school! You're just throwing your life away!"

Ignoring his father, Kaimo rushed upstairs to his room. Closing the door behind him, he locked it and took a deep breath. He removed his filthy clothes and lay on the bed, tears welling in his eyes. His mind was scrambled with countless thoughts plaguing him. He wondered why he was still living in a makeshift town so far from the heart of civilization. Why had his mother abandoned him? Was she dead? Why did she ever put up with his crude, unreasonable father? His life was worth more than that of a gunsmith or miner.

Kaimo had many dreams in life. To him, leaving Icdarus and attending his residency at a university to become an ophthalmologist was at the top of his list. He also desired the life of an adventurer but by no means had enough money to leave, explore the vast world, or establish a medical practice in a great, industrial metropolis.

"I won't give in," he whispered to himself. "I'll prove him wrong."

Battling exhaustion, Kaimo curled up on his rickety bed. His father continued to yell and blurt random insults from downstairs, as if still in conversation with him. Trying hard to be the better person, Kaimo quelled his inner rage and ignored Gabriel. As he lay in silence, he closed his eyes and soon fell asleep.

III
Memoir: Inner Conflict

As usual, I don't know where to start. I'm not much of a writer. I woke in the middle of the night and can't sleep. There's so much on my mind. My father's random insults are expected, but hitting me was unacceptable. I have the right to speak my mind. I'm not fond of conflicts and do not approve of war. There is no sense in it whatsoever.

The empire has many faults. Women are looked down upon for working unless it's selling food or being a waitress. Only men can vote, which has angered a great many people. There's not much of a court system for crime. Most suspects are either shot on sight or sent to prison without a trial whether innocent or not. Yes, these are serious issues but not enough to spark a revolution.

Insurgents are no better than the imperium. Both factions are brutal. They're all killers. I detest violence. We need to prosper and keep progressing. I still cling to aspects of the old world and maintain faith, but I realize science is the future. The war needs to end, otherwise, it'll just be an endless loop, an absurd paradox.

If only I had the money to attend medical school or open an optometric boutique. I want to help those who suffer, especially veterans. Most resemble broken clocks, no longer chiming with life. But just as clockwork can be repaired, I want to help restore their vision. To see is a gift. It's essential. My purpose is to improve their safety and quality of life.

I may not be a surgeon, but I'm still a doctor despite what people think. The empire denied me a scholarship to become an ophthalmologist. I worked hard for my doctorate in optometry. I couldn't even obtain a business loan as an optometrist. The denial was frustrating, but I don't hate the empire for it. I will just have to do things the difficult way.

Since I don't have the money to obtain my residency or open an optical emporium, I'm stuck being a miner until I save enough qauras. Perhaps things will change soon. I am an optimist and will forever have hope. Sooner or later something decent will come my way. Well, it's hard keeping my eyes open now. Writing did the trick. Boring and tiring. Goodnight, future me.

IV
Cause for Concern

Kaimo woke to the sound of a rumbling engine. He yawned, got out of bed, stretched, and looked out of his window. In the distance, a motorized coach drove through the already busy market district. Despite the early hour, the world was wide awake and waiting for him to join its madness.

He went to the bathroom and used a mechanical toothbrush to clean his teeth. Even a small contraption such as this made him thankful. He rinsed his mouth, then twisted a corroded valve and stepped into the shower stall. One foot worked the bellows, pumping out tepid water as he bathed with a block of soap. When finished, he closed the squeaky valve and dried himself with a towel.

The house vibrated while he dressed in clean

clothes. Rushing to his father's room, he found it empty. Hesitant at first, Kaimo stepped inside and approached the large telescope by Gabriel's window. Unable to see anything, he increased the magnification on the scope and looked through the lens. Initially blurry, he used an adjustable wheel on the side of the optical tube to focus.

"There you go," he muttered. "I see you."

Far off in the sky, he spotted a massive steam-powered airship. The flapping masts bore a circular emblem of interlocked gears surrounding overlapping triangles. It was no surprise to Kaimo when he noted the alchemical insignia—science was vital to the world's evolution and the empire's success.

Turbines and pistons propelled the steam-powered vessel, and several metal masts with full-rigged sails embraced the wind. Kaimo noted imperialists accompanying the ship's crew, transporting dozens of stacked crates. He assumed they contained food, weapons, and, of course, kogal.

"If only I could leave this backwater town and be on one of those."

The vibrations stopped, at which point he glanced at his fob watch—he still had time but he'd be late for work if he didn't hurry. He went downstairs and peeked into the living room. His father lay asleep on a recliner, three empty wine bottles at this side. Revulsion carved on Kaimo's face, he stepped away.

"Nothing changes."

In the dingy kitchen, he cooked a couple of eggs and toasted a croissant for breakfast. He ate his sandwich quickly, then hurried to the dilapidated hallway where he grabbed his hat. Dashing out of his house, the route he chose took him to a tram station in front of the town's brothel.

"Good morning," he said to a fellow miner who was already waiting, tipping his coppola.

"Morning."

"Did you by any chance see that airship?"

"Those things are above the clouds," he said, hawking and spitting.

"I know but..."

The man turned, and Kaimo took the hint. He waited in silence for his transportation to work, welcoming the gentle breeze. Soon, more miners joined the duo. After ten long minutes of listening to moaning behind them, a trolley arrived. Kaimo paid the fare and climbed aboard, sitting in the back of a carriage.

Picking up speed, the tram roared with steam and exhaust. As it reverberated through the raucous market district, a grubby boy selling printed newspapers caught Kaimo's attention with the headline: THE WAR CONTINUES. He forced his eyes away from the grim news while the trolley left town, toward the excavation site.

Kaimo stared at the railway, drifting off in deep thought. *Mom, where did you go? The war is getting worse. Is that why you didn't take me with you? Are you also against the war? Maybe that's why you abandoned us. I'm trying to be my own man, but you should have taken me with you.* He stilled his dreary monologue for a moment, aware of going off on an unknowable tangent. *Today will be another backbreaking day. Then again, anything is better than following in my father's footsteps.*

As soon as the tram reached the mining valley, Kaimo disembarked. He gazed up at a tower atop the central mountain, acknowledging a metal pylon flaunting lenses and shutters; the panels, capable of being rotated to block or pass light from the sky, conveyed information to airships. The empire relied on such communication and controlled it, soldiers permanently stationed there.

Grimacing at the heliograph station, Kaimo battled against his zeal for optometry. He refused to join the imperium just to build, service, or use optical pylons. Filled with resentment, he joined his fellow miners and made his way down the uneven pathway. By chance, he saw his older friend nearby and waved. Liam walked with a steady limp, approaching him.

"Good day, Doc," he said warmly, in contrast to the usual sarcasm from others. "Ready for another taxing day?"

"Why not? The workload will probably make it go by faster."

"Hurry up, people!" Lord Beaumont shouted. "The supply train will be here by midday and we must be ready!" He scanned the area. "Kaimo!" Making eye contact, he added, "You'll be in sector three today."

He responded with a salute.

"That's way deep," Liam muttered to him. "More dangerous for the lungs. You be careful down there."

“Will do.”

Entering the dim mine, Kaimo strode away from his only friend; he was new there and many of the miners considered him eccentric. It wasn’t just the anecdotes of his strange tendency to feel or see unnatural things such as a city in the sky but more because he resented his ingenious father, as well as anything remotely related to violence. To everyone else, war seemed to be a natural part of the world.

Deeper into the narrow cavern, Kaimo stepped into an elevator shaft with a group of workers. Filled to capacity, the liftman pushed a lever that caused the platform to screech. Hydraulic legs spun to life, gears and cogs rotating as the miners descended a couple of miles underground.

At the bottom, everybody exited the platform and scrambled to their mandated places. Kaimo had to reach sector three, a deeper zone inside the cavern. He passed a drill teeming with mechanized wheels and whistling pipes. The deafening machine, facilitated by its steam engine, rotated and cut through the ground at an angle, creating yet another section to mine.

Kaimo hastened to his assigned area. The supervisor in the vicinity saw him and pointed at a wall without uttering a word. Truth be told, he considered the gesture rude regardless of not hearing him because of the noise produced by the machinery. He joined several miners and raised his tool, chiseling at granite.

At times, Kaimo used a pick and struck with great power. As soon as he spotted delicate kogal, however, he switched to a chisel and tempered his strength. He applied just enough force to carve out the precious stones. It took hours for him to make real progress, his body drenched in sweat.

When he had procured enough resources, he used a shovel to lift the kogal, then hurled everything into a nearby mine cart. He wasn't sure which was more tiring, hacking or shoveling—both were backbreaking work. To his surprise, by the middle of the day, he had filled the cart to capacity.

Lord Beaumont descended from the lift, observing the miners. "Not bad, Kaimo. Take fifteen to eat."

Kaimo responded with a faint nod, breathing heavily. Meandering through one of many tunnels, he approached the elevator shaft. Moments before he stepped in, an explosion shook the cave. Heavy boulders collapsed, crushing the liftman. Several miners lost their balance and tumbled to the ground.

Dust filled the cavern. Kaimo coughed violently and backed away in disbelief, his ash-covered face an expression of absolute dread. Numerous miners darted through the dim, stifling passage, checking to see what had happened. At the sight of the destroyed elevator, panic set in. Screaming and yelling filled Kaimo's ears while he stood stock-still, acknowledging how narrowly he had escaped death.

"I'm...alive?" he muttered aloud.

Vibrations pulsed throughout his body. Another explosion, followed by a tremor, threw him against a jagged wall. The knobby ceiling cracked, dust and rocks falling. In mere seconds, the fretful workers resembled survivors of a meteor shower. Galvanized by the disaster, Kaimo broke into a run and joined the others, searching for another way out. By chance, he saw the overseer sprinting not far from him.

"Lord Beaumont!" he called out, struggling

to breathe as he ran. "Lord Beaumont! What's happening?"

"The hell if I know!"

"It's those damn insurgents!" blurted a running miner.

"Don't be ridiculous," Lord Beaumont retorted, slowing down. "It's probably just an accident."

"A malfunctioned drill?" Kaimo said.

"Precisely," Beaumont replied, reaching a cavernous chamber where a large pit lay. He jostled his way to the front, standing before a rail bridge. "Silence!" The overseer waited for everyone around him to hush. "News flash! Accidents happen. We are inside a damn mountain. Cave-ins are to be expected."

"We're not being attacked?" asked another miner.

Lord Beaumont laughed. "This is a shit town in the middle of nowhere. Terrorists attack strategic locations like cities that would potentially cripple the empire, not a dump where people dream of leaving. Now listen up. I will activate the railway. We can use the mine carts to get across. Four people at a time. No more than that."

The miners followed his advice, working together to empty the ore-filled carts in their sector. Most of them struggled to remain composed; a group of them accidentally toppled a cart, causing a thunderous echo. Despite their crippling anxieties, they lifted it back in place, climbed in, and used a lever to accelerate down the railway.

Others followed their lead, getting in different carts. Kaimo, meanwhile, was among the first waves of miners to cross the rickety bridge. Out of curiosity, he gazed below and stared into the pit—it was too dark for him to determine how deep it went. Fear gripped him, but he had no space to cower away.

"If you don't like what you see, don't look down," one of the miners said.

Kaimo unexpectedly released a subtle laugh as he responded, "Sound advice."

Eventually, they left the cavernous chamber. No longer above a pit, Kaimo calmed down and focused on what lay ahead. He took control of the lever, picking up speed and zooming through the darkened tunnel. When they reached a fork, Kaimo remained straight instead of switching tracks.

The cart almost zigzagged because the railway line had too many twists and turns for comfort. Erring on the side of caution, Kaimo attempted to decelerate; the carts were not meant for transporting groups, and his companions were ill at ease, especially when going up and down an uneven ramp. Trepidation overwhelming Kaimo, his skin crawled.

By good fortune, the cart did not derail.

"Thank the gods," he said.

"No," a miner retorted. "Thank science."

Kaimo flinched at the remark. He didn't consider himself a religious zealot. In fact, as a doctor who aspired to be more than a lens-maker, he embraced science. Yet he could not deny the watchmaker argument—the intricacy of creation was akin to the design of a fob watch; such complexities of the gears were not self-created. Then again, he was equally aware the same could be said about the gods, as they were infinitely more advanced than a watch; ergo, another greater force of intelligence must have created them too…

The argument could go on in an endless loop, no different from a temporal paradox. In this debate within his scrambled mind, he was stuck in an elaborate foxhole, and there was no atheist in a foxhole. Truth be told, Kaimo was more of a neutralist but did lean towards faith. He didn't, however, want to argue, especially at a critical time like this, and so he kept his rebuttal to himself.

Though a clockless interval to Kaimo, the miners spotted natural light. When they reached a corner, the cart made a sharp turn and exited the mine. They emerged onto a gravelly ridge, relieved to be outside. While decelerating, Kaimo noted smoke rising from the opposite side of the mountain, but slopes of granite blocked his view. More alarming was the scheduled imperial train approaching on the main railway below.

"Shit," one of the miners blurted out. "It's already here?"

"We're in serious trouble," another said.

Kaimo sighed. "Maybe they'll be forgiving because of the cave-in. I mean, we've already mined the ore to meet their quota. All we need to do is load it on the train."

"Yeah and how're we gonna do that?" the same worker snapped.

"Calm down," Kaimo said. "We'll explain what happened and then get these carts back inside to transfer the ore once everyone is sa—"

Another strange vibration. At first, he thought it was a tremor, but he realized the pulse had come from within him. An eerie, burning sensation filled his tightening chest as he and his companions spotted a biplane emerging from the mist, descending toward them.

"What the hell?" sputtered one of the men.

Shock flashed across their faces as the pilot opened fire at the train. Bullets rained down on multiple carriages like a devastating blaze, destroying a turret and riddling the metal hull with holes in a matter of seconds. Kaimo stopped the cart and hastily got off, followed by the others. Terror clutched them as they ran for cover.

"It *is* an attack," Kaimo said, no one hearing him. *Why would they strike here? Is it the ore? The kogal?*

"Why is this happening?" a miner cried out.

"The resources," Kaimo said, a tense expectation hanging in the air. "They need them." Appalled, his eyes widened, horror creasing his pale face. "The train! They're going to hijack the imperial train!"

Pulling out his retractable spyglass, he looked through it. The refracting telescope offered greater detail of the pilot. The insurgent's features were masked by the helmet and thick goggles, but Kaimo fixed his gaze on the long hair and pursed lips. Stunned, he lowered his monocular with a slack-jawed expression.

"Even women are a part of the rebellion..."

After waiting for the plane to ascend into the sky, Kaimo sprinted ahead. He heard the others call out to him but ignored them. Reaching a precipice, he leapt off a crag. Sprinting downhill, he followed the mine cart track and jumped down another bluff that led him to the mountain's base.

Taking cover by a cluster of boulders, Kaimo surveyed the area. There, he waited and watched the aviator descend and open fire again. Even though he was still a safe distance from the advancing train, pure instinct drove him to the ground, motionless until the biplane rejoined the sky. Several imperialists climbed the train and attempted to shoot the pilot with their flintlock rifles.

Kaimo remained in hiding. *I need a gun.* "No," he sputtered, shame overpowering him. "I didn't just think that!" He let out a frustrated sigh. *I'm stupid and naïve. I can't afford to be so damn idealistic.*

Cursing under his breath, he whispered, "I must get back somehow. Dad will panic if he finds out what's happening."

Despite the immediate threat, Kaimo darted across the barren footpath toward the dense smoke he'd seen earlier. He stared at it as if looking down the barrel of a gun—a personification of fear. The eerie vibration lingered within his chest, lending him the necessary courage and willpower to move. After all, the path before him was the only way home.

V
TRAUMA

Kaimo arrived at a crossroads, where he caught a glimpse of wider tracks. The freight train was upon him, its reverberating engine within earshot. Ignoring his nausea, he wiped beads of sweat from his glistening forehead and sprinted ahead as the braking locomotive of brass and copper-colored accents started to pass him. He stopped, steam engulfing him. A force of zephyr embraced him, his clothes and hair flapping wildly.

With no cover in sight and the aviator about to

shoot, he broke into a run, gripped a sidebar attached to one of the many wagons, and leapt aboard. He noted a sliding door wide open and rushed inside as a torrent of bullets streamed down. Rounds penetrated the carriage, one missing him by a hair. He winced, falling back on his buttocks.

"The gods are either dead, or they have a sick sense of humor."

Staring at the numerous holes, he checked his body for wounds. Not feeling pain or finding any blood, he pressed on. In the adjacent cart, he found a dead soldier sprawled on the grated floor. No matter how much he hated warfare, it seemed to him that his destiny could not be rewritten.

Kaimo's heart raced with anxiety at the sight of the soldier's rifle. He approached it, filled with dread—not because of the dead imperialist, but in acknowledgement that if he didn't grab the weapon, death would be a certainty. Disgust plastered on his perspiring face, he picked up the rifle.

"I cannot escape fate," he said to himself, aware of his own hypocrisy. "Is this what happened to you too, father?" Despite his inner conflict, he armed the gun that conquered his principles.

Bolstered by the weapon, Kaimo entered the rumbling carriage ahead. It was completely empty, ready for the mine's resources. He pressed on into the next wagon. Inside were a multitude of crates. Before checking them, he heard soldiers shooting from above. They shouted among themselves, reloaded their rifles, and fired again. Expecting a counter-strike, Kaimo searched for cover. To his astonishment, no bullets came his way.

"I shot it!" one of the soldiers exclaimed.

"The insurgent's going down!" another bellowed, just as ecstatic.

Hearing the imperialists through the bullet holes, Kaimo sighed with relief. "Thank goodness."

While the soldiers cheered, Kaimo tugged on the next cart's door. It wouldn't budge. Locked. Shaking off his frustration, he turned to the side as the train gradually halted. The mine's main entrance came into his view. He was about to jump off and run but stopped short as rebels emerged from all directions of the valley and shot at the remaining soldiers returning fire.

Kaimo winced again, bullets whizzing by him. He ducked and crawled back into the previous carriage when a soldier descended from the roof of the train. Without hesitation, the soldier turned and aimed his gun at the intruder. Instinct took hold as Kaimo simultaneously raised his own weapon in self-defense and pulled the trigger. A single bullet launched from the smoky barrel, piercing the soldier's hauberk. Blood leaked from the sentry's breastplate as he dropped his rifle and collapsed.

"No!" Kaimo blurted, rushing over to the lifeless soldier. He checked for a pulse, dread crushing him. Horrorstruck, he backed away and leaned against a wall. "I'm...I'm so, so sorry. I'm sorry."

Time stops for no one—not even the gods; that is, if such deities exist. And yet for Kaimo, it felt as though time had indeed stopped. The bubble he'd been living in burst as his world turned upside-down; his worst nightmare a reality. All his life, he believed that killing wasn't just wrong or immoral but inhuman and outright evil. He trembled, transfixed by the atrocity of his own actions. Fingers splayed, he retched, and a stream of vomit surged from his mouth.

"Forgive me," he muttered, wiping his lips.

Gagging at the acrid smell of his puke, Kaimo

backed away from the dead man. Afraid other soldiers would spot him and, more alarmingly, label him a rebel, he left the carriage. Returning to the sealed door, he examined the padlock and struck it with his gun's stock. Gunshots interrupted his concentration, but he didn't withdraw. Again and again, he bashed the lock until it finally broke.

Inside the carriage, he stood before an abomination: an unnatural, column-shaped prison with cylindrical pipes and semitransparent tubes whose syringes had been inserted into the veins of a young woman. Kaimo wasn't sure whether the tubes were draining fluid or injecting some kind of serum into her. Unconscious and suspended by the mechanical contraption, she hung in rags that scarcely covered her modesty.

"Suns of Zykard!"

Indifferent to any consequences in the immediacy of the horror before him, Kaimo removed all the needles from the young woman. He grimaced at the manacles that entrapped her. Taking a step back, he reloaded his weapon, aimed with care, and shot at the shackles. Ignoring the deafening reverberation, he reached out to catch her.

"I've got you. You're safe now."

Slinging the flintlock rifle over his back, he placed her over his shoulders and made his way outside of the cart. Bullets whizzed in all directions as Kaimo summoned the courage to jump off the smoldering train. He checked his flank and took cover, waiting for the precise moment to leave.

In the clear, Kaimo broke into a run. He panted and wheezed, struggling to maintain his pace. Adrenaline pumping, he escaped the mountainous valley and sprinted back to town. His feet and legs burned. Throbbing pain shot through every nerve, but he refused to slow down.

Other miners joined him, running for their lives. Kaimo struggled against the urge to double over, his sharp vision blurring. Muscles cramping, his legs threatened to buckle. Before collapsing, he caught a glimpse of a war veteran; the gaunt silhouette of an old, sullied man whom he resented.

"Father..."

"Kaimo?" Gabriel called out, approaching with a pistol in hand while other miners passed them by without so much as a glance. A heartbeat later, his son collapsed, inadvertently dropping the young woman. "Son!" Holstering his gun, Gabriel reached him. "The town's siren went off. Every soldier in Icdarus rushed off to the mine. Are the rumors true? Has there been a terror attack?"

Kaimo managed an imperceptible nod before fainting.

CHAPTER TWO

Shifting Gears

I
RECUPERATE

Kaimo woke after a couple of hours, finding himself back home. He struggled to move, his legs still throbbing. His vision returned with the realization that he lay in his bed and was not alone. It took him a few moments to consider how he'd returned—his father. Yet the person at his bedside wasn't Gabriel.

"Mother?" he mumbled.

Seated on a chair beside him was a woman wearing his mother's clothes. An image of her flashed in his mind. Together, they walked through the market while she held his little hand; he gazed at her as if she were an angel, delighting in the rustle from her black satin corset and bustle skirt. Her bonnet hid her auburn hair as she reached for a fruit. Before inspecting it, she glanced at her son and gave him the warmest smile.

The image of his mother's smile was burned into his mind. Though, when he blinked, the cherished memory vanished.

Breaking out of his daydream, he stared at the woman he'd rescued. She took off the bonnet, revealing a strong visage with brunette hair that shone like autumn. To his surprise, her countenance gave him the impression that she'd never been injured. Truth be told, she had made a remarkable recovery, he thought. Her gentle blue eyes met his, and her warm smile calmed his nerves. She extended a hand, gripping his fingers.

"You..."

"Rest," she said, her voice firm but equally soft. "You've done enough today. Now it's my turn to look after you."

"Ma-may I know your name?"

"Zylpha," she answered. "Zylpha Bess Wrayburn. And you're Kaimo, right? Kaimo de Morté?"

"Yes," he replied weakly. "I take it my father told you." At her nod, he went on, "It's a pleasure to make your acquaintance. I mean, well, it's a pleasure to officially meet you now that we're both awake and safe."

She let out a soft chuckle. "*Enchantée*."

An awkward silence descended in the room.

"So, um, what happened?" he asked, breaking the stillness.

Zylpha hesitated but soon answered, "Gabriel brought us back. He was kind enough to let me stay. We didn't talk much. He was mostly concerned about what had happened. At first, I thought he saved me. As it turns out, you're the one who freed me from that nightmare."

"Actually, what I meant—"

"I know," she interjected in a composed but grim tone. "I know you're wondering about me. You can be trusted. Otherwise, you wouldn't have freed me." She paused, eyes fixating on her scarred forearms. "Xelvok Von Cazar, Grand Marshal of the Imperium,

Duke of Enbertum and Sword of the Emperor, found me and burned my village in the process."

"That's inhuman," he said, revulsion carved on his face.

"Xelvok isn't human. He hasn't been for a long time. If ever. I was to be the emperor's prize. You see, the grand marshal believes my blood has something called the *aether*, a mythical power that coursed through the veins of a forgotten dynasty." Like a celestial hammer wreaking havoc, Kaimo felt his head pounding while she went on, "I always knew there was something different about me. Don't think I'm crazy, but at times I can feel it."

"Feel what?"

"Something inside me," she said, her eyes downcast. "Something unnatural. My mother never told me much about our past. She thought it was for my own protection. Unfortunately, he still found us. It seems the emperor wants my blood. Lord Cazar tried to transport me in secret, but I think the resistance knew something and interfered."

"Moons be damned," he said, his voice cracking in utter shock. "I thought they were just hijacking the train for resources."

"I honestly don't know. Though it *is* possible they were trying to kill two birds with one stone, I have a terrible feeling they weren't there to rescue me. I'm lucky to be alive."

Kaimo's brows knotted. "This is an atrocity. We need to do something. Is my father downstairs?"

"Um, no," she replied, her tone disconcerting. "I'm afraid he's gone. Before leaving, he told me after serving in the war that this town has been the only real peace he's ever known and that he needs to preserve it."

"No," he groaned, forcing himself up.

"Please rest," Zylpha said, pressing her hand on his chest.

"I can't. My father's irrational. He still thinks he's some kind of war hero. I need to stop him."

"He's trying to protect you and maintain whatever peace is left here."

"It's too dangerous. I can't let him do that. Not by himself." He spotted his gun and grabbed it. Seeing her follow him with concern, he held out his hand in protest. "I need you to stay here until we're back."

"What if someone comes looking for me?"

"Not a chance. I snuck out of the train without

incident. Anyone who knows of your existence is probably still at the mine. But hey, if anyone knocks or rings the doorbell, don't answer. Matter of fact,"—he dug into his pocket and pulled out a key—"here. This is for the attic. If anyone suspicious prowls around, go upstairs. You'll be safe."

"Please be careful."

"I'll...I'll try."

II
Crisis

Defying his own credo, Kaimo went downstairs to his father's workshop and searched for weapons. Grabbing two pistols, he holstered them on either side of his belt. He also took a bandolier of rifle ammo and slung it across his vest. After arming his rifle and testing its scope, he abandoned his home. Kaimo limped toward the town square, a few onlookers stunned to see him wielding a gun.

Disbelief written on her face, Clara called out, "Kaimo? What are you doing with that? Are you all right?"

"No," he said flatly, not making eye contact.

Ignoring the onlookers, Kaimo advanced toward

a mechanized trolley, its passengers all soldiers. As he boarded it, they gazed at him with acceptance. By all appearances he was volunteering to fight the terrorists. A minute later, the steam-powered tram accelerated. As they approached the mine, many imperialists checked their rifles.

Weighed down by terrible anxiety, Kaimo held his weapon tight. His heart thudded, emotions rising and jolting him akin to high voltage. *Why am I doing this? My father is scum. He deserves to...no. I'm the scum for thinking this way. He's not the best father but the war isn't his fault, and now I am no different from him. I have blood on my hands.* Tasting nausea on his lips, he leaned out of a window, on the verge of vomiting. Yet his queasiness dissipated when the trolley turned—he saw an imperial airship docked by the mine.

The soldiers cheered at the sight of the massive vessel. Kaimo squinted, slack-jawed and overawed.

"Impossible," he muttered aloud.

Pulling out his spyglass, he viewed the steam-powered zeppelin with great detail. Unlike others he'd seen in the sky with masts, this was a rigid ship clad in metal with a cylindrical shape and armed with cannons and turrets. It also had massive turbines on either side, attached to the casing that provided an almost impenetrable hull. Even though steam engulfed the vessel, he noted dozens of soldiers on the lower deck, arming cannons along the gunport.

"*Iron Cloud.*"

The trolley reached the mine. Kaimo got off with the troops, acknowledging the imperial train was missing. He assumed the rebels had succeeded. In theory, the train should've still been there so he and his fellow miners could load up the empty containers with the resources they'd mined.

"Doc!" a raspy voice called out.

Kaimo turned, the sight of a friend calming his fear. "Liam!" He sprinted over to him and embraced him like a brother. "You're all right!"

"Luck," he said. "Pure luck."

"What happened?"

"Bombs were just the start of this nightmare. Those damned insurgents came outta nowhere. They took the train. Didn't even bother to take any of the kogal we mined. Crazy if you ask me."

"Is it over?" Kaimo asked.

Liam grew sullen. "I'm afraid not. Half those sumbitches are inside the mine. They've taken a few hostages."

"*What?*"

"It's a real tragedy. But listen, your father came to help. That's why I ain't freakin' out to see you alive. He told me you escaped the cave-in. He's in there now with Lord Cazar...the Duke of Enbertum. Brave man, your father. Still a hero, even though he's retired."

Kaimo's world turned upside-down as his befuddled mind absorbed Liam's words. "Wait a minute. Wait. Lord Cazar is here?"

"Yup."

"And my father's with him?" At the old man's nod, Kaimo went on, "In all the world, why would rebels attack this backwater town...and why out of everyone in the empire would the grand marshal himself be here?"

"Beats me, Doc. I've never seen anything like this before. We'd best stay clear until they resolve the crisis."

"I can't," Kaimo responded, unnerved by the hostage situation. "My father's not young anymore. I'm getting him out of there."

Liam's face contorted at his companion's words.

Rifle in hand, Kaimo walked off and followed the imperial troops. Reaching the mine's entrance, he mimicked others by raising his gun and rushed inside. Blood shrouded the cave's knobby walls and ground. Corpses from both factions lay sprawled along the pathway. Kaimo slowed down, observing each one. His father was nowhere to be seen, so he advanced through the dim tunnel.

He eventually caught up to the soldiers at a fork littered with more lifeless rebels and imperialists. Most of them had been fatally wounded from gunshots, while others had lost their limbs. Unable to believe his eyes, Kaimo wondered, *What menacing weapon could have done that?* The brigade stood amid a bloodbath and hesitated until they heard echoing voices from one of the passages.

"This way!" a soldier yelled.

Sprinting ahead, they went through the left passage and arrived at a cavernous chamber filled with ore.

"Drop your weapons and surrender!" one of the insurgents shouted.

Witnessing a standoff, the soldiers lowered their guns and remained still. Kaimo froze in place for another reason—his beaten father was a hostage, his lips cracked and rimmed with blood. Dozens of miners, along with a few imperialists, lay in partial sitting positions, their arms spread wide.

Only one man stood opposite them without fear—Lord Xelvok Von Cazar. Different from all the other imperialists, Xelvok wore a mechanical vizard over half his face, as if to hide scars. Its bronze detail of gears and metal tubes spliced together made him appear more like an industrial construct rather than human. His military garments matched the tint of his mask, and his burgundy cape added a regal air. Kaimo kept a healthy distance, anxious to resolve the situation without further violence.

"Where is she?" Xelvok demanded, his voice gruff. At the lack of a response, he gripped the handle of his sheathed sword. "Do not test my patience."

"I have no idea what you're talking about, Cazar," one of the rebels said. "You're the incompetent fool that let us take your precious train. Now, if you want these people to live, you'll evacuate the mine and let us—"

Unconcerned with hostages, Xelvok raised his pistol and shot Gabriel in the head. Kaimo let out a distorted scream that sounded like a pitiful "*No!*" and helplessly watched his father collapse. Without hesitation, the rebels aimed at the grand marshal who clicked a button on his armored wrist, a mechanized shield taking form.

Bullets dented Xelvok's brass shield. Flaunting a venomous smile, the grand marshal holstered his gun and unsheathed his chainsaw sword, swiping the nearest rebel in a curving arc that severed his facial features. Maneuvering the fearsome weapon sideways, he cleaved an insurgent who attempted to flank him.

With no time to reload, the remaining insurgents unsheathed their blades and charged at the imperialist. Lord Cazar parried their attacks. His reverberating sword shattered the first enemy's weapon, tearing through skin and bone until her body split diagonally. Pirouetting, he dodged an attack from one of his other foes.

Seizing the chance, the grand marshal parried, riposted, and thrust his vibrating blade straight into the man's heart, shredding it. Lord Cazar's derisive smile broadened as he veered aside while hurling his shield at another terrorist, its gear-like trim decapitating him. Only one rebel stood alive.

"Where is she?" Xelvok demanded. "I won't ask again."

"Go to hell," the insurgent retorted, pulling out a pistol from his back and shooting at the grand marshal.

The unarmed imperialists gasped, fearing the worst. Xelvok, however, waved a hand in the air like a madman, as if he repelled the bullet. Kaimo was too distraught to see the unnatural distortion around Lord Cazar that deflected the bullet. The soldiers' helmets hid their slack-jawed expressions.

Taking a step back, the remaining insurgent reached for his sword despite his lack of strength to lift it. Crippling anxieties gripped him as he struggled to stand—blood seeping from a bullet hole in his chest. He fell backwards, horror wreathing his face.

Kaimo rushed over to his lifeless father, holding him in his arms.

"Dad!" he cried out. "You killed him! After everything he's done for the empire! You killed him!"

"His noble sacrifice served a higher purpose," Xelvok said. "What was his name?"

"Gabriel!" he shouted. "Gabriel de Morté! He was a respected war veteran, you sadistic murderer!"

"May his soul find peace," one of the surviving miners said grimly.

Xelvok ignored the miner, indifference in his eyes. "Soldiers, we have a stolen train to find."

With languid deliberation, Xelvok sheathed his sword and abandoned the mine with his brigade. Kaimo continued to sob, unable to comprehend what had just happened. His aspirations dwindled and died in that moment, replaced with emptiness. Numb from within, he was barely able to smell the musty air inside the shaft or feel the grainy, coarse ground.

Remaining at his father's side, he cried uncontrollably. Writhing in agony, his stomach churned, an infinite wave of sorrow gripping his soul as he regretted the rift between them. First, he'd lost his mother. Now, his father. *Forgive me.* His oath and ethics as a doctor to do no harm ebbed to nothingness. *What am I going to do?* An image abruptly blazed into his mind—Zylpha. *The grand marshal is undoubtedly looking for her.*

"I need to get back to her," he managed to mutter.

III
Bereavement

With the help of surviving miners who'd been waiting outside during the hostage situation, Kaimo brought his father back to the town's crematory. Unable to preserve bodies, the cremator initiated an immediate cremation. Many stood together in the dim chamber lit only by kerosene, tear-eyed and in silence, watching Gabriel's body burn until nothing but ashes remained.

The cremator eventually gave Kaimo a brass urn. He stared at it blankly while the others around him expressed their condolences. Clara was one of them, hugging him. Barely acknowledging her, he withdrew from her embrace. Saddened by his coldness, she left. Kaimo brought his father's remains to the columbarium next door. A few people followed him, passing through the graveyard to enter the dome-shaped building.

Once inside, Kaimo stood in an ornate room containing recessed compartments with decorative jars inside most of them. He scanned for one with his father's name and spotted it on the left. Fixing his eyes on the engraving, he gently placed the urn in the niche and touched it one last time.

Liam placed a hand on his shoulder. "I'm so sorry, Doc. He died for a cause he believed in and will live on in our hearts."

"He was betrayed by the empire," Kaimo said, clenching his fists.

"I beg your pardon?" the old man asked.

Thinking twice, he kept the truth of his father's murder to himself. "The grand marshal should have protected him."

"They will find that train and avenge him."

"I somehow doubt that. The insurgents are much smarter than we think. I'm positive they have some kind of contingency plan. Otherwise, they wouldn't have hijacked the train in the first place."

"Either way, it's out of our hands."

"Not entirely. I'm sick of waking up every day doing the same thing and wondering if I'll ever make a difference in the world. Now it's clear to me. I must take matters into my own hands."

"Don't do anything you'll regret. Your father's in a better place. You just focus on your dreams and get to medical school."

"My father's dead, Liam. Murdered. I can't just pretend that didn't happen."

The old man nodded, his eyes downcast. "Be careful, Doc. The path you're walking is dangerous. Believe me, I've had my fair share of tribulations. What you're hinting at has consequences. There's a price to pay, and sometimes that price can cost us our lives."

People paying their respects drifted away as Kaimo responded, "I was naïve and ignorant. My dad wasn't perfect either. Still, he didn't deserve such a horrible fate. Now that my eyes are open, I need to make things right."

"I'm not sure I follow..."

Kaimo's world was crumbling fast, countless thoughts scrambling in his distraught mind. Though it pained him that his father had been killed, that wasn't the source of his motivation to retaliate. In truth, it was because of the woman he'd found in the train. Whether it was a coincidence or they were aware of her presence, he didn't know. One thing, however, was certain—he had to ensure her safety.

"My apologies. You may not agree with me. My mother would've definitely forbidden this. But I need to leave and find a way to convict the one who killed my father. Call it justice, revenge, or something else entirely. I don't know. Perhaps when all this chaos is over, I'll find a way back to my vocation. But now, there's only one path I can see."

Liam kept quiet for a moment. "Follow your heart, Doc. Just please, at least for your parents' sake, keep yourself alive." He embraced him. "Stay safe, my friend."

"You do the same."

Bidding him farewell, Kaimo made his way out of the columbarium. He took a deep breath outside in the cemetery, beside an abandoned church. One of the dilapidated building's rock-hewn walls revealed faint but still legible, chiseled letters that read: *a pox on the gods!* Old statues that once depicted ancient deities lay toppled, mostly destroyed. No one buried their loved ones any longer, but a few tombstones from the old world remained.

Grief coursing through him, Kaimo was compelled to take his resentment out on the primeval graves. Before kicking one down, he noted the still-legible name on the stone and resisted the temptation to destroy it out of respect for the dead. Melancholy weakened his countenance as he left, making his way to the town square.

The market was bustling again, people milling about. Pedestrians jostled through the cobbled street, one of them mindlessly shoving Kaimo and accusing him of being blind. Anger burned in his chest, but he ignored the unpleasant incident and reached his residence. A sympathetic voice called out to him as he was about to enter the house.

Kaimo turned and saw Clara. "Oh, hey," he said, his hand on the doorknob. "What're you doing here?"

"Don't be like that," she said, disappointment flashing across her face as she caught her breath. "I felt terrible not saying anything at the funeral. To be honest, I didn't know what to say. Even now, I'm not sure—"

"There's nothing to say," he interjected. "Something horrible happened. Horrible things happen to us all. We will never be prepared and may not always find the right words."

"I'm so sorry."

"You have nothing to be sorry about. None of this is your fault. My father and I were at the right place at the wrong time."

Clara stared awkwardly at him. "What I mean is...I'm sorry for your loss."

"Thank you," he said, his composure ebbing; he looked away in a desperate attempt to hold back his tears.

"Listen, you're not alone. I lost my dad to the war when I was seven. You know it's just been me and mom trying to make a living. So, if there's anything you need—anything at all—I'm here for you."

Shaking off his melancholy, he made eye contact with her. "Thank you, Clara. I just need to be alone right now."

"I understand," she said, her eyes downcast. She looked around aimlessly and glanced up when a frayed curtain fluttered. "Oh, do you have company?"

"Huh?" he muttered, his eyes fixing on the bedroom window that failed to reveal anyone. "No. Of course not. Look, I really need to be alone right now."

"Okay. Well, if you don't mind, I'll check on you in the morning. If you need me for anything, don't hesitate to come over."

"Thank you. Truly."

Kaimo entered his house, closed the door behind him, and peered through the peephole until she disappeared into the crowd. Taking a deep breath, he took off his hat and grabbed his father's spare keys on a wall-mounted rack. Rushing upstairs, he checked both bedrooms but found them empty. He then remembered that he'd given his guest a key for before leaving and unlocked the hatch to the attic, lowering its foldable ladder.

"Zylpha?" he called out, climbing the creaking steps. "Zylpha? Are you here?"

At the top, Kaimo stepped inside and bent under the eaves of the ceiling. His eyes cast over dusty containers and a locked chest to a few feet beyond the boxes where, hidden behind them, Zylpha peeked out.

"Kaimo," she said, relief in her voice, getting to her feet. "I wasn't sure if that was you outside. All I could see was that hat. I was so scared and came up here to hide. Thank goodness you're back. Where have you been?"

"My father," he started, doing his best to maintain composure. "He—"

Unruly emotions lodged in his gut, tears escaping him. Like an uncontrollable tidal wave laying siege to a bastion, Kaimo drowned in his bottled emotions that betrayed him. He had always succeeded in portraying himself with a calm countenance in front of others, but this time, he lost control.

Zylpha stared blankly and without any gift of clairvoyance surmised what must have happened. Sadness consumed her like a black hole, coupled with fear and dread. She reached out and held him, patting his head softly. He leaned on her shoulder, eventually pulling away as he attempted to recompose himself.

"I am so, so terribly sorry," she said.

"No," he responded, waving a hand. "I'm the one who's sorry. I didn't mean to break down like that."

"You have every right. He was your father."

Kaimo cleared his throat and hid a sniffle as he turned to the hatch. "It's not safe here anymore. We need to leave."

"*Leave?*"

"Yes," he said, descending the rickety steps. "Grand Marshal Xelvok was there with an entire brigade. He...he is the one responsible for killing my father." At her gasp, he went on, "I don't even know why he spared me. It's only a matter of time before he finds that train and realizes you're not there. He'll be back for sure. And when he returns, we need to be gone."

"Where will we go?" she asked, joining him downstairs.

"Don't know. Guards are probably stationed at the port, so definitely not by air. Damn it! Everything's happening so fast." He paused, thinking hard. "My father has a lot of supplies in his workshop. Follow me."

IV
Treacherous Escape

The duo went downstairs and entered Gabriel's garage. Tools and gun parts lay on a couple of benches in the back. Racks along the walls held rifles and pistols. Although reluctant at first, Kaimo approached the weapons and knew all too well that he couldn't avoid them. Seizing a bandolier of ammo, he wrapped it around his vest and slung a flintlock rifle over his shoulder. He took a Grimtol—a revolver with a sword attached to the barrel of the gun. Sheathing it, he turned to Zylpha and handed her an extra pistol.

"For emergency."

"Thank you," she said, accepting it.

Kaimo strode to Gabriel's safe. Using one of his father's spare keys, he unlocked it and found stacks of qauras. In the meantime, Zylpha holstered her gun and turned her attention to something elongated and large in the center of the workshop. A brown tarp covered it, with several tight straps. Its width and overall size left the pair no choice but to walk along the sides of the garage.

"What is this?"

Though engrossed in gathering his father's money from the safe, Kaimo turned to look at what had held her attention. Pulling out a sleek knife, he approached the tarpaulin, cut all its straps, and pulled it off to reveal his father's steam-powered automobile. Zylpha's eyes brightened, taking in its beauty. The vehicle's thickened, steel body gave it a hulky appearance; yet it looked stylish with wing-like fenders and bumpers, two sporty doors, and wheels with onyx rims.

"It belongs…it belonged to my father."

"*Très chic*," she responded with glee, touching its elongated hood. "Kaimo, this is it. This is our way out."

"What? No way."

"Why not?"

"To be honest, I've never driven before."

Zylpha appeared somewhat smug. "But I have."

"Seriously? Considering the imperium's discrimination against women, I didn't realize there're so many accomplished ladies in the world," he said, remembering the insurgent who piloted a biplane.

"Don't exaggerate," she said gaily. "We definitely live in a man's world, but I've done my part to overcome that. Just not so much with guns. Now, if we're to get as far away from Xelvok as possible, we'll need this. And we both know how hostile the Canyons of Rezekos can be. I'll drive while you navigate. Sound like a plan?"

Hesitation seized him, but he silenced his indecision and surrendered the keys. Making haste, he put his rifle in the trunk and then walked over to the front of the garage, lifting the wide overhead door. His companion, meanwhile, unlocked the sedan and slid into its leather upholstery. Putting the key into the ignition, she activated it. The engine rumbled and roared with life, steam spewing from the vehicle's twin exhausts as Zylpha drove the car out of the garage.

"Get in," she said.

"Ambitious *and* pushy, huh?"

Upon closing and locking the overhead door, he got in the car. Before he fastened his seatbelt, Zylpha pressed the throttle. The vehicle accelerated onto the street. People gawped, unused to anyone owning an automobile. Checking both ways to ensure the path was clear, Zylpha motioned eastward—away from the mine. Kaimo lowered his tinted window and leaned out, looking back once more.

Fumes filled his nostrils while the automobile left the town, descending a rocky hill. Throughout his life, he'd often dreamed of venturing out and leaving. Through tragedy, one aspiration was materializing. Now that it was finally happening, bizarrely, he wondered if he'd ever see his hometown again. An overwhelming mix of exhilaration and apprehension shot into his stomach as reality kicked in.

"Are you all right?"

No longer leaning, Kaimo shook his head. "It's hard to believe I'm leaving Icdarus," he said, glancing at the rearview mirror. "Truth be told, my ambitions are simple: Return to school, receive my medical license, and open up my own optometric clinic.

But revolutions against the imperium? Raging war? Killing? No." He stopped for a moment, pensive. "I mean, don't get me wrong, I've always wanted to leave. Just—"

"Not like this?"

"Right..."

"Well, we're not out of the woods yet," she said, gesturing at the town's closed entrance where two imperialists stood guard.

Zylpha slowed down. The soldiers marched forward, ogling the approaching vehicle. One of them gestured to turn around. The escapees glanced at each other, apprehension etched on their faces. Zylpha sighed heavily but halted the automobile and opened her window, waiting for the guards to reach her.

"You need to turn around," one of the soldiers commanded.

"But there's no other way out of town," Zylpha replied.

"Correct," the other soldier said. "Haven't you heard? The town has been on lockdown since yesterday. It will stay this way until the insurgents are found. Grand Marshal Xelvok's orders himself."

"We need to leave," Kaimo mentioned. "It's an emergency."

The first soldier lifted the mechanical visor of his helmet, eyeing the passenger. "I know you. You're that gunsmith's son. He makes good weapons."

"He's…thank you."

"I wasn't complimenting you. State your business."

"And explain why *you* are not the one driving," the second soldier demanded. "Who is this lady with you?"

Kaimo stuttered for a moment as he responded, "Th-this is my fiancée, Zy-Zelly." Her features were deadpan as he continued, "We're on our way to Bogdar to visit my mother. She's sick."

"You didn't answer my question. Why is *she* driving?"

"Sorry," he blurted, looking at the other soldier. "What can I say? Times are changing fast, and women are bolder these days. She's been asking me for a while. So, I promised I'd teach her."

"During an emergency?" the first soldier said rhetorically. "You'll need to wait until the lockdown is lifted. No exceptions."

Zylpha nodded and shifted her gears, reversing. Maneuvering the wheel, she turned the car around and drove back up the hillside. Disappointment creased Kaimo's face, discouraged and lost for words; he accepted that leaving was too good to be true. His companion didn't speak either. All she did was drive.

After half a mile, at the top of the mountainous road, she stopped abruptly, reversed sharply—the rear wheels encroaching on the precipice—and shifted the gears, accelerating toward the guards. Kaimo veered to the side, a metallic taste in his throat. The soldiers, meanwhile, gazed at the car in disbelief.

"Gods be with us!" Kaimo gasped, afraid they were plunging headfirst into yet another foxhole.

"I'm afraid only your father's car can help."

Kaimo winced and ducked, regretting his wayward decisions as the soldiers raised their flintlock rifles. They opened fire, one bullet shattering a headlight and the other destroying Zylpha's side-view mirror. She shrieked when it blew off but maintained her course. The guards attempted to reload their guns before leaping out of the way as the automobile zoomed past them. It smashed through the gate, the escapees promptly exiting Icdarus.

"Get to the motorcycles!" one of the soldiers shouted.

Adrenaline pumping, they rushed over to their steam-powered motorcycles to pursue the escapees. From behind, the imperialists drew pistols from their holsters and opened fire. Zylpha shrieked again, ducking along with her companion.

"This is crazy!" Kaimo blurted. "At this rate, we'll be dead in seconds!"

"Then do something!" she snapped, rotating the wheel and swerving the automobile left to right.

Bullets punctured the hull of their vehicle. One pierced the rear windshield, shattering it. Kaimo feared the next bullet would end up in his skull. Again, his mind spun like an unforeseen force knocking his world off its axis. Conflicted by his principles, a part of him withered and died as he came to terms with what he needed to do.

"Keep the automobile steady."

"I'll try," she said, focused on the zigzagging path that opened up into a barren expanse as she descended the mountain.

Checking his intact side-view mirror, Kaimo saw the soldiers gaining on them. Unbuckling his seatbelt, he drew his Grimtol and cocked it as he leaned out of the window. He aimed and shot at the guards. Though he missed, the imperialists nonetheless swerved away.

Spared a few seconds because of their fear, the lens-maker pulled out his spyglass and attached it to the top of the gun barrel. He adjusted the magnification until the objective lens gave him the clarity he needed. Kaimo aimed with precision, degradation peeling away at his soul, and fired. The targeted soldier let out a distorted bawl as his bike smashed against a crag and exploded.

Reloading his gun, the second imperialist shot at Kaimo, who simultaneously returned fire. To his surprise, Kaimo remained unscathed. One bullet, however, pierced the hood of the automobile and penetrated its gadgetry. The smoking engine screeched as pistons halted—the bullet jammed inside.

"Shit!" Zylpha blurted, trying not to lose control of the wheel.

Cards stacked against him, Kaimo closed one eye and looked in the ocular lens of his spyglass. His view limited, he relied on the power of his scope and pulled the trigger; the Grimtol cocked back, its last bullet propelling out of the smoky barrel and lunging straight into the soldier's neck. He, too, bawled and fell sideways along with his motorcycle.

Zylpha cheered, ignoring the car's heinous noise. "You did it!" She steered the automobile northward despite its severe damage. "Come on, get back in. No one else is tailing us."

"I'm...still alive?"

Horrorstruck by his actions, he stared at the dying man. Like a bullet tearing through his heart and bleeding him out until numb and dead inside, his sense of ethics dissipated. He wasn't sure whether or not he had the right to consider himself a doctor or even human for that matter. His soul darkened, mortification dissolving his integrity.

Kaimo sat back inside the car and pondered, *What have I done? I committed murder. Just because they looked like automatons doesn't mean they were lifeless machines. Could there have been another solution to this madness?*

"I had no idea you were so good with a gun."

"I'm not," he said, staring at his weapon as though

he wanted to toss it out. "It's optics that saved us."

His background in optometry had helped him stay alive. Yet it also aided him as a killer, which sickened him. He wondered, *Is this how my father first felt? Will I turn into him…a biological machine with no remorse?*

Zylpha glanced at him, his pain evident. "There's a war out there, Kaimo. The imperium is ruthless, and it's affecting the world and everyone in it."

"I know."

"Do you really? I don't understand why, but you saved me from Xelvok. He is arguably the most powerful man alive. These are the consequences for rescuing me, and this is only the beginning."

"*I know,*" he repeated, frustration touching his voice. "There was no way I could leave you. That would've been just as inhuman."

"You can still go back," she said, passing an arched rock. "There aren't any witnesses. I can do this by myself. If you return home, just report your father's vehicle as stolen. You'll be vindicated."

Kaimo faltered, allowing her words to sink in. "Where would you go?"

"Only one person can help me. Professor Oswald

Briknoll. He's a scholar of the old world. My mother told me that if anything ever happened to her, I should find him. That was before…before Xelvok killed her. Not to sound heartless, but I'm trekking the Canyons of Rezekos with or without you. My life depends on it."

"I won't let you go alone," he said, his voice firm.

"Are you sure about this? There's no turning back. If anyone in the imperium sees you with me, you'll be hunted."

"It's too late for me. I can't go back. Not after this."

Zylpha glanced at him for a moment. "What do you mean?"

"I can't pretend none of this happened. The terrorist attack. Being trapped in a mine. Almost getting killed by rebels and imperials. Finding you hooked up to that ungodly machine. My father murdered."

"I'm so, so sorry."

"Don't be," he said, checking the rearview mirror out of paranoia. "None of this is your fault."

"I beg to differ," Zylpha whispered so quietly she might as well have thought it.

She said nothing more on the matter, steering the automobile northeast. With the exception of the engine's unnatural, regurgitating sounds of cylinders and pistons struggling to move, silence enveloped the pair. Kaimo let out a deep breath as he gazed at the polluted heavens, acknowledging the twin suns westering. The sky's orangey-red tinge calmed his troubled soul.

"Well, at least we're not driving through a storm."

"That we can both agree on," she replied.

As they regained their composure, the engine ignited. The pair jolted, startled by the outburst. Inky steam escaped from the hood, accompanied by reverberations. The car decelerated at an alarming rate. Zylpha pressed her foot on the throttle, but it failed to respond. Then it shut down and came to a stop, fire leaping from the damaged gadgetry.

"Get out!" Kaimo yelled.

They jumped out of the burning vehicle and ran in opposite directions until it exploded. Gathering their bearings, the pair rejoined beside a crag and stared blankly at the ruined car. Riddled with bullet holes and making unsettling sounds, Kaimo wasn't surprised it blew up.

"I think we're fated to die," Zylpha said, her expression lifeless.

"My rifle was in the trunk, so you may be right," Kaimo replied, rubbing his throbbing head before observing his surroundings. "Hmmm...seems like we're in the outskirts of Rezekos. How far are we from Bogdar?"

"Excuse me?" she said with both hands on her hips. "I thought that was just a part of your weird cover story, which reminds me, where in the world did you get Zelly? And, um, I'm your fiancée?"

Kaimo let out a rueful laugh. "It was a decent cover story." At her nod, he went on, "So, not Bogdar? Where do we need to go?"

"Enbertum," she said.

"*What*? Isn't that across the continent? I mean, we need to start somewhere. How far are we from Bogdar?"

"Not even halfway."

Turning to hide his unavoidable gulp, Kaimo noted the expanse of a canyon so immense it made him appear like a grain of sand. Colossal escarpments paved the way from east to west, a gorge so massive that it appeared unending to him—even with the use of a telescope. Kaimo detached the spyglass from his gun and lowered it.

"We're screwed," he mumbled.

They stood together in front of the burning automobile, wondering if this would be their last evening alive.

CHAPTER THREE

Trekking Rezekos

I
Surviving

The pair advanced toward the gorge littered with dead trees, fossils, and a dry basin. Natural arches in various, exotic formations filled the terrain. Soaring spires of rocks and wind-faceted granite, carved like mushrooms, scarred the desolate landscape. Kaimo spotted a non-rigid airship drifting high above; he assumed the denizens aboard the aerial vessel would see an expanse that resembled a natural wonder with immense gashes tearing through the old, dry earth of Zykard.

Steep banks of schist grew around the fatigued duo. And far ahead stood mountains, massive stone pedestals, and a mesa here and there. Despite the day nearing twilight, it was still scorching hot. Two suns beaming down on their backs would do it, Kaimo thought. Nevertheless, the pair pressed onward and made their way north. The path soon narrowed, and the split escarpments of siltstone drew closer until almost kissing.

By now, the steam-powered blimp was long gone. The pair slowed their pace, hiking a zigzagging plateau walled off by elevated cliffs where steep, rugged crags protruded like daggers. This region, essentially a barren wasteland, was why civilization wasn't prospering much in the southern continent of Quradale.

Leaving the backwater town of Icdarus behind, however, gave Kaimo the motivation he needed to venture out into the world and leave the arid badlands; he simply wished it wasn't under such dire circumstances. Enbertum, from what he'd learned, was the only grand metropolis in all of Quradale. He daydreamed about the great city until they arrived at a dead end.

"Wonderful," Zylpha said with a sigh of frustration. "What now?" Before her comrade even suggested climbing, she heard a howl. "Uh, what the hell was that?"

"I'm afraid *that* was a veyra'nem. They usually hide from us and just stay in the outer wilds hunting smaller animals."

"We're already in the wilds, and it's just two of us. What if there's a pack?"

Kaimo reloaded his Grimtol. "They'd be stupid to prey on us, but they can try."

"Unbelievable," she frowned, pulling out her pistol.

"Either way, our situation isn't getting any better standing here. Whether they attack or not, we best be on our way."

"Right," she said. "Where to?"

He ruefully pointed up.

"You can climb?"

"There's a first time for everything."

Not having much choice, they holstered their weapons and tackled the crag. Several times, Kaimo feared he'd lose his grip and fall to his death. Despite his distress, he kept silent and persevered to keep up with his companion, who'd been scaling the rock face with relative ease.

"You're pretty good at this."

"My oh my, how *ever* did you notice?" she responded with a wink. "Don't stop now, first-timer."

They continued up the crag, pieces of rocks crumbling. Kaimo, and even his skilled companion, struggled to maintain their grip, searching for safe footholds. Though challenging, both of them reached the top of the plateau, panting until they caught their breath. The pair gazed at each other, sharing a mutual look of relief.

"I never wanna do that again," he wheezed.

"You said it," she replied. "Where to now?"

"Truth be told," Kaimo began, "I'm only familiar with Icdarus. Getting to Bogdar is a bit beyond me."

"Darn…I keep forgetting."

"I do, however, have a little trick up my sleeve," he said, pulling out his spyglass and adjusting its magnification. Manipulating the convex lens, he brought it to the appropriate focal point to see an object suspended near the swollen clouds. Bringing it into focus, he pinpointed the airship that had passed them earlier. "I see the blimp that was above us from before. With any luck, we'll reach town if we follow it."

Zylpha's countenance brightened. "That's remarkable. You really do know a thing or two about optics."

"I'm a certified lens-maker and want to study ophthalmology," he said, walking east. "They say optometrists who become ophthalmologists are the best eye doctors. Funny that we're attempting to reach Enbertum because it's well known for having the finest university. I even heard rumors that the grand city has an observatory with a telescope so massive you can see the fourth moon."

"That's claptrap."

"Why because three is enough? Just because we can't see it with the naked eye doesn't mean it's not real. I know for most people these days seeing is believing. But there's a lot more to life than what our senses reveal...consider the aether within you that Xelvok is after."

Zylpha was almost speechless. "Okay, you piqued my curiosity. When we get there, we'll check out that observatory."

"Sounds like a plan," he said, his voice filled with enthusiasm.

To their dismay, another howl echoed—much louder, and joined by others from all directions. They pulled out their guns again and scanned around. Not seeing anything, they broke into a run and passed several more rock spires. Within earshot of them, more hungry howls resonated.

Kaimo looked skyward, acknowledging that the twin suns had almost set. With little light remaining in the twilight sky, and still in the heart of the wilds, anxiety took hold of the pair. Adrenaline kicked in as they fought against throbbing pain shooting through their calves and thighs. Their lives on the line, they refused to slow down and soon reached the top where another rock face loomed.

Cursing under his breath, Kaimo prepared to climb it when a veyra'nem emerged from the higher precipice. Zylpha took a step back, slack-jawed. The muscular, four-legged creature revealed a luxuriant blood-red mane that embellished its gray fur coat. Horns spiraled from its cranium, and its protruding claws looked so sharp, Kaimo assumed they could mince him like butter.

The beast's horizontal pupils gazed down on its prey, growling and unveiling oversized fangs. Before it pounced, Kaimo raised his Grimtol and fired. The sound resonated with the creature's roar as a bullet tore through its flesh. When he shot it again, his gun kicked back—the whizzing bullet piercing its skull. To his surprise, the animal lay dead one foot away from him.

Whimpering from all directions filled their ringing ears. The pair opened fire, letting out a salvo at other beasts charging from behind. Though they eliminated the threat on their flank, more veyra'nems approached from the same precipice above the frightened duo. Out of ammo, the pair darted westward and jumped down a ridge, landing safely a few feet down.

Legs intact, they broke into another run. Sprinting ahead, Kaimo acknowledged that they should've been dead by now. He slowed his pace and checked his flank; the pack of flesh-eating creatures had ceased pursuing them. Panting heavily, he stopped to catch his breath. Zylpha turned to him, wild-eyed.

"Have you lost your mind?"

"They stopped chasing us," he said. "Veyra'nems are territorial. Maybe we were near their den and pissed them off. I think—"

The loudest howl silenced him. He shuddered, a tense expectation hanging in the air. Something stirred above them. From sheer instinct, Zylpha gripped his arm and hid behind him. Daunted by the alpha veyra'nem, which was thrice the size of the others, Kaimo failed to notice the grip she had on him.

Perspiration glistened on Kaimo's forehead, goosebumps erupting on his skin. Despite the Grimtol's empty chamber, he lifted it in an angle and switched a gear that extended its barrel-bladed edge. Kaimo stood his ground, treating his hybrid gun like a sword. The ferocious beast growled, as if expecting him to flee. Instead, its prey boldly took a step forward.

"I'll at least die a man."

The alpha veyra'nem pounced when a cracking, thunderous sound tore through the air like a sonic boom. A projectile zoomed past the pair at lightning speed and buried between the alpha's eyes. Snatching the chance, Kaimo pierced its heart and roared in unison with the dying creature, but not before it collapsed on him.

Zylpha, frozen in place, skimmed the barren environs.

A cloaked man rose from a boulder and approached the duo, wielding a sniper rifle. “Isn’t it a bit late for either of you to be hikin’ here?” he asked, his voice guttural and muffled through his gas mask.

“You saved us!” Zylpha said, astonished.

“Not really. I’ve been hunting veyra’nems for their pelts. To be honest, you were the perfect distraction and bait needed to lure the alpha out.”

“Well, thanks anyway. I think.”

“Um, a little help?” Kaimo muttered.

“Oh!” Zylpha sputtered, running to his aid. “I’m so sorry!”

Amused, the huntsman watched her struggle and fail to lift it. He shrugged, gripping the dead creature by its limbs. Together, Zylpha and the hunter lifted the carcass and tossed it aside. Kaimo gasped for air, inhaling and exhaling heavily.

“Thanks again,” Zylpha said.

“Like an angel from the heavens of old,” Kaimo rasped, getting to his feet and extending his hand. “Thank you.”

“Mmhmm,” the hunter uttered, not shaking his hand. “The name’s Dumont Fen Cogen.”

"Kaimo de Morté. And this is—"

"Zylpha Bess Wrayburn," she finished, curtsying. "We're not, by the way, hikers. We left Icdarus in the morning and are traveling to Enbertum."

The hunter stared at her blankly for a moment. "Do you have a death wish?"

"Of course not," she said, irked. "Our automobile…died on us. And believe me, it's not repairable. So, we continued on foot."

Dumont turned. "Does your woman always do the talkin'?"

"*We're not together,*" they said in unison.

The mask Dumont wore hid his grin.

"She's a proud feminist," Kaimo replied. "But I do get in a few words." No one laughed at his humor, so he cleared his throat and went on, "We're well aware how far Enbertum is from here. We're trying to reach Bogdar first. Hopefully, we can catch a blimp there to take us to the northern city."

Dumont was about to respond when howls pierced the air. "As you can hear, it's not safe in these parts. Luckily for you, I know this land like the back of my hand and can be your guide…for a price."

"I think we can find our way," Zylpha said. "But thank you."

"Ya think?" the huntsman responded. "These gorges are like a maze, let alone the Jiwan River. If you're travelin' by foot to my town—"

"I'll pay as long as it's reasonable," Kaimo interjected.

"I wouldn't be a successful hunter if my prices weren't. It'll be sixty qauras." At their unexpected elation, he stopped them short with the wave of a hand. "Don't get too excited. First, we need to survive the night. The veyra'nems are vengeful beasts. They won't let us simply go off on our merry way after killin' their alpha. I say we make camp and wait 'til mornin' to move."

"Right. They don't like fire."

"All right," Zylpha said. "Well, let's get it started."

The trio gathered flint near an arched canyon. Without enough twigs for combustion, Dumont sacrificed one of his bullets. Opening it, he removed the gunpowder and sprinkled it over the stones and scarce branches. Rubbing them together, he ignited a fire; the encroaching veyra'nems hesitated and eventually backed off.

To their relief, the howling stopped. Dumont brought out meat from his knapsack and cooked it, sharing it with the others. Famished after such a long day without eating, the escapees gratefully accepted and ate with relish. The huntsman drank water from a bota bag and then offered it to his company. Kaimo gestured at Zylpha to drink first. Parched, she grabbed it and took several gulps, then gave it to her companion.

"Thank you," he said.

Zylpha nodded in agreement, chewing and swallowing the last of her food. "Yes, thank you so much."

"It's all in the payment," the hunter replied.

"Of course," Kaimo said, understanding.

They finished eating and curled up by the fire. Kaimo used this time to explain what had happened in Icdarus—except for the sensitive details concerning Zylpha and how he'd found her. The young woman remained quiet for a change, listening to his story; this was the first time he'd gone into such detail.

"My condolences for your loss," Dumont said.

"Thank you."

"It makes sense for you to start over. I reckon

you'll be happier in Enbertum. Quite a trek, though."

"It'll be easier once we find an airship," Zylpha said.

A tranquil silence descended over the camp. They embraced the hard-earned peace, listening to the crackling fire. Zylpha stargazed for a while, taking in the heavenly expanse that gleamed like a collage of glittering angels. To her astonishment, a shooting star flickered; the meteorite burned with an orange glow through the dark sky. Excited, she turned to share the experience with the others, but they had already fallen asleep. Gazing down at Kaimo, she smiled and lay down to join him in deep sleep.

II
Outer Frontier

The following morning, Dumont finished skinning the alpha veyra'nem for the pelts he needed and then woke the others. Kaimo and Zylpha gathered their bearings and briefly scouted the area for dangerous wildlife before venturing north through the rocky, eroded land. The huntsman led the way, rifle in hand. Together they trekked a mountainous footpath, both suns beating down on their sweaty backs.

"The heat is unbearable," Zylpha said.

"You think this is bad?" Dumont put in. "It gets worse by noon."

"Unfortunately, he's right," Kaimo replied, briefly stopping to catch his breath. "It's not so different in Icdarus."

Despite the scorching temperature, they advanced uphill. The passage soon narrowed and curved downhill, affording them some relief. A surge of adrenaline pushed them forward when they heard a waterfall nearby. At the base, the trio found themselves in an oasis with cascading water.

For the first time since his departure from Icdarus, Kaimo saw a tree on one of the lower plateaus along with bushes. Most captivating to him, however, were the passive animals drinking from the springs. Startled, the two-legged mammals trotted to the opposite side. They were the same species; however, the array of coat colors—crimson, amber, black, teal, and pearl-white fur—gave them an exotic appearance. They also had onyx tusks growing beneath their snouts.

"Are those uy'kaja?" Kaimo asked.

"Right you are," Dumont answered.

Zylpha tilted her head, giving a sidelong look of surprise. "You've never seen one of these beauties before, Kaimo?"

"Never," he said, his eyes still fixed on them. "Honestly, all I've seen are birds, airships, and more airships. See, up on Icdarus, all we have for show are mountains, buildings, and machines. We barely even have trees there."

"I keep forgetting. Anyway, they're tame. Let's see if we can ride them."

"No need," Dumont said, approaching the falls and pulling out his wineskin. "My boat is just around the corner."

"Wait," Zylpha said, dumbfounded. "You have a boat?"

"Of course," the huntsman said. "I wouldn't be able to earn a livin' without one. Quality game ain't easy 'round these parts. And trust me, these animals, great as they are, wouldn't do the job. Not even the best uy'kaja. Now drink up fast so we can be on our way."

Kaimo and Zylpha took advantage of the natural springs, drinking and splashing water on their perspiring faces. The hunter drank as well and then refilled his bota bag. Ready, they left the hidden sanctuary and followed the stream of water until reaching a corner where it opened up to a river.

Ahead was a canoe moored to a small wooden dock. Careful of missing planks, Zylpha and Kaimo crossed it and boarded the boat. Dumont untethered the rope and joined them. Taking control of the oars, he rowed north. By good fortune, the Jiwan River lacked the ebb and swirl exhibited by most wild tributaries. Instead, calm waters trickled with occasional boulders scattered about.

"We finally caught a break," Kaimo said.

"You keep saying that as if I'm doing this for free," the huntsman said suspiciously. "Mind if I get paid now?"

Kaimo shrugged. "Sure."

Reaching into a pocket in his vest, he pulled out sixty qauras and handed the currency to Dumont, who tucked it inside his duster. Satisfied, the hunter continued rowing the boat. The lack of a current meant he didn't struggle. Despite his unease after Dumont's comment, Kaimo waived it off and gazed at the panorama in awe. The gorge coursed between escarpments with steep slopes that soared so high, they provided shade for the trio.

"My back isn't sizzling anymore," Zylpha said.

Kaimo let out a soft chuckle. "Yeah, thank goodness."

"We're almost there," Dumont said. "Just another couple of miles and Bogdar will be in sight."

Excitement took hold of the lens-maker, triggering him to pull out his spyglass. Looking through the lens, he adjusted the barrel and brought the monocular telescope into focus. The objective lens provided him with the perfect view of the town, built within the stony crags of the escarpments.

Bogdar appeared like twin gems, expertly carved and chiseled out from rocks on either side of the slopes. Built neither too low to be affected by the streaming water nor too high for the suns to overly burnish the town, it lay centered along the steep rock faces. Arched bridges of metal high above the river joined both sides of the sculpted settlement.

"Incredible," Kaimo muttered.

"That's a nifty monocular you've got."

"Thanks," he said, handing it over to Zylpha who'd been gesturing to have a peek. "I studied optometry and crafted it myself."

"Truly? Now *that* is impressive."

"He's being modest," Zylpha said, wiping the lens. "Kaimo is a doctor."

"Optometrists are doctors? Who'd have thought. Congrats, kid."

Zylpha adjusted the focus for herself and looked through the lens to see the rock-strewn town. She noted a wharf at its base, where two elevators with cogs and gears cranked to take people up and down. High above, an airship descended between both sides of Bogdar, steam engulfing the town.

Before her view blurred, she glimpsed metal platforms beyond the rocky ledges of the buildings where people milled about, as well as catwalks at the center of town for people to disembark the arriving vessel. Steam billowed like a cloud of smog, obstructing her vision. Zylpha lowered the monocular and handed it back to Kaimo.

"Thank you," she said with a warm smile. "I've never relied on telescopes before, but they really do seem useful."

"How did you get into craftin' them?" Dumont asked, paddling.

Kaimo was pensive for a moment. "In a strange way, it started with my dad. He was a retired veteran and an accomplished gunsmith. He eventually opened a shop and had me help him make weapons. I never liked guns or agreed with the war, so he finally let me just craft the scopes that are attached to rifles."

"I like you, kid. You're smart. Do me a favor and stay that way."

"I'm technically a young man but thanks. I'm definitely trying my best," he replied, putting his spyglass away.

"Just how old are you?" Zylpha asked the huntsman.

Dumont laughed through his mask. "Old enough to be your father, but I ain't got no kids of my own, so don't worry about me scoldin' much. Overall, I agree with the *young man*. The war is nonsensical."

"I'm glad you agree," Kaimo said. "There are no moral grounds to justify it."

Zylpha gazed at him with fondness.

"Careful not to get preachy 'round here. Anyway, we've arrived. I'm gonna hand over these pelts and get myself to the bar. If you need me to hunt a beast or anythin' else in general and have the qauras, don't hesitate to find me."

III
Bogdar

The pair thanked Dumont and climbed to the wharf where other boats had docked. At one of the elevators, they entered and waited for the liftman to activate it. Ascending four hundred feet, the duo watched the hunter moor his canoe until clouded by the airship's steam. Their attention turned to the suspended vessel and adjacent heliograph station whose optical shutters clanked an encrypted message to a sister town.

As soon as the platform reached Bogdar, the pair exited and joined the crowd. Most women wore corset-style bodices, ruffled blouses, buckled boots, and top hats, while many of the men sported dusters and fedoras. Some even had gas masks with flip-up goggles, uncannily similar to that of the huntsman. Jostling by them, Kaimo regarded the buildings set into the cliff like lit-up caverns, roaring with machinery.

"Spectacular," he said, appreciating every detail.

Midway through the grated walkway, they crossed an arched bridge that brought them to the other side of town. Several boutiques reminded Kaimo of home: a bookstore, an apothecary filled with tinctures and potions, a smithy displaying swords, an emporium specializing in guns, and stalls with merchants selling a cornucopia of produce. The pair stopped to buy food. They ate fast, observing the people and lifestyle.

"Shall we move on?"

"It's exciting here, but I know we're not safe yet," Kaimo said, gesturing for his companion to lead the way.

The duo advanced, leaving the market behind. They came across the town's saloon where a tumult of jubilant voices resonated with piano music. Near the wooden louver doors, Kaimo's eyes were riveted on a woman whose snug décolletage flaunted her plump bosom with off-the-shoulder sleeves and a low-waist, ruffled skirt. He blushed when she brazenly eyed him.

"Want a picture with her?" Zylpha asked, poking his stomach.

"Huh? What? No! Of course not. I'm just not used to seeing a lady revealing herself like that."

"That's not a lady. That's a prostitute."

"Goodness," he gasped, picking up the pace.

Joining a catwalk, they realized the vessel connected to it was suspended in the air. Kaimo had never seen a flying ship so close before and gawked at its masts and hull design in awe. On the catwalk, their footwear clanked on the metal grating. Crippled by extreme paranoia, Kaimo glanced down to see how stable it was, uneasily acknowledging it to be nothing more than a makeshift boarding ramp that the captain laid down while his airship remained suspended.

"Well, that's disturbing."

"Afraid of heights?" she asked, amused.

"Tickets," the stationmaster called.

"Sorry," Zylpha started, "we don't have them yet. I was just wondering...are we able to reach Enbertum from here?"

The captain overheard and shook his head. "The imperium is restricting travel to major cities." At their shocked reactions, he went on, "I take it you haven't heard? Rebels attacked Icdarus and hijacked a train. There's still some fugitive or insurgent at large, so we're restricting long flights until she's caught."

"She?" Kaimo said, his pupils dilating.

"I know," he answered with scorn. "Hard to believe, but there are apparently women in the resistance. Their leaders must be desperate if you ask me."

"Times are changing," Zylpha blurted out, burning with anger. He stared at her oddly, and she caught herself. "But you're right. For women to be soldiers, the rebels are a bit too desperate. Just don't be surprised if you see a female professor one day."

The captain laughed. "That wouldn't be so bad. I just can't accept women fighting for a lost cause. Anyway, my ship is leaving for Icdarus in fifteen minutes. If you want to head north, there's a zeppelin due here this the evening. But it's only going as far as Vinestead."

"That's the countryside," Zylpha said, sulking.

"We can't stop trade," the captain responded. "Farmers need to make a living, and we all gotta eat."

"Thanks for the information, Captain," Kaimo said.

"*Bonne chance.*"

The duo moved away, dispirited. Off the unstable catwalk, they returned to the rusty, elongated grating of Bogdar and wandered aimlessly. They eventually found themselves in front of the tavern. Upbeat piano music wafted toward the busy footpath, at which point they exchanged awkward glances.

"I'm not sure what to do now."

"Don't worry, we've already made great progress."

"This isn't an adventure," Zylpha snapped. "I'm a victim. Tortured. Your father was killed. Remember?"

Kaimo flinched at her words.

"I'm sorry. That was insensitive. I shouldn't have said that. Please forgive me." At his weak nod, she went on, "With the slightest lead, Xelvok can use his airship to find us in an instant. Then we're both as good as dead."

"I understand," he said while someone accidently shoved him. "But despite what you may think, I stand by my words. It's honestly not that bad. Vinestead is a safe place. Endless swards with so many farms you can get lost in them...and maybe we should."

"Get lost in them?"

"Why not?" Kaimo said with a shrug. "The countryside is the last place Xel—" He stopped and glanced around; too many people lingered near them. "Listen, let's get a drink to calm our nerves.

There's something that's troubling me, but we can't talk about it here."

"All right," she sighed. "Got nothing else better to do."

The pair went up the tavern's stairs and stepped through the louver doors. Inside was filled to capacity with gamblers, drunkards, prostitutes, and a few others like them, lying low for a couple of hours whether to get a drink or simply relax. Not a single seat was empty by the bar, so the duo squeezed through to the back and found an empty table. They sat down and groaned in unison, relieved to rest their feet.

One of the waitresses approached them. "Need anything?" she asked.

"Brandy, please?"

"Just water for me," Zylpha said haggardly. She waited for her to leave and then turned to Kaimo. "So, what's troubling you?"

Checking to ensure no one was eavesdropping, he responded, "Something's amiss. Think about it. Why were you on an imperial train heading to a backwater town like Icdarus?" Since his question was rhetorical, he went on, "If you were truly meant for the emperor, Grand Marshal Xelvok would've had you on his airship. Instead, he was sneaking you around on a cargo train."

"But why?"

"Truthfully? I have a terrible feeling the grand marshal has other intentions for you and the aether in your bloodstream. Otherwise, why all the secrecy? Your image should technically be plastered on countless posters by now. Well, maybe it's too soon for that." At her frightened expression, he quickly added, "I'm not trying to jinx us." The waitress brought their drinks and left. Kaimo sipped his brandy and continued, "Still, I can't shake this feeling that Xelvok has other purposes."

"Enough of that. You're scaring me."

"You should be. Truth be told, I'm scared as hell. But fear means we're alive. Please listen to me, Zel. Either way, Xelvok wants your soul. This is why Vinestead works out. The countryside is the last place he would expect you to be. That's exactly why there're travel restrictions. He expects you to flee to Enbertum or book passage to another continent where other huge cities are."

"This is crazy. I can't nestle up on a farm for the rest of my life."

"Nothing of the sort," he said, rejecting the thought with a wave of his hand. "This isn't long-term. We just need to let the heat die down a little. Then we make our move and show our faces in the big city."

Zylpha didn't respond, quaffing her water. By chance, she saw Dumont enter the saloon and watched him get a drink by the bar. Her eyes wandered all over the dingy tavern. The piano player's jubilant tune barely registered with her; nor did she get drawn to a table where rowdy men gambled their money away.

Sipping his brandy, Kaimo embraced the music and vibrant ambiance of the place. The only thing he wasn't fond of was the creaking floor above him—the wild moaning and thumping made him feel uncomfortable. To drown out the disturbing noise, he concentrated on the pianist who'd just started a new melody.

"Okay," Zylpha said. "We lay low for a while and then what? Pretend to start new lives? Become farmers, get married, and have a family?"

For a moment, Kaimo looked as though he wouldn't mind that idea. "Funny," he replied, finishing his drink. "We can probably look for work in one of the plantations and just stay there until things calm down."

"Things will *never* calm down. Xelvok will search to the ends of the world until he finds me."

"Moons of Zykard. You're too pessimistic."

"I'm a realist. You should be too. I say we hire Dumont as our bodyguard, take that airship to Vinestead, and make our way to Enbertum no matter the consequences."

"It's really loud in here, but didn't you hear anything I said?"

"I did," she answered, her voice calmer. "I'm beyond grateful for your help and your ideas. You may be right about Xelvok's intentions. It makes sense. But it's imperative I get to Oswald before it's too late."

"The professor?"

Zylpha nodded. "I don't know about you, but I trust Dumont. Money aside, he saved us and got us here in one piece."

"I feel the same."

"Right then," she said, confidence in her eyes. "Let's bring the old man over and tell him everything."

CHAPTER FOUR

Fields of Hope

I
Growing Trust

The duo gestured at Dumont, getting his attention. With languid deliberation, he joined them. For the first time, he removed his helmet. The huntsman wasn't a machine after all, Kaimo humorously thought to himself. He sported a gray beard, salt-and-pepper hair pulled back in a ponytail, and slightly wrinkled skin with a coarse face that went well with his dark brown eyes.

Time on her side, Zylpha told him the truth about herself and how they scarcely escaped Icdarus alive. Chin resting on clenched fists, he listened intently, his barrel-aged whiskey untouched. When the young dissident finished her story, Dumont glanced at Kaimo and then back at her as if expecting to be told that this was just a gag.

"Aether?" he finally said. "Do you really expect me to believe this?"

"I swear it's the truth," Zylpha answered. "It's dormant in me, as it was with my mother before me. Only the professor knows a way to help me."

"This is all a bit too much for me."

"The grand marshal killed every insurgent in the mine," Kaimo said. "Even some of the hostages. My father included. I saw it with my own eyes, Dumont. Whether any of us believe in the existence of the aether, Xelvok believes it's real."

"I know your father was included in that massacre, and I'm sorry he was at the wrong place at the wrong time, but if you were there too, why are you still alive?"

Kaimo paused for a moment, his eyes welling. "I wasn't a hostage. He didn't see me or other miners as a threat. Otherwise, I'd be dead too. Those in his way were killed without hesitation. To him, we are nothing more than expendable pawns in his campaign."

"War's ugly, Doc," the hunter replied. "Though he may've gone too far slaughterin' hostages just to kill those bloody terrorists—"

"They're not terrorists," Zylpha interposed. "They are freedom fighters."

Dumont scoffed. "Still stupid of 'em to hijack a train."

"It was a cargo train, *not* a passenger train," she said. "And quite honestly, I'm beyond grateful because if they hadn't done that, I'd still be in that hideous cage."

"So, you didn't hear anythin' vital from Lord Cazar?" Dumont asked.

"I arrived only at the end...at the worst possible moment. All I heard was him enquiring about the whereabouts of a woman. No one seemed to know what he was talking about. Then he just went crazy, cutting everyone down. Not a single arrest."

"Even if I do believe you, I'm a hunter. I handle game. Guidin' you both here was just pity."

Zylpha scowled at his words. “Isn’t it about the qauras?”

“We can pay you,” Kaimo said.

The huntsman cursed under his breath. “Money’s great but I’ve got a life here. Sure, no kids or a woman to come home to every night. Still, I can’t just abandon my home and go off on some wild escapade.”

“Name your price.”

“Forget it, Kaimo,” she said, standing up. “We’ll do it ourselves. I don’t need anyone to pity me.”

Dumont grabbed Kaimo’s arm as he attempted to leave. “Not so fast,” he said, his tone hinting scorn. “I thought you were a smart young man. Getting yourself mixed into this mess is not sensible.”

“I can’t let her go off alone. And my father may not have been the best role model, but I can’t accept what happened to him. Something needs to be done.”

“Real stupid, Doc. Real damn stupid.” The hunter let out a frustrated sigh. “I guess I’ve got no choice but to be as dimwitted as you.” He ignored the gleam in their eyes and went on, “Five hundred qauras.”

“*What?*” Zylpha blurted, her heart skipping a beat.

“It’s okay, Zel. I’ll handle this,” Kaimo said.

"Listen, we need coin for food and travel. How about four? Half now and the other half when we arrive at Enbertum." The hunter hesitated as he considered the offer but eventually nodded, at which point Kaimo sat down and handed over the money he'd taken from his father's safe. "Here's two hundred."

Dumont gulped down the last of his alcohol and counted the qauras. "So, the airships are only goin' to Vinestead, huh? Funny thing is, my sister has a farm out there...east near the third station at Rollin' Grove. I want you both to get your arses there and look for a red barn. When you find it, tell Maggie that I sent you and stay put 'til I arrive."

"You can't leave now?" Zylpha asked.

"I already told you, I can't just waltz out of here. I've got a complicated life with debts to pay. But you can get a head start. Find my sister, and I'll find you in a couple of days when I settle some things."

"Thank you, Dumont," Kaimo said, shaking his hand firmly. "I knew we could rely on you."

"Get outta here before I change my mind."

II
Heights Abound

Kaimo and his companion left the saloon in a hurry. In the hectic street coursing one of the many ledges of an escarpment, they strode toward the skyport building, adjacent to the airship. Like other structures in Bogdar, the ticket booth was carved out from granite. The duo approached it and waited in line. Zylpha looked at a billboard showing scheduled departures and reconfirmed that all flights to Enbertum had been canceled.

"Next," the stationmaster called out.

Kaimo stepped forward. "Two for Vinestead."

"Forty qauras."

He paid the fee and took the tickets.

"Thank you so much," Zylpha said. "You've done so much for me. I don't know how to repay you."

"Don't worry about it. We're helping each other."

"I know. It's just...I don't have any money." Shame creasing her features, she looked as if she were about to cry. "I'm used to being in control, but now I feel so helpless."

"Hey," he said softly, placing a hand on her shoulder. "You would've done the same for me. Besides, you pull your weight. You managed to take down a few of those veyra'nems. And you're certainly a better driver than I am."

Zylpha let out a chuckle, wiping a tear from her eye. "You're a good person, Kaimo. I just hope this isn't all for nothing."

"Ah, there *is* something you can do for me," he said, revealing a wry smile. "No more pessimism."

She let out a rueful laugh, beaming with a nod.

With an hour to spare before their departure, Zylpha took advantage of the extra time and returned to the market district. Since the garments she wore neither belonged to her nor fit her properly, she purchased new ones and dressed in the fitting room. Emerging from the clothing boutique, Kaimo took in the polarized goggles on her forehead, the sleeveless corset, fingerless gloves with brass buttons on the knuckles, and knee-high buckled boots over her leggings.

"Very nice."

"Don't make me blush. Been a while since I had my own clothes. Anyway, shall we be on our way?"

"There's no time like the present."

The pair went back to the skyport. Together, they waited by the gated entrance with dozens of others. To Kaimo's surprise, a non-rigid blimp emerged rather than a zeppelin. It floated from the haze and smoothly descended between the mountainous escarpments until midway down the crags. As soon as the captain aligned his airship with the platform, he signaled his crew to lower the ramp.

"Tickets out!" the stationmaster yelled, unlocking the gate and extending the catwalk.

Travelers showed their receipts and scrambled onto the suspended vessel, Kaimo and Zylpha included. First-class travelers went inside to the lower deck with private cabins, while the rest of the passengers remained on the poop deck. The duo made their way aft and stood by the gunwale.

"All aboard!" the stationmaster shouted, gesturing at the captain to draw back the ramp as he locked the gate.

The crew untethered the ropes along the platform and took their mandated positions. Taking the helm, the captain moved the airship and departed from Bogdar. As it ascended, the twin suns shone on the squinting passengers. Zylpha lowered her goggles, gazing at the maze-like gorges of Rezekos below.

"We're finally making real progress," she said.

"Yes," Kaimo replied, pulling out his spyglass. "It's refreshing to have luck is on our side for a change."

"You said it."

Adjusting the focus of his telescope, Kaimo looked through the eyepiece and observed the battered plateaus, cliffs, and canyons of the harsh region. He noted a peligrida—an amber-feathered bird whose single eye alone had more visual acuity than humans with 20/20 vision; its fluffy, multicolored feathers gleamed as it cawed, its squeal more of a whistle. Ascending, it soon disappeared into the smog.

"Beautiful," he whispered to himself.

Kaimo brought his attention back down to the gulch. Even though the Jiwan River coursed through many of the zigzagging ravines, it didn't reach other gullies, where the arid trenches contained enormous columns of steel jutting from the ground. Zooming in, he identified that they supported an incomplete network of railways being built toward Bogdar; however, the railway connected from Icdarus to another far off town built atop one of the many plateaus.

Upon further observation, Kaimo spotted *Iron Cloud* stationed there. "Thank goodness we didn't end up in Callopeak," he said, pointing westward.

"What do you mean?"

"Here," he said, handing her the telescope. "Have a gander." As she looked through it, he added, "The grand marshal's airship."

"But no train in sight. Why is Xelvok there?"

"Who knows," he responded with a shrug. "Maybe he's attempting to see if a train will pass through?"

"If that's the case," she began while giving him back the spyglass, "I say let him keep searching."

"We need a solid plan. Let's be realistic. It's only a matter of time before he finds it. He has an entire empire at his disposal. Soon every imperial zeppelin will be roaming the sky to find it. And when he realizes you're not there, every town and city in Quradale will be crawling with soldiers."

"I know," she said, her voice hinting apprehension. "Let's just hope we get to Enbertum before that."

Kaimo agreed. Squinting, he turned his gaze north as the blimp soared high into the clouds.

The gullies lessened, signs of life growing from the mostly dry landscape. Patches of withered shrubs sprang from the cracked ground, a few still alive. An occasional bristlecone pine tree stood firm, scattered about in their natural, twisted form with warped trunks and curled branches as though nature itself condemned them from birth.

Both suns began to set, and the canyons disappeared. Parched meadows atop the rocky summits of rising plateaus vanished, and the land flattened. The terrain revealed more greenery, plants, and grass. Kaimo and Zylpha welcomed the change, relief flowing into their calming hearts. They stared out into the orange-red sky, appreciating the pink-tinged clouds.

"Stunning view."

"It's absolutely beautiful."

"Beautiful is the perfect word," he replied, staring at her. She noticed him gawking from the corner of her eye and looked at him; embarrassed, he turned away. "The world is wondrous, and we are miracles living on it."

"Yet there is too much political unrest," she said, disappointment obscuring her lovely features.

"It's tormenting the very spirit of our civilization."

"We can only hope that the war will end soon."

Sure as day follows night, the blimp reached Vinestead. It passed verdant fields ripe with vegetables and fruits. In the distance, a white uy'kaja trotted across the eastern grassland, its gait relaxed. Birds flew below, perching on vines where grapes grew in abundance. The duo saw plantations that spread for miles, animals grazing throughout each farm.

"Good evening, ladies and gents," the captain announced via a horn-shaped loudspeaker, "we have reached Vinestead and are approaching our first stop. Gather your belongings and be sure to leave in a timely fashion. Thank you."

By now, twilight arrived. Under normal circumstances, it was rare for anybody to spot a star with the naked eye; the polluted atmosphere made sure of that. Drifting among the clouds, however, Kaimo spotted dozens upon dozens of them. The starry heavens shimmered like an assortment of priceless jewels in a hidden cave waiting to be mined. Without needing his telescope, he gazed at them and a distant moonbow in complete awe. Then his eyes wandered over to his companion as an inexplicable sensation of déjà vu came over him.

"You are a prism through which the beam of life refracts," he murmured, in a trance-like state. He promptly shook his head, blushing and hoping she had not heard him. "Um, did you see that moonbow?"

"What? Really? Where?"

"Uh, I can't see it anymore," Kaimo replied, scratching his head. To avoid awkwardness washing over the conversation, he promptly added, "It was just there. Strange. But it reminded me of a prism, no different from when I'm correcting refractive errors in a scope."

Sensing his shyness, Zylpha shared a quizzical expression that leaned more towards amused.

Approaching a tall metal tower with an elongated platform, the airship began its initial descent. When the steam-powered vessel drifted below the clouds, Kaimo, or anyone else for that matter, could no longer see a single star. Despite his disappointment, he tried to look on the bright side.

"We're almost there," he said.

"I almost want to get off here."

Kaimo couldn't blame her. He was tired and wanted to rest. Still, he fought against the exhaustion that came over him like a spell and shook it off. Adrenaline kicking in, he paced back and forth until the airship reached the next skyport tower, where it floated along the platform. The crew moored the suspended vessel to the dock and lowered the ramp while the stationmaster extended his catwalk.

"We have arrived at Green Pastures," the captain announced via loudspeaker. "This is the first stop in Vinestead. Next is Shady Oaks."

Several people disembarked while others boarded the ship.

After a couple of minutes, the stationmaster yelled, "All aboard!"

The crew untethered the blimp, at which point the captain took the helm and steered his vessel away. Traveling northeast, the airship rose into the sky but only a few feet above tree level, regardless of the paucity of trees. Swathed in greenery, the terrain was rich with wheat fields, round straw bales of hay, vineyards, windmills, growing crops, and irrigated canals.

Illuminated only by gentle gleams from the visible moons, which reflected soft light from the twin suns, Zylpha and Kaimo struggled to view the panorama. Needing to locate the ranch owned by Dumont's sister, a wave of distress came over Kaimo. Despite it being difficult to see details of the environment, he knew the pale light was better than none.

"Evening, ladies and gents," the captain announced again. "We're approaching Shady Oaks."

"So close," Zylpha said, her anxiety tangible.

The blimp approached a skyport identical to the previous one. Kaimo used his monocular and spotted a brick building whose chimney exhaled smoke. He failed to identify a barn but didn't see anything else before the crew lowered their ramp. The stationmaster unlocked a gate while the captain connected his hovering airship to the tower's platform.

"We have arrived at Shady Oaks," the captain said. "Gather your belongings and move along. Don't forget anything. I confiscate lost articles. Love 'em, quite honestly. Next is Rolling Grove."

Zylpha and Kaimo shared amused glances, eager to reach their destination.

III
Pursuit

Meanwhile, in the dusty town of Callopeak, imperial soldiers searched a train that had just arrived. It rested on steel columns twelve feet below the plateau's gorge. The highest-ranking officer exited the locomotive and scaled cracked steps along one of the canyon's escarpments that led to Callopeak's surface. Leaving the station's entrance, he passed an optical pylon and crossed an arched bridge that took him to the other side, where the *Iron Cloud* was suspended.

Several gunslingers near a saloon eyed him but kept to themselves as he strode through the rutted main street, wooden buildings erected on either side. Most townspeople and merchants were engrossed in their businesses, trying to ignore the empire's presence. The officer scanned a few of them, his helmet concealing a scowl. Reaching a water tower adjacent to Callopeak's skyport, he turned at a corner to where Xelvok stood, reviewing a logistics packing list beside an eroded ramp leading to his rigid zeppelin.

"Lord Cazar," the officer called out.

"One moment, Commandant," Xelvok replied, examining a certificate of origin. He eventually flipped the page and inspected another document. His eyes poured over a list of weapons and resources scheduled to ship to Enbertum. Without expression, he handed the packet back to the town's official and turned his attention to the officer. "Speak."

"We have yet to find the insurgents, Milord," he said, lowering his head. "I fear this may be another train that came through Rezekos. In which case—"

"If not here," Xelvok interjected, "then the rebels are bound for Pavebaro, just north of Vinestead." His eyes narrowed, fixing on his steam-powered airship. "They have grit, I'll give them that. Strange, though, the effects of the transfusion process should have left the dissident disoriented. She won't get far. Not unless the aeth..."—the grand marshal realized he was thinking aloud. "Inform your contingent to disengage and return to Iron Cloud for immediate departure."

"At once, Grand Marshal."

IV
Sojourn

Kaimo and Zylpha disembarked the blimp at the Rolling Grove skyport in Vinestead, along with a dozen other people. Stepping onto the grated platform, they descended a corroded, box-shaped staircase that spiraled down fourteen flights. At the base, the pair scanned the area while fellow travelers went on their way.

"See anything?"

In spite of the poor light, Kaimo surveyed the region with his spyglass. "I don't, but Dumont said his sister's farm is east from here. So, let's go that way."

Zylpha didn't argue. Together, they followed a grimy road. Not long after, however, it ended. Before them lay a sward whose lush-green grass filled the entire region for miles. Flowers bloomed throughout the field, vegetables and fruits abounded, and not a single weed in sight.

They eventually came across a canal with irrigated land. Not wanting to get wet, they walked alongside the shallow water to an arched overpass.

Crossing the bridge, the pair continued eastward. After passing a tractor they came across an old barn; but it was too dark outside for them to distinguish its color. The traveling duo sprinted up a narrow footpath within the plantation, between aisles of seemingly endless crops. Though haggard and panting, they reached the timber-framed storehouse with dark red, vertical siding.

"Could this be the one?" she asked, catching her breath.

"I think so," he replied, his raspy voice filled with hope.

Just then, they heard the cocking of a rifle. "Ya two vagabonds go turn round now 'n steal sum other persons food," said a coarse, middle-aged man from behind. "Go on. No other warnin' fer ya. Now git!"

"Dumont sent us," Kaimo blurted, his hands raised.

"Say what now?" hawked the plantation owner. "Dumont? Well, shit. I haven't seen the bugger in almost a year." He lowered his weapon, eyeing the pair. "Where's he at?"

"He's planning to join us in a couple of days," Zylpha answered.

"My name is Kaimo de Morté, and this is Zylpha Bess Wrayburn. We hired Dumont as our guide. We're trying to reach Enbertum. Since the imperium restricted flights to major cities, we have no choice but to travel on foot. He told us to come here while he settles some debts and will come as soon as he can."

"The name's Nestor Legget," he grumbled, turning toward his homestead. "Well, ya'd best get on over."

The duo followed him through the field, away from the barn. No longer surrounded by crops, they walked along a dirt-filled path leading to another cobblestone house with a smoking chimney no different than others throughout Vinestead. The home also had a porch whose beams held up a wooden ceiling.

Nestor stepped into his house, gesturing his guests to follow. "Maggie?" No one replied, causing him to groan. "Maggie!" he repeated, raising his voice.

"*What?*" she shouted from upstairs.

"Get yer wrinkled arse down here!" he responded. "Ya got guests, 'n another comin' yer way in 'bout a day or two."

"Guests? What're you talkin' about?" She appeared at the top of the stairs and made her way down, squinting at the uncomfortable pair. "This is *our* house, ya ninny! That means they're yer guests too."

"Nah uh," he grumbled. "They be folks from yer brother. I reckon he comin' in a couple of days. Camio Martey and Bessy Burns."

"Nice to meet you, ma'am. I am Kaimo de Morté, and this is my good friend, Zylpha Wrayburn. We hired your brother to help us get to Enbertum safely. Dumont told us to come here."

"I know it's awfully late," Zylpha said. "If it's a problem..."

"Nonsense!" the woman said, waving her hand. "Margaret Cogen-Legget. If Duwey sent ya, then it's cus yer a nice lovin' couple."

Kaimo flinched. "We're not toge—"

"Come!" Margaret interjected, making her way to the kitchen. "Ya must be hungry. I'll fix ya somethin' to eat."

Candles and kerosene lamps lit the way to the dining hall. The floor creaked as they entered the adjacent room. Nestor gestured at chairs opposite him and took a seat, putting on spectacles to read a newspaper. The pair sat down, noting an oil painting of a sailboat in stormy seas.

"You have a wonderful home," Zylpha said.

"Yes, it gives me a warm feeling."

Barely acknowledging their compliments, Nester grumbled. "These shitty glasses ain't workin' fer me...wasted money! What? Oh, thank ya. Been here 'bout twenty years."

Kaimo rose from his seat and approached. "May I?" he asked, reaching out for the spectacles. Nestor raised an eyebrow but gave the frame to him. "Do you know your PD or visual acuity?"

"Huh? Wha? Beats me. I ain't no doctor."

The optometrist examined the temples characteristics of the lenses. Squinting at the glasses, he reached into an inset pocket in his vest. Realizing it was empty, Kaimo touched his chest to find something dangling around his neck. He grasped the monocle and pulled it out, reexamining the spectacle eyewear.

"Let me guess...wrong size?"

"Actually, it's not that. These are usually crafted in a standard size. The frame is good quality—nickel with spring-hinged temples and soft nose pads. But the question is how many diopters is it?

"Dio what?"

"Diopters. Units of measure, which are different from the usual magnification powers in telescopes. From what I see engraved on the inside of the temples, your glasses are a plus 4D with a pupillary distance of sixty-five. If you're having trouble with visual acuity, I recommend 6D with 8D prism in."

"Thanks, *Professor.* I'll be sure ta get 'em after I win the lottery."

"Oh, um, I'm sorry," Kaimo said, scratching his head. He sat back down next to Zylpha who stared at him strangely. "What?"

"Nothing," she said, turning away.

Moments later, Margaret entered with sandwiches and two cups of water. "Here you go."

"Thank you," the guests said in unison.

Together, they ate the much-needed food and gulped down the water. Margaret chuckled and brought over a jug for them. When their stomachs settled, they shared their grim story with the farmers. They kept it simple, explaining that they wanted to get as far away from the terror attack as possible.

"That's dreadful," the wife said.

"How come it ain't in the newspaper yet?"

Margaret smacked her husband's balding head. "Are ya daft? It just happened. How're they gonna write an article like that and print it worldwide in three days?" She snorted and added, "I swear…"

"Bah!" the husband blurted. "I'm goin' ta bed."

The wife ignored him as he left, focusing on her guests. "Any friends of Dewy are friends of ours. Make yerselves at home. Shower if needed. We got towels in the closet. Sorry to say, we don't have another bedroom. But yer more than welcome to sleep inside the barn. Plenty hay there for beddings."

"We can't thank you enough," Zylpha said.

"Sure ya can," Margaret replied. "Ya can help my husband in the morin' out in the field. So much work to be done."

"I'll be happy to help," Kaimo said.

"*Wonderful!*" she said excitedly. "Well, I'm gettin' myself to bed too. Holler at us if ya need anythin' else."

They bade one another good night. Shortly after, the pair took individual showers upstairs and cleaned themselves. Slammed with exhaustion, they strolled to the barn. Just as Margaret had told them, stacks of straw blanketed the hayloft. Climbing up the ladder, they settled down and rested on a mound of it. The second floor had an unglazed window through which they saw a couple of windmills and grassland lit by the cratered moons.

"Your plan wouldn't have been so bad," Zylpha said.

"Huh? No, I wasn't thinking clearly. I've already lived most of my life up in the middle of nowhere." He paused, pensive, "Zelly, have you ever heard about the subconscious?" At her nod, he went on, "Like an ophthalmologist who peels down obscurities of the eye, psychiatrists are gaining respect by explaining mysteries of the brain. Anyway, I think my subconscious mind turned to the countryside because maybe somewhere deep down inside, I'm scared of civilization."

"No, just smart," she said. "Those bigger, grandiose cities are not as perfect as they're painted out to be. There's a lot more corruption, the crime rate is higher, and imperialists rule them with an iron fist. Well, except for Drenengarde...mafia gangs have mostly taken over that one. Hence, crime and corruption."

"And yet you still want to reach Enbertum?"

"Only because of Oswald Briknoll," she said. "He's an esteemed scholar and professor who knows about aether. Whether anyone believes me or not, he's the only one who can help me."

"I believe you."

Zylpha gazed at him, seeing determination in his eyes. "I know," she said, placing a hand on his. "Kaimo, why do I have this lingering feeling that we've met before? I feel as though I've known you for a lifetime. I know it sounds strange, but it's part of the reason why I trust you so much."

"*C'est* bizarre," Kaimo said, a pensive tenderness coming over him. Embracing her hand, he continued, "I cannot explain it either but…I have the same feeling."

Like a refreshing breeze on a humid day, Zylpha leaned in and kissed her companion. By nature, Kaimo flinched as a parade of wild thoughts stampeded through his mind. Yet he was smart enough to cast them aside and kiss her back.

"What does this mean?"

She smiled warmly at his question. "It means I like you, and you like me. We trust each other enough."

"Okay," he said, stroking her hair.

They kissed again while the moonlight shone on them. Zylpha proved to be bolder than most women, taking the initiative; however, she wasn't bold enough to undress him. Kaimo, on the other hand, was altogether more reserved. He embraced this new, fresh moment without spoiling it with lust. Sinking into the hay, they held each other in their arms, closed their eyes, and fell asleep.

V
Country Life

A couple of days of waiting for Dumont turned into a few. During this time, the guests helped the farmers on their plantation. Kaimo used a steam-powered tractor, plowing and fertilizing the land. He also, on occasion, used it to gather and haul bale hay. Zylpha, meanwhile, helped Margaret harvest her crops throughout the fields.

Airships came and went. Their powerful engines, and the dense steam they produced in the sky high above the farmlands, reminded Kaimo that living in the countryside was only one spectrum of life. The world was waiting for him, and though eager to see the rest of Zykard in its full glory, he needed to wait for the huntsman.

On the eighth and final day of the week, Kaimo breakfasted on eggs and juice. Motivated as if the farm were his own, he left to use Nestor's tractor. Plowing back and forth, he cultivated the wide fields. Zylpha watched him from a window in the living room, sitting on a rustic couch by the hearth.

As she sat there, she also wondered how life in the country would be; but she knew all too well that choosing a permanent life here would be tantamount to suicide with the empire searching for her. She brushed it off, knowing what had to be done. Still, she appreciated sojourning in Vinestead.

Yet another blimp arrived at the nearby tower. A few people disembarked from the vessel, at which point it flew away in a rush, smog filling the heavens. If a meteor were to flash across the firmament, no one would be able to see it. And though beaming behind the haze, not even the twin suns revealed themselves to the farmers and guests.

Thunder bellowed its presence like an enraged

demon. Lightning struck and flashed a dozen times. Kaimo saw the sky's wrath and realized it was approaching the homestead. He returned the tractor to the barn and went back inside the house, rejoining Zylpha in the living room. Sitting together, they watched as rain pummeled down like a salvo of daggers.

"My goodness," Margaret said, flinching from the thunder. "I haven't seen a storm like this in months."

"Not bad, kid," Nestor said. "Ya made short work of things."

Zylpha kissed her partner on the cheek. "How are you?" she asked, holding his hand.

"Tired," he said, his eyes fixed on the rain as if it were therapeutic to watch.

Out in the distance, he noted someone advancing. Sure as day, he pulled out his spyglass to see the man in greater detail. Despite the weather, the cloaked traveler sauntered through the field. He breathed with ease, the filters in his breathing apparatus giving him the clean air his blackened lungs needed. With a rifle slung on his back and two pistols holstered on either side of his waist, he meandered over to the homestead.

"What is it?" Zylpha asked, seeing his face brighten like a spot of sunshine escaping the clouds.

"It's him!" he answered with excitement. "Dumont!"

"Oh, crap," Nestor said, groaning while getting to his feet. "I thought we'd git 'nother day of peace."

"Quit complainin' ya wanker 'n git the door for 'im."

Her husband grumbled but walked over to the door and opened it. "Well, look who decided to show his face after a year."

"Howdy, Nesto," Dumont said, patting Nestor's shoulder while stepping inside the house. Right away, he gestured at the young couple with a wave; they greeted him with a bow. "So, I see you've met my company."

"Met?" his sister said, emerging from the living room. "Heck, they've become quite the farmers waitin' fer ya to show yer annoyin' face." When she reached him, they gave each other a tight hug. "Still using that hideous mask?"

"Not always," he said, lifting the visor. "Happy now?"

"Ya look better with it sealed," Nestor said, snickering with a cough.

"Careful, Nesto," he said. "You may need one too. After all, we both broke our backs hauling kogal before the farm life."

"You both used to be miners?" Kaimo asked, taken aback.

"No, just transporting resources," Dumont replied. "Though that would be just as lethal, especially for anyone mining for a living. Kogal is far worse than coal. It'll kill yer lungs within months."

Concern flashed across Kaimo's face. "It's a good thing I wasn't a miner for long," he muttered, placing a hand on his chest.

"That's why them imperials be wearin' those devil masks," Margaret said.

"Except mine's a lot more elegant than theirs," the huntsman responded.

"Any mask gives me the creeps," Zylpha said.

Though forthright, the group laughed at her comment.

Dumont sniffed the air as his stomach let out a growl. "What's cookin' now, sis?"

"Um...shepherd's pie?"

"Sounds good 'cus I'm starvin' and ain't goin' anywhere 'til I've got somethin' in the stomach."

The quintet sat in the dining room and shared a feast together. During the scrumptious meal, the farmers told Dumont how their guests helped them around the plantation. The coarse huntsman complimented the pair, but they both modestly waived it off as nothing more than a job.

"So, what's the plan?" Kaimo asked.

"Plan?" the huntsman said. "My sister's gonna lend us her finest steeds." He ignored his brother-in-law, who cursed under his breath, and continued, "We'll use 'em to reach the grand city. Enbertum, that is."

"Yer think ya'll can just waltz in here 'n take our stuff?" Nestor snapped.

"Don't be such a drip, Nes," Margaret said. "This between me and my brother." She paused for a moment. "Ya never pay me back, little brother. Why should I go outta my way to sacrifice three of my precious steeds?"

"Uh, 'cus this time I got the money," Dumont said.

"Since when are ya helpin' others?" Nestor asked.

"It's a job," he said curtly. "I'm gettin' paid for it. Four hundred qauras. I already got half, which I used to pay most of my debts yesterday. Just one left." He reached into a pocket and tossed over fifty qauras on the table. "Now you can't say I haven't paid you back, sis. I'm gettin' the other half when I get 'em to the big city. Ain't that right, kids?"

"Yes, of course," Kaimo said.

"I trust 'em like I'm sure ya do, too. I'll split half those remaining two hundred with you both. Then you can get a dozen steeds or a month's worth of food."

Nestor no longer argued.

"Humph," his wife snorted, taking the money. She glanced at her guests and turned to her brother. "All right. Ya got yourself a deal, little brother."

No longer raining, the farmers took them to one of their stables where they revealed a pack of grazing uy'kaja. Dumont assisted Nestor with putting saddles on the chosen steeds. His uy'kaja had a black coat that matched his raggedy outfit. Kaimo's and Zylpha's steeds had light, sky-blue coats.

"Thank you so much for everything," Zylpha said to the farmers.

"Yes," Kaimo concurred. "We cannot thank you enough for your incredibly generous hospitality."

"Yer more than welcome," Margaret said.

"Remember, their generosity wasn't free," the huntsman said, his mask concealing a smirk.

Awkwardness briefly took hold of Kaimo as he nodded and then approached his uy'kaja. The traveling trio used stirrups, mounting their animals while an airship passed them from the high heavens. To their surprise, it wasn't a passenger or merchant blimp, but, rather, an imperial zeppelin. Though it flew fast, the group looked up and gazed at it.

"It's happening," Zylpha mumbled.

Kaimo heard her, also acknowledging that this was the first time he'd seen a military vessel flying around the countryside since their arrival. Though troubling, he remained focused on the present and gripped the reins of his steed. Like him, his companions took control of their uy'kaja and then waved at the farmers.

"Come back soon, little brother," Margaret said, waving back.

"Not *that* soon," Nestor said. "But when or if ya do, bring these nice chaps of yers back so they can help me some more."

CHAPTER FIVE

Journey's End

I
Road to Progress

The trio traveled north, their steeds galloping as swiftly as the brisk winds that come and go with every season. Vinestead gleamed as the twin suns shone on it. Lush green flatlands surrounded them for the next couple of hours. When dusk arrived, however, the terrain became bumpier. Trees grew in abundance, hills rose, and the seemingly endless strands of grass diminished, as did the skyports and their associated blimps that roamed the clouds.

Leaving behind the plantations of Vinestead, Kaimo and his companions raced toward a valley. The peaceful countryside soon faded in the back-lands. In the distance, the trio saw a vista of mountains. From west to east, the mountain range filled the region. As they strode farther north, the rising valley took form and teemed with life.

"This must be the Vale of Lei'halm," Zylpha said.

"Right you are," Dumont replied. "Lots of critters here, and not all friendly. So, we'd best be extra careful."

"May the wind be at our backs," Kaimo put in.

They strayed from the woodlands and eventually came across a stream that flowed from one of the far-off mountains. Riding beside it, they smelled clean air, wet grass, and a refreshing aroma of lavender. Flowers bloomed around them, shrubs growing with an occasional tree rich with leaves.

The creek stretched between earthy knolls for miles, curving through the gulch. Atop one of the verdant mounds, Kaimo used his spyglass and fixed on an optical pylon in a remote village. Despite the existence of sprawling cities ruled by a vast empire, the age of industrialization was still young. Cobbled streets and terraced houses were being built—that much he could see—but a great deal of the old world still existed there, such as thatched homes and old-fashioned wells without city pipes or even a septic system.

One thing, however, caught his attention: the imperial railroad. In the distance, he saw its tracks coursed through the land like the river he and his companions rode beside. Though a train wasn't in sight yet, Kaimo knew it was only a matter of time before one with soldiers would arrive. The village also had a skyport for airships, so there was evidence of progress.

"See anything?" Zylpha asked.

"Just a remote village. Nothing out of the ordinary."

"That's an upcomin' town called Pavebaro," Dumont said. "Imperial trains frequent it with supplies for construction. We'd best stray from it."

Continuing onward, they couldn't avoid a forest that grew in their way. Not wanting to travel in the direction of Pavebaro, the trio breached the thick woods. The smell of pine and spruce filled their nostrils as they passed clusters of trees through which the lively stream flowed.

The steeds slowed their gait, careful not to overexert themselves or hurt their fragile legs by cantering along the gritty path. A chorus of myriad insects filled their ears, resonating in the minty air like a sweet lullaby. As soothing an intonation as it was for Kaimo, he didn't care for bugs and hoped not to see one. What he and his companions did appreciate, however, were the crown of trees whose twisty branches shaded them from the suns.

Three days passed while the trio traversed the woodlands. Dumont hunted for food each day. He caught fish from the stream on a couple of occasions; other times he used his rifle to hunt wildlife tucked away in the forest, such as a boukaphant—a beast with an azure fleece, an elongated tail of many thongs, one horn protruding from the cranium, and hooves. Every evening, Dumont set up a campfire, roasting meat. Each of them took turns to watch the camp.

On the fourth day, the winding foothills led them out of the uneven forest. No longer in hazardous terrain, the uy'kaja increased their pace and galloped fast. The travelers broke away from the narrowing creek and left the valley. Distinct spires rose in the distance like split mountains.

"Is that it?" Kaimo asked.

"That it is," Dumont responded.

"I can't believe we're almost there," Zylpha said, her heart pounding with anxiety. "We're actually getting there."

"We ain't there 'til past the entrance," Dumont threw in.

"Fair enough," she said, controlling her apprehension.

As they drew closer, the smell of nature died. Swathed in what seemed like mist, the trio embraced the pseudo fog. Yet as the spires reshaped into soaring buildings, they realized there was no fog or mist—it was the ubiquitous smog from steam engines that engulfed the region. Again, the land flattened. It smoothed out, absent of trees and grass. Shrubs and flowers scarcely revealed themselves. The trilling of insects dissipated. And the occasional barks and howls of animals tucked away in the wilderness vanished altogether.

Only one species of beasts reigned supreme within the rambling, expanding city—the uy'kaja. They roamed the cobbled roads in their colorful coats, hauling carriages. Despite only having two legs, they were powerful creatures man still relied on. Yet the passing of a car, the engine of which reverberated past the galloping trio, reminded them that it was only a matter of time before such animals would also be shunned by humanity.

Kaimo stared at the automobile, remembering his father's vehicle and wishing it hadn't been destroyed. Those thoughts dissipated when he acknowledged the city's clock tower, which soared almost as high as the docking airships. Incredulity left his mouth agape. The gargantuan metropolis itself was filled with brick buildings of industry, terraced homes, a high-rise wall spreading across the perimeters of the entire city, and power plants whose counterweighted clockwork churned with kogal.

Slowing down, they reached the gated entrance of Enbertum. Masked soldiers gazed at them, not with suspicion but with pity for riding on steeds instead of at least having a carriage. Not seeing them as a threat, they gestured to the trio to proceed. With the exception of Dumont, the travelers were unnerved while entering the city limits. Away from the whispering guards, they recovered their shaken intentions and focused on the path ahead.

The cobbled street was simply one of myriad streets, built like a cosmic web that spread for miles on end. Buildings proliferated every road from left to right. Quite frankly, Zylpha didn't know where to start. She pulled on the reins of her steed and halted, prompting the others to stop as well.

"Where to, Zelly?"

For the first time, she was mystified. "The truth is, I haven't the faintest idea. All I know is Oswald lives here and we need to find him."

Dumont grunted under his gas mask.

"He's a famous scholar, right?" At her nod, Kaimo went on, "Then we search for a renowned institution. Whether we come across the legendary observatory or the University of Krenanstein, I'm more than sure someone in either place will know who he is and where to find him."

"Good thinking, darling."

"Let's get to it," Dumont said.

II
Roaming the Metropolis

Kaimo and his companions advanced into the sprawling city. Carriages filled the paved streets, and an occasional automobile drove by at a surprisingly controlled speed. Despite congested streets jammed with people and machinery, the trio cantered ahead with relative ease. Soaring buildings blocked the ever-radiant twin suns, but Enbertum still beamed despite the musty steam, vented air, smog, and gothic architecture enveloped with gloom.

As usual, people milled about the majestic city. Many of the men had fine garments with striped trousers, buttoned shirts with vests, ascot neckties, and fitted tailcoats. Some gentlemen even wore brocade jackets exhibiting shawl collars. As for the women, they boasted embroidered frocks, tailored skirts, swallowtail coats, collared blouses, and laced corsets. To top it off, just about everyone owned a bowler hat.

To the lens-maker's disappointment, soldiers were the exception to the elegant fashion. Clad in full-plated armor and helmets with breathing apparatuses to filter the air, they prowled the streets like lifeless husks. Others stood guard akin to statues near the train station, harbor, and skyports.

The trio ignored them, searching through bustling avenues in an intricate design of interlinked cogs. Emporiums and boutiques triumphed with customers looking for various goods ranging from food, herbs, potions, kitchenware, and antiques. Kaimo found two bookstores on different boulevards, an impressively large library near the police station, a museum showcasing armor and swords of knights from the old world, and a few small publishing houses, as well as a newspaper company called *Liberté au Crépuscule*.

Kaimo and Zylpha felt like tourists, absolutely clueless where to go. Truth be told, the huntsman shared their disorientation but kept it to himself. Despite being ignorant, he led them through the concourses until his eyes caught a sign with an arrow that read: *University of Krenanstein*.

Without saying anything, he guided his companions to a boulevard lined with trees and flowerbeds. Though scarce, Kaimo and his partner were happy to see some form of nature in the vast metropolis. Passing an open gate, they followed a road bringing them to a park-like campus.

Unlike other parts of the city where homes and businesses were crammed together, these gothic buildings stood out like monuments. Each revealed intricate portals showcasing carved effigies of knights serving a primordial king long before the empire's existence, stained-glass windows along the façades, spire-shaped corners, and crenellated roofs. The structures were distanced from one another throughout the plaza but in relative walking distance.

The gated passageway, however, forced Kaimo and his company to ascend a staircase leading to the institutional building; they needed to enter it to gain access to the outer plaza, which was where most students resided. Dismounting their steeds, the trio tethered the uy'kaja to a post while pupils and professors passed by. Afterwards, they went up the stairs and reached the main entrance where an imperialist stood guard.

"Excuse me, good sir," Kaimo started, "are we allowed to enter?"

"That depends," he responded in a reasonable tone. "Are you a student here or applying to attend Krenanstein?"

"Sorry, no. Not yet."

"Then what business do you have here?"

"We're lookin' for a *real* smart guy," Dumont said.

"Some kind of savant, librarian, or professor."

"There are more than two dozen professors on the campus..."

Zylpha took a step forward. "Can you tell us where we may find the renowned scholar Oswald Briknoll?"

"I can't help you, ma'am," he said. "Hundreds of people come and—"

"Pardon the intrusion," intervened a passing educator who stepped aside while showing his identification to the guard. "You're looking for Professor Briknoll?"

"Yes," Zylpha said. "It's extremely important."

"Might I inquire as to why you seek him?"

Zylpha glanced around out of habit. "It's regarding his research into the existence of aether."

"I see," the educator said with intrigue. "I'm not surprised. He used to work here at the university. We worked on a couple of academic experiments together...at least until a string of horrific, unnatural murders started taking place. It's a bit beyond what the police can handle. With his background in forensics, the emperor appointed him as a researcher of sorts in the investigation."

"Then we check the police headquarters," Dumont said.

"Not quite," the educator responded. "Come. Walk with me." He strayed from the guard and went down the entrance's flight of steps with them. "It is a sensitive matter. Officers tend to shun him. You see, they want to be the ones who catch the criminal. They have their highfalutin reasons, but they're humiliated if you ask me. Hence, like many other researchers, he is stationed at the observatory." At their dumbfounded expressions, he added, "East of here."

"Thank you so much," Zylpha said.

Kaimo shook his hand. "Thank you."

"You are most welcome. Good luck."

The trio hurried to their steeds. Untethering the reins from the post, they mounted the uy'kaja and galloped out of the campus. Returning to the congested labyrinth of streets and buildings, they made their way east. As usual, Kaimo and his companions remained vigilant what with the incoming traffic of carriages, automobiles, and crowd.

Dumont cursed under his breath, slowing the gait of his steed. The others followed his actions, their stomachs growling and aching for sustenance. By chance, after passing several more avenues, they located a café. Famished, they stopped for lunch and tied the reins of their uy'kaja to an adjacent post.

"You two find seats while I get us some food and drink," the huntsman said, pulling out a few qauras.

The others complied, finding a table outside.

In the meantime, Dumont stepped inside and approached the barista. "Three coffees, and tell the baker we want beef crêpes."

"Anything else?"

"No."

"Twelve qauras."

The hunter paid her and waited by the counter as she prepared the coffees. By chance, he glanced at his employers seated at a table outside. Seeing them holding hands, he snorted and rolled his eyes behind his mask. Thinking about the situation, he turned his attention back to the barista.

"Say, whereabouts east is the observatory?"

"Near the harbor...beyond the clock tower. It's the only dome-shaped building. You can't miss it."

"Thanks," he said, tipping her with a qaura.

Receiving his order, he joined the others outside

and gave them their food and drinks. This was the only time Dumont lifted his visor. Together they ate quietly, satisfying their parched lips and empty stomachs. The scrumptious flavors of their crêpes mixed with grilled beef, sautéed vegetables, and sizzling cheese melted in their mouths. Balanced with the bitter, nutty taste of their drinks, they were revived.

"I can't believe I'm here," Kaimo said, breaking the silence as he sipped his dark roasted coffee. "All my life I've dreamed of this moment."

"You want to attend medical school, right?" Zylpha asked.

"That's the goal. I aspire to be an ophthalmologist. It's just...I just don't know if it's still feasible with everything going on."

"Don't worry," she said calmly. "When all this is over, you will."

"Thank you, Zelly. I sure hope so."

Dumont cleared his throat. "Are you two lovebirds finished?"

The couple blushed but didn't retort. Instead, they emptied leftovers in the trash receptacles and returned to their steeds. Dumont untethered them from the post as Zylpha mounted her uy'kaja. Before mounting his, Kaimo spotted an optical emporium named *Optometric Haven.*

Eyes wide, he sprinted across the busy street and was nearly hit by an automobile that beeped at him. He waved apologetically and carried on. Unable to control himself, much like a child with toys, Kaimo placed his hands on the glass window and examined some of optics' latest inventions—opera-style binoculars, monoculars, larger telescopes with tripods, hand-held magnifiers, and monocles with lanyards.

"Hey, Professor," Dumont called out. "I know all this science stuff is exciting, but we've got places to be."

"Right," he said, snapping out of his trance. "Sorry."

Zylpha simply smiled at him with affection.

"We make for the harbor," the huntsman said.

Together the group rode past rows of houses, smoke rising from their chimneys. Though most of the buildings stood at least twenty to thirty feet high, the trio saw an elongated structure of a colossal bridge in the background. Dumont used its wired ropes as landmarks, making his way toward it.

At an intersection, they halted their steeds while an automobile drove by. The path clear, the trio advanced north. After a few turns through the concourses, they arrived at the arched bridge and crossed over it. One of many schooners drifted beneath them, and an airship hovered high above.

Kaimo abruptly stopped midway. Since their arrival at the grand city, he'd caught glimpses of a statue in the far-flung distance; but the buildings had blocked his vision. Now on the highest rise of the bridge with a wide view of water, he saw a distant island and what was built on it.

"Whoa," he said, overawed.

"Mother of science," Zylpha said. "It's actually real."

Dumont glanced at them as though they were behaving in a ridiculous fashion but also understood why. Before their eyes stood an effigy of gargantuan proportions. Yet it wasn't just any sculpture; it was a statue of Emperor Dalfein Af Ereganen himself. He held a sword that nearly kissed the clouds. Military garments with spaulders expanded his shoulders, and a cape almost swayed with the wind.

"It's quite the sight," Dumont said, hawking at

the water. "Can we go now, your royal majesties?"

Crossing the steel overpass, they reached the other side of town that comprised a great deal of warehouses and factories. Kaimo and his companions arrived at the harbor where the quayside was filled to capacity with boats. From a distance, they saw a paddle steamer approaching, its wheel slowing down as the captain prepared to dock and allow passengers to disembark.

"Look!" Kaimo said, pointing east.

At the edge of the wharf—built beside a lighthouse and heliograph tower—atop the cliff of Enbertum's coast, stood an astronomical observatory. A shimmering beacon akin to a white pearl, its open dome-shaped roof revealed the tip of an enormous telescope. Kaimo noted the massive objective lens, speechless.

"I guess you can show me that fourth moon."

"I'd love that," he said, beaming at his partner.

Dumont scoffed. "Nobody's gonna let us near that bloody thing," he barked. "We'd have to be researchers like the esteemed professor here. But we can at least get ourselves inside 'n ask if anyone knows 'bout that scholar of yours."

"Makes sense..."

"You don't need to be so dismissive," Zylpha said.

Ire creased the hunter's face. "Let me remind ya again that this ain't an adventure," he snarled. "You're being hunted by the most dangerous man alive. Get it?"

"Life is short and precious. It's fleeting moments like this that make life worth living. Even if they're just snippets, we need to fight for every moment to be alive."

"Exactly," he said. "I'm fighting to live long enough to get paid."

A rueful laugh escaped Kaimo.

"I don't want to seem ungrateful," Zylpha said. "You saved us and guided us all the way here. Albeit, for money. But you still helped. I only hope that one day you see more to life than qauras."

"Probably not," he grumbled to himself.

Zylpha shook her head and, similar to her partner, let out a chuckle. "Fine. Have it your way, Mr. Robot. Let's go."

The travelers cantered across the pier, the hooves of their steeds thumping on the wooden planks. Most workers were busy unloading imported goods from various continents while others prepared to set sail. As the trio passed an approaching ferry, they guided their mounts up a staircase that spiraled up Enbertum's cliffside.

Reaching the top, Kaimo and his companions advanced toward the observatory. It stood out like an ivory gem, a shooting star that had traversed the glistening cosmos, only to be hurled unto Zykard, carving itself into the ground. Kaimo couldn't take his eyes off it, halting at the guarded entrance; inside the stargazing building contained a means to see the mysteries of the universe.

The trio dismounted the uy'kaja and approached the guard.

"Greetings," Kaimo said, beaming like a little boy. "We're here to see Professor Oswald Briknoll."

"I'm afraid he's not available. Police business."

Dumont scowled under his gas mask. "Knew it..."

"We're, um, actually a part of the investigation," Zylpha said. "He requested assistance with those horrific murders."

Lifting his visor, the guard stared at her suspiciously. "Women helping now, too? What is this world coming to? Fine. Go ahead."

"Thank you, *good sir*," she said, containing her anger while passing him.

III
Fragments of a Legend

The travelers entered Enbertum's observatory. His heart bursting with excitement, Kaimo gazed up at the vaulted ceiling. Elevated on a metal platform at the center of the chamber, the largest optical telescope he'd ever seen in his life stood before him. The entryway of the ramp leading to its splendor, however, was blocked by mechanical gadgetry. Ignoring consequences, he approached it.

"Hey!" shouted a voice opposite him. "What is the meaning of this intrusion?"

Across the aluminum floor stood an old man attired in a sack suit whose brown, loose-fitting jacket complemented his blue floppy bowtie. Boasting a white handlebar mustache, he approached in a rush, waving his hands in protest as if shooing insects. As the old man drew closer, he stopped and gawked at the young woman. Pulling out a monocle, he placed it on his left eye while slowly approaching her.

"Science be damned," he rasped, pale as a lich.

"Do my eyes deceive me? Zylpha? Is that really you?"

"Yes," she said, her hands shaking. "I'm still alive, Professor."

The scholar made haste to the door, locking it. "Miracles amid dubious times. Where is your mother?"

"She...she's gone from us."

Professor Briknoll scowled. "Hoping she was still alive was too much to ask. How did you escape the emperor's grasp?"

"I fear the emperor does not even know of my existence."

"You fear?" he replied, raising an eyebrow in response. "If that is truly the case, then that is another miracle."

"No," she said despondently. "I fear something much worse. The grand marshal hid me from the emperor and had me transported elsewhere by train. He imprisoned me in a poisonous, alchemical machine. If it weren't for the actions of this man,"—she gestured at Kaimo—"then the aether within me would probably be flowing through Xelvok."

"The duke? To say that such a thing would be treason is an understatement. Improbable. He is

Emperor Dalfein's sword." Silence descended upon them for a moment. "If this is true, it could mean a coup d'état."

"Isn't that already happenin' with them insurgents?" Dumont asked.

"Not exactly," Kaimo answered. "They outright formed a resistance to eliminate the imperium entirely. It's an all-out war."

"I hope the resistance wins," Zylpha put in.

Kaimo stroked his chin. "There's no doubt the empire is out of control. Unfortunately, the resistance is fighting evil with evil."

"But which faction is the lesser evil?"

"I understand, Zelly," he responded, his eyes downcast. Wanting to change the topic, he quickly turned to the scholar and extended his hand. "Forgive me. I am Kaimo de Morté, and this is Dumont Fen Cogen."

"A pleasure to meet you both," he said, shaking Kaimo's hand. "Impressive that you managed to free Zylpha and bring her here unscathed."

"Barely," he said, his nerves twitching again as he recalled the grim incident. "During the terror attack in Icdarus, Xelvok cornered a group of insurgents in the mine and killed them despite a hostage situation. My father…he was a war hero for the empire and the grand marshal killed him without hesitation just to get to the insurgents."

"By the four moons," the scholar gasped. "You witnessed the hijacking of the imperial train at Icdarus?"

Kaimo nodded. "I was mining kogal at the time. When we heard explosions, I got out of the mine and witnessed the attack. I somehow thought it'd be safer to hide in one of the train's carriages. That's when I found her."

"Therein lies the problem," the scholar deduced.

"Right…because if she was meant for the emperor, Xelvok would've personally brought her aboard Iron Cloud and hand-delivered her to him."

"Crikey," Dumont blurted.

Professor Briknoll grumbled. "Immortality," he said in a pensive tone. "We have always been obsessed with it. Why else did man create religion? We imagined greatness, deeming our makers immortal. But they have faded away into extinction no different from our ancestors. For decades the emperor has searched the primeval world, digging into its esoteric secrets by means of science. It's been his goal since the beginning—his raison d'être—to succeed where the gods have failed."

"Rasu what?" the huntsman asked.

"To lift man from the trenches of his mortal coil and vanquish that which is unnatural to conquer...death itself," the scholar reiterated. "Though it would seem Lord Cazar knows more about the old world than even Emperor Dalfein and has ambitions of his own: to snuff out His Imperial Majesty and steal such glory for himself. Alas, you are the only ones who can put an end to his yet-to-be magnum opus."

"How the heck are we gonna do that when there's an entire resistance strugglin'?"

The scholar acknowledged Dumont's question, conflicted about an answer. "Have any of you ever heard of the Etherstone?" When they shook their heads, he gestured them to follow him to the back. He moved autopsy reports on his table and revealed an ancient tome. "All my life, I have studied the aether."

"Pardon my ignorance," Kaimo began, "but what exactly is the aether? I mean, from an intellectual point of view."

"*Ah*," the scholar uttered, his eyes brightening with life. "The perfect question. To the uneducated, it is mere myth—an impossible power considered as magic. To the fully educated, its nature is undefinable. Something...not of this world."

"What exactly are you implying?" Zylpha said. "That those who possess the aether are not—"

"Nothing as bold as what you're thinking," the scholar interjected. "If we can actually define it, then the true nature would be parasitical to the spirit like a leech is to the body. More frightening is the fact that it needs overwhelming sustenance. Fuel, so to speak. Think of a train with coal or an automaton with kogal. Steam engines need energy. And just as is stated in theoretical physics: matter is energy, and energy is matter. That very substance and fuel for the aether is none other than the Etherstone."

"I'm not quite sure I follow," Kaimo said.

Professor Briknoll pondered for a moment. "The aether flows through one's body like the subconscious. You know it's there and feel it but cannot touch it. Yet it is alive. Consider man's spirit. I theorize it is brain and mind combined that create *soul*. Just so, the aether is a malleable thing akin to soul, and the stone its body. Merge these constituents and..."

"An aggregate of insurmountable power," Kaimo concluded. "Immortality."

"Precisely," Briknoll said.

"Now we're getting somewhere, but my mother never told me anything of the sort. And this still doesn't explain what exactly the Etherstone is and how it came to be."

The professor grimaced. "Hence, why I asked if any of you had ever heard of its legend before. Millennia ago, during the days of old—long before the empire's reign—there exists an ancient tale of a valiant paragon who became king, unifying knights across the world to fight a darkness that was said to be unnatural. Legend has it, he even commanded a legion of golems. Alas, and alack, superstitious minds of that time could not comprehend science."

Dumont scoffed, not sure why he was still there.

"Who was this paragon?" Kaimo inquired.

"I could only find one parable that shared his name: Ma'vak Zaar. Call him the world's only sorcerer or magus in written history. Alchemist. Chemist. Warrior. King. There are far too many superstitions to weed out from the truth. What I do believe is that he existed. That much I am certain."

"Such a foreign name," Kaimo said, an uncanny sensation rippling through him.

"Tch," Dumont uttered. "Sounds more like an elaborate title if ya ask me."

"The primeval legend is ten thousand years old," the scholar said snootily. "I'm afraid everything in the tale *is* foreign and elaborate. Ma'vak Zaar was a force to be reckoned with. As for his power..."

"What of it?" Zylpha asked, her voice eager.

"It is said Ma'vak Zaar was on the cusp of divinity. He was the first and last to wield the power of the gods by means of alchemy. It is assumed, but *never* proven, that he was the one to formulate an amalgamation of celestial proportions—the Etherstone itself."

Zylpha stared at him in disbelief. "The aether that flows through my veins was the very power he wielded?"

Professor Briknoll nodded. "With the omnipotent gem, he was somehow able to harvest the aether that flowed into his bloodstream. Then the story alters and gets murky. From what I pieced together,

Ma'vak Zaar became the very darkness he hunted. It is said his greatest knights slayed him before the world's imminent destruction."

Kaimo shook his head in dismay. "If any of this myth is true, then the Etherstone is the most deadly, terrible thing in existence. What happened to it?"

"United under one banner, our beloved heroes gathered together and used their swords to shatter it. But destroyed, it wasn't. Nay. The gem split into fragments, and those very pieces were cast into the throes of oblivion—hurled into the deepest parts of our earth—never to be discovered again."

"Until now," Zylpha responded, her voice gruff.

"So it would seem. To this day, only your mother claimed to feel the inner vibrations of the aether. It pierced her soul and spoke to her mind like a maddening whisper. Evidently, despite such power remaining dormant, it has been passed on to you. Lord Cazar must know it flows within you, Zylpha. There's no other reason for his obsession with you. Yet the aether is useless to him without the fabled gem. Ergo, he clearly believes in the Etherstone's misbegotten existence."

Dumont groaned through his gas mask. "But ya

just said a moment ago that the damn thing was destroyed."

"Shattered. Not destroyed. Remnants still linger."

"Damn it all," Kaimo said, unnerved as fear surged and gripped him. "For all we know, Xelvok may've already unearthed some of the shards. If he reforges the Etherstone, the world won't live to see another day."

"If the legend is even half true," Dumont replied, suspicion touching his voice.

"Of course it's real," Zylpha snapped. "Xelvok was an alchemist before the war and killed my mother in his twisted experiments. Now he's after me. I feel the aether inside me. This isn't an illusion. We need to do something."

"But where do we start?" Kaimo wondered aloud.

"You can begin right here in Enbertum," Professor Briknoll answered. At their stunned expressions, he went on, "Why do you think this city thrives so much? You can't possibly think steam engines and kerosene do all this. Could it be mere coincidence? Or is it possible Emperor Dalfein Af Ereganen unearthed one of the insatiable fragments and ignorantly uses it to further enliven this ever-so-prosperous city?"

"Is this claptrap real?" Zylpha said, finding it difficult to accept her heritage.

The scholar remained silent for a moment. "Inconceivable as it may seem, there is only one way to discern the veracity," he finally said. "Wait until midnight. When the city falls asleep, find your way into the central clock tower and—"

"This is insane," Dumont interjected. "Give me my money, kid. I'm done with this fairytale."

To his chagrin, Kaimo reached into his pocket.

"Thank you for everything," Zylpha said earnestly. "I know we don't see eye to eye. I realize we can't live in this world without money or following laws. You're a hunter and keep your feet on the ground. I respect that."

Kaimo nodded, disappointment carved on his face. "Thank you for coming this far with us, Dumont."

"Yeah…whatever," he said curtly, taking his money and leaving.

"I have problems of my own," the scholar said. "My soul, tangible or not, belongs to the imperium. That was the vow I made when receiving my doctorate. I am old and feeble now. No escaping my fate.

Therefore, this quest is up to you two."

"There must be something more. My mother told me to find you if anything happened to her. Surely she didn't want me to come all this way just to hear a tale?"

"Your mother was a wondrous person, Zylpha. She protected you. Now the past becomes the present, and we are thus hurled into the future of an unknown paradigm. Your incorporeal heredity cannot be denied. It is entirely in your hands."

"But why start at the clock tower?" Kaimo asked, his head spinning.

"Like any great mechanical invention, it needs occasional tinkering. About seven years ago, by mere chance, when I was repairing one of its cogs, I felt something unnatural. It cannot be described. Now leave me. I have an investigation of my own that needs tending, and it's far more gruesome than exploring the heart of Enbertum."

IV
Destiny Reforged

The weary pair retired to an inn not far from the harbor. They paid for one night, went upstairs to their room, and closed the door behind them. The couple rested on the bed, holding each other until nightfall, not uttering a single word. Their minds shut down like jammed gears, preventing them from thinking straight about the midnight excursion.

Although dispirited, Zylpha had the urge to break the comforting silence. "I wasn't looking for all this." Her partner stayed quiet, listening as she went on, "I'm not sure if all those details are true."

"It's overwhelming," Kaimo replied. "Quite frankly, I don't know how or where to put all that in my head."

"Do you think it's just a legend?"

"To be honest, I'm not sure. It's clear Xelvok believes it. He wouldn't be obsessed with you otherwise."

"I'm scared."

"So am I," he said, caressing her curled hair. "In truth, I'm frightened. But we can't run from this."

"Are we really going to break into the clock tower?"

Kaimo sighed and thought about everything. "There's a reason why your mother trusted Professor Briknoll. His academic research into the aether is sound. Despite our fear, we need to know for sure."

Zylpha agreed as a tight, constricting sensation formed in her stomach. "I know Dumont was all about money. Still, I can't believe he left."

"Yeah…this madness started with just the two of us. Yet somehow having him around made everything seem feasible." He paused, pondering again. "I can't blame him. Maybe it's because he's older and set in his ways."

"You won't leave me too, right?"

"*What?*" he responded, caught off guard. "No. I'll never abandon you. I'm here to stay no matter what happens."

"But what if your life is threatened?"

"Nothing will change my feelings."

"Nothing?" she said skeptically. When he shook his head, Zylpha let his words sink in. "Thank you, Kai."

He smiled at the nickname. "No need to thank me, Zelly. We'll get through this."

The couple gently kissed and held each other until midnight arrived. Despite their growing fear and anxiety, they left the room and went downstairs. Dozens of men, gambling and drunk, barely paid any mind to the pianist or the departing couple.

As the duo stepped out, a city of lights greeted them. Kaimo stopped for a moment, his mouth agape at Enbertum's nightlife. Lamp posts with gleaming fixtures lit up the roads, and the lighthouse beamed with tremendous luminosity. The water shimmered in the distance, reflecting the glow that rippled with docked boats.

Not wanting to draw attention, the pair left their steeds behind as they ventured south. Though smog mingled with the clouds, the three moons still revealed themselves in the gloom. As the duo walked through one of many boulevards, steam enveloped them. Leaving behind the harbor and factories, they traversed Enbertum's bridge.

On the other side, they reached a neighborhood whose homes brightened even the darkest alleyways, the windows emitting soft light. Carriages had stopped for the day, the paved streets empty for the most part. A few people still lingered, but not a single animal trotted through the mostly sleeping city.

The pair was about to cross a main intersection when an automobile drove by, its headlights temporarily blinding them. When the path was clear, they continued onward. Farther south, they looked skyward and gazed at Enbertum's greatest marvel—the smog-kissing clock tower. Adjoined with a reservoir linked to the city's waterworks and sewer system, its pinnacle revealed a radiant turret with clock faces in four directions, the cast iron dials bolted together with revolving pointers.

"This is it, Zelly. Are you ready?"

"No, but do we have a choice?"

He couldn't disagree with her, continuing onward. Together they approached one of the stone façades with a brass door. Kaimo examined it, trying to figure out a way to open it without making noise. In the meantime, Zylpha lifted her pistol and shot the chained lock.

"Women power," she said, winking at him.

Using a great deal of force, the duo pulled the slab-shaped door aside and entered the reservoir. Before them lay a dimly lit cylindrical tunnel with damp brick walls. Musty air caused them to crinkle their noses, and dripping water echoed in their ears. Though faint, they were within earshot of a clanking sound resonating from above.

"Do you hear that?" he asked.

Zylpha nodded. "It's just ahead."

Conscious of their urgency, the duo advanced through the dark passage. At each of the junctions, Kaimo chose paths where the reverberations were louder. Zylpha followed, putting her trust in him. They had no choice but to step into puddles here and there because of leaky pipes. One of the conduits along the ceiling spewed hot steam, forcing the pair to duck and scoot past it.

Turning at a corner, they found a rusty metal ladder. Kaimo clutched a rung and shook it first, making sure it wasn't loose. Satisfied it was secure, he started climbing. Zylpha let out a sigh and soon went up too. As they ascended, a guttural dirge of mechanical clunking surrounded them.

Rising above the reservoir, the duo breached the innards of a spire where massive gears spun. The revolving, interchanging cogs rotated with great strength. Larger wheels moved slowly while smaller ones rotated quicker, every gear inside the tower moving in perfect synchronization.

Midway up, Kaimo scanned the few catwalks along the sides. From the corner of his eye, he thought something moved. Looking closer, he recognized shadows of turning gadgetry. For a moment, he blundered by glimpsing down the mechanical spire and felt his heart sink.

"Don't do that, silly!"

"Sorry!" he blurted.

The bitter taste of nausea shot up his throat like an unforeseen storm, filling his parched mouth. Fighting the urge to vomit, he continued climbing. Zylpha was right below him, refusing to make his mistake. The pair stayed focused, maintaining a tight grip on the eroded rungs of the fixed ladder.

Just then, a rung broke off in Kaimo's hand. He gasped and almost let go with his other hand. Zylpha shrieked. Drowning out her voice, he regained his grip. In haste, he reached the top and extended his hand. Zylpha accepted it, emerging on the catwalk.

"Thank you," she said.

The narrow, grated platform twirled around the tower like a spiraling ramp. Holding on to the railing, they strode up toward the pinnacle. For reasons unknown to Kaimo, his chest burned with an inner vibration. Behind the clock face, its repeating tick-tock echoing in their ears, they saw a spinning apparatus whose mechanical guts glowed dark green.

Such intricacy, however, did not cause the radiance; rather, it was what hid behind the conduit of intertwining gadgetry.

Standing in front of the contraption, they stared at the partially concealed fragment of a gem that flickered with life. Its shape resembled a rigid jewel composed of glass, metal, and granite compressed into one stone, the edges sharp with cracks. Despite lacking the luster that it must have had in its full glory, the pair stood slack-jawed and speechless.

Before either of them spoke, someone clapped.

Craning their necks, they saw the silhouette of a man behind one of many rotating gearwheels. To their dismay, Grand Marshal Xelvok Von Cazar emerged. Zylpha took a step back at the cocking of multiple guns. Kaimo glanced around—a dozen soldiers revealed themselves on different catwalks around the sides of the clock tower.

"Well done," Xelvok announced, boasting a twisted smile. "At first, I could not believe my eyes. I told myself: They deceive me. It must be an illusion. But here you are, a mere miner and simpleton thwarting the empire. I still cannot believe it. You are truly the last person in all of Zykard I'd have ever expected to tamper with my campaign."

"How?" Zylpha said. "How did you know where we'd be?"

Stepping out from the shadows, Dumont emerged. "As soon as that mad scientist of yers started ramblin' about legends, I knew it was stupid to go against the empire. They own the world. No point in crossin' them."

"Folly indeed," Xelvok said.

"Traitor!" Kaimo bellowed, anger flooding him for the first time since he last argued with his father.

"*How could you?*" Zylpha said, shaken by such treachery.

The huntsman merely scoffed. "It's all 'bout money."

"Ah, yes," the grand marshal responded. "Your reward."

Xelvok pulled out a revolver and shot him from the back. Zylpha shrieked and cringed, watching him reel over and fall. Snatching the chance, Kaimo struck his elbow into the conduit and grabbed the Etherstone's fragment. With the exception of the grand marshal, every soldier aimed at him.

"Shoot us and whatever's left of your precious stone gets crushed."

"Steer your weapons," Xelvok commanded. He squinted at Kaimo, intrigued. "That gem is the property of His Imperial Majesty. Hand it over, along with the dissident, and I promise to grant a swift execution."

"Swift? Like this?" Kaimo shot Xelvok's brass revolver out of his hand. In greater haste, he turned and shoved the shard into his partner's hand. "Run!"

Zylpha raced back down the ramp while soldiers abandoned their positions to seize her. In the meantime, Xelvok raised his shield and deflected Kaimo's salvo of bullets. Aware it could only resist so many projectiles, he lifted his hand and waved at the next round, deflecting it as if by sorcery. Kaimo backed away in disbelief but remembered the professor's tale about how mankind once confused science with magic.

"Impressive trick," he added, his fear ebbing. "I'd like to see you do that again."

With one bullet left in the chamber, he aimed for the marshal's forehead and pulled the trigger. Like before, Xelvok lifted his arm in defiance and repelled the bullet. This time, Kaimo concentrated on the unnatural phenomena as the bullet propelled backwards, as if rebounding off something solid; yet it appeared to ricochet in mere air.

"Your wish is my command."

Kaimo hastened to reload his weapon while Xelvok unsheathed his machine sword, swiping it in an arc. The active chainsaw-like blade sliced off Kaimo's bandolier—it dropped on the grated floor—and Xelvok kicked it down the tower, raising his reverberating weapon. His adversary swiftly activated his gun's built-in sword.

"You murdered my father in cold blood."

"I remember all too well," Xelvok replied, his twisted grin making him appear more like a mechanical devil what with half his face covered by a grim, metal vizard. "Now's your chance to avenge him."

"En garde!"

Blade to blade, on the grated platform atop the soaring clock tower, they struck at each other with passionate strength. When both swords clashed, raging sparks flared and illuminated the dim catwalk like flashes of lightning. Kaimo maneuvered to the side, against the rusty rail, and blocked another attack. The grand marshal leaned forward, his chainsaw sword beginning to cut into his target's weapon.

Letting out a loud groan, Kaimo pushed Xelvok back and withdrew a few steps to recompose himself. The grand marshal sprinted forth with a maniacal gaze and struck multiple times; his reverberating blade tore through the railing on both sides as he swung left and right in an attempt to mutilate Kaimo.

"Have you no prowess?" Xelvok commented, rage overwhelming him as he pressed onward with his fiendish sword.

"I'm still alive, you filthy cur!"

Seizing the chance, Kaimo riposted but missed Xelvok by a hair. Wrath burned on the grand marshal's already demented visage, confirming his foe had almost wounded him. With fury, Xelvok struck in an upward arc; the teeth of his spinning blade sliced through the left side of Kaimo's face in a vertical movement, cutting into his eye.

Kaimo screamed in agony, blood spurting everywhere. Instinctively, he gripped his disfigured face and covered the ruptured eye socket. Using his other hand, he thrust his sword forward with the last of his strength. Despite his worthy attempt to gouge the grand marshal, he failed miserably.

"Pathetic."

Adrenaline pumping, Xelvok grabbed his adversary's thrusting arm and snapped it backwards. Kaimo let out a bawl, dropping his bladed gun as pain assailed every vein and nerve. Overwhelmed by the unbearable twinges throughout his body, he lurched toward unconsciousness.

"Give your father my regards."

Eager to end the pitiful battle, Xelvok kicked him off the catwalk. In his final breaths, he smashed against the many rotating cogwheels as he plummeted down the tower. The grand marshal peered over the sawed-off banister, watching with extreme pleasure as Kaimo fell to his death.

CHRONICLE II

GILDED AGE

CHAPTER SIX

Fate Unbound

I
Revenant

When the Grimtol dropped, it landed on a rotating cog interlocking with another wheel. The spinning gadgetry jammed, and the gridlock malfunctioned. All four clocks stopped moving and forced stored water in the reservoir to release into Enbertum's sewers.

Zylpha, meanwhile, had just reached the base of the tower when soldiers emerged from the dark tunnels and gripped her. She roared in defiance, fighting to free herself. Growing pale, she shrieked at the top of her lungs as Kaimo fell, smashing against a dozen gearwheels. Shuddering, she helplessly witnessed him drop to his death.

"*Kai!*" she cried out.

Kaimo's lifeless body splashed into a smelly pool at the base of the tower, the current pulling him into a channel where the once fresh waters mingled with an array of putrid garbage—rotting food, dead rats, broken trinkets and gizmos, and other random litter. The lens-maker's corpse bobbed in the contaminated canal, carried by the flow with infested wastes until it reached a rusty sewage drain. Pumped into a bulky pipeline, his body navigated through the corroded waterworks for a long moment into an underground sewer.

In the stinky, cylindrical tunnels, an automaton, attired in an elegant ditto suit that brandished a red bowtie, approached the pouring wastes with delight. Its copper body shone with splendor, and its mechanical head revealed an aluminum visage with a vented mouthpiece, slits for a nose, and a bioptic, monocular telescope drilled and mounted into one eye socket while the other appeared empty. Excitement propelling through the automaton's gears, it rummaged through abandoned baubles and discarded jewelry when Kaimo slithered out of an adjacent pipe.

"*Bonjour*," the automaton said, tipping its black top hat. "Or is it *bonsoir*? Anyhoo, how are you on this extravagant evening?" Kaimo failed to respond. "I suppose you had a long day too and wish to retire."

The mechanical construct of gears, cogs, and overall humanoid design did not have emotions or feelings of any kind, but it wasn't an unintelligent creation. Staring at the battered body, it acknowledged something dreadful was wrong. Though it only had one eye, its telescopic vision provided immense clarity; it analyzed Kaimo's corpse and felt him, acknowledging the absence of a pulse. Aware of the urgency, the robot hurriedly pulled him out of the water and performed cardiopulmonary resuscitation.

"I dare say it may be too late for you, young chap."

In spite of the automaton's failed attempt to revive Kaimo, it persevered and continued to press its copper hands in a series of compressions. Although not equipped with a built-in ventilation system, the mechanical being used its mouthpiece to artificially pull in air and expel it into the dead man.

Despite not opening his eye, Kaimo coughed out water and gagged, unexpectedly breathing life once more.

"Splendid!"

Even though Kaimo remained unconscious, he had regained a pulse. He wheezed, his breathing distorted. Understanding the man's health was deteriorating fast, the robot laid him over its shoulders and sprinted through the reeking tunnels of sewage until returning to the surface.

Making its way home, the automaton rushed across the expanse of steam-filled streets and buildings. It paused once to allow an automobile to drive by. While waiting, the mechanical savior observed *Iron Cloud* flying out of the city, toward the ocean. The path now clear, the robot continued its journey toward a portcullis that automatically opened.

Ahead of the gate lay a cobbled path that led to another cliffside where a manor house stood. Its stained-glass windows, crenellated roof, and general stonework shone in the brilliant night. No clouds in sight, the three visible moons provided a natural blue tinge of light over the dark sleeping city. Only one man, whose auburn hair matched his brown sack suit, was still awake; he opened the front door when the robot approached.

"Bartholomew lu Vogmorton, where have you been?" he demanded. "And who in the wretched world is that?"

"My sincerest apologies, Master Edgar. I was searching for parts when—"

"By all the heavens," Edgar lu Vogmorton interjected while pinching his nose, "what is that *horrible* stench?"

"Alas, I cannot smell it," Bartholomew responded. "However, it is simple deduction to conclude that the aroma to which you refer is a form of putrefaction from this man, whom I found dead in the sewers."

"*Dead?*" the master said, following the robot out of the marble foyer.

Bartholomew walked through an elongated, carpeted hallway as he responded, "I was exploring the underground realm for potential replacement parts to strengthen my frame when he emerged from the waterworks. I surmise the poor chap must have been trying to repair the clock tower and accidently fell into the reservoir."

"Repair the clock tower?"

The automaton flinched as if glitching. "I dare say you enjoy taking my statements and turning them into questions. Yes, the clocks stopped functioning. I would go myself to fix them, but this dashing bloke needs medical attention first."

"Are you blind?" Edgar glanced at the robot's one eye and reconsidered his question while following him up a spiral staircase. "There is no possible way this is a watchmaker or repairman of any sort. Look at his face!"

"Master, you told me manifold never to judge a book by its cover. This idiom, however, is a double-edged sword. I dare say it makes us hypocrites. Because on one side, you looked at his features and assumed the worst. I, on the other hand, see the potential of a renaissance man. He has a certain… what is that famous, distinguishing human phrase?"

"*Je ne sais quoi.*"

"Yes! There it is. Do you not agree?"

"No," Edgar said, strolling through another corridor decorated with paintings and lit sconces along the walls. The pair entered an extravagant chamber boasting a magnificent chandelier, velvet drapes, and a canopy bed. Edgar ogled at the unconscious man, pensive. "He must be some kind of...hooligan."

"I think not," Bartholomew said as he laid Kaimo down. "Perhaps something is amiss in the city and he was at the wrong place at the wrong time?"

"You think? I mean, look what happened to his arm."

The automaton examined the awkwardly bent arm. "How astute of you, Master. Yes, it appears to be broken." With little effort, his robust arms snapped it back in place. "There! All is well again."

"Not so," Edgar replied, searching Kaimo's pockets and finding a spyglass. "We have no idea who this would-be watchmaker is, and I don't want to find out."

"Master, we should give him the benefit of the doubt. I shall take full responsibility and nurse him back to health. Perhaps a day's rest here will do him some good. Then, tomorrow, I can bring him to my laboratory. Why not take full advantage of the equipment we have and see what he has to say when he awakens?"

Edgar sighed. "If he even wakes up. The man looks to be at death's door. Anyway, do as you like. But please hurry. I am rather famished and wish for you to prepare a platter of ahi tartare before I retire."

"Of course, Master," the butler said, checking Kaimo's pulse.

"And take my extravagant hat off," Edgar said, leaving the room. "You look utterly ridiculous with it."

The automaton ignored him, keeping the stovepipe hat on.

II
Gearstorm

Morning came, and Bartholomew prepared *le petit-déjeuner* for his master—a crunchy tartine and coffee with a dallop of steamed milk. Afterwards, the automaton returned to the bedroom where Kaimo lay in a comatose state. As planned, he carried him upstairs to another chamber filled with steam-powered machinery, bookshelves along the walls, acrylic paintings of Edgar's ancestors, and a desk sprinkled with herbs and empty vials.

The robot slid the patient onto an exam table and strapped his limbs to the operating platform. He examined Kaimo's body and assumed the discolored patches of skin on his back were bruises. He realized that if his patient had in fact fallen, it would explain the broken arm. Concluding his analysis, he also deduced that Kaimo probably ruptured his ribs and may have even injured his spine.

"There is much to do," Bartholomew said to his unconscious patient.

Getting started, the automaton brought over a multitude of gears and cogs. With all the old, discarded pieces of metal he'd found in his travels to the sewer, he set about creating a contraption with attachments for one's back and limbs. At times, he made a great deal of noise by using drills to fasten screws.

Throughout his experiment, he glanced at Kaimo's disfigured face and eventually stopped. Using his bioptic telescope, Bartholomew measured his patient's head. With due diligence, the automaton finished crafting a leather buckled harness. He inserted an experimental monocle with telescopic power that he'd been working on for himself.

Bartholomew knew that if his patient survived, he'd need it more than him—this was based on logic, not emotion or altruism.

"I am making progress."

Adjusting the diopters of the lens by means of the focus knob, he fastened the headgear to his patient's scarred face. Despite the odd contraption taking away a piece of his humanness, Kaimo no longer looked disfigured. The automaton returned to drilling and piecing his collected metals, gears, and cogs together. In two hours' time, he fashioned a mechanical brace and placed it on a desk. Although his wheezing dissipated, Kaimo still struggled to breathe in his comatose state.

"Hang tough, young chap."

Moments later, Edgar walked into the chamber. "Thank you for breakfast, Bar—gods be damned! His face!" A mechanical monstrosity greeted his eyes: half of Kaimo's handsome features were covered in gears; an advanced lens with sophisticated optics replaced his eye socket. "What manner of ungodly experiments have you been doing this morning? He looks like a machine!"

"*Au contraire*, he looks rather appealing for a

human. More importantly, I implemented this facial contraption to save his reputation."

"His reputation? You're a butler, not a psychiatrist."

"Pardon the correction, Master, but I think in this situation, I would be more of a psychologist."

"Tomayto, *tomahto*," Edgar said, stepping closer to study the bizarre but fashionable monocle and mechanical brace. "Well, all things considered, quite ingenious. I just hope all of this was worth it."

"I have done all I can," Bartholomew said, his otherwise robotic voice hinting a lament that overrode his indecipherable gaze. "The rest is up to him."

"Indeed...*qui vivra verra*."

A week passed. Kaimo recuperated in the original bedchamber where he'd spent his first night at the mansion. Bartholomew checked him every day, providing sustenance via intravenous tubes. Despite how peaceful he looked to Edgar and the automaton, he remained unresponsive.

After one long month, Bartholomew walked into the room, as on any other day, with his master. They checked on their guest again. The robot focused on injecting food and water into him, while

Edgar examined his body—now absent of bruises. He lifted Kaimo's legs, bending them at the knee to ensure blood circulation. Staring at him for a long moment, he let out an unexpected sigh of frustration.

"This is madness. He should've been taken to the hospital. I don't even know why I let you experiment on him."

"I think you were drunk on the first night, Master."

"Drunk?" he said, taken aback. "I most certainly was not. I'll have you know I'm always of sound mind."

"Then why did you allow him to stay?"

Edgar remained quiet for a moment. "I don't know," he said pensively. "Perhaps it all seemed rather suspicious. There was no mention in any newspaper of foul play at the clock tower, and yet it took the city two weeks to have it repaired."

"Quite the conundrum."

"It pains me to say this," Edgar started, empathy washing over his apprehension, "but I think he may be brain dead. I think...I think it's time we consider surrendering him to *Notre-Dame de la Miséricorde*."

The automaton was about to protest when Kaimo groaned. Edgar flinched as if an apparition had manifested before him. Though a mechanized phantom of sorts, Kaimo was alive. Bartholomew may have been a robot, operating on burning kogal inside his plated chest, but he gazed at his patient with incredulity. Together, the duo witnessed him move for the first time since his fall.

"*He is alive!*" the automaton shouted with enthusiasm. "*He is alive!*"

Edgar tossed him a long look. "Don't be absurd. He was always alive, you metal clown. Quick! Fetch him water and food!"

"Right away, Master," the butler said, leaving in a hurry.

Kaimo groaned again. "Zelly..."

"I beg your pardon?" Edgar said. Approaching the bedside, he placed a gentle hand on his guest's shoulder. Kaimo, however, screamed in hysteria. Edgar gasped. "Goodness, are you all right?"

He stopped shrieking, finally opening his good eye. "Was it a nightmare?" he rasped.

"Can you hear me?" Edgar asked. "Sir? Are you—"

"What happened, Master?" intervened the automaton, entering in a frenzy with a tray of water and soup.

"I don't know. He just started screaming."

"Zelly," Kaimo muttered again. "Whe…where am I?" He touched his face and felt the telescopic monocle, as well as the leather harness holding it together. "What have you done to me?"

"Please calm yourself," the master said firmly. "My name is Edgar lu Vogmorton, and this is my butler, Bartholomew. He found you in the sewers about a month ago and resuscitated you."

"I believe the correct word, Master, is *reanimated*."

"That's not possible," Kaimo muttered, remembering his final moments of falling to his death. "I was attacked at the clock tower and fell."

"Quite frightening," Edgar replied. "Well, this would've never been possible if you landed on the ground. Bartholomew is a genius but cannot revive a pulverized corpse. The water must've broken your fall. After all, the tower is adjoined to Enbertum's reservoir. I'm calling it a miracle."

"No," he whispered, his strength threadbare. "It's no miracle."

"Here!" the automaton said lively, bringing over a tray. "You must eat and drink. Regain your strength. By the way, are you able to see well?"

"It's...my vision is...blurry."

"It is evident that the vitreous humor is beyond restoration. And believe you me, there is nothing funny about it. Despite your condition, however, your retina is still intact but operating at minimal capacity. You may be experiencing chromatic or spherical aberration. This is the first time you are using your new monocle, so there may be a form of dispersion that is affecting the refractive index of the lens."

"Blimey," Edgar blurted. "Speak plainly, Bartholomew. He's a humble watchmaker, not a doctor."

"Optometrist," Kaimo said. "I am an optometrist."

Edgar stared at him, deadpan. "That's one hell of a coincidence. So, you mean to say that you understand all that gibberish?"

"Mmhmm."

"Brilliant," the automaton said. "Adjust the focus slider on the right to obtain your required diopters and optical power. I am certain you will find the magnification and optics quite posh. One might even think you are *bon vivant*."

Kaimo gave a weak nod. "Thank you," he said,

tweaking the dial. The objective lens focused all colors to the same point. By eliminating the severe distortion, the monocle enabled him to see with incredible clarity. "Extraordinary."

"Well, now that that's settled, may we know your name?"

"Ka—" he gave a violent cough. "Kaimo de Morté."

"Well met, Sir Kaimo," the robot said, feeding him a bowl of vegetable soup. "That is most definitely a marvelous name. Truth be told, after repairing you, I was going to name you Gearstorm."

Kaimo spat soup all over Bartholomew's arm.

"Gearstorm?" Edgar said, wild-eyed. "Heaven's sake, he's an ordinary man of flesh and blood like me. If anything, that should be *your* name."

"Bartholomew will suffice," the automaton replied. "In point of fact, I cannot explain in greater detail how exciting this moment is to me. You see, it is most fascinating that you only have one eye. In a manner of speaking, you are almost just like me. One could even say that we can pass for brothers."

"Brothers?" Edgar said, unable to contain his laughter. "Ignore him, Kaimo. I fear some of his cogs are loose."

"He rather enjoys repeating some of my fine words."

Kaimo unintentionally ignored the automaton, eyeing the soup to satisfy his groaning stomach.

"And yes, brothers," Bartholomew added. "We are both not only experienced in optics but also capable of repairing machines. That, my dear Master, is not a coincidence."

"Repairing machines?"

"Ah, yes," Edgar responded. "I do not mean to pry, especially since you've only just awakened, but since you are not a watchmaker, what were you doing at the clock tower and at such an ungodly hour?"

"I was..."—he thought fast and considered lying—"Professor Briknoll told me to find an artifact hidden there."

Edgar's eyes widened. "Professor Briknoll, you say? Unfortunately, he's been missing for a few days now." Assuming that Kaimo was about to enquire about him, he curtly went on, "The good professor was assisting the police and I with an investigation. You see, I am a hired detective. There have been grueling murders as of late, and we cannot catch the killer."

"Yes," the bedridden man rasped. "I heard of the murders."

"Perhaps the perpetrator assaulted you, Sir Kaimo?" Bartholomew posed. Awkward silence washed over the conversation, motivating the automaton to continue. "More clues to investigate, Master."

"I suppose that's a start. The blackouts are not making it any easier. In any case, our patient needs much rest. Kaimo, take as much time as you need. You're a welcome guest and can stay as long as you'd like until you are restored."

"Thank you," Kaimo replied. "I cannot thank you enough."

"Nonsense! You'll be up and about in no time," Edgar said in a nonchalant manner, leaving the bedchamber.

III
Memoir: Acceptance

This night is merely one of many during which I cannot sleep. My mind is a clutter of storms. Dread has infected me. Yet how I am still alive evades me. It is either some miracle or curse. Maybe both conclusions are superstitious? In my current condition, I find myself losing faith in the gods like everyone else.

In the end, it was science that saved my life. Not even a human doctor but an automaton. Even now, my body fails me. I can barely move my other arm unless I rely on this mechanical contraption. Worse, low vision has crippled me. I'm no different from a retired veteran from the war.

Each passing day, I wonder if I'd be better off dead. Could you ever look upon me again without revulsion, Zelly? The feelings we shared seem like a distant dream or memory from a lifetime ago. Alas, it might as well have been. I am but a ghost to Zykard.

What kind of doctor affected by low vision enters medical school to become an ophthalmologist? Unfortunately, no one has discovered a means to treat a vitreous hemorrhage. Hence my aspiration to study ophthalmology. But now, I can barely even practice as an optometrist unless I rely on this bizarre contraption on my face, which is a crutch for the eye. Residency is out of the question now. No one would accept me. It'd be the blind leading the blind. I'll never be the successful man I envisioned myself becoming. I have failed in every way imaginable.

I write this not out of self-pity, or for someone to find this illegible letter and demonstrate clemency. This is literally all I can do to keep myself from going insane. Zelly is always on my mind. It pains me to acknowledge the possible truth that I may never see her again. But why should I even have such a privilege? I failed her and should be dead. No, I need to cast out this spell of melancholy and find a way to save her.

Whether by a miracle or mere luck, the fact remains that I am alive. That counts for something. Sir Edgar is a refined gentleman, and his automaton is certainly resourceful. Having them is a blessing…a godsend. Oh, drat. I'm being superstitious again. I am a man of great fortune. No, not if people start calling me Gearstorm. What a horrendous name. At least Sir Edgar turned that around rather quickly.

Goodness, I fear I'm going off on another

tangent. I could have very well been dead, in which case I'd be of no use to Zelly. Breathing means there is hope. Even if this recovery takes me weeks, months, or I dare say even a year, I'll be restored one day and shall find you.

The empire is indeed corrupt. I see that now. The Duke of Enbertum has poisoned the Imperium with his obsessions of the arcane and must be stopped. I'll do whatever it takes to rise up again. This I promise you, Zelly. But, first things first, and that's a good night's rest.

IV
Bal Masqué

Another couple of weeks passed. During that time, Bartholomew aided Kaimo with physical therapy. Though an arduous journey to recovery, he strived to remain disciplined. With the aid of Bartholomew's mechanical brace, his body movement improved, enabling him to feed himself and even stand on his own two feet.

From time to time, Kaimo read newspapers to keep up with current events. For the first time, he was curious to learn if there had been any new attacks perpetrated by the insurgents. His appetite for reading, unfortunately, was short-lived; headlines of a missing chemist in one article and an astrologist in another, and the rise of a sadistic serial killer, quashed his interest.

He maintained physical therapy sessions with Bartholomew. On other occasions, he drank concoctions that the automaton prepared for him; the remedies allowed his wounds to heal quicker. Every day, the automaton spent hours with his patient, helping him from his bed to limp across the room. Upon this triumph, Kaimo brazenly removed his leg braces and stood firm without mechanical crutches.

"Bravo!" the automaton said, clapping.

"Thank you, Bart."

That same evening, the lens-maker took advantage of his renewed strength to tweak his new monocle. It took a moment for him to loosen the straps of his leather harness, humiliation pouring over his dignity. Battling his embarrassment, he removed the hardly chic headdress and modified it by improving the aperture with an experimental autofocus. As he finished working on the optical device, someone knocked on his already open door.

"Kaimo," Edgar called out, entering the room. He inadvertently flinched upon seeing his guest's disfigurement but caught himself and continued, "Ah, I see you're putting your expertise in optics to use." His eyes wandered for a moment, his expression sympathetic. "Forgive me, I should be calling you Doctor."

"I'm not an ophthalmologist. Kaimo will suffice."

Edgar produced a warm smile, putting a hand on his shoulder. "Optometrists are doctors, too, my friend."

Hearing those words soothed his shame quicker than endorphins or decoctions.

"I am deeply honored by your words. Alas, my greatest fear has come to pass. I'll never be able to advance into medical school, much less utilize my existing doctorate. Truth be told, a part of me doesn't even want to greet society with this face."

The detective stopped him from donning the leather apparatus. "You won't have to worry about that this evening."

"Pardon?"

"Tonight, every fine citizen in Enbertum is

equal," Edgar barely reiterated. "Now that you are back on your feet, I thought it would be therapeutic for you to attend an event with Bart and I."

"Sounds promising. What is the occasion?"

"Fraternizing with the enemy," he said, clapping twice to call Bartholomew, who emerged with a prestigious mask on his face. Edgar tossed him a look of ridicule, pulling off the flamboyant vizard. "House Cazar is hosting a masquerade. Care to join us?"

It took a moment for Kaimo to acknowledge the invitation. "House Cazar? The Duke of Enbertum?"

"Lord Panzy," Bartholomew said.

Edgar let out a rueful laugh. "Well, these days he's either known as Grand Marshal of the Imperium or Sword of the Emperor. But yes, the one and only Lord Cazar whose endless titles have resulted in an overinflated ego."

"I'd love to attend," he replied, tightening his fists.

"Excellent," the detective said, his jubilant voice barely audible because of the butler's abrupt cheer. He handed Bartholomew's regal mask to his guest. "By now you must have a few suits that Bart tailored.

Put on your best one, because it will certainly be a night to remember."

Kaimo gave a faint nod, suppressing a smirk. He used the next hour to dress. His usual wavy hair was tamed, and he wore a crimson vest over an ivory ruffled shirt—a jabot decorating his neckline. He donned a tailcoat, the frock laced with intricate embroidery. Then, he put on the vizard Edgar had given him and stepped outside while using a sword-like cane as a crutch.

"*Ouh là là*," the butler said, wearing an equally stunning suit. "You look magnificent, *Monsieur*."

"What happened to Sir Kaimo?"

"Welcome to my world," Edgar intervened, emerging from the shadows with a cape over his aristocratic, embossed coat. The golden, shield-like bauta mask over his face gave him a kingly appearance. "Shall we depart?"

The trio entered a carriage, at which point Bartholomew took the reins; he nudged his steeds to canter out of the manor. On the city's streets, the uy'kaja picked up their pace and changed their gait to a gallop. The coach raced past numerous people at great speed, outmatched only by an occasional automobile.

"So, are you and the grand marshal acquaintances?" Kaimo asked.

Edgar shook his head. "Invitations were sent to all nobility. Believe me, I'd much rather be attending the première of *Vieux Divinités Déchues* at the opera tonight. Oh well. Fortuitously, I have a contact I'm supposed to meet at the ball. 'Tis why I'm a private eye. But while I work on my challenging case, you can savor the night with hors d'oeuvres and fine wine."

"And dancing!" Bartholomew threw in.

"I can hardly wait," Kaimo replied through his princely, black mask lavished with motifs.

They turned at a corner, mingling with other carriages and a couple of automobiles that approached the duke's mansion. Dozens of citizens flooded the gates of House Cazar, dressed in the most elaborate frocks Kaimo had ever seen. He noted their masks, many of which were clownish or even demonic. Though, without his advanced monocle, it was too difficult for him to see their detail.

Arriving at the entrance, the trio descended their carriage while one of Lord Cazar's servants tended to the coach. They walked up the stairs, approaching the mansion. Kaimo's legs throbbed with pain. He struggled to scale each step, but determination mixed with the fear of being derided and laughed at fueled him to reach the top without needing help.

Classical music filled their ears as they passed the carved giltwood doors. The three guests stepped into the grand foyer, their shoes gliding on marble. Erring on the side of caution, Kaimo scanned for his nemesis but failed to spot him. With his companions, he entered the ballroom, a chamber of spectacular opulence. The symphony soothed his enraged soul like a balm. Looking ahead, he saw a group of musicians playing violins, cellos, flutes, and clarinets.

"Well," the detective started with a sigh, "he always knows how to impress."

"Where is he?" Kaimo asked, his tone more demanding than innocent. "I mean..."

"The host? I'm sure Lord Cazar is somewhere around here, no doubt mingling with the other houses. No need to thank him for the invitation. This ball is more political than a genuine party. But enjoy yourself. You deserve it after what you've been through. Bart, tend to his needs while I find my contact."

"Of course, Master."

Kaimo watched Edgar walk off into the crowd and stood still for a moment as more guests flooded in, jostling past him. He walked toward a cornucopia of fruits and fresh meats that looked more like decoration than edible—*à la française* as opposed to *à la carte*. Despite being ravenous, he turned away from the delectable food and scanned the ballroom, where a great many patrons performed an elegant waltz.

Most noblemen showed off, dazzling in their glamorous frockcoats and cravats. One man leaning on a balustrade above, however, looked quite different; an ominous man wearing a long-nosed, beak mask. Without his experimental monocle, it was difficult for Kaimo to confirm, but he had an uncomfortable feeling that the patron clad in black had been gawking at him since his arrival. He blinked, and the sinister man was gone.

"Are you all right, Sir Kaimo?"

Nodding at the butler, the lens-maker drowned out the music and raucous voices as he used his good eye to observe the guests. To his surprise, one of the nobles resembled a jester whose vizard boasted teal horns. Many other patrons wore fascinators and animalistic gnagas—cat- and pig-shaped masks that only covered the upper half of their faces. Though affected by low vision, he had a strong impression that some men were dressed as females.

Real women, however, had elaborate papier-mâché masks painted with acrylics and adorned with crystals, and glitter embellished their head-dresses. Among them, one woman planted the notion in Kaimo's mind that she was a deity who'd descended unto Zykard to bless the world; it was, of course, simply an artistic illusion. There was only one angel who'd fallen from heaven, and she had been taken from him.

Kaimo eventually spotted a man in a military outfit. His mask stood out from all the others—he'd seen it before—a mechanical vizard of metal tubes and gears spliced together; the imperialist was more like an industrial construct than a human being. Bartholomew was the only one not sporting a mask, and yet, to Kaimo, he was the only entity that seemed human at the ball.

"Stay here, Bart."

"But I want to dance."

The automaton tilted his head, intrigued by his companion's behavior. He nevertheless listened and stood stock-still.

Kaimo's heart raced as he sneaked a table knife into his ruffled cuff. Perspiration glistened on his forehead, hidden by his royal mask. An eerie vibration called out to him—this wasn't the first time; it was as if a voice whispered to him. He turned to see if the ominous man from upstairs had called out to him. Alas, the peculiar murmurs were in his head, a tongue of unknown origin springing from his burning chest as he approached his target.

Courtesy of the masquerade and elaborate braces on his arms and back that made him resemble a half-assed automaton created by a madman, Xelvok glanced at the approaching patron without any recognition. Nevertheless, he turned to greet the incognito cripple who limped closer to him when an explosion erupted. People screamed and scrambled for their lives as gunfire from insurgents spread across the chamber.

Caught off-balance, Kaimo used his cane for leverage and pulled out the knife he'd taken. A voice of reason called out to him—the voice of ethics—but he waived it away, wrath overcoming apprehension. Without a doubt, he knew this was the moment to strike. In a single action, he lunged and heaved the tip of his blade toward Xelvok's throat. The world around him slowed, and he felt himself decelerate; he wondered if this was anxiety.

No. This wasn't emotion. His eye locked on the knife, just a hair away from gouging the grand marshal's exposed neck, but he halted against his will. People falling to their deaths were suspended. Blood and flame froze. Everything stopped, including a salvo of bullets that had just found their way into Kaimo's chest—no doubt the result of misfire.

He strangely pulled away from the grand marshal. No, he didn't pull away. Something forced him back. His lexicon reversed, distorted as if dyslexia seized him. Nausea smeared his lips, the demarcation between his human impulses impossible to distinguish. Numbness took over. The cold, detachment of machinery clutched him in a long, clockless moment. Dead bodies lifted. Blood seeped back into corpses, life returning to their pale, contorted faces. The bullets embedded in Kaimo's chest whizzed out of him, returning to the barrels of the guns.

Kaimo breathed naturally, flame dissipating behind him. Never in his life had such an abnormality happened. On second thought, he had in fact witnessed an anomaly akin to this moment: the massacre before his father died. And again, during his last moments with Zylpha. He kept moving backwards, and there was nothing he could do about it. Just as he realized the impossible—time being reversed—even his thoughts regressed like a film rewinding. Then, he blanked out altogether.

V
Distorted Symmetry

Kaimo woke, wheezing. He gripped his unwounded chest and panted, realizing he was back in Edgar's mansion. Discombobulated by what he considered to be a vivid dream, he rubbed his pulsating head. As his breathing returned to normal, he got out of bed.

"Strange," he said to himself, noting his leg braces were back on. "I thought..."

Shaking away his bewilderment, he removed the apparatuses that supported his feet. He struggled to walk but leisurely prepared himself for the day like any other in his life. After a refreshing shower, limped through one of the hallways on the second floor, determined to explore the mansion on his own. Distant music motivated him to search each chamber, yet he did not find a musician. He went downstairs, hearing it louder.

"What is that beautiful melody?"

In the living room, he found Edgar sitting on a couch. To Kaimo, it looked as though he was staring at a wall while waving a hand. He looked around the den, hearing the most serene symphony of violins; but for the life of him, he could not figure out where it came from.

"You like music too?" Edgar asked.

"It is wondrous. But where is your musician?"

Edgar chuckled. "I know my eccentric butler found you in the sewers but surely you did not live in a cave all your life."

"I might as well have. Born and raised in Icdarus."

"That would certainly explain it," Edgar said, standing up and approaching a desk near an open window that overlooked his garden. Atop the table rested a wooden box with a swirling horn attached to it. "This, my good friend, is called a phonograph. It plays recorded music as a pastime for the weary mind."

Kaimo stared as if it were magic. "It's like a musician trapped inside a machine."

"Hah! Yes, it is quite astounding. With just an ounce of kogal, it can play for days or weeks on end."

"We had nothing of the sort back home."

"Icdarus will catch up soon," Edgar said just as Bartholomew entered, prancing around the room. He grabbed his master's hand and spun him around, but Edgar pulled away. "How many times do I have to tell you: Men don't dance together!"

"I am not a man, Master."

"Ugh," Edgar grumbled. "Sometimes you're as ignorant as a child. Dance with a woman next time."

Kaimo smiled, finding their squabble amusing. "I wouldn't mind dancing with you, Sir Bartholomew. That is, if I weren't in this condition," he said, failing to rotate his once broken arm that was still healing. A heartbeat later, strident ringing filled his ears. He jumped back in terrible fear. "Is that an alarm? Does the empire know I'm here? Are we under attack because of that damnable masquerade?"

"The ball was canceled," Edgar said, guffawing.

The butler mimicked his master, producing a fake but hearty chuckle. Kaimo stared at them with a befuddled expression, his memory of the ball vague and dissipating like a lost dream. Relishing the moment, Edgar walked across the living room to a box hanging on one of the walls and lifted two tin cans attached to non-electrical acoustics and rotating cogs.

"Yes?" he said to the lower apparatus near his mouth. The other piece near his ear, he listened intently. "Correct. Everything is as scheduled. I'll be there in the evening." Again, he paused in silence for what seemed to be no reason. "Thank you. Good day to you as well."

"I was in a coma for just a few weeks, right?"

Edgar laughed again. "Yes, my dear friend. Do not forget we're in Enbertum, and I am, after all, of royal descent. So—"

"He would be our king if monarchy prevailed!" Bartholomew interjected with pride and passion.

"Is that true?"

The detective waved it off. "I come from a noble lineage, that much is accurate. One of my great fore-fathers was indeed a king before the empire formed. But to say I'd be king now is a bit farfetched. Anyway, don't be surprised to see some of the world's latest inventions in my home. I have a habit of collecting ephemera. Though, I have a strong feeling some of these glorious inventions will stay with us for the long-haul."

"The sound that gizmo made was extremely disturbing. What is it?"

"It's called a telephone," Edgar responded. "Telephones and telegrams are the way of the future, my friend. Like the phonograph, it relies on kogal and uses an acoustic engine with magnetism to send a live telegraph of sorts. How else can I explain? Ah! You do know what an optical telegrap—"

"Of course," Kaimo intervened with a sigh. "That we *do* use to send messages. In fact, I am positive guards at Icdarus sent an optical telegraph via the pylons when insurgents hijacked the imperial train, which is the only explanation of how Iron Cloud arrived so quickly."

Edgar stared at him blankly. "Iron Cloud? Wait a minute. You witnessed the hijacking at Icdarus?"

"Our enigmatic guest becomes even more fascinating!"

Kaimo gulped. Accidently, he had revealed too much about his past. Deep in his paranoia, he wasn't sure if he could trust them. He'd made a terrible mistake confiding in Dumont, who'd betrayed him. Yet he couldn't shake the feeling that there was something quite different about the master of this manor, as well as the butler. He felt his head spinning again.

"Are you all right?" Edgar asked.

"No," he responded, walking over to a window next to the phonograph. He fixed his troubled eye on the garden of trees and flowers—a rare sight to behold in the industrial metropolis. "I've been hiding something terrible that has been haunting me. I fear it will eventually catch up to me. No. Those are the wrong words. On the contrary, I intend to catch up to it."

"Out with it, Sir Kaimo."

"Yes," Edgar agreed. "I am rather curious, especially since I investigated the clock tower weeks ago and only found evidence of imperialists there… not the Midnight Mutilator whom we thought attacked you."

"So, you knew all this time and didn't turn me in?"

The detective scoffed. "I *hate* the imperium. Besides, there was nothing to suggest you were or are a criminal. Only that whoever attacked intended to kill you. Essentially, you should be dead. Tenfold dead."

"Grand Marshal Xelvok."

"I beg your pardon?" Edgar said, absolute shock flashing across his face.

"Forgive my master," the robot began, "he claims to hear well but often needs sentences and words repeated. I deduce he has a minor hearing impairment."

"Shut it, Bart. This is serious."

Kaimo took a deep breath, facing them. "What I am about to tell you will make me seem like a madman. I assure you and swear on my father's ashes that everything I say is the truth and nothing but the truth."

No longer withholding the truth, Kaimo explained in complete detail what had transpired since the rebel attack in Icdarus. His companions listened attentively, the intense story drowning out the serene symphony playing in the background. At the end of his account, silence descended for a moment.

"Professor Briknoll told you about this... Etherstone is it?" Edgar asked.

"Whether myth or not, the grand marshal

believes it to be true. The entire clock tower was surrounded by imperial soldiers. There was no escaping. He already possesses one of the fragments and most definitely has Zylpha now. With a direct link to the aether, there's no telling what he can do."

"This sounds like the beginning of an incredible escapade we must embark on," the automaton stated.

Edgar hushed him and sat quietly for another moment. "Without meaning to sound harsh or indifferent, Kaimo, the sad truth is you failed to protect Zylpha. If you venture out to save her or collect the other shards, you might fail again. And there won't be another chance. If the grand marshal realizes you are still alive, he will end you for good."

"Of that, I have no doubt. Which is why I intend to have allies this time around. My mistake was thinking myself a hero. It nearly got me killed. In fact, I *was* dead. What's more terrifying is that I didn't see a light or feel anything warm. Death was cold and unforgiving. Bart brought me back for a reason."

"The reason is to live, not die again," Edgar said. "No one confronts the Sword of the Emperor and lives."

"I cannot waste this second chance by hiding. Will you help?"

Bartholomew started, "It would be my hono—"

"We cannot rush into such an ordeal," Edgar reasoned. "One false move will get us killed. Fortunately for you, I have connections with the resistance." Before he heard any objections, he added, "I know you're not fond of their methods, but as you explained during your tale, they are the lesser evil."

"Well said, Master."

Kaimo considered everything, logic prevailing. "When do we begin?"

"Not so fast, my friend," the detective said. "My hands are tied to a case that is beyond me. I told you I'm a private investigator. The police employed me to find the Midnight Mutilator. If we cannot even solve this investigation, then we won't stand a chance against the might of the imperium."

Rubbing his chin's stubble, Kaimo couldn't help but look troubled. "What do you suggest?"

"If you want my help in rescuing Zylpha and ending the crazed ambitions of Xelvok, we start by finding the mutilator. Fortuitously, I have a solid lead. Part of the reason for that phone call you heard earlier."

"Master, you are invaluable as always."

Edgar gave his automaton a smooth wink.

"All right. I am at your disposal. Besides, we'll need the professor. If he's missing, then time is of the essence. What's your lead?"

"The opera house. Tonight."

CHAPTER SEVEN

Symphony of Madness

I
Investigation

Evening arrived, and the trio dressed in their best suits. Kaimo stepped outside, his ornate cane decorative with a sword-like design of precious metals and jeweled accents. Edgar climbed into his black carriage and lent a helping hand to his guest, while Bartholomew took hold of the reins and tugged on them.

Their steeds sprinted fast across the city as though galloping when, in fact, they each only had two legs. The tiny, fluffy wings that grew on their backs acted as rudders, allowing them to swiftly maneuver around wandering citizens and effortlessly turn at street corners. Their incredible speed was only matched by the occasional automobile that drove by the coach.

"Edgar, how come you don't have a car?"

"I do," he answered. "But we're going to the opera, not across Quradale. If you didn't know already, I like to conserve my resources."

"Very smart."

"*Merci beaucoup*, my good friend."

Arriving at the theater, Bartholomew halted the carriage and opened the door for his companions to step out. Several coaches were already stationed there, guests flooding into the building embellished with an inscription above its entrance: *Lieu du Majestueux*. The well-dressed pair waited for Bartholomew to park the carriage, tether both steeds to a post, and return.

Reunited, the trio made their way up the wide staircase. Passing an arch of stone pillars, Kaimo gazed up at the architectural carvings of intricate musical notes and the angelic statues atop the roof.

They reached the portal whose doors revealed a relief of ancient knights, which was also where several guards stood. Edgar showed his badge to the imperialists and ticket collector, at which point they allowed him and his guests entry.

Kaimo thought the art he'd seen at Edgar's mansion was the epitome of style, but he changed his mind upon entering the opera house. Before him hung a massive crystal chandelier that sparkled and lit up the lobby. The entrance hall unveiled an extraordinary mural of a king and his knights charging toward an ominous darkness that enveloped the land across from them. Walking on a royal blue carpet, they ascended a spiral staircase.

At the top, another guard checked everyone's tickets. Again, the sleuth displayed his badge and was allowed entry to an elongated corridor. Arriving at their box, Edgar opened the curtains and took a seat with his butler. Kaimo, awed, stood for a long moment, staring at the auditorium.

The stalls below had aisles with terraced seats. Balconies with golden balustrades and scroll-shaped brackets hung along the sides, boasting reliefs of children playing on vines. Above the mezzanine,

Kaimo scanned the other boxes, as well as the theater's crowned ceiling that showcased an illustration of paradise with floating gods and goddesses.

"Remarkable, isn't it?" Edgar said.

"*Oui*. Truly splendid, Master."

"I wasn't asking you, Bartholomew. You've been here a hundred times. I was asking our new companion."

"It's breathtaking," he answered, taking a seat.

As they waited for the performance to start, people continued to swarm into the building and find their seats. The crowd grew loud with a continuous rumbling of murmurs and grumbles throughout the auditorium. Kaimo, meanwhile, relaxed in his cushioned seat, which was more comfortable than his bed back in Icdarus.

The lights eventually dimmed, and the patrons hushed. Pleated curtains swooshed open, unveiling a verdant grove with flowers and trees whose branches were ripe with fruit. The backdrop revealed a starry sky where a dense mist filled the stage, followed by a beautiful plump woman who emerged from the misty orchard.

Dressed in an off-the-shoulder sheer gown, she

gazed up at the decorated ceiling as if witnessing a celestial being descending before her eyes. Absolute silence filled the auditorium. To Kaimo's astonishment, an orchestra of musicians surfaced from a platform beneath the lady to accompany her as she sang.

The woman's voice soared throughout the entire theater. Her singing seized Kaimo, digging deep into his tormented soul. The intense music conjured tears, his good eye and hybrid monocle transfixed on the singer. Raising her vocal pitch shook the very foundations of the building. And then she abruptly stopped, looking away from the audience. Clad in leather garments, a man appeared on the other side of the misty grove and gave voice to the silence.

Like the woman, his tenor pierced Kaimo's soul. He had only heard rumors of singers but never imagined they would be so divine. The pair approached each other and held hands, singing together. Their voices mingled with the emotional symphony that touched the heart of every listener.

To Kaimo, the opera singers bore a resemblance to fallen angels searching for a way back to paradise. His advanced monocle allowed him to see the show in detail. Using gears on the side of his harness, he changed its function from diopters to magnification. Tiny cogs shifted as lenses switched out, the apparatus turning into a monocular. He adjusted the sliding wheel, zooming in. Others relied on opera glasses. One of them was Bartholomew, using a gold-trimmed pair whose sleek brass handle complemented his jointed hands.

"Give me those!" Edgar said, yanking the binoculars from his automaton. "You don't need them."

"How rude," Bartholomew said, using his bioptic eye to continue watching the singers.

"Kaimo," the detective whispered while using the glasses, "I believe there are two things all the victims have in common."

"What would that be?"

"They're esteemed citizens of Enbertum and, interestingly enough, have all attended the opera house before they went missing."

"Can you elaborate on esteemed?"

"Those of the academic mind," he reiterated. "Physicians, scientists, scholars...the list goes on. Anyone involved in this case, especially when they might have a lead, gets taken. Professor Briknoll was the most recent."

"Do you mean to tell me that you could be next?" Kaimo asked, unable to hide his bone-swallowing gulp.

"Precisely," Edgar replied. "Strangest of all is that the victims have always disappeared after attending an opera. I have a hunch the very killer we seek is among us in this building. Right now."

"Quite unsettling, Master."

"The killer loves opera..."

"Indeed," Edgar replied. "Akin to this extraordinary performance that reeks of tragedy and the epic tale of *Vieux Divinités Déchues*—our old fallen gods—in the ancient tongue, the mutilator is compelled to put on a grand show of his own. Why else would we discover bodies with the skin flayed from their faces?"

Hearing such horrific information, Kaimo drowned out the angelic voices and scrutinized the audience with his monocular. As more actors and actresses appeared on stage, they flaunted white and black wings while performing a waltz to the instrumental ballad that brought tears to a great many people. Bartholomew clocked his head about and noted their emotional responses.

"I dare say this grand event is beginning to get a tad melodramatic," he commented. "Do you not agree?"

"See anything?" the detective asked, ignoring his butler.

"I don't know," Kaimo said. "I'm not so good at this."

"When dealing with a psychopath, no one ever really is," Edgar responded, utilizing his opera glasses. "Bartholomew, go and investigate the corridors on each floor."

"How about the property's perimeter?"

"Yes, great thinking. Do that afterwards. Be thorough but not so obvious as to cause suspicion."

"I'll be as quiet as a deaf man and as invisible as a blind one."

"Blindness doesn't make you invisible, they just can't…forget it. Just get the heck out of here."

The butler bowed and left the box, closing the curtains behind him. In the meantime, the detective pretended to be engrossed in the extravaganza while Kaimo scanned the balconies and every detail of the auditorium. His inclination was to watch the staged drama, but he knew all too well what was at stake.

Unnerving thoughts filled his mind because the patrons seemed normal to him. If anyone had a countenance that could possibly reveal somebody to be of dubious character, it would be him what with his disfigured face. Though the leather harness hid those mutilated features, he still felt self-conscious.

Despite how hard the lens-maker concentrated, he wasn't as proficient in surveilling as the detective. Nevertheless, he did his part. Just before the intermission, their curtains opened again. Edgar turned to rebuke the butler for making noise but gasped as a needle stabbed him. Kaimo tried to holler for help, but the individual clad in a long-nosed, beak mask was already upon him, wrapping his nostrils and mouth with a chloroform-soaked handkerchief.

II
Crimson Labyrinth

Several hours later, or so it seemed to Kaimo, he woke and found himself in an underground dungeon. His vision hazy, he battled grogginess as he clambered to his feet and slammed against the brick wall. Faculties returning, he adjusted his blurry monocle until it focused. Stuck in a locked cell, he realized his legs and arms were shackled to chained manacles.

"Where am I?" he groaned, nausea on his lips.

The gloomy cell contained a makeshift bed, a toilet, and a bowl of water on the floor for him to drink from as if he were a pet. Still leaning on the dank wall, he smelled the scant musty air and felt a chill. At a sharp sting in his grumbling stomach, as if a knife pierced him, he keeled over and vomited.

Hearing someone scream in agony, Kaimo experienced heart palpitations. He wiped beads of sweat off his forehead, his mind bizarrely lucid, as if overdosing on an alchemical remedy—that was how agonizing the voice sounded. Rubbing his mouth clean, he pulled on the chains; they did not budge at all. When he tugged them again, however, the gears on his arms rotated and strengthened.

Kaimo took a deep breath and yanked a third time. Cogs and wheels spun, the mechanical brace attached to his arms and back reacting to his exertions as he hauled against the shackles with considerable force. The chains broke. His disabilities, he thought to himself, were a miracle in this rare instance.

Through the bars of his cell, he looked around and spotted many others like his. To his disappointment, they were all empty. Staring at the gate, an idea came to mind. At first, Kaimo assumed he was stupid for even thinking it. Yet he had nothing else to lose; he gripped the bars and took another deep breath.

"All right, let's see what else you can do."

Mustering all his strength, he pulled on them. His loud and distorted groan shifted to a roar. Gears whirling in synchronization, he bent the iron bars just enough to slip out of his prison. As a consequence, the gizmos on his right arm broke. Hastily, he disconnected the damaged mechanical parts from his movable hand and maintained the other half of the brace because his back and previously broken arm were still healing. Hearing another scream that echoed throughout the murky dungeon, he grimaced and limped out of the detention sector.

Exploring the concrete hall, he encountered a junction. Kaimo paused to consider which path to take. Before deciding, he heard footsteps. A hooded and masked figure emerged, much like the one who'd seized him at the theater. The man stopped but did not cower. Instead, he tilted his head, as if amused to see his prisoner free, and unsheathed a machete.

Absent of panic or concern, the masked man charged his prey, the bloodied blade raised. No longer experiencing chromatic distortions in his monocle, Kaimo saw with great clarity and waited for the perfect moment to react. The assailant swiped his razor-sharp blade sideways to decapitate Kaimo, who promptly veered aside and grabbed his hand.

Using his free arm, he punched the masked man in the stomach and seized the blood-soaked machete. Without hesitation, he cut down his foe. The man did not scream in pain. Kaimo found this odd and removed the beak-shaped vizard to identify the perpetrator, only to discover a reanimated corpse.

Kaimo shrieked, falling on his buttocks while backing away. Looking more closely, he realized it was not a cadaver but, rather, a wooden mannequin or automaton of sorts; however, attached to its head was the facial skin of a recently murdered chemist. Whoever the insidious mutilator was, he'd carved off the faces of his victims and used them for despicable experiments. *But how can such an abomination move? It's more doll than robotic. Is it the aether?* Another terrifying thought plagued him: *What if there are more of these wretched dolls?*

Challenging the discomfort from his limp, machete in hand, Kaimo broke into a run and chose the passage where the mannequin had emerged. A metal door blocked his way; he opened it and stepped into an antechamber littered with bones, guts, tissue samples in vials, organs in jars, and a collection of lacerated bodies hanging like meat bags. Kaimo shrieked, horrified by the atrocities before him.

"What manner of devil has done this? No, it isn't a demon. We are the only devils in this cold, cruel world. It is the work of a human...a demented man or woman turned monster. I must end this madness."

Fighting back the urge to vomit again, he left the chamber and advanced through another dim corridor. Midway across, he heard the same person scream. Kaimo painfully ran toward the agonizing screeches and found a torture chamber where he stumbled upon a different reanimated corpse cutting Professor Briknoll, who hung upside down.

"Professor!"

The masked creature of horror turned and swung at Kaimo. He parried the attack, skidding on a pool of blood. From the corner of his good eye, he saw another machete and grabbed it. Wielding two blades, he struck down the doll that perverted nature and hacked until it lay in pieces. Not a single gear hid in its frame. A wave of terror seized him, escalated only by the genuine possibility that his face would be plastered on one of these monstrosities if he were to be caught again.

Kaimo wheezed and panted, heavy rasps echoing in the chamber as he caught his breath, perspiration glistening along his forehead. He checked his surroundings for other creatures of horror, then freed the professor and laid him down on a table probably meant for another form of torture. Barely conscious and in utter shock, Oswald did not speak. Kaimo tore parts of his white shirt from under his brown vest and bandaged the professor's wounds.

"Stay here, Professor. I'll handle this."

He gave him one of the machetes and got to his feet. Searching the room, he found a pair of keys and a Grimtol with a box of ammunition. Ensuring the gun's chamber was fully loaded, he holstered it. With the newly discovered keys, he removed the cuffs on his wrists and left the room. Ahead, he met several more junctions and picked a different path each time.

The dungeon was an underground maze—an abandoned network not meant for laymen. He was quickly losing what little composure he'd regained in this realm of unknown horror. An epiphany about Zylpha and the fate of the world granted him the needed courage to transcend his trepidation: this ghastly nightmare, terrifying and gruesome as it may be, was trivial compared to the true menace at hand.

Facing fear head-on, Kaimo broke into another run and charged through random passages. Lights flickered. Blood decorated the old walls and concrete floor. He ignored rooms showcasing severed body parts, entering a detention block with several cells. At first, he wondered if this was the same prison sector where he'd woken. Kaimo was about to leave when he spotted someone else curled in one of the cells.

"Edgar?" he called out, hopeful.

The prisoner groaned. "Ka...Kaimo?"

"Oh, thank goodness!"

Approaching the jail, he shot the lock with his Grimtol. Stepping inside, he helped the shackled detective to his feet. Kaimo used his newfound strength in an attempt to break Edgar's manacles, but he failed because the robust cogs in the mechanical brace only functioned for one arm.

"You do realize that you're not literally Bartholomew's brother, right?"

He snorted. "I turned into Gearstorm about thirty minutes ago. How else you think I freed myself from this nightmare?"

"Impressive."

A heartbeat later, Kaimo facepalmed. "I think you're about to take back that compliment."

"Huh? Why would I do that?"

To the detective's surprise, Kaimo pulled out keys and unlocked the cuffs. Despite their appalling situation, the pair laughed. Edgar patted him on the back and stepped out of the cell, scanning the area. Holstering his Grimtol, the lens-maker followed and handed his companion the machete.

"You're more resourceful than you led on, my friend," Edgar said. "We may survive this nightmare yet."

"I found the professor."

"*What*? You found him?"

"Yes. He's quite shaken up but should be fine. Can you rendezvous with him while I find us a way out of this hellhole?"

"All right, but be careful."

"I'll try," he said, shaking his hand and parting ways with the detective. "Okay, you demented son of a bitch. Where are you?"

III
Puppet Master

Lights flickered sporadically as Kaimo sped through putrid and bloodied halls. Adrenaline pumping, he fought against the pain in his legs and explored the dim corridors until he found a barred door. Bolted on the other side, the keys he'd found earlier were useless.

Reluctant to waste his limited ammo, he lifted his recovering arm. The intact mechanical gears gave him the strength to bash a hole in the wooden frame. He put his hand through the opening, lifted the bar, and unlocked the barrel bolt latch. The damaged door squeaked aside as Kaimo climbed stone treads that led up to a hatch.

Fortune on his side for a change, the trapdoor was open. He stepped into a storage chamber filled with aisles of shelves containing ingredients for herbalism, alchemy, and chemistry. Kaimo exited the stockroom, finding himself in a modern structure of gothic design, where the stained-glass windows lent no light—it was far beyond the hours of working men.

"Could this be one of the buildings at the university?"

He cast a glance over his shoulder when he heard a familiar symphony. The music played in every room in perfect harmonization. Gazing at the corners of each chamber he'd entered, Kaimo saw gramophones strung up in the form of loudspeakers, which broadcasted the classical ballad.

Static abruptly mixed with the graceful song as a husky, demented voice said, "I made a blunder assuming you were a cripple."

Kaimo raised his gun and turned, ready to shoot. No one was in the room with him. He continued through the building and reached the atrium, which would have been beautifully lit were it daytime. The main entrance was sealed. Turning, he faced two curving staircases that ascended several floors on opposite ends of the atrium.

Static integrated with the song again as the husky voice added, "So deceitful! Look at you walking. I see a slight limp. Other than that, you are a perfectly molded human. Delicious and ready to become one of my toys."

"Show yourself!"

"Tsk-tsk-tsk. For a man who enjoys theater, you are no fun. Where is the revelry? Like any play, there must be mystery. Otherwise, it becomes dull and boring. Allow me the honor to add some entertainment."

The music grew much louder, and the lights brightened in the atrium. As the entrance illuminated, Kaimo looked up and saw an abomination atop one of the staircases. Unlike the others, this one did not have a mask. It boasted the carved-out face of a female astrologist who'd been missing for months.

A heartbeat later, the mannequin raised its machete and ran down the stairs, screeching. Monocle set to focus, Kaimo lifted his Grimtol and blasted the doll off the steps. Without a moment's respite, two more wooden figures emerged—one from each staircase.

"Animated puppets," he said, taking aim. "I guess that would make you their master. What's your secret? Is it the aether?"

"Lord Cazar has great plans, my beloved cripple!" the mutilator announced. "Those who thwart his ambitions are dealt with summarily. This is where I come into the grand scheme of things. Bring his gorgeous face to me, my pretties! I must carve it off and add it to my collection!"

"Sorry to disappoint," Kaimo retorted, shooting both dolls before they could reach him, "but half my face has already been taken. You'll need to figure out something else."

Three mannequins sprang out from above, rushing down the staircases to stab their prey as he reloaded his gun. Kaimo's experimental autofocus failed. Manually adjusting the diopters of his objective lens, he aimed at the hellish creatures and shot them one by one. The last puppet was mere feet away from gutting him. Up close, its head exploded.

"Can we hurry this up a bit? I'd like to skip to the finale."

"Patience!" the gruff voice said through the instrumental music. "All in due course, my sweet love!"

Snatching the chance, Kaimo checked the chamber of his gun. Three bullets. With haste, he refilled it as a horde of eight abominations came at him from the stairs and side doors. Some of them had body parts attached to their wooden frame, while others simply flaunted the face of a dead person.

Kaimo spun his gun, blasting six of them to the floor. Their carved frames splintered and broke apart with ease. In haste, he activated his gun's built-in blade, parried the attack of one while kicking it down and then pirouetted away from the other. Reloading his gun, he aimed and shot them.

"I fear your toys are going to be on back order soon."

"Duplicitous cripple!" the mutilator shouted via the loudspeaker. "Perhaps it's time to raise the stakes!"

All the lights turned off. Only illumination from the moons beamed into the glassed atrium. Tension hung in the darkness. To Kaimo's surprise, the mutilator emerged from behind, slicing his stomach. He yelped in pain while turning and plunged his sword into the beaked mask that split in half.

The mutilator cackled, withdrawing with a contorted grin; his exposed features revealed disfiguring sores oozing with pus. Kaimo gasped at the sight. Caught off guard, he fired his Grimtol but missed as the killer retreated into the shadows. With only six bullets left, he reloaded for the last time.

Gazing into the shadows of the columned arcade, he glimpsed the mutilator prancing between the pillars and fired multiple times into the darkness. Between wheezes, Kaimo thought the terrifying battle with a background of the most beautiful melody played out like a psychotic waltz.

The killer let out a maniacal laugh. He scuttled in a quadrupedal galumph toward his prey who pulled the trigger of his Grimtol, only to realize it was empty. Pouncing on him like a wild animal, the mutilator hissed and placed his hooked blade along the good side of Kaimo's stunned face.

"Such marvelous features! I shall create a true masterpiec—"

Blood, brains, and severed lumps filled with pus poured over Kaimo as a machete spliced the killer's deranged head from behind. Nausea seized him as he kicked off the twitching body before acknowledging the wounded professor and Edgar, who'd just saved him.

"Well, I guess the show's over."

Edgar gave him a long look. "Careful there, Kaimo. With such humor in dire situations, you may very well be Bartholomew's long-lost brother."

CHAPTER EIGHT
New World

I
Respite

Photographers wielding bellow-designed cameras, as well as journalists, lined up on the following morning to speak with Detective Edgar lu Vogmorton. He stood in front of the police headquarters with a regiment of imperialists behind him. Attired in a black sack suit and bowler hat, he presented a strong countenance while answering questions.

"Without a doubt, this investigation was the most difficult yet in my entire career," the sleuth said. "But with due diligence, my team and I put a stop to the criminal. Rest assured, citizens of Enbertum, the killings and mutilations are over."

"Detective," called out a reporter, "what clues made you look into the theater?"

"Each who has fallen prey to the perpetrator had attended the opera. As we all know, most victims were murdered in the most heinous way. I realized we needed to follow in their footsteps to find him. I gambled with my very life and feel a modicum of relief knowing we have prevented further deaths."

"Could there, by any chance, have been a way to apprehend the Midnight Mutilator instead of killing him?" one of many journalists asked.

"I'm afraid it was a life or death situation," Edgar said firmly. "Self-defense."

Another newsperson pushed forward. "It's my understanding that you were able to rescue Professor Oswald Briknoll." At the private eye's nod, the reporter added, "Brave work, Detective."

"But how did you escape?" asked an inquisitive journalist, suspicion in her eyes.

Edgar cleared his throat. "I have an ingenious butler to thank for that," he said, lying. "If you examine the crime scene at Krenanstein University, you will locate one of the cells with bent bars. No human, my dear reporter, could ever do that. Sir Bartholomew saved the day."

The crowd's excitement rang in his ears as he stepped down the staircase. Imperialists guarded the detective as flash powder ignited, explosions capturing him as he passed a slew of reporters. They attempted to hurl more questions at him, but he forestalled them with the wave of a hand and his overly dashing smile. Getting to the bottom, he slid into the backseat of his automobile, beside Kaimo, and signaled Bartholomew to drive.

"Thank goodness that's over," he said, letting out a sigh of relief.

"Goodness is right, Master," the robot responded while accelerating the vehicle. "I went looking around as you instructed, but by the time I returned, both of you were gone. It was quite frightening, really."

"You don't have emotions, Bart."

"Oh, but I do, Master," he insisted. "For a moment, I thought my gears were going to rotate backwards and malfunction."

"I would've loved to see that," the detective said.

"So, did they accept your story?" Kaimo asked.

"Indeed. I'll be on the front page of the newspaper tomorrow, and the imperium will never know of your involvement. Quite ingenious, my friend. Xelvok still thinks you're dead, and now we can meddle with his campaign."

"'Tis a jolly good plan, Sir Kaimo."

"Thank you. Both of you."

"Don't you dare thank us," Edgar said. "My handsome face would be plastered on one of those twisted puppets if it weren't for you. Now we just need to wait for Professor Briknoll to recover. Then we'll consider what to do next."

The trio returned to the Vogmortan Manor. Bartholomew parked the vehicle and entered the mansion, preparing food while Edgar checked on the scholar. Kaimo, meanwhile, went to the lavatory to examine his wound. Thanks to the butler, he had stitches in the gash he'd received when battling the mutilator.

Not seeing any signs of an infection, he took a shower and dressed himself in fine garments. Returning to his room, he lay on the bed for a while, staring at the canopy. It was his intention to take a nap, but he couldn't fall asleep. Feeling restless, he eventually walked across the hallway. He stopped at the end where a bay window, nestled into the stonework, showcased the entire metropolis. Experiencing a rare minute of calmness, he focused on an airship flying across the ocean.

"Hang in there, Zelly. I'm coming for you soon."

II
Strategy

Kaimo took in the view for a little longer. His eye wandered over to the blue ocean, watching tidal waves crash against the cliffside of the observatory. He wanted to hold on to this sight and tranquility. So, he continued to stand until hearing voices downstairs. Smiling at the scenery, he stepped away and joined the others on the first floor in the dining hall.

"Ah, there you are, Sir Kaimo," Bartholomew said. "I was just about to call upon you for the midday entrée."

"Thank you, Bart," Kaimo said. Seated at the table, he greeted the others who smiled and nodded back at him. He unfolded a napkin, placed it on his lap, and waited to be served. "How are you feeling, Professor?"

"*Comme ci, comme ça*. But all things considered, I'll be fine. The important thing is we are safe."

"Well said," Edgar put in.

Without further ado, the butler revealed dinner. "*Et voilà!*"

Bartholomew served chicken stew laden with spices, green olives, jeweled couscous, caramelized onions, and a savory, juicy lemon sauce. As a side dish, he brought them roasted vegetables. The professor salivated at the rich fragrance of every flavor. Kaimo found it amusing, but he was starving too. Together they had a feast, drinking wine and eating to their hearts' content.

"Delicious as always."

"Thank you, Master."

The professor burped, resting both hands on his stomach. "Quite frankly, I didn't think I'd ever experience another meal again."

"Agreed," the detective responded, sipping on his red wine.

"I still can't believe what we witnessed," Kaimo said. "What do you make of those fiends, Professor? Do you reckon it was the aether?"

"Indubitably," he answered. "Despite the imperium's growth and all kinds of elaborate inventions being patented these days, there is no technology in the world that can stimulate inanimate objects."

"How do you explain me, Monsieur?"

"You're an automaton," Oswald replied. "No different from the steam-powered engines of a train or paddleboat that rely on coal, or an automobile or zeppelin that use kogal as liquid fuel, your engine relies on the same chemical resources. That is your sustenance, which allows your cogs and gears to spin with life."

"Quite an astounding invention. Me, that is."

"Yes, very innovative for mankind. Ergo, you are a complex but animated, walking, talking machine. You didn't just start functioning without some form of combustion. To the lesser mind, those devil dolls literally walked and acted on their own like magic. But we all know the source of their wretched life wasn't sorcery but rather, a parasitical substance none other than aether."

"I know little of the ancient legend," Edgar said, grabbing a piece of meat. "Only one name comes to mind: Ma'vak Zaar."

Oswald snorted, quaffing his wine. "Rest assured, that's the only name you need to know. Zaar wielded the Etherstone itself, which was the only alchemical artifact ever to be fused with the aether. It is said in the days of old that he used its power to harness the aether into his bloodstream."

"What good does that do?" Kaimo asked.

"As you've witnessed," the professor began, "the aether is an extraordinary power that's beyond our comprehension. One who has the blood of Ma'vak Zaar and wields the Etherstone is destined to conquer this world."

"Are you insinuating that Zel—"

"Is a descendent of Ma'vak Zaar," Oswald theorized. "Yes, she has the aether within her bloodstream."

"Hmm...and Xelvok wants to possess it for himself," Edgar surmised.

"Dammit all to hell. That explains why she was hooked up to that ungodly contraption. I thought something was being injected into her, but it's the other way around. It's some kind of blood transfusion machine!"

Edgar narrowed his eyes. "*J'ai pas les mots...*"

For a while, Bartholomew kept clocking his head

at whoever spoke but couldn't keep quiet any longer.

"This insightful conversation translates to me that we are destined to be destroyed."

The professor tossed him a look of disdain and then turned back to Edgar. "Is there a way to deactivate him?"

"Codswallop!" Bartholomew gasped.

"Settle down, Bart," the sleuth said. "And no, we're not destined to die. Destiny has nothing to do with it. You of all…thingamajigs should know this to be true. Nothing is written in the stars. We will forge our own paths."

"I couldn't have said it better. Together, we must find a way to stop Xelvok and prevent the Etherstone from being reconstructed."

"Well, what are we young chaps waiting for?"

The professor scowled while swallowing his food. "I'm not young. I can't even have coitus anymore."

"We need a solid lead," Kaimo answered the butler.

"I have a contact in the continent of Faraheydein," Edgar suggested.

"Drenengarde," the professor responded. "It's another city parallel to Enbertum except the imperium isn't fond of it. Too many mafia gangs. We can search there for another fragment of the Etherstone."

"Overseas it is," Edgar said, finishing his wine. "But, of course, only when the good professor has been restored."

III
Nautical Voyage

Over the next few days, the lens-maker continued to tweak his achromatic monocle, enhancing its hybrid functionality as a monocular telescope. Working on the barrel itself, he replaced the plastic material with glass, installing multifocal diffractive lenses and prism in between for both the ocular and objective lenses. In addition, he upgraded the gearwheels and cogs on the side of his leather harness to improve the autofocus, eliminating optical aberrations.

Optometry, however, wasn't the only thing Kaimo indulged in. On occasion, he practiced fencing with Bartholomew to become a competent swordsman. Not wanting to just rely on his telescopic eye, he also spent time increasing his proficiency with guns, such as target practice with Edgar. In the mornings and evenings, he jogged through the manor and along the harbor; it was another form of physical therapy because, much like the professor, he was still recuperating from his wounds.

By the end of the week, the professor had recovered enough to leave. Morning came, and the twin suns gleamed at the hazy metropolis that stretched all the way over to the northern coast of Quradale. The quartet was already in Edgar's automobile, the butler driving toward Enbertum's wharf.

Passing a few people and carriages, Kaimo looked out of the window and smiled at the city that he'd only dreamed of visiting before. Now, he was leaving the bustling metropolis to reach even greater places. But this journey wasn't for pleasure. Looking ahead, he saw the pier and took a deep breath.

One of the many guards approached the advancing vehicle, at which point Bartholomew lowered the windows and slowed down. Edgar flaunted his badge at the imperialist, who snorted and gestured for them to pass quickly. The butler accelerated along the quayside and drove to a steamer.

Again, they halted while Edgar showed four tickets to the stationmaster. Their admission accepted, they boarded the ship and parked at the aft. The quartet exited the vehicle, walking by the gunwale. Together, they patiently waited while hundreds of authorized citizens boarded the seaworthy vessel.

Within thirty minutes, the captain blew his boat's horn. Steam engines rumbled as the ocean-faring ship propelled away from Enbertum. Kaimo stared at the fading metropolis and nearby island whose statue of the emperor still impressed him. He didn't take his eye off Enbertum until it disappeared from his sight.

Turning around, he noticed several people staring out into the seemingly endless ocean. Unsure where the others had gone, he searched for them. On the top deck, beyond the vessel's dual smoke stacks, Kaimo joined Edgar. For a while, they stood by the bow and stared at the calm waters. The gentle breeze embraced them, mingling with the rising steam.

"Is this your first time on a boat, Kaimo?" the detective asked.

"Essentially," he replied. "I've been on a canoe of sorts through the gorges of Bogdar. It was just a short distance, though. Never imagined I'd be on a steamer as big as this and venture out into the world."

"I'm sure there's more to come, my friend."

"Aha!" the butler blurted, approaching from behind with a tray. "There you are, Sir Kaimo. Food and refreshments for both of you. *Bon appétit!*"

"Did you tend to the professor?"

"Yes, Master. I did exactly as instructed and dare say he's beginning to warm up to my nuts."

Edgar burst out laughing. "Bartholomew, next time say 'gears,' not nuts. You're my butler, not a robotic gigolo. You don't want to give people the wrong impression."

"You're a gentleman and a scholar, Master!"

Kaimo patted Bartholomew on the back. He took a sandwich and glass of water, sharing the meal with Edgar. It was difficult to stay busy aboard the ship, especially during an intercontinental voyage. They would be under steam for six days and hoped boredom wouldn't set in.

Their wish partially came true, because two days later a storm brewed near them. As it encroached, the crew struggled to keep the vessel from capsizing. Water filled the lower deck, and the tempest struck against the narrow, thick hull. To exacerbate matters, the side-wheeled paddles struggled against wild, swelling waves. The ocean-going steamer strained, fighting the storm that seized it; ear-shattering thunder and pummeling rain terrified the passengers.

Fed up with one misfortune after another, Kaimo was about to scream at the top of his lungs in frustration. Then, to his horror, he witnessed lightning strike a merchant vessel flying high above him. Flickers in the dark heavens revealed the fiery airship descending fast into the ocean. His guts roiling, sorrow filled his heart as he watched helpless people fall miles away, only to drown in the madness of the hurricane.

The mountain-ripping thunder and lightning, turbulent winds, and stabbing rain persisted. Kaimo felt as though such forces of nature would tear through his skin. He and his companions helped the crew bail water, especially near Edgar's automobile. The surging water overwhelmed them, but after an hour of relentless work, their efforts were rewarded.

By chance, the storm waned and moved away. Twilight was long gone. Kaimo and his comrades stayed on the upper deck, watching the departing squall. Despite the recent problems that had beset them, they were grateful to be alive.

Kaimo sighed. "All those people…"

"It's a terrible tragedy," Edgar said.

The robot attempted to understand their emotions and replied, "Perhaps it was fate."

"Fate is a fickle thing," the professor commented. "I normally detest sailing and almost requested we travel by air. I get seasick too often during such rocky voyages. And yet, if I had given in to my ego, that might have been us. Dead and lost in the depths of the ocean."

"Dreadful," the butler said.

Morning arrived, and the peaceful weather embraced all the passengers. From time to time, the quartet spotted full-rigged, merchant airships with three or four masts. Then, on the final day, they witnessed a flotilla of imperial zeppelins soaring among the gray clouds.

On impulse, Kaimo pulled out his spyglass but stopped short. Instead, he relied on his enhanced monocle, switching it to a monocular and using its telescopic power to view them with greater clarity. Even though the *Iron Cloud* wasn't among them, Kaimo felt uneasy seeing such a large armada in the sky.

Beyond them, he glimpsed a mysterious phenomenon. It billowed within the hazy smog that obscured his vision, even with the highest setting of diopters or magnifying power. In that moment, Kaimo acknowledged an enigmatic shift in the firmament, as if it reflected something immense by means of glass—a megalopolis floating in a parallel sky—detached from known reality. The lens-maker wasn't sure if he was experiencing an enigmatic sensation swathed in unworldliness. Yet, as fast and abruptly as it had peeked out from the heavens, it dissipated altogether.

"Did you see that?" he asked, a subtle vibration rising within his chest.

"Their formation was a glorious sight, Sir Kaimo," the butler said. "The imperium grows stronger by the day."

Oswald frowned. "We're fighting against them."

"Bloody scoundrels! I hope their ships burn!"

Embarrassment creased the private eye's face.

"I meant Welkin," Kaimo said. "Did you see it?"

The professor gazed at him with incredulity. "No one can see the emperor's abode. It's concealed from the naked eye. One might as well say it's a false rumor."

"Perhaps," he said, a troubled expression taking hold of him. "I don't know. Thought it was there… thought I saw it in Icdarus once too. Maybe just an illusion due to the light or some other aberration."

"Don't worry," Edgar said. "You'll eventually adjust to the apparatus."

"Indeed, Sir Kaimo," Bartholomew added with confidence. "It is a hybrid telescope that allows a monocle to also act as a monocular. It uses diopters and magnification power. In point of fact, it is even more advanced than my bioptic eye."

"Thanks, Bart," he said modestly, equally educated in optics and regretting he mentioned seeing a floating castle.

The professor eyed him again, suspicion etched on his face. After a moment, however, he waived it off, distracted by the sight of landfall in the far-flung distance. Standing by the railing of the upper deck, they anxiously gazed ahead. Kaimo, meanwhile, zoomed in with his telescopic eye.

At first, Kaimo had difficulty summoning the words to describe what he saw. To his surprise, the imperial capital appeared more like a fortress built atop a mountain of industry. Factories blanketed the heart of the metropolis, and its majestic bulwark ascended like an escarpment. The impenetrable-looking fortification surrounded the imperial city, opened only at the harbor.

Warships equipped with full-length flight decks surrounded the harbor, each carrying a dozen biplanes. The carriers also wielded cannons and turrets at every corner. And high above roamed an armada of zeppelins, similar in size to the *Iron Cloud*, reconnoitering sky, sea, and land.

"Holy mother," Kaimo said, slack-jawed.

Edgar scoffed at the sight. "Vel-Qatal…heart of the ignoble imperium. Be prepared for interrogation by an officer in the upper echelons. Even with my badge, they do not so easily allow entry into the capital."

"Just tell them the Midnight Mutilator has an accomplice in Drenengarde," Professor Briknoll said.

"Truly brilliant, Sir Briknoll!"

Kaimo nodded at the professor, hopeful that he and his companions would be granted entry into the capital city so they could reach Drenengarde. Advancing to a vast quayside, the captain docked his vessel. Steam dispersed as the paddlers slowed down until stopping altogether, along with the engine.

The quartet jostled through the crowd of passengers on their way downstairs, toward Edgar's automobile. To his disappointment, Kaimo noted a long line forming by the ship's exit. Struggling against irritation, he cursed under his breath and stepped into the vehicle with the others.

Bartholomew activated the car and slowly drove to another exit dedicated to automobiles. The group waited by the departure platform until prompted to accelerate to the decorated guard who had three hulking automatons standing beside him. He approached, his face concealed by a gas mask.

"Windows down," the imperial officer said, observing the quartet until fixing his eyes on the detective's badge. "Move along."

"Huh?" Edgar blurted. "You don't need any documentation?"

"Are you not here regarding the terror attack? Insurgents blew up one of our power plants near House Dutré and the Hall of Justice."

"Indeed," the sleuth replied, managing to maintain a composed expression despite the hurricane in his mind. "Rest assured, we will get down to the bottom of this lunacy. Thank you, Officer."

"Move along."

Professor Briknoll grunted. "You heard the officer. Get going, Gearstorm."

"How uncouth of you," Bartholomew said, accelerating while closing the windows. "I am Sir Bartholomew lu Vogmorton."

"Gearstorm," coughed the detective.

"Did the resistance seriously attack the capital?" Kaimo asked in disbelief, unable to focus on their humor.

"Apparently," Edgar said, somewhat surprised while scanning the imperial metropolis in hopes of spotting the destroyed building. "It must've happened just after we left Enbertum."

"They're getting bolder."

"It's a civil war, Doctor," Professor Briknoll said. "There are bound to be a great many casualties."

"*Excusez moi*, but what is so *civil* about war?"

"On a slightly brighter note," Edgar started, ignoring his butler, "we were able to use that incident to our advantage."

"Right," Kaimo said in agreement. "No interrogation."

"The gods are with us!" Bartholomew proclaimed, driving past a multitude of industrial skyscrapers.

"Must you be whimsical all the time?" the professor snapped.

"*Savoir faire*, Bart," Edgar said.

"If I were human, he'd probably make me cry."

The professor rolled his eyes, restraining himself.

In the meantime, Kaimo observed every detail possible of the capital whose buildings boasted neoclassical architecture. Several basilicas decorated the sprawling city, but they no longer held religious value—they had all been refurbished and resplendent for court. Tanks with multiple turrets on their wings guarded noble houses that exhibited elegant façades with marble pillars and granite treads. Flagpoles anchored into the concrete stood on every other boulevard, banners depicting interwoven gears surrounding an arsenic symbol. And regiments of soldiers marched along many of the paved crossroads.

"This is unsettling," Kaimo said.

"Without a doubt, they are preparing for a massive strike," Edgar replied, his composure ebbing.

The professor grumbled. "Or worse..."

"They plan to invade Drenengarde?" Kaimo surmised.

"Anything is possible," Edgar said. "We'd best make our move fast. On the double, Bart."

"Good grief, there is never a dull moment to being a tourist. Gosh darn it! I just caught myself using an oxymoron. There's a reason why the word moron is in it. Well, that is just my unbiased opinion. Ah! Another! They make my cogs want to reverse."

Edgar hid his face in the palms of his hands. "Believe me, when I requested an automaton with panache, this is not what I had in mind."

"Do not deny your unbridled love for me, Master."

The others laughed, Kaimo playfully patting Edgar, soothing his embarrassment. Kaimo turned his attention back to the city. It was impossible to ignore the disturbing number of automatons there, but he also couldn't take his eye off the mountainous fortress whose pinnacle almost kissed the clouds. It was, however, nothing more than an optical illusion from his depth perception. What did embrace the swollen clouds was the hovering fleet of military airships, which cast massive shadows over Vel-Qatal.

"Do you think there is or was a fragment of the Etherstone here?" he asked.

"Of that I have no doubt," the professor answered. "And believe you me, it's long gone. Either in the emperor's or Xelvok's hands."

"Should we not search this magnificent city?"

"Appearances can be deceiving, Bart," Edgar said. "This city thrives on corruption. We weren't joking before. I'm afraid the wisest thing for us to do is depart from the capital as quick as possible."

"Drenengarde is a suitable location," the professor put in. "There is an unavowed rumor that the emperor lost his grip on the city. Hence, why they may invade it to maintain pretenses. I not only believe a shard of the stone is hidden there, but Edgar has a contact who can broker an introduction with leaders of the resistance."

"It's hard for me to fathom the idea of working with insurgents," Kaimo said. "My father fought for the empire and was a respected veteran. I never, *ever* liked war. Always hated both factions. But when Xelvok killed my father in cold blood, something snapped inside me. I just hope the rebels are more humane than what I hear and see."

"The truth is ugly, Doctor," the professor hawked.

Bartholomew turned at a corner, reaching a sealed gate. When guards on either side of the entrance saw them approach, they opened the mechanical portcullis. The automaton drove past them, leaving Vel-Qatal and entering a freeway. On the opposite side, the quartet noticed a seemingly endless line of vehicles and coaches—people waiting to be interrogated before being allowed entry into the imperial capital of Zykard.

Edgar whistled at the sight. "It's good to be a detective."

"Thank goodness," Kaimo responded, feeling lighthearted. "I would've lost my mind stuck on a line like that."

"*Bon voyage!*" the butler said, his sonorous voice ecstatic.

IV
Traversing

Val-Qatal at their backs, the quartet experienced a modicum of relief. Increasing the vehicle's speed, Bartholomew zoomed through Faraheydein's curving turnpike at would have normally been an alarming velocity. In the hands of a trusted automaton, however, Kaimo and his companions were relatively relaxed. The path ahead revealed a verdant wilderness with dense opako trees whose thick trunks brandished crystals embedded in the bark, as well as branches flaunting purple leaves.

Several trees arched across the road, their elongated boughs creating a crown above the highway that formed a natural tunnel. Thriving shrubs and colorful flowers grew over the railings from both sides. Despite the manmade passage carved out of the wilds, the region teemed with life. The quartet drove past six pagado—bug-eyed, furry marsupials with cone-shaped faces and long tails—fighting to get in their mother's pouch.

When the forest dwindled, the twin suns illuminated the sparkling throughway. As the road curved, one of the luminous stars beamed directly at Bartholomew. Like clockwork, he flicked a clip-like filter over his bioptic lens, transitioning the achromatic telescope of an eye into an absorptive, polarized lens that allowed him to drive without glares from the suns obstructing his vision.

The paved highway shifted into a grainy road, forcing Bartholomew to decelerate against the harsher terrain. Shortly after, the ground opened to a crisp white flatland with a backdrop of creamy hills and soaring mountains to the east and west while the quartet drove farther south.

Hours passed. The group stopped from time to time at mechanical outhouses serviced by automatons. They also occasionally went off-road to refuel at dingy kogal stations guarded by imperial soldiers. Then the quartet continued their journey. The passengers were by no means comfortable, but they managed to take naps.

Nightfall came and went. As dawn arrived, Kaimo woke and enjoyed the scenic path. It shifted again, becoming a kaleidoscope of green, auburn, and golden-yellow rocks interspersed with steaming geysers and salt pans. The passengers assumed that this bizarre but exotically beautiful landscape had probably formed when the nearby volcano was active millennia ago.

When the clayish road flattened with signs of loam and rocks, Kaimo spotted a hot air balloon. It drifted in the sky above a far-flung town. In time, Bartholomew drove beside tracks that connecting most villages and towns throughout the continent of Faraheydein. The railway eventually ended, but construction workers were expanding the tracks so trains could one day reach Drenengarde.

Twilight emerged. Fuel was running low again; however, the weary travelers did not encounter another kogal station in the region. Anxiety gripped Kaimo. To him, sitting in an automobile for hours on end became less charming and more unmanageable, crushing his high spirits. Then he looked ahead, acknowledging the obscure outline of a smog-filled city.

"Please tell me that's Drenengarde."

"Do you want false information or the unadorned truth?" Edgar said. At his companion's flagging expression, he let out a hearty laugh and added, "I jest, Kaimo! Indeed, our destination is upon us."

"Think we'll make it with the kogal we have left?" he asked.

"Beyond the shadow of a doubt," Bartholomew said, accelerating.

"We should find a decent inn and rest first," the professor suggested.

"Agreed," Edgar replied. "With those infamous gangs that keep insurgents and imperials at bay, we'll need daylight on our side."

The suns finished setting, replaced by the visible moons, stealing light and reflecting soft rays to pave the way for nightwalkers. Drenengarde lit up in the night, reminding Kaimo of Enbertum. The city's ambiance and architecture appeared gloomier and yet glamorous at the same time. Lamp posts that gave an extra glow lined the roads. And dark, gritty alleyways seized the crossroads with an occasional black automobile passing.

What caught Kaimo's attention the most was the setback buildings whose exterior, step-like walls made them look slightly narrower as they soared to the sky. The city had one onyx-stained skyport, a zeppelin soaring over an adjacent skyscraper. Other less important structures displayed decorative entrances with lit-up logos and bas-reliefs, including the inn they had just reached.

"Finally," Kaimo sighed, getting out of the vehicle and stretching with incredible relief, pliable joints cracking.

"I'll park the automobile and rejoin you, Master."

"Thank you, Bart," Edgar said, saluting his butler. "Okay, let's rent a room or two." He stepped inside the shadowy inn, unexpectedly drawn to a finely dressed woman singing. Her voice was accompanied by two musicians—one playing a piano and the other, a saxophone. He eyed her for a moment while walking over to the busy bar. "Good evening. Can we get a couple of bedrooms for one night?"

"Seventy-five qauras," the bartender said flatly.

"What a voice," Kaimo commented as his companion paid the fee.

"Her tone is as melodious as the music," the professor said.

Edgar shared a beatific smile. "Years ago, I used to visit more often and always relished the live entertainment Drenengarde offers. Remarkable artists are among us." He turned, his eyes scanning the establishment. "Barkeeper, do you by any chance have a telephone I can use?"

"Ten qauras," the owner answered, gesturing at a corner past the bar.

The detective gave him coins displaying the emperor's face embossed on them and then walked over to the corner where two tin cans hung against a wall. Grabbing both metal devices, he dialed a code on its keypad and waited as the earpiece rang in his ear. After a long moment, someone answered.

"It's me," Edgar responded. "I'm in Drenengarde with some of my compatriots." A feminine voice spoke back, her words muffled. "I figured you'd be surprised. Yeah, it took more than a week to get here. I'm still not used to leaving my comfort zone, but it had to be done." The woman replied again, her voice inaudible. "There's only one reason why I'd be here. I need to speak with you know who."

"Who's he talking to?"

Oswald merely shrugged, grabbing a drink.

"All right," Edgar continued, "I'll be there. Thank you. I owe you one." He hung up, turning his attention to the others. "It seems we'll get our meeting."

"When?" Kaimo asked.

"Tomorrow afternoon."

Just then, the butler entered the building. "Your vehicle is safe and secure, Master." At the detective's nod of gratitude, Bartholomew fixed on the singer. "What a remarkable voice. She sounds almost as eloquent as me!"

The group ignored him, going up a flight of steps. Bartholomew promptly joined them, at which point Edgar gave Oswald a separate key. After the professor thanked him and went into his room, the others entered theirs. With the exception of the automaton, fatigue hit them hard. Kaimo and Edgar collapsed on the beds while the butler stood by the window, keeping watch for the remainder of the night.

V
Crossfire

At midmorning, Kaimo was the last to wake up. He took a much-needed shower and joined his companions for breakfast. To his surprise, Bartholomew wasn't among them. Unlike last night, they were the only ones sitting at a table beside the bar. Citizens seemed to prefer the nightlife more, he thought to himself.

After eating toast with crushed avocado, he stepped outside with the others. "Goodness, it's on the cold side."

"Bonjour!" Bartholomew said with elation, vacating the vehicle. When the others greeted him, he opened the trunk and pulled out a few trench coats. "I bought these fine tunics exactly as instructed."

"Well done, Bart," Edgar responded, taking his double-breasted coat. "Put these on, gentlemen."

"Good thinking, Detective," the professor said. "These should help us fit in more."

"And stay warmer," Kaimo commented, wind blowing the flaps of his caped coat. "It's quite ridiculous. The suns are beaming without a single cloud in sight and yet I've never been so cold in my life."

"I don't like it any better than you, Doctor," the professor replied. "But we are, after all, in another continent."

"*Touché*."

Time being of the essence, the quartet got in the automobile. Bartholomew started the engine and merged onto the main road. Just about every man was clad in a trench coat and fedora. The women looked similar, except for their cloche hats. A few of them were chatting at street corners. Some loitered in front of businesses, while others chatted and smoked cigarettes.

"So," Kaimo started, "where are we headed?"

"Le Beau Monde," Edgar answered, glancing at a black car passing by on the two-lane road. "It's an art gallery. Our contact has an underground network there, which is where we'll have our meeting."

"A sound plan."

The professor grimaced. "An audience with leaders of the resistance is no trifling matter. If the parley bodes well, we will also need to investigate Drenengarde's heart, the cloc—"

A salvo of bullets interrupted his train of thought as the group ducked for cover. Bartholomew instinctively swerved the vehicle when a white automobile emerged from an intersection, gangsters shooting up an adjacent black car until it flipped several times on the road. In a vain attempt to avoid the upside-down vehicle, Bartholomew accidently slammed into a lamp post.

"*Pardonnez-moi!*"

Edgar groaned, rattled.

"Moons of Zykard, what just happened?" Kaimo muttered, blood dripping from his forehead.

"Hooligans," the professor rasped, opening his door to crawl out.

Two white automobiles across from them stopped, eight goons attired in trench coats stepping out. Advancing toward the black automobile, they opened fire again until it exploded. Seeing the detective's vehicle and realizing it was the same color, they reloaded the magazines in their experimental, blowback submachine guns and aimed at the automobile.

"Shit!" Kaimo blurted. "They think we're with them!"

"Defend yourselves!" Edgar shouted, jumping out of his car.

In seconds, bullet holes riddled the vehicle. Shattered glass sprayed the passengers, setting off Bartholomew to exit the automobile. He nonchalantly lifted a shotgun from within his overcoat, aiming it at the goons. Startled by his presence, they fired at him. Pumping his weapon, the butler blasted one of the gangsters off his feet.

"They've got a freakin' automaton with 'em!" one of the thugs said.

"Take it down, boys!" commanded another, unloading his magazine into his target without mercy.

Bartholomew jolted back from the gunfire but blasted two more gangsters as he walked across the street without fear. In the meantime, Edgar rose from behind the trunk of his vehicle and shot at them but missed. The private eye cursed under his breath, searching his pockets for a clip of ammo. When return fire came his way, he leapt down for cover and remained next to the professor.

"I don't suppose you have any ammunition?"

"My sincerest apologies," the professor started, "I ran out of magazines during my last lecture."

"Those guns," Kaimo said, flustered. "I've only seen them on planes."

Tackling his trepidation, the lens-maker emerged from the vehicle's hood and drew his Grimtol, fixing on the gangsters. To him, such hooligans were no different than the deceased mutilator or crooked imperialists. He cocked his gun and took aim. Autofocus enabled, he shot a goon with solid accuracy. Targeting another without remorse, he shot him too. In tandem, the automaton pumped his shotgun, blowing away every last one of them. Then he overturned both cars.

"No one messes with Gearstorm! But my friends call me Bartholomew. Or just Bart."

"They can't hear you," Edgar said. "They're dead. Now get back in the car and drive us the hell out of here before more come."

"Understood. Make haste slowly. Drat! I did it again."

Returning to the bullet-riddled car, the quartet continued toward their destination. Steam billowed from the hood, and the automobile vibrated. Its engine produced a dirge of rattling and whirring sounds as if it were regurgitating cogs. To Kaimo's extreme surprise, the vehicle still functioned and moved.

"Everyone all right?" Edgar asked.

"I am operating at ninety—"

"Not you, metal-head."

"The crash left me rather bruised, but I'll be fine," the professor said. "How about you, Doctor?"

"Same," he said, wiping his forehead clean of blood and sweat. "I just can't believe what happened. In broad daylight, too."

Edgar glanced at him from the rearview mirror. "That was some impressive shooting back there, Kaimo."

"It's all in the optics."

"Doc the Sharpshooter," the sleuth added.

Despite the tension hanging in the air, Kaimo let out a soft laugh.

A couple of miles into the metropolis, Bartholomew turned and entered an underpass. The elongated tunnel curved several times. Surprisingly well lit, Kaimo was impressed with the concrete passage. For the first time, more than a few cars drove around them.

Ascending from the tunnel, the butler turned at an intersection near the spire-shaped clocktower. One mile later, Bartholomew merged onto a boulevard named *Chemin de l'art.* They passed an opera theater, two museums, and then reached their destination. Bartholomew parked in front of the building, which exhibited diverse geometric-shaped sculptures of art and stained-glass windows that rose from the first floor to the crown.

"Le Beau Monde," Edgar said, relief in his voice. "It's nice to be back in one piece."

"To be precise, Master, we are actually composed of myriad parts. So, the correct syntax would be that we are back in pieces."

"Someone smash him apart, please."

"*Anyway,*" Kaimo began, "there's no time like the present. Best we'd get on with this meeting."

Getting out of the severely damaged vehicle, Kaimo stood by the art gallery's entrance with Edgar and Professor Briknoll, waiting for Bartholomew to park and rejoin them. Several passersby stared at the badly damaged automobile, which looked like it were about to explode.

When the butler reappeared, they approached the building's entrance. As before, the detective showed his badge to a guard. Free to enter the gallery, the group stepped inside and avoided the queue at the atrium. Abstract art adorned the walls of the marble corridor in the eastern wing. Edgar led them to a sealed door with a gold-plated sign that read: "Employees Only." He knocked on it as if using an enigmatic code.

"*Le mot de passe?*" said a gruff voice.

"Avant-garde," the detective answered.

A masked guard opened the door and ushered them inside. Unlike imperial soldiers, the individual lifted the intimidating visor and gave a nod of respect. Kaimo was stunned to see a woman clad in imperial armor but understood that she must be an insurgent. An uplifting sensation swept over him, her robust presence amid the conflict of civil war easing his nerves.

"Good to see you again, Edgar," she said.

"It's been too long, Viviane," he said, shaking her hand. "You'll have to visit Enbertum more often."

"I like it here just fine. No imperium. Well, the others are waiting. This way."

The quartet followed her through a dim hall and descended a creaking flight of steps to an underground warehouse. Sealed containers filled the storeroom. Walking ahead, Viviane brought them to her office where four insurgents stood waiting. One of them was a woman, her bug-eyed face contorted, as she stared at Kaimo whose countenance shook as much as hers, shock carved on his visage.

"All right," Viviane said. "I've done my par—"

"Mother?" Kaimo interjected, gazing at the woman as fierce bitterness washed over him like a lament.

An awkward silence enveloped them. In that harrowing moment, Kaimo wasn't sure if he was crazy. A furious compulsion to lift and bash the storage crates came over him, indignation burning in his chest. He started to shutdown like an automaton, empathy and love draining from his fatigued mind.

Regret flashed across the older woman's face. "Kaimo..." she responded, teary-eyed as she approached her son.

"Marisa?" the contact said, raising an eyebrow. "You know them?"

She failed to respond, losing her struggle to remain composed. Tears of pain, remorse, loss, and love escaped her.

"What's happening?" Kaimo said, taking a step back. "Is this a hoax or some kind of sick joke?" When she shook her head, he went on, "You abandoned father and me for the resistance? Explain this madness!"

The others were bemused, shock creasing their features as they gawped at Marisa and her son.

"Are we missing something, Master?"

"I think so."

"Your automaton is clearly missing a few too many cogs," the professor whispered. "I reckon things are about to get very serious."

CHAPTER NINE

Zenas Solma

I
Reasons

Kaimo removed his leather harness, revealing his disfigured face and eye. "Look at me! Look at me!" He watched his mother's countenance shift. Her calm and strong features contorted, horror carved on her face. "The same man who did this killed father. Yes. That's right. Dad's dead. Murdered in cold blood. I'd be dead too if it weren't for the automaton that has cared for me more than you ever have."

"I deserve this," she said, breaking down. "Every painful word." Marisa fought against her tears and shuddering sobs. "But I would do it all again. Leave and join the resistance. I'd do it for every child in the world. For you."

"For me?" he repeated, frenzied.

"Your father and I loved each other very much. We never saw eye to eye on the war. Yet it wasn't until he returned that I realized how much he changed."

"So, you thought it'd be best to leave me with a cretin and fend for myself?"

"This war is bigger than us," she said, her voice firm. "If the imperium could turn the gentle man I once ardently loved into an emotionless monster, they could do that to you too. Every child is endangered. I sacrificed all of my happiness in the high hopes that we may one day put an end to their draconic and chauvinistic society."

"Why couldn't you have taken me with you?" he asked, his hands trembling.

Marisa shook her head, wiping tears away. "No child deserves this life. Not you. Not anyone. I left to be a part of something greater." She abruptly stopped, shuddering. Controlling herself, she went on, "Despite the horrible afflictions that have befallen our family, you are here. My son."

"Don't call me that. I am *not* your son!"

She gripped him by his forearm. "Then why did you call me mother? No amount of time or affliction can wipe away the bond of mother and child. You are my son."

"Lies!" he bellowed, weeping with her.

Marisa embraced him and held her son tight. The others stood outside the office but heard everything, silent as mice. It was an awkward moment, and more so for Kaimo who'd learned to forget his mother. Yet just when he'd become a man, she'd unexpectedly come back into his life. For better or worse, he let go of his anger and embraced her.

"Who did this to you?" she asked, daring to caress his scarred face.

He turned away when she touched him. "The grand marshal himself. Xelvok Von Cazar."

"That's…how could this be? I have only dreamed of confronting him."

Kaimo donned his harness and made eye contact with his mother. "Something terrible has transpired. Something that I fear is beyond all of us. Even the resistance. Xelvok's ambitions threaten not just us but the world itself."

"What have you learned?"

"Gather your fellow leaders," he said. "They must all hear the story I need to share with you."

II
Imminent Threat

At her son's request, Marisa brought everyone back into the office where Kaimo explained everything that had happened since the beginning at Icdarus. For greater detail about the mysterious aether and Etherstone, the professor took over what with the archaic period being his area of expertise.

"You expect us to believe that the grand marshal plans to overthrow the emperor?" said Rengis, one of the other leaders.

The professor grunted. "It is a simple matter of deduction."

"Xelvok already has at least one of the fragments. And if he has the same knowledge as Professor Briknoll, then he most definitely has another from Vel-Qatal. We need to save Zelly before it's too late."

"This would explain the blackouts in the capital," Marisa said. "That's the only reason we were able to successfully attack one of the kogal power plants."

"Have there been any blackouts here?" Edgar asked.

"No," another insurgent leader answered. "Not yet."

"This is our chance," Kaimo said, fired up. "It's only a matter of time before Xelvok steal's the fragment here. We saw an army at the capital. We'll need to use this city's central clock tower as bait. Then, when he least expects it, we launch an attack."

One of the other leaders scoffed. "What you're suggesting is suicide. Iron Cloud is the most lethal airship ever built. It's a fortress in itself."

"What makes you think one of the shards is in the clock tower?" Marisa asked.

"I am no simpleton," the professor grumbled. "I'm an esteemed professor at Krenanstein and don't need to validate myself to the likes of you."

"Indulge them, Professor," Kaimo said. "This is why we've gathered together."

Oswald glanced at him and snorted. "My doctorate is in ancient mythology, particularly the aether and its origin. During my research, I studied at Vel-Qatal. Have you not ever wondered why such grandiose cities have power beyond steam engines? Searching for clues, I found my way to the capital's clock tower. It resonated with the same power as in Enbertum. It was there, too. The clock towers are the heart of each city. Literally. You see, once the fragment was removed from Enbertum, we experienced blackouts."

"Even if you're right," Rengis began, "we are not ready to challenge Grand Marshal Xelvok. He possesses far more power than that Etherstone thingamajig. We need to strike the imperium like ghosts."

"I concur," said Alastair, another leader. "Confronting the duke is certain death."

"Why are you all so terrified? What power can possibly be more frightening than the Etherstone?"

Marisa turned to her son. "Kaimo, forgive me for asking, but, when you confronted him, was there anything unnatural that you experienced?"

"Think hard," Rengis threw in.

Kaimo didn't need to do that. He recalled the frightening battle at Enbertum's clock tower, as if it had taken place mere hours ago; he remembered the excruciating pain when Xelvok slashed his face and disfigured him; he remembered when his arm snapped backwards, and how he fell to what any logical person would conclude was certain death. Before that, however, he recalled one thing that was, in fact, unnatural.

"Yes," he finally said. "I remember now. Before he struck me down, I shot at him. Yet the bullets... they ricocheted without hitting anything."

"If you think you're crazy, you're not," Marisa responded. "We have heard of this too. In fact, one of our moles witnessed it firsthand during a failed assassination attempt. The bullets did not ricochet, Kaimo. Because there was nothing in the air. Nothing at all to stop them. What you saw was a—"

"Manipulation of physics," the professor intervened, pensive. "Or rather, a manipulation of reality."

"So, you know of it too, Professor," Marisa said.

"I have only heard rumors of it from my fellow colleagues at Krenanstein. The quantum mechanics of it seemed impossible. Yet if the legends of the aether and Etherstone are true, then science can reveal something even more mystifying."

"Can you speak plainly?" Edgar snapped. "I don't want to be a detective every second of my life."

"Temporal distortions," the professor reiterated.

"The bullets that 'ricocheted' as Doctor Kaimo saw it, were not repelled by something as dubious as magic. It was the Zenas Solma...a device that theoretically creates chronological deformations in time."

"Bloody hell," Bartholomew blurted.

"I've been told the temporal engine reacts to a crystalline key embedded in Xelvok's hand," Marisa said. "From what we have gathered, it needs to be recharged and has limited power. But it is nonetheless detrimental and outright unnatural. That is why it's impossible to confront him and survive."

Though a timeless interval to Kaimo, his mind was stuck—deep in thought—as he seized an abstract memory that had betrayed him. Fate dealt kindly, the lens-maker peered through the looking glass within his distorted memory and recalled a surreal moment in which he stood amid a ball, masked nobles performing a waltz around him. Details eluded him as he desperately tried to hold on to the opaque recollection, then it dissipated altogether like a faded dream.

"He cheated death..."

"I beg your pardon?" Edgar said, seeing the troublesome expression on his companion's pale face. "Speak your mind, my friend."

Kaimo shook away his maddening thoughts. "It's obvious I wasn't meant to live, but if we let fear dictate our lives, we will never truly be free. You call yourselves freedom fighters. You say this *resistance* is supposed to remove the shackles of humankind that the emperor has placed over the world. Yet these words mean nothing if we cannot truly battle against the real threat."

"Eloquently put, Sir Kaimo. Though, I am quite buggered with the mention of the Zenas Solma and quantum mechanics. Or perhaps I'm just a knob."

The leaders ignored him and glanced at each other, silent.

"Why did you hijack the imperial train at Icdarus?" Kaimo asked.

"One of our spies told us something critical to the Duke of Enbertum was on it," Marisa replied, her eyes downcast. "We sacrificed a great deal for that information."

"Good people," Rengis said with regret.

"It wasn't for nothing. I would've never found Zelly or learned of Xelvok's diabolical scheme. Everything happens for a reason. If you don't want those horrendous sacrifices to be in vain, we need to act. Impractical. Impossible. Staring down the very face of suicide. Whatever you want to call it. Now is the time to strike big."

"Who are you to come here and bark orders at us?" Rengis snapped. "I respect that you are Marisa's son, but we have been fighting this war for decades. Millions of people throughout the world look to us with hope."

"Exactly," Alastair said. "We are their leaders. Are we to just stop our efforts against the emperor's tyranny and drastically change our plans because an *optometrist* marches in here talking about Xelvok's deranged obsession about some antediluvian mythos?"

"Yes," the detective said flatly. "Think about it, my friends. Emperor Ereganen has already obtained what he wanted. He conquered the former kingdoms and united the world. Albeit, it's not the utopia we dreamt of. Hence, why you are hiding here. The fact remains that the emperor is practically on his deathbed and empty of ambition."

"Dalfein Af Ereganen is not a threat anymore," the professor affirmed.

Kaimo nodded at his comrades. "I couldn't have

expressed that better. Xelvok is the true menace at hand. It's only a matter of time before a coup. Every minute wasted is a chance for him to succeed. If we don't save Zelly, she will keep suffering. I implore all of you. Help us attack Iron Cloud and save her."

"And if we don't?" one of the insurgents said snottily.

"It's not a demand," Kaimo said. "But if you don't, I fear the world and all who inhabit it are doomed."

Marisa and her fellow leaders let his words sink in and deliberated in private for half an hour. The others waited outside the office. Uneasy, the lens-maker paced around the storeroom. Just when anxiety and angst gripped his innards, his mother and coconspirators emerged from Viviane's office. Galvanized, he approached them, sharing the same grim expression on their pale faces.

"You have our support," Marisa said. "We'll make preparations now and have the Stormguard pick us up. If we do locate a shard of that Etherstone, we'll use it as bait."

Kaimo beamed, filled with genuine hope.

"Don't look so elated," Alastair commented, scowling at them. "If what you say is true and Xelvok does indeed come looking for that…gem, fragment or whatever it is, then we may very well all die."

"We won't," he said confidently, raising his enhanced arm. "I'll make sure of it."

III
For Freedom's Sake

Parting ways with Viviane, Kaimo and his companions followed the insurgents through an underground network of tunnels. The dim, musty subway led them beneath the city's skyport where a rebel stood guard. Disguised in imperial armor, the soldier guided them to Drenẹngarde's surface. He confirmed there were no gangs or troops within the vicinity and escorted them to an elevator.

"Thank you," Marisa said, activating the lift. "Inform the others via telegram that we'll need reinforcements on standby."

"Right away, ma'am," the disguised rebel said, saluting her and leaving.

Kaimo resented his mother, and he knew that he'd probably hold a grudge against her for a long time; but in a broken world dominated by men, he was equally proud to see that she was well respected and in such a powerful position. In a strange way, her strong will reminded him of Zylpha. He deeply missed her and grew anxious, hoping there was still a chance to save her.

At the skyport's rooftop, Kaimo broke out of his reverie. On a grated platform, they waited for the insurgents' primary vessel, the *Stormguard*. When the full-rigged airship arrived, the group embarked. Together they soared into the dense clouds, further masked by the steam their enormous vessel produced.

Marisa introduced the crew to her son and his companions. She and her fellow leaders also informed them of their plans. By early evening, reinforcements joined them. Alastair left in a blimp of his own with a regiment and descended to investigate the city's clock tower to see if a shard of the Etherstone was in fact there. In the meantime, Bartholomew refilled his engine-heart with kogal and used his bioptic telescope to survey the region. Kaimo and his comrades were eventually shown to their quarters below deck. Relieved to rest, they surrendered to deep sleep for the remainder of the night.

The rebels probed Drenengarde for the next couple of days, remaining above the swollen clouds.

With plenty of rations on board, all they needed was patience. No one knew how long they'd have to wait, but Kaimo intuited that Xelvok would make a move sooner rather than later because of the army he and his friends had seen at the capital. A bomb was ticking in Drenengarde, and it was ready to go off.

At the end of the week, the insurgents were on edge; they hadn't expected to wait so long, but Kaimo used his time wisely to build a reflector telescope for the airship. He asked for assistance, and Bartholomew obliged. Together, they used silver to craft a metal-on-glass mirror. Though a prototype, when finished, the insurgents' telescope was absent of aberrations and enabled them to see for miles on end.

Yet another day passed. By midmorning, however, Kaimo used the airship's telescope and spotted an imperial zeppelin approaching. In ship's aft, the lens-maker adjusted the slider to zoom at maximum power. To avoid two suns burning out the retina in his good eye, he reangled the oculus. Thanks to the large aperture and its multi-coated optics, the light transmission during daylight was exceptional; he saw that the approaching airship was none other than *Iron Cloud*. He immediately alerted the crew.

"I'm coming for you, Zelly..."

Edgar sprinted across the deck, over to his comrade. "This is it, Kaimo. It's all or nothing."

"I've never been more ready," he said, his resolve strong.

The flotilla of rebel ships hid in the clouds, waiting for *Iron Cloud* to reach Drenengarde's clock tower. Just as Kaimo assumed, the imperial airship aligned itself with the spire's pinnacle and remained suspended while Xelvok disembarked with an entourage of eight soldiers, entering the clocktower.

Marisa signaled the other vessels to descend further. The armada revealed themselves and aimed their cannons at *Iron Cloud*. Moments before they attacked, the imperial crew sounded their alarm. Too late. The insurgents released a bombardment, the effect sending the ship careening and smashing against a nearby building, an optical pylon on its roof tumbling.

Explosions erupted throughout the fiery sky. Half of the building adjacent to the clock tower collapsed. Kaimo cursed and turned away from the sight, hoping no innocent lives were taken other than gang members. Despite his internal moral struggle, he charged toward the gunwale as his ship approached the *Iron Cloud*.

Side by side with the dreadnaught vessel, Kaimo aimed at soldiers who'd been shooting at insurgents and fired with flawless precision. Edgar assisted him, a pistol in each hand. Shotgun ready, Bartholomew leapt across from the *Stormguard* to the *Iron Cloud*, landing on its deck. Soldiers targeted the butler who merely jolted from a salvo that made him think he was dancing. He returned the favor, blasting them off their feet.

In the meantime, inside the clocktower, Xelvok heard his ship's alarm and turned to vacate the building when Alastair emerged with his regiment and opened fire. The grand marshal saw the insurgent leader holding a shard and rushed behind a wall, gritting his teeth while his entourage counterattacked. Pressing hard on his left hand, a tattoo-like symbol glowed. He donned a glove, concealing it, and charged out with his chainsaw blade and shield, blocking bullets.

"You dare attack the Sword of the Emperor?" he bellowed, cutting down a rebel.

The grand marshal blocked bullets with his shield. When it dented and took too much damage, he waved his glowing hand. Courtesy of the Zenas Solma's temporal distortion, projectiles reversed in all directions. The insurgents, strategically positioned in Drenengarde's clock tower, forced Xelvok to leap down to lower platforms. Repelling bullets, he raised his resonating blade and gutted his foes with vehemence.

Back on the *Iron Cloud's* outer deck, Bartholomew cleared it of imperialists. With the path clear, Marisa raised her steam-powered airship high enough for the insurgents to aim grappling hooks at the enemy vessel. Metal flukes piercing its hull they swung across, Kaimo included.

"Freedom!" the dissidents shouted in unison.

Edgar patted his butler on the back and then joined other insurgents to fire at a wave of imperial soldiers emerging from the upper exterior of *Iron Cloud's* cylindrical hull. The dreadnaught's firepower from many turrets destroyed several rebel ships. Only the *Stormguard* and two others remained from the original ten. In spite of shaken morale, the insurgents fought on, silencing fear. Rallying, they summoned the means to survive with the will to overpower.

Kaimo, meanwhile, rushed toward a sealed door and shot the lock open with his Grimtol. He entered the airship's attached gondola, descending a flight of steps to a corridor with several cabins on either side. Guards stood by the doors of the private quarters. Confronting the sentinels, he unloaded every bullet in his chamber into them.

Reloading his weapon, he checked each cabin. To his frustration, they were all empty. Sprinting down the hall, he reached the grand marshal's cabin and raised his enhanced arm. The mechanical brace of gears and cogs clanked in harmony, aiding him with unbounded strength as he smashed the door open. Inside, the found Zylpha hooked up to a dialysis machine akin to the one on the imperial train.

"Zelly!"

Kaimo freed Zylpha, laid her over his shoulders, and gazed at the inhuman machinery. Disgusted, he bashed the mechanical abomination until it stopped humming with energy. He cringed as Zylpha's blood poured out of a metal container. Conquering his nausea, he vacated the room to rejoin the others.

Charging through the corridor, the strange vibration in his chest returned; it was as if another presence that had a mind of its own lay dormant within and spoke to him. Whether by instinct or some other force unbeknownst to him, he knew that the Zenas Solma's temporal engine was aboard the *Iron Cloud*.

He wondered, *Could such power truly be here? Where can it be? Such an ungodly invention must be destroyed!*

Time against him—this being his only chance to save Zylpha—he ascended the staircase and exited the gondola. On the outer deck, the surviving insurgents reused their grappling hooks. Edgar waited, gesturing him to hurry as Xelvok emerged from the clock tower, his reverberating chainsaw sword and military garments blood-soaked. Shard in hand, Xelvok stared at Kaimo in utter disbelief.

"You?" he said, lunacy etched on his face. "Impossible!"

Kaimo cracked a smile at him and charged toward the gunwale. Edgar joined the lens-maker, waiting for him to disembark while he shot another approaching soldier.

"I'm right behind you, Sharpshooter," the sleuth said coolly.

Spotting the grand marshal, Edgar fired both guns at him. With languid deliberation, Xelvok sheathed his sword and pulled out a pistol, aiming as his initial target swung from the *Iron Cloud* to the *Stormguard*. Kaimo landed safely, ready to take Zylpha to the infirmary when Xelvok's bullet caused an uproar.

"Master!"

Pale as a wraith, Kaimo whirled and witnessed Edgar fall before reaching the airship. Bartholomew hurled himself down, gripping the detective's grapnel device. With his other hand, he seized his master and relaunched the grappling hook back up as the *Stormguard* flew away. Despite the butler's incredible dexterity in rescuing his master, Kaimo saw that Edgar had been shot.

"Put me down," the sleuth whispered, his words barely audible.

Bartholomew rested him on the deck. Gently handing Zylpha to a nearby insurgent, Kaimo rushed over. He acknowledged the severity of Edgar's wound and broke down, gripping his hand. The professor saw the commotion and approached, impotent to help. Edgar, meanwhile, used the last of his strength to gaze at his friends. Blood trickled from his mouth as he struggled to smile.

"Kaimo...you...sa-saved...her," he rasped. "Ke-keep it...that...way."

"I will," he said, unable to control his tears. "I promise."

"Gearstorm..."

"Yes, Master?"

"Tha-thank...you...for..."

The detective breathed his last breath. Bartholomew, although, essentially nothing more than a collection of metal cogs, understood death and produced an artificial, deafening lament. Kaimo and the professor shared tears of anguish, clutching their lost comrade.

CHAPTER TEN

Struggles of War

I
Feelings Rekindled

The insurgents experienced a bittersweet victory. Following the detective's death, they left Drenengarde and swiftly traveled south before Grand Marshal Xelvok returned to his damaged battleship to pursue them. As they escaped, Kaimo brought Zylpha to the vessel's infirmary and laid her on a bed.

Unlike before in Icdarus, she remained in a comatose state for days. With the help of fellow insurgents, Kaimo nursed his partner and waited for her to regain consciousness. He barely left the room, and Bartholomew often checked on him while also providing him with sustenance. Despite saving Zylpha, the death of Edgar plunged him into a state of melancholy. Bartholomew, although incapable of demonstrating genuine emotions what with him being an automaton, emanated an uncanny emptiness, as if he truly felt human anguish.

Stormguard drifted high in the clouds, above the southern continent of Faraheydein. A range of misty mountains stretched below for thousands of miles, opening up into a curving valley similar to the one in Quradale; yet it was unique, especially its narrow fjord whose unspoiled beauty paved the way with erosive glaciers.

Marisa helmed the vessel, following the fjord's long, narrow inlet of water between the icy cliffs. Patches of snow blanketed the environment. The fresh air dissipated, replaced by a harsh coldness only tolerated with thicker, warmer coats. Properly attired, the crew operated their ship at full capacity, embracing the frosty atmosphere that stung their skin.

On the sixth morning, Zylpha stirred for the first time. Kaimo held her hand, tears of joy escaping his good eye. She groaned in pain, weakened by the loss of so much blood. Puncture wounds along her arms and neck testified to her ordeal, but she was healing. When she moaned again, Kaimo's face contorted as if he were the one experiencing her agony.

At twilight on the same day, Zylpha finally opened her blue eyes. She coughed and wheezed, barely moving. Though slow and weak at first, she touched her arm and felt a needle. Not realizing it was nourishing her, she tore it off while gasping and struggling to get out of bed.

"It's okay!" Kaimo said, reaching out to hold her.

Zylpha gazed at him for the first time and sat still, shock flashing across her face. "They said there is no beyond. I felt nothing. Saw nothing. Yet here we are. Is this heav—"

"You're alive and well," he intervened, holding her hand.

"But you died," she said, tears welling up in her eyes. "I saw you..."

"In a matter of speaking, I did die. By some miracle, I fell into the reservoir. It carried me to Enbertum's sewers. An automaton found me there, performed cardiopulmonary resuscitation, and experimented on me. Sort of horrific and yet strangely warm-hearted at the same time if you ask me."

"An automaton?" she said weakly, coughing again.

"Yeah. His name is Bartholomew. He tried calling me Gearstorm, courtesy of these extravagant apparatuses,"—Kaimo showed her his mechanical brace that supported his left arm and back and then turned his face sideways to show his headdress—"but the amusing nickname quickly backfired on him."

Zylpha touched his leather harness in disbelief and started to cry. To his surprise, she pulled him in and kissed his lips. She moved her hand to remove the attached monocle, but he gently stopped her. Though hesitant, she ignored him, lifted it off, and saw his disfigurement. Despite his terrible embarrassment, she stroked his scar and passionately kissed him.

Surviving as they had, after all they had been through, the couple found release in their affection, grief, joy, trauma, and happiness.

"I'm so sorry," she said, stopping. "I am so terribly—"

"Please don't say sorry," he softly interrupted, caressing her hair. "I'd do anything for you. I would do it again an infinite amount of times to keep you safe."

She stared deeply at him. "No one has ever looked out for me so much. Not even my mother. I..."

"*Je t'aime*," he whispered.

Hearing those words from the old tongue, a wave of passion surged through her. "I love you too, Kai," she responded, ignoring her pain. "I'm so in love with you."

They kissed again, slipping out of their clothes. Zylpha forced her lover down on the bed, their bodies pressed together. Kaimo delicately caressed her as though she were divine. Sinking into a state of euphoria, he fondled her breasts and heard her moan with pleasure, arousing him further.

"You are the radiance of every star."

"And you are my world...my everything," she purred.

As they kissed, Kaimo regained a part of his lost humanity; it had gone adrift after so much suffering and degradation.

"I only want to show you how much love—"

Bartholomew opened the door, watching Zylpha reel aside and hide. "*Ouh là là! Enchanté. Mademoiselle*, you have been restored!"

"Bart, get out!"

"Right!" he said, flinching as a human might. "I'll guard the door. Enjoy your delightful copulating. Both of you, that is. Cheerio!"

Zylpha lowered the sheets from her eyes when the door closed. She abruptly burst into laughter with Kaimo. They kissed again and then simply held each other for the remainder of the night.

II
Regrouping

Back in the northern capital of Vel-Qatal, the *Iron Cloud* docked at an imperial skyport for repairs. Across the city, at the pinnacle of the central fortress, Grand Marshal Xelvok stood in a marble chamber beside a pane of glass, watching his precious vessel be serviced. He sipped his wine, listening to classical music from a phonograph atop a furnished desk when someone knocked on his door.

"Enter," he commanded.

An imperial general walked in with an entourage

and knelt briefly. "Lord Cazar, we returned from our investigation at Icdarus and have the information you requested."

"Well," began Xelvok, turning his attention to the brigadier general, "speak."

"His name is Kaimo de Morté," the officer replied, handing him a dossier. "That file belonged to his father, Gabriel. He was a well-respected veteran during the emperor's campaign and retired shortly before the resistance formed. Based on what we heard from citizens in Icdarus, the doctor's mother abandoned him when he was young."

The grand marshal scanned through Gabriel's records. "Is that all?"

"It seems Kaimo de Morté was something of an outcast, My Lord. I discovered from a certain Liam at the quarry that his original intention was to become an ophthalmologist and open his own optometric practice, treating veterans with low vision."

"Is that so?" Xelvok said, raising an eyebrow behind his mask. "What prevented him from achieving this all-encompassing goal?"

"Financial difficulty, Lord Cazar. He worked as a miner to save money for medical residency to obtain his surgical license. To all intents and purposes, he seemed quite harmless and avoided conflict. I think—"

"Kaimo de Morté is a traitor to his father and the empire," Xelvok interjected, throwing the dossier on a desk. "He is an accomplice to the resistance and shall be dealt with no differently from any other dissident. I want him found immediately. Reconnoiter land, sea, and sky. Search every city and town for the infamous doctor. Leave no stone unturned."

"Forgive me for asking, My Lord, but will you not honor us with your presence?"

"I will join the fleet when Iron Cloud is repaired. Until then, I want every available soldier scouring the firmament. All of Zykard. Bring him to me...alive."

III
Remembrance

The following day, Kaimo told Zylpha everything that had happened after his apparent death back in Enbertum. After bringing her up to speed, he officially introduced her to Bartholomew, as well as the crew. And though it pained him, she met his mother, who was engaged in other matters but took the time to speak with her son's lover. Zylpha was especially happy to see the professor, embracing him.

By midafternoon, *Stormguard* passed over ancient castle ruins blanketed by detritus and landed in Faraheydein's southernmost town known as Weneghen. With the exception of snow, it reminded Kaimo of Icdarus. Most citizens there resented imperialists and gladly kept quiet about the insurgents among them.

Kaimo and his company escorted Edgar to the town's crematory for cremation. Out of respect, his remains were put in an urn and given to Bartholomew. They labeled it: *Edgar lu Vogmorton a.k.a. Master.* Gathering together at the old cemetery, the insurgents shared a moment's silence.

"Let us remember the wonderful life of Edgar lu Vogmorton," Kaimo said, breaking the stillness. "He was a gregarious man, always retaining his sangfroid. When all seemed lost, he took me in—a mere stranger—and helped me get back on my feet. In such a short time, he became my best friend and brother-in-arms."

Kaimo paused, glancing at his partner and close friends.

"Edgar wasn't just a private eye handling any investigation to earn qauras," he went on. "He was a wealthy man with a noble lineage. Regardless of his riches, he ventured out into the troubled world and risked his life countless times, especially during the Enbertum murders. The dreadful case was solved thanks to him."

He stopped, fighting back his tears, and mustered the strength to smile at Bartholomew.

"Those who were privileged to know Edgar understand what I've said is true. Edgar, you were a brave soul and a true friend. We shall forever keep you in our hearts. We'll continue the fight. The world will be put right again. It may not be today or tomorrow. But rest assured, my wonderous friend, we shall succeed. So, rest easy now, brother. Rest easy."

Despite the forlorn mood at the funeral, Kaimo's friends and fellow insurgents clapped at his words. Zylpha embraced him, feeling his pain. Even his mother comforted him with a hug. It took all his willpower to remain composed, hiding the tsunami of emotions that ebbed and flowed through his devastated mind.

"I've thanked Gearstorm so many times," Zylpha

began, "but I wish I could've at least been able to thank Edgar once for saving you."

"Audacious until the end," Marisa said.

"I knew the amiable sleuth for years and even worked several cases with him. Still, I never could have presented such an encomium that extolled his charm and spirit as eloquently as you have expressed."

"Thank you, Professor."

"Indeed, 'twas a fine eulogy, Master Kaimo."

"His spirit lives on in you, Bart," he said, hugging him like a brother. "Let's remember him always."

Bartholomew agreed, standing at the old cemetery with the urn in his hands. He remained in the stillness for the following hour.

Time on their side for a change, the insurgents took advantage of their momentary respite in Weneghen and restocked on vital supplies. The lens-maker purchased optical materials at an emporium, intending to tweak the *Stormguard's* reflecting telescope further. Zylpha would have normally been at his side, but she was helping his mother gather rations for the journey ahead. Having what he needed, Kaimo was ready to rejoin them when he glimpsed a boutique. At the corner of his good eye, he saw something glittery and stopped.

IV
Covert Operations

For weeks, the empire searched the skies for insurgents. They halted multiple merchant ships and passenger blimps, interrogating captains. Yet none could find the rebels. Searching an entire planet was unrealistic, but the imperialists persevered.

In the meantime, Marisa and her fellow leaders spread out with their airships. Most of them hovered above the clouds. When imperials least expected, the rebels attacked and raided military zeppelins. *Stormguard's* carrier-size deck contained half a dozen biplanes—Kaimo and Zylpha shared one and assisted in taking down larger vessels. Zylpha sported tinted, fluorescent goggles with polarized lenses and helmed the fixed-wing plane while her lover handled its weaponry.

"We make a good team, darling," she said.

"That we do!" he responded, destroying a row of turrets without missing—courtesy of his improving skills and hybrid monocle.

"Sweet shooting."

"It's all in the optics."

The insurgents knew when to strike and when to stay hidden. In hiding, the rebels regrouped and formed new strategies against the imperium. In the course of a month, they armed an imperial train and detonated it; they hijacked another zeppelin, using it against the enemy; and they even blew up a court building in Vel-Qatal. They avoided direct confrontation to avoid loss of life, attacking from the shadows at any given opportunity.

Marisa and her leaders were running out of provisions. They regrouped in the northeastern continent of Horbentayle. Their primary goal was to stock up on rations and weapons at the resistance headquarters. Although heavily involved in dismantling the empire's grip on the world, the insurgents did not forget the grand marshal's ambitions.

Professor Briknoll aided them, studying texts regarding the primordial legend of the aether, Ma'vak Zaar, and the mysterious Etherstone. Though his task required extensive research, he was confident that he'd eventually pinpoint where on Zykard to search for the next fragment of the mythical gem.

Kaimo and his beloved occasionally checked on the esteemed scholar but mostly left him alone to his research. The loving couple spent most of their days together to the point of being inseparable. Their feelings for each other rose above the mud of tragedy like a lotus, love and beauty overcoming everything.

On one evening during twilight, Kaimo took her to the airship's aft to watch the half-light of dusk. It was one of those rare days when they could watch the golden suns setting without needing to squint. The scattering light revealed a vibrant sky with an orangey, red tinge and pinkish clouds.

"It's so gorgeous," she said.

"That is the perfect word." Kaimo stared at her, unable to look elsewhere. "I never imagined life would be as colorful as this sky. But it's because of you that my life is so meaningful. I've grown so much, and you make me a better man every day." He reached into his vest and continued, "Most people wait months or even years, but there's no doubt in my mind that you are my soulmate." He went down on his knees, proffering a diamond ring. "Zelly, will you marry me?"

Tears welled in her eyes as she ogled at the ring and then back at him. "Yes!" she sputtered, covering her mouth in utter shock. Realizing her response was somewhat muted, she lifted her arms to embrace Kaimo and repeated herself. “Yes! Yes a thousand times!” Zylpha gave him a heartfelt hug, kissing him with passion. “Je t’aime, *mon âme.*”

“Je t’aime, *mon amour.* So much more.”

“No,” she said lightheartedly, tilting her head. “That’s not fair. Neither of us loves more than the other. We love one another equally.”

Kaimo gave her a warm smile. “I can live with that.”

They embraced again, cherishing the evening together.

By nightfall, the couple had announced their plans to Bartholomew, Professor Briknoll, Marisa, and the rest of the crew. This was uplifting news everybody needed to hear in the midst of a grim war. The wedding was set for the end of the month, which was only two weeks away. But first, they would have to travel to the resistance headquarters, where the marriage would take place.

The northern region where the flotilla hovered over resembled an ashy terrain because of the active volcano. Seismic activity stirred throughout the province. Sulfur gasses rose from the open mountain, a stream of magma sizzling down. As the *Stormguard* and its entourage descended from the black clouds, volcanic ash filled the humid air.

Advancing toward the volcano, Marisa's steam-powered vessel and her colleagues flew directly into the fuming column of smoke that billowed into the gray heavens. Beneath them, a fountain of lava erupted not far from where lifeless trees stood. Severe cracks incrusted the stale, charcoal environment. The mixture of water vapor, smoke, and the dreadnaught's steam blinded onlookers like Kaimo from other bleak details.

Stormguard and its company remained suspended deep within the murky fumes while an armada of imperial zeppelins reconnoitered the barren expanse. The rebels remained calm, the strong, metal hull and rumbling engines of their ships withstanding the searing heat. With great resilience, the crew maintained their positions.

"What in the world are they looking for out here?"

"Patience is a virtue, son. After what we did to Xelvok and the renowned Iron Cloud, they will be searching every grain of dirt for us."

Not long after, the zeppelins changed directions and flew south. When the imperialists abandoned the region, Marisa and her fellow insurgents drifted out of the billowing smoke and turned west. Passing over the desolate wasteland wrought with molten lava, geysers, steam vents, and hot springs heated by geothermal activity, they eventually arrived at much more hospitable terrain.

Beyond the mud domes blanketed by dry lava channels, steep slopes formed into columnar basalts. They rose from empty pockets throughout the intersecting formations of rocky joints. Up ahead, eroded granite sprawled upward like a monolithic tower. Similar to the volcano, a deep mist engulfed the area, along with the surrounding and seemingly endless rock masses that covered the province.

Marisa aligned herself with the steamy spire of columnar basalt. Directly above it, she halted the ship again. *Stormguard* was still detectable in the concoction of natural mist and manmade smog. Kaimo, standing outside on the gunwale beside his fiancée, wondered why they had abruptly come to a full stop, hovering in the middle of nowhere.

"What's mother doing?"

"Maybe we should find out."

"I second that, Mademoiselle," Bartholomew said. "The insurgents are indeed acting most peculiarly. On second thought, I suppose we are insurgents now, too."

"I suppose we are, Bart," Kaimo replied.

Using his hybrid monocle, the lens-maker activated the monocular and zoomed out. He scanned the area for imperial vessels in the haze. A minute later, his mind transitioned from bewilderment into a state of pure amazement as the layers of basalt shifted.

Adjusting the gears on his facial apparatus, Kaimo homed in on the odd movement. Beneath them, the flat summit of granite opened up like an abyss. Billowing steam that, at first glance, resembled sulfur gases mixed with sulfuric acid, consumed the flotilla of airships that descended into the batholith-shaped tower.

"I don't believe it," Kaimo said.

"It's an underground hideout," Zylpha said, slack-jawed.

"Blimey!" the automaton blurted. "These clever blokes astonish me. I must meet with the architect at once."

Kaimo expected to find a cavernous chamber of magma as if he were in a volcano but instead discovered a steam-powered city of staggering proportions. Yet the metropolis wasn't the typical province laid out from east to west or north to south; rather, it was a mechanical construct built from the ground up, stacks of steel rods and beams uniting a multitude of floors.

Buildings stood atop buildings, rising higher and higher like turrets on a castle. One of those metal-strewn ramparts revealed an elongated docking bay for the airships. Marisa and her army docked there, their ships moored and suspended. Kaimo disembarked the catwalk with his fiancée and the automaton. The trio were bedazzled, overawed at the immense headquarters of the resistance.

"Magnificent," Bartholomew said.

"Yes," Kaimo agreed. "Truly incredible."

Zylpha beamed at them while nodding in response.

"It gets better," Marisa said, joining them with an entourage of crewmembers. "I reckon you'll want to see this, my son."

"All right," he replied. "You have my undivided attention."

Marisa signaled the captain who stood in an adjacent control tower; he helmed controls with levers, dials, and a shiny steering wheel whose metallic axis and spokes turned with graceful ease. The city's cogs rotated, resonated, and echoed in a reverberating dirge throughout the gargantuan cavern.

Machinery spun with life and produced dense steam; a power-driven platform cranked skyward. Though it moved in gradual levels, the metropolis elevated all the way to the surface. Within minutes, it stood atop the monolithic columnar basalt, swathed in both mist and steam.

Just when Kaimo thought he'd seen everything, pipe-shaped apparatuses emerged from buildings edging the sprawling city. Each of the jointed limbs expanded and bent to the ground, gripping the earth like crampons. In smooth and gentle steps, the metropolis moved downward. With the exception of Marisa, who looked smug, the adventuring trio stood speechless.

"Welcome to Mystwalker."

Camouflaged in dense steam, imperialists roaming the skies would need to get too close to the strange moving phenomenon before comprehending its true nature. One zeppelin, in fact, made that mistake. Moments before the crew discerned what lay hidden in the manmade mist, a salvo of cannons obliterated it. In short, the rebels were safe for now.

Security assured, Marisa took the time to announce to everybody her son had not only officially joined the resistance but that he would also be getting married. With only a week left before the ceremony, preparations were already underway. Invitations went out to the leaders and highest members of the rebel force.

Kaimo was impressed. Although the resistance had formed a council of generals to act as prime ministers, he believed his mother was regarded as the most important of them all. Having time to breathe, he shared his thoughts with Zylpha at a café.

"My mother said she's just one of many leaders of the resistance, but don't you think it's strange how just about everyone is always seeking her approval or following her lead?"

"Women power," she said, winking at him.

In the meantime, Mystwalker trekked the coarse continent of Horbentayle, a vast land whose surfeit of kogal made it an industrial mining haven. It prowled north through the infertile, charcoal badlands for days. Time on their hands, Zylpha and Kaimo explored the mammoth city; they especially liked its booming market district that thrived along grated walkways.

Mystwalker reached a swamp engulfed in a dense fog. The mobile city added to the haze, its bulky and metal apparatuses thumping on the clammy marshland. Nightfall arrived, and a chorus of insects sang with the passing mechanical construct. The pair climbed several ladders to a balcony where the steam and mist evaporated. Holding each other, they watched the moons and a few stars.

"Tomorrow you will be my husband."

Kaimo turned to her, a tingly sensation igniting in his pounding chest. "Second thoughts?" he asked.

"Never, my love."

"I am yours."

"As am I…yours now and always," she added emotionally, kissing him.

The lovers stayed for a while, stargazing. By midnight, they returned to their quarters and unleashed their passion. Unable to keep their hands off each other, they slipped out of their clothes and found comfort under the blankets. Kaimo kissed her breasts. He kissed her fingers, toes, and neck; he kissed every part of her body. Consummating their ardor drove them both to exquisite heights.

The gods had been forsaken long ago by the majority of humanity, and Kaimo recently became a skeptic too, but he made love to Zylpha as if she were a goddess. Her feet pressed against his back. Embraced by warmth, wetness, and a burning sensation foreign to him, he moaned as loud as her. There was nothing awkward about this new, magical experience. Zylpha loved him more for it. Affection blossoming, it became a night they'd never forget.

V
Parley

Back in Vel-Qatal, the grand marshal boarded his repaired warship. The strident turbines roared as he used a catwalk to reach the upper deck, entering the inner rigid structure. Striding a narrow platform, he passed rumbling engines and fast-moving pistons. Xelvok approached the aft of the *Iron Cloud* to where the Zenas Solma was installed.

The spherical device rotated, amplified by a humming resonation. Attached to a cradle mount, identical to a globe, it spun on its axis and metal spindle with unnatural energy that sporadically fizzed. Xelvok tested the temporal engine to ensure it still worked when he heard footsteps from behind.

"Lord Cazar," a masked soldier called out as he approached with an entourage of two soldiers.

"What is it, General?"

The imperial officer halted and saluted him. "The Emperor himself has called upon you," he said.

"I will report to His Eminence immediately."

A wave of revulsion rushed through the grand marshal as he vacated the *Iron Cloud's* rigid structure. Outside, he walked across the deck while his warship disembarked from the capital. His black cape flapped in the wind. Near the bow of the vessel, he entered the gondola and reached his quarters at the end of the lower corridor.

Standing before a crystalized contraption, he pulled a lever and dialed a code attached to its diaphragm. The coils around the frame activated and pulsed with magnetic energy, draining kogal. The glassed capsule whirled with ashy residue as the prismatic crystals aligned, spawning a humanoid being none other than the emperor.

Xelvok knelt before him, lowering his head in reverence. "You have called upon me, Your Imperial Majesty?"

"Rise," Emperor Dalfein commanded. As the grand marshal rose to his feet, the emperor continued, "News has spread fast that the Immortal Empire has weakened, allowing insurgents to run amuck."

"Their tactics are novel. But fear not—"

"You disappoint me, Lord Cazar. I've spent decades establishing the imperium. My victory allowed me to ascend into paradise. Where the gods failed, I succeeded. The world looks to me now as their one true God. However, there are still those who resist the new world. I tasked you with finding the misguided dissidents. Yet they have not been dealt with. Instead, my beloved Iron Cloud, which I entrusted to you, has been damaged in a recent attack."

"Forgive me, Your Eminence."

"Of all the houses, you were the only duke I trusted. That is why I chose you to become my Sword as Grand Marshal of the Imperium. Throughout my entire campaign, Iron Cloud was *never* touched. Not a single graze. You have failed me despite such power in the palms of your hands. Errors are contagious, Lord Cazar. If the citizens and denizens of our glorious empire see such flaws, they will question my divinity."

"Your divinity can never be questioned, Sire."

The emperor scoffed. "Even your countenance is filled with weakness. I see it in your eyes. Purge your shame and dispose of those pesky insurgents. Take drastic measures if need be. Supersede their ethics. Now is not the time to be judicious. Use the innocent as bait. Either way, I want them dealt with once and for all."

"I shall not fail you again."

Though hazy within the grainy residue, a cross between disdain and loathe seized the emperor's face. Kogal no longer consumed, the luster of the device's prismatic crystals dimmed, and the humanoid collapsed into a formless pile of ash. Xelvok gazed at the residue through his mechanical vizard, gritting his teeth.

"Very soon, you will see *my* divinity, Emperor. Until then, stay in your celestial abode and rule like a blind fool."

VI
Unity

At the crack of dawn, the camouflaged metropolis left the swamp behind and traversed through a lagoon. Reconnoitering the region, Kaimo sighted a town that stood afar. He clicked gears on the side of his leather harness, turning the monocle into a monocular. Switching from diopters to magnification, he zoomed in on the distant settlement known as Cogbarrow, which was under imperial rule.

Built over a reed-infested lagoon with canals stretching for miles, from his vantage point, all the buildings appeared to float. A grand harbor brought trade to the otherwise isolated settlement whose bending, narrow streets bustled with activity. With several regiments of imperialists stationed there, it was no surprise when the insurgents moved away from it and continued northwest.

Mystwalker advanced to an arid expanse with strangely colorful cacti, a refreshing sight to Kaimo compared with the wet, spongy mires he and his crew left behind. The savannas and grasslands thrived with vibrant cacti, dry shrubs, scattered trees, and crystal shards jutting from the ground.

The city shifted toward another rock mass. Unlike the columnar basalts, the granite protruded from the land like an intrusive monster; the hardened magma plug derived from a volcano that ceased millennia ago. Carved in a manner to resemble an onyx gem, the colossal stone soared like a god among mountains. The clunky, mobile metropolis scaled the rock mass as its summit opened, the city setting itself atop the gargantuan spire.

"You have more than one of those hideouts?" Kaimo said, thunderstruck.

"Despite the camouflage, we can't stay in one place for too long," Marisa said. "It helps us stay concealed from the enemy."

"Absolutely brilliant," Bartholomew said.

Zylpha realized Mystwalker did not descend into the cavernous chamber, "Are we not going inside?" she asked.

"Well," Marisa started with a sly expression, "since we made it safely across and have more than enough smokescreen to camouflage us, I figured why not have a beautiful view for a certain wedding."

Her future daughter-in-law beamed. "You're so wonderful!"

Kaimo smiled too, grateful that his mother was trying to connect with him and his beloved fiancée despite, the resentment he'd shown toward her. The anger that once burned in his chest was waning, but he still didn't understand why she hadn't taken him with her when she'd left so many years ago.

Playing devil's advocate for the sake of being objective, he admitted to himself if life had played out that way, he would have never met Zylpha. In a strange way, he came to terms with his past, instead of letting his mind swim between numerous what-ifs and wishes that he no longer cared to imagine. To end his inner struggle, he embraced reality.

Another night came and went. The suns rose from the horizon. It looked the same as any other day, but it wasn't. Kaimo and Zylpha's wedding day had finally arrived. The groom, bride, and guests gathered together at the crown of their mechanical metropolis. Kaimo wore a pearl-blue tuxedo, while Zylpha dazzled in an off-the-shoulder, white décolleté dress embroidered with silvery sequins along her bosom and ruffles that rolled down to the floor.

The happy couple didn't have a fancy basilica like the imperialists in Vel-Qatal, but they appreciated the mist- and steam-free panorama as they stood on the highest balcony. The twin suns shone on them, and calm breezes embraced the crowd. Marisa walked Zylpha down the aisle as serene organ music played. As best man, Bartholomew stood beside the groom, who gulped in awe when his bride lifted her sheer veil.

"Today," intoned the scholarly professor officiating the marriage, "we are all gathered here to bear witness to a love rarely seen. The secret behind a lasting marriage is not simply attraction but friendship. With genuine companionship, love can blossom and continue to cultivate through the test of time and until death. I stand before you, privileged to say that these fine people deserve no less. Should anyone disagree, speak now or forever hold your peace."

The guests remained silent, their hearts filled with delight and excitement.

"Splendid," the professor said. "Now it's time for those tear-jerker vows." A few people chuckled at his comment. "Rings!" he added.

"Righto!" Bartholomew responded.

Reaching into a pocket, he gave the groom his diamond ring. With great care, Kaimo took it and placed it on his bride's finger. She blushed and presented a wedding band of her own, putting it on him. After a series of *awws*, the crowd quieted down. Now the couple stood together, ready to exchange their vows.

"Kai, you are my best friend," she said between subtle sobs. "You are my world. The light of my life. Pure hope in my darkest hour. A cure to the hollowness that haunted me for years. You saved me when I was a stranger and cared for me when no one else would. You're my eternal star. My everything. No matter what happens in life, I will cherish you forever, *ma chérie*."

"I take it that's a yes?" the professor said.

"Yes!" she responded, sharing a soft laugh with the guests.

Swallowing his anxiety, the groom braced to express his deepest emotions. "Before you, my life was black and white. From the day I met you, Zelly, you brought color to my life. I was a blind man cured. With you, I can see the world as it truly is. I may have rescued you, but you also saved me."

Kaimo paused for a moment, wiping a tear away.

"You are a beacon guiding my way," he continued. "You are a woman of extraordinary measure. My treasure. Together, we will confront the struggle of life. We'll face it all. Good. Bad. Order. Chaos. Hope. Sadness. Happiness. Love. I will stand by your side always. My answer? Yes. Yes to infinity."

"Je t'aime," they said in unison.

"Well, I think that about settles it," the professor said. "With the power vested in me, I hereby pronounce you husband and wife. You may—"

"Kiss the groom!" Bartholomew threw in.

Zylpha grabbed her husband and yanked him to her lips, kissing him passionately. Many of the guests shouted accolades, while others cheered and clapped. Marisa and her fellow leaders threw confetti, and children scattered rose petals. The married couple looked out into the crowd and waved at them, gleaming in the sunshine.

The celebration continued in a ballroom. Musicians played classical music, stirring the guests to dance. Many of the women wore flamboyant, taffeta gowns while men boasted their best suits. Everyone gathered in a circle to watch the bride and groom's first dance before joining the waltz.

"I feel as though I'm ready to gambol."

Zylpha laughed softly. "You dance well, Husband."

"I practiced in secret," he said, gesturing at Bartholomew who, cheekily and unconcerned, pranced alone and demonstrated the most elaborate spins. "Since it seems I've got it down, I suppose you can teach me how to drive or even fly a plane."

"My oh my, you make it seem like we're living in a woman's world."

"I dare say that may be the case *when* my mother wins the war," he said, twirling his wife and smoothly lifting her off her feet. "Many things will change, and that includes a new world for humankind."

"Well, aren't you the feminist," she said, allowing her husband to spin her.

"Jolly good, Master Kaimo! You dance with great *élan*!" Bartholomew said in a cheerful tone, forcing down a glass of wine that simply made his kogal effervesce with bubbles. "I say, this drink raises spirits. Pun intended."

When the waltz ended, Marisa called for everyone's attention by clinking glass with a spoon. "First and foremost, I thank you all for being here. Our morale has never been stronger. But equally important is what this day means to me. Having my son here and seeing him achieve his dreams could not make me happier. Finding love is a rarity in this day and age. Hold on to it, Kaimo. Treasure your wife, because she truly is a gem. I am proud to call her my daughter." She raised a chalice of champagne. "To the bride and groom!"

"To the bride and groom!" everyone repeated joyfully.

"This is the happiest day of my life," Zylpha said, her eyes glassy.

"I don't want to steal your thunder, but it is mine as well," Kaimo replied, wiping a tear from her cheek.

"*Our* thunder," she beamed, winking at him.

United in matrimony, husband and wife danced the night away. Marisa insisted on at least one dance with her son; she also shared one with her daughter-in-law. Kaimo honored Bartholomew with a waltz. The automaton then danced in a circle with children as if he were a tot himself. Delicious cuisines filled everyone's bellies. Harmonious string instruments produced merry music that filled the columned halls festooned with flowers. Guests chatted, shared jokes, and tears of happiness. It was a sacred day that would live on in their hearts forever.

CHRONICLE III

Theoretical Paradox

CHAPTER ELEVEN

Clockwork Alchemist

I
An Aeronaut Born

Though the wedding was over, the bride and groom luxuriated in a few days' respite. As reality would have it, this wasn't a time for them to embark on a honeymoon, but they enjoyed one day at the northwestern beach of Horbentayle. The shore may not have boasted golden sands or cerulean water, but the couple gladly accepted the murky beach. By midafternoon, Bartholomew joined them. He watched them swim until forced to bang sand out of his metal soles, inadvertently kicking a couple of mussels.

"*Excusez moi.*" He inspected the shells, confirming no damage. "I must say, you chaps have quite the muscles with that exoskeleton. No wonder the sea is so strong."

On another occasion, the newlyweds shared an evening on a hot-air balloon that took them above Mystwalker's smog. It would have been romantic if Bartholomew wasn't positioned between the couple, stargazing with his bioptic eye. The automaton at least had the right idea, Kaimo thought. He and his wife shared a warm smile and gazed at the heavens for the remainder of the flight.

For the most part, the couple sojourned in the mobile city and enjoyed every moment they had together. With the mobile city still in hiding and a little more time to spare, Zylpha indulged her husband by granting his wish during their first dance.

First, she taught him how to drive an automobile. Upon him bragging about his new skill to Bartholomew, Zylpha decided to take it up a notch by teaching him how to pilot an aircraft on his own. She started with aerodynamics from a theoretical standpoint. He keenly listened to her and scribbled notes, studying them. When ready, she graduated him to practical application.

On days when Marisa and her crew scouted the northern expanse aboard *Stormguard*, the couple joined them to borrow a biplane. Kaimo disembarked every morning with Zylpha, and each time he returned a better pilot. To him, becoming an aeronaut wasn't as meticulous as his studies in ophthalmology, but it wasn't as straightforward as driving an automobile either. After a few test flights, however, he handled a biplane by himself without crashing.

"Well done, Master Kaimo," Bartholomew said as the aspiring aeronaut vacated the cockpit on the *Stormguard's* deck. "Mademoiselle, you are an outstanding instructor. I considered the idea of an award for your husband, but coming back alive is accolade enough, wouldn't you say?"

Zylpha nodded with laughter.

Kaimo gave the butler one of Edgar's long looks. "Thanks, Bart."

II
Titan

The insurgents continued their strategic campaign against the empire. Several airships disembarked from the main base to ambush military zeppelins patrolling the southern region of Horbentayle. Altered via optical telegraph, the imperium's industrial factory of Gatterstanz sent an armada to investigate the rebel attack. Rebels in the mobile city used the distraction to their advantage and accelerated Mystwalker off from the mountain—near the eastern dunes of Yulfa'qas.

The insurgents rapidly arrived at Gatterstanz, an industrial metropolis mass-producing automatons. No longer holding back, Marisa disembarked the mobile city using *Stormguard*, laying siege to the fortification by bombing an entire sector and blacking out the industrial zone. Despite such a bold ambush, hundreds of soldiers and robots from other sectors prepared for battle. Quicker than the insurgents expected, tanks emerged and took aim.

In tandem, Mystwalker unleashed a bombardment from its turrets. The salvo decimated a dozen tanks. Imperialists nevertheless opened fire, shooting at the rebel airship that withdrew into the heavens. When the *Stormguard* mingled with the clouds, troopers below repositioned themselves and focused counterstrikes on the mobile city. Bullets pierced its thick hull, denting it but not fully penetrating its robust metal.

Satisfied with the damage she inflicted on the empire, Marisa helmed *Stormguard* away from the industrial metropolis. Using clouds to hide, she retreated without incident and regrouped with Mystwalker. The insurgents were about to leave when the ground ruptured; the mobile city staggered.

Aboard the *Stormguard*, Kaimo used his telescopic vision to determine what had precipitated such a catastrophic event. Homing in on the damaged factory, he noted mechanical sectors from the center of Gatterstanz shifting. Gears and cogs clanked in different ways, a cacophony of motorized layers rising and merging together.

"What the hell is that?" he said, horrorstruck.

The metropolis unfolded, frames of buildings and interlocked wheels soaring until they molded into a robotic titan that stood as high as a skyscraper. Had the *Stormguard* not withdrawn, it would have grabbed and crushed the dreadnaught. The steel automaton stepped forward, the land trembling. Its entire stomach revealed a massive rotary turbine, and its glassed chest displayed a heart of liquid kogal.

"Goodness gracious," Bartholomew said. "It's God!"

"No, silly," Zylpha responded. "It's a clockwork machine no different from you. If man can build such a thing, then we can tear it down."

"Are you thinking what I'm thinking?"

"Let's do it, darling."

Despite their overwhelming trepidation, they piloted a biplane and flew off the *Stormguard*. Kaimo aimed and fired at the titan, synchronizing with Mystwalker. In tandem, Marisa signaled her crew to attack. Barrages of cannonballs blasted the clockwork behemoth, but it barely recoiled.

In retaliation, the colossus of Gatterstanz released an optic blast: the alchemical beam devastated a part of Mystwalker. Countless insurgents screamed in hysteria as they witnessed a multitude of their comrades disintegrate. Buildings on the side crumbled, and one of the moving apparatuses blew off.

Zylpha gasped. "This is an atrocity!"

"So many good people lost," Kaimo said, heart-stricken. "Zelly, we need to do something drastic or more will suffer the same fate. Can you get me closer to its chest?"

"I'll try," she said, changing course.

Throttling hard, Zylpha accelerated at full speed toward the mammoth automaton, which attempted to swipe them like an insect. She maneuvered in a smooth summersault, dodging its fist. Kaimo fired his machine gun at the glassed chest. To his astonishment, it failed to shatter.

"Damn it!"

"Did you miss or is it bulletproof?"

"Unfortunately, it's the latter. Must be two tempered and laminated sheets. The refractive index for both coated panes of glass is probably identical. This would explain why it's optically transparent. There isn't a single distortion. Whoever constructed its frame knew what they were doing."

"Should we find another weak spot?"

"I'm afraid there isn't one. The kogal would corrode the metal and clockwork design, so it's contained in the glass heart. We'll need to get close again."

"*What*? Why? Its hand nearly blew us up."

"Bulletproof doesn't mean invincible."

Zylpha sighed with frustration. "You're lucky I love you."

Turning sharply. she flew toward the clockwork behemoth again. As it prepared to swat them a second time, Kaimo opened fire. Thanks to the pilot's skill, the pair evaded certain death. Fighting optics with optics, the optometrist used his monocular telescope to identify the weakest part of the glass, shooting nonstop until it cracked like a spider's web.

He gritted his teeth. "Come on!"

Moments later, other insurgents from the *Stormguard* boarded biplanes of their own and joined them in the fray. They followed Kaimo's lead, attacking the automaton's heart. The titan, however, destroyed several planes with its optic blast. Zylpha nosedived, evading the alchemical beam. Without mercy or reprieve, the massive automaton struck down another three aircraft with its hand. Despite an armada of pilots bombarding it, the interlayered glass failed to shatter.

"That abomination will be the end of us," Marisa said. Witnessing how much firepower the colossal automaton could withstand, she turned to her crew. "Rengis, signal Mystwalker and the others to retreat."

"Aye," he said, leaving the flight deck.

Meanwhile, the titan was mere steps away from crushing the mobile city. Zylpha swung around yet again, enabling her husband to unleash another magazine of bullets. This time, the robot's swipe was so robust that currents of wind tossed their biplane aside. Zylpha struggled to regain control, careening from left to right. Descending a couple of miles, she balanced the aircraft and breathed heavily.

"*Okey-dokey...*I'm not doing *that* again."

"Good idea," he said, his heart palpitating as he reloaded. "We'll need to figure something el—"

"Leave it to me, Master Kaimo!" the butler announced. "Kamikaze style!"

Piloting his own biplane, Bartholomew flew past them at maximum speed. He zoomed by so fast that even Zylpha was caught off guard. Sharing shocked gasps, they watched him fly directly into the titan's heart. Crashing through the glass, Bartholomew propelled inside as his plane exploded.

"Bart!" Kaimo cried out. "*No!*"

Dark green kogal poured from its punctured

heart, staining the sand beneath its brass feet. The titan emitted a mechanical dirge that resonated like a straining groan. Steam billowed from its jointed fingers, arms, legs, and bioptic eyes. It then gripped its neck as if choking, falling backwards and crushing half of the industrial metropolis.

"By all the moons," Zylpha muttered, incredulity flashing across her face.

Kaimo panicked, scanning through his monocular. Against better judgement, his wife flew closer to the burning debris. She ignored the few remaining soldiers who still shot at them while Kaimo fired back. As his bullets tore through the troops, he kept hoping to spot Bartholomew. Sensing her husband's anxiety, Zylpha force landed near the titan's remains.

"Bart!" Kaimo yelled as he vaulted from the cockpit. "Bart!"

Zylpha gasped. "Look out!"

Quick as a gunslinger, Kaimo drew his Grimtol and put down three soldiers. Seeing another regiment of troops emerge, he leaned against one of the titan's bent fingers for cover. Zylpha rose from the cockpit, shooting two of them with her pistol. She swooped off the plane and joined her husband, bullets flying their way. While they reloaded their weapons, a pump-action shotgun blasted the remaining imperials off their feet.

"Death cannot court the mighty Gearstorm!" Bartholomew said, his metal frame sizzling but still intact.

"Bart!" Kaimo shouted, elated as he ran over to hug him. "You crazy bastard!"

Zylpha embraced him too. "You did it, Bart! You destroyed the one thing that would've hurt the resistance."

"It was rather exhilarating," Bartholomew said.

"Well, fun time is over. My mother's plan of distraction was calculated to give us just enough time to attack the factory. By now, Iron Cloud and the entire fleet of the imperium must be on their way."

"Don't worry, love," Zylpha said. "I'll get us back."

With Bartholomew gripping one of the biplane's stacked wings, they returned to the *Stormguard* where insurgents cheered them on. Her son safe, Marisa brought her ship back to Mystwalker, at which point the mobile city returned to its nearest mountain base and descended into the cavernous chamber. Within one hour, the other airships returned and concealed themselves.

Though underground, artificial steam vents allowed air to seep inside. Secreted from the imperium, Marisa and her fellow insurgents focused on new tactics and stratagems. And just as anticipated, more than a hundred warships scoured the continent, reconnoitering every nook and cranny in Horbentayle for signs of the resistance. But despite Xelvok's determination, he and his armada failed to trace them.

III
Revelation

Professor Briknoll continued his tedious research in Mystwalker's library. Digging deep into a history spanning over ten thousand years was a mammoth if not meticulous task even for a scholar such as he. One week later, however, Oswald had a breakthrough. The professor summoned the leaders of the resistance. By the next hour, they gathered in the library with him, waiting for him to speak.

The professor cleared his throat. "My sincerest apologizes for the impasse," he said, his voice raspy. "It has taken longer than expected, especially after that battle. However, it seems my research has finally paid real dividends."

"You have a lead?" Kaimo asked.

The professor nodded. "At first, I was at my wits end. To say it has been meticulous and problematic to distinguish myth from historical accounts in the overall mythos herein is an understatement. One parable even claimed Ma'vak Zaar had a doppelganger or that both entities were one and the same. Absolute hogwash! Still, I dug deeper to find one potential truth."

"What have you discerned, Professor?" Zylpha asked.

"For reasons unknown, the knights of old could not destroy the Etherstone completely. Whether it be a will of its own that possessed the heroes to prevent its annihilation, I cannot say. If we stray from myth and focus on the facts at hand, then it's a simple matter of finding the remaining shards wherever they may be. Most seemed to have been found in archeological dig sites and esoterically used to further power our grandiose cities. I have no doubt one of them is Welkin."

"Welkin is claptrap," Marisa said. "We have searched endlessly in the firmament and could never find such a floating castle."

"I have seen it," Kaimo responded. The insurgents stared at him, intrigued. No longer feeling like an oddity among men, he went on, "It's a matter of optics, but within the smog I've seen it. The rumors are true. Hidden as Mystwalker is, it roams the skies instead, and most likely because of the alchemical fragment we seek."

Bartholomew started, "It would indubitably be taxing to locate such a—"

"Apologies for cutting you off, Gearstorm," the professor interjected, "but we can worry about Welkin another time. There is another shard we can search for on Zykard." Marshalling everyone's attention again, he continued, "The tomb of Ma'vak Zaar."

"That legend is as much rubbish as Welkin."

"*Mother.* Professor Briknoll has never failed us. Let us give him the benefit of the doubt."

"I'm sorry, my son. It's just risky committing to this mission when so much is at stake."

"The cards are indeed stacked against us," the

professor said. "But you have witnessed the grand marshal's obsession firsthand at Drenengarde."

"Of course," Marisa agreed. "I lost some of my best men."

"We also lost Master Edgar," Bartholomew said, his voice emulating grief.

Sorrow gripped Kaimo, remembering his friend. "If we ignore this any further, Xelvok will eventually obtain the remaining fragments and reforge the Etherstone. We cannot stand idle in the face of this madness. What say you, mother?"

"Do we even know where to go?" Rengis asked.

"The legend of the final battle against Ma'vak Zaar points to the island continent of Jyu'Bakyi."

Marisa shook her head. "It seems we have no choice. Rengis and I will assist you while the rest of our council remains dedicated to our primary cause against the imperium, as well as to protect Mystwalker."

"When do we leave?" Zylpha asked.

"I reckon now," Kaimo said with resolve.

IV
Primordial Discovery

In agreement, the insurgent leaders embarked on what was to prove a treacherous journey. Marisa and her crew left Mystwalker aboard the *Stormguard.* The steam-powered airship ascended to the clouds, flying north to wrap around the planet and reach the southeastern continent known as Jyu'Bakyi. Geographers often disputed whether it was an island or a continent. Professor Briknoll affirmed it was neither but rather both—an island continent.

Drifting above, Kaimo and his companions hovered over a sunken, volcanic landscape wrought with acidic hot springs, sulfuric ponds, toxic vapor, and sizzling lava. The inhospitable terrain soon turned into dunes that covered the other half of Horbentayle. Dust devils roamed the vast region of Yulfa'qas, a dust storm brewing.

Eventually, the vessel reached the desert's coast and flew over a dark ocean. The crew stared at the sea for days. It seemed endless. Yet, according to Marisa, to avoid passing through Quradale and Faraheydein, this flight trajectory was better. They maintained their course, patient but equally eager to see land.

Two more days passed, and the crew spotted what appeared to be a dot in the far-flung distance. Marisa descended just below the clouds for a better look. Her son stood aft and used the dreadnaught's telescope. Miles away, he sighted a misty island. Adjusting it, he saw more isles interspersed, separated only by shallow water and coral reefs.

Farther ahead, he picked up on something larger. Like the isles, a fog of sorts enveloped the mainland. At first, he couldn't grasp its circumference. But as the *Stormguard* drew closer, Kaimo discerned its size when putting his prototype telescope to the test, its near-astronomical power superseding the diameter of the island continent. Surrounded by the ocean from all sides, it stretched from east to west for at least three thousand miles. If it were an island, it was surely the largest he'd ever seen or heard of in his life.

A white, sandy beach blanketed the nearest shoreline. Here, the water was crystal clear like turquoise with no signs of plankton or pollution. Light from the twin suns reflected on the clear water, showcasing a pure blue ocean. Palm trees garlanded the oceanfront, growing deep into the jungle beyond the tranquil beaches.

"Exquisite!" Bartholomew said.

"You said it, Bart," Zylpha replied.

"When all this is over," Kaimo began, "we'll come back here and experience our real honeymoon."

"That would be perfect, *mon chérie*."

Marisa helmed her ship in gradual descents. The rainforest beneath them flaunted a lush-green wilderness that looked like paradise to the crew. Cascading waterfalls poured into an emerald lake where a glimmering rainbow hung. Kaimo deeply appreciated the natural spectrum of light caused not only by dispersion but also refraction—identical to the prism within his lenses.

Rocky outcrops surrounded the waterfalls, and moss carpeted every nook and cranny in the jungle. Endless clusters of gnarled trees created an illusion that grew on top of each other. Perennial vines hanging and sagging from the branches fashioned an intermingling effect. Vibrant foliage with shades of crimson and violet sprinkled the ground. And animal life freely roamed the tropical biome.

Jyu'Bakyi was essentially the final frontier. But all the same, the empire regulated it like any other place in the world. They controlled Kaal'al, a region of interspersed villages. Kaimo saw the mountainous dwellings where thatched homes stood on top of soaring pillars of onyx and metamorphic schists.

Rope bridges joined the verdant spires, uniting the villages. At the peak of the highest central rock column stood a skyport. Fortunately for the insurgents, there were no zeppelins. Imperialists, however, spotted their vessel and grew suspicious. When the ship flew overhead, the general realized it wasn't a merchant vessel and used a kogal-powered machine to initiate an emergency distress signal.

Deeper inland, the villages came to an end. *Stormguard* strayed from the sleek, towering spires, drifting above Mula'nandis—luxuriant mountains that ranged from vertical peaks to nappes, rock layers folding back on themselves. Tetragonal crystals jutted out like pillars, and partially uprooted trees leaned toward a pit where the kaleidoscopic spring resembled a sunken ring of seething decoctions.

Beyond the mountains of Mula'nandis, the insurgents crossed a region of soft and lush hills. The grassy, conical, and dome-shaped mounds appeared manmade but were as natural as the blue sky. The knolls rolled for miles, gradually lowering to a flat sward.

One more mountain stood ahead, its summit as high as where *Stormguard* drifted. The crew recognized it as Mount Windom. Carved like a titan with wings curving inward, it looked ready to engulf a forest blanketed with bluebells. The concealed, enchanted-looking grove wielded some of the lushest vines Kaimo had ever seen.

Homing in with his prototype telescope, the lens-maker examined slabs of stone rooted in the ground, showcasing as if the formation was deliberate rather than by nature. One of them had faint markings etched into it. Farther ahead, he studied a monolithic structure swathed in moss. Despite his powerful magnification, the plushy and velvety flora prevented him from seeing finer details.

"I found something!" he announced, pointing northeast.

"What do you see?" Professor Briknoll asked, his voice hinting enthusiasm. His eyes wandered to the independent mountain, where Kaimo had pointed. "If there is a temple or tomb as it is written, then that location is as good as any to investigate."

"I'll let Marisa know," Rengis said, making his way to the helm.

V
Tomb of the Magus

Stormguard landed in the sward directly below the obscured structure. Marisa had wanted to touch-down closer, but the collection of gnarled trees and rocky growths prevented her. From there, the crew of insurgents disembarked and entered the woods. Zylpha fixed her eyes on the exotic flowers that paved the way, lending the grove an enchanted feel.

The calm wind grazed the adventurers. To Kaimo, it was as refreshing as the clean air. Invigorated, he took a moment to stop and breathe deeply. The insurgents heard a distant creek flowing within the wood-lands. They reached an area where upright slabs of stone rested in strange formations.

"This is definitely it," the professor said, approaching one. "Excellent find, Doctor."

Inspecting it with his facial apparatus, Kaimo studied markings that had faded over the course of millennia.

"Do you see something?" Marisa asked.

The professor let out a frustrated sigh, using a

cheap monocle of his own. "Yes, but the language is either illegible or I'm blind."

"How about you, Kai?"

"I'm sorry, it's difficult for me too. I converted the lenses from diopters to magnification, but even with my monocular at maximum zoom, I can't make out the words."

"You're all buggered because these are not words, but, rather, symbols," Bartholomew said, looking at another with his bioptic telescope. "There are inscriptions on each of the stele. Terribly sorry, though, it is impossible for me to decipher their meaning."

"Can you grasp some of it?"

"I am afraid not, Master Kaimo. However, if you have ink and parchment, I can jot them down and provide everything to Professor Briknoll."

"Hallelujah," the professor blurted. "The automaton is not being facetious. You do impress me, Gearstorm. From time to time, that is…"

"You will find me full of surprises, old chap."

Armed with a quill and paper, Bartholomew went to each stele, writing whatever symbols he was able discern and make out on the weathered stones. It took him a few minutes, but when finished, he gave the parchment to the professor to translate.

Oswald furrowed his forehead, deep in thought. "*Vieux*—my apologies, I need to double translate." He pondered again, his already wrinkled face creasing further. "Blood of old. Rebirth? No. Recurrence. Time unbound. Kindred anew. Let thine soul mend past and present." He stopped, struggling to interpret the remaining words. "Ye hath forged the path. Now, upon happenstance, thou shalt conquer the future."

"Eh?" Rengis muttered, raising an eyebrow.

Hands on hips, Marisa scoffed. "What in the world was that nonsense?"

"'Tis a riddle of sorts," Bartholomew said.

Rengis cursed under his breath. "Leave me to strategies and mapping out plans for an assault against the empire. But riddles? Not my forté."

"Is there nothing more, Professor?" Kaimo asked.

"I can essentially paraphrase it." It took him a moment to decipher the last set of symbols. "Should the world fall into darkness again, let the chosen one's descendent redeem us."

Bartholomew rubbed his metal chin. "Hmm..."

Zylpha felt her heart sink into her stomach, her head spinning. "Blood of old and new," she said, unsheathing an ankle knife. "My past is catching up to me. Whether I accept the truth, I am the kindred in this conundrum."

"Zelly, wait!"

Ignoring her husband, she gently slit the palm of her hand and sprinkled blood on the central obelisk. The aether reacted, an earthquake striking the region. Several insurgents lost their balance, falling on the rumbling soil. Trees toppled. A monstrous, thundering roar filled their ears that sent a chill down their spines; yet no creature or animal appeared. The land cracked and ruptured, splitting open as a mechanical mausoleum rose from the loam.

"Bloody hell," Bartholomew said.

The professor gasped. "By the core!"

"I didn't want to believe it," Zylpha said, her eyes downcast.

"Rengis," Kaimo called out. "Fetch me your wineskin." Taking the bota bag, he poured alcohol on his wife's wound, ripped off part of his shirt, and bandaged her hand. "There now. It shouldn't get infected."

"Thank you, love. But...what if I am the same darkness?"

"Perish the thought," he said, gently placing his hands on her cheeks. "You are not your ancestor. Ma'vak Zaar chose his path. Today we forge a new one for you."

She nodded, his words giving her strength.

"What now?" Rengis said to Marisa. "Shall we enter?"

"That's my son's decision to make," she answered.

"We do not wait for destiny," Kaimo responded, the first to take a step forward. "Destiny waits for us."

The insurgents grabbed branches to use as torches and advanced toward the dirt-filled mausoleum, its metal frame rusted as if concealed underground for thousands of years. Despite such an impossibility to Kaimo, considering its technology, intrigue coursed within him as he entered with his fellow insurgents. Torches lit, they descended a broken staircase that led them to a pitch-black corridor.

Dust filled the musty air. Grains of dirt fell from the fractured, uneven ceiling. Many of the insurgents coughed but carried on. Blazing light on their side, they strode through the grimy passageway and up another flight of old steps. Numerous treads broke upon impact, but the insurgents persevered to the other side.

Atop the stairway, they passed a cracked portal empty of reliefs that had crumbled from age. The insurgents strode through the archaic entrance, finding themselves in a decrepit temple. Ahead of them stood a cracked but intact tomb, guarded by bronze statues wielding swords and shields.

"Gentlemen, and ladies," the professor began, his mouth agape, "we've just made history."

Before anyone else investigated what might be hidden in the sarcophagus, the reverberating sound of a steam engine filled their ears. Cogs and gears behind the walls spun like clockwork. The wired frames of the metal statues twitched. Horrorstruck, the insurgents unsheathed their swords and guns, aiming at the knights of old that sprang to life and shambled toward them.

"What's happening?" one of the rebels sputtered.

In a trice, a knight sliced him in half. The other insurgents fired their guns. Bullets penetrated metal, and the statues recoiled. Still, they shambled toward their prey. Kaimo took aim and emptied the chamber of his Grimtol into one. The mechanical construct twitched and collapsed. Conserving ammo, Kaimo activated his gun's blade, striking the wired frame of another monstrosity.

Putting his newly learned fencing skills to use, Kaimo parried and riposted with athletic prowess. Wielding an épée, Bartholomew fought beside him. Keeping her distance, Zylpha reloaded her pistol and shot at the clockwork horrors. The professor stayed back, letting others handle the battle.

One of the statues beheaded another insurgent. Fury creasing her face, Marisa blasted it apart with her shotgun. Kaimo and Bartholomew struck two more with their swords, causing them to malfunction. Adrenaline pumping, the insurgents reloaded their rifles and shot down the remaining knights.

"Can someone tell me what the hell just happened?" Marisa snapped. "Two of my best men are dead!"

"The design of this place," Rengis said. "The technology..."

"Yes," the professor responded. "It predates our civilization."

"That's not possible," Kaimo said. "We only

invented steam engines and automatons in the last century."

Zylpha grew pale. "Something's not right."

"Something unnatural," the professor affirmed.

"I am as mystified as you lot," Bartholomew said. "But we came for the fragment. Let us search the tomb and be gone from this peculiar place."

Kaimo agreed, focusing on the situation. In front of him lay the tomb of Ma'vak Zaar. It seemed impossible. Fiction on this day—in this very moment—became reality. There were no legends or myths. It was something beyond his comprehension, an epiphany that gripped him and warped his sanity.

"There's no time to cower," he muttered to himself, scaling the steps.

In front of the carved sarcophagus ornamented with faded images of knights, Kaimo heaved open its lid. The concrete slab fell sideways, shattering. Dust rose to his face. He waved it away while coughing and looked down. Gazing at one of the shards of the Etherstone, the lens-maker reached for it. Yet he stopped midway, staring at the primordial skeleton whose deformed skull revealed bone fractures. Dry air escaping, the remains broke apart and collapsed into ashes. Confused and uneasy, Kaimo shook away impossible thoughts, grabbed the shard, and backed away from the tomb.

"I have it," he said, wheezing for fresh air when there was none.

"Then we're done with this insidious place," Marisa said. "Let's go, soldiers."

Zylpha held her husband who softly stroked her pale face. They joined the others, leaving the tomb of unknown horror. The professor was the last to leave. By mere curiosity, he glimpsed into the sarcophagus and squinted at the ashes. Near the splintered skull was a piece of convex glass. Reaching for it, the achromatic object cracked and disintegrated in his hand. He thought himself crazy, wrestling maddening thoughts while sprinting down to regroup with his comrades.

VI
Showdown

The insurgents rushed through the dark, underground corridor. Vacating the mausoleum, relief filled their demoralized spirits as they breathed fresh air again. Kaimo hugged his wife and gently kissed her. Afterwards, as they strode toward their airship, *Iron Cloud* abruptly emerged from Mount Windom, hovering over them.

To the insurgents' dismay, Xelvok and a regiment of fifty imperial troops surrounded them in the rustling forest. Zylpha took a step back, the vivid memory of torture burning into her mind. In tandem, both factions drew their weapons and targeted each other.

Kaimo scowled at the grand marshal.

"Ah, the famous optometrist who escaped certain death," Xelvok said. "I must admit, surviving that fall in Enbertum was quite impressive. More so, your brazen ambuscade at Drenengarde with these bunglers. I commend you for such heroics. Alas, your incredible luck has ended."

"Turn back to whatever dustheap you came from, or I destroy this," Kaimo said, his gun point-blank at the shard.

"Is this the part where I beg you not to?" Xelvok asked, his lips cracking a twisted smile. "It would be rather foolhardy for me to oblige. We both know that the fragments of the Etherstone are indestructible. The knights of old could never truly obliterate it. How they even shattered it into shards is the greatest enigma."

"There's no mystery. If the stone shattered, then its pieces *can* be destroyed. It's only a matter of time."

"Time is on my side, de Morté," the grand marshal said, irked. "In fact, I have become the god of time." He shot a baleful glance at Zylpha, letting out a subtle cackle. "Déjà vu, is it not? Hand her and the fragment over, *Doctor*."

"Or else?" he said, cocking his gun. "You'll grant me a swift execution? That didn't really work before."

"Eradicate them all! But save the merry couple for me!"

The imperialists and insurgents opened fire, taking cover behind trees. Xelvok unsheathed his resonating chainsaw sword and charged Kaimo who shot at him. The grand marshal let out a wicked laugh. Protected by the Zenas Solma, time distorted around him and repelled the bullets.

If reality surrounding Xelvok had not shifted in such an unnatural way, the bullets may have very well killed his intended target. Ricocheting out of place, the projectiles killed both imperial soldiers and insurgents. With no concern for who died, Xelvok lifted his sword and swung with feverish intent to behead his opponent. Reflexes set in motion, Kaimo pirouetted away and struck back with his sword.

"Damn it," Zylpha said, aiming at the grand marshal. Unable to get a clear shot, she targeted other imperialists, assisting fellow insurgents.

Kaimo and Xelvok continued to do battle. Their swords clashed, the reverberating sound thunderous. The sharp teeth of the grand marshal's blade started cutting into his adversary's weapon. Sparks flared and flew all around. Kaimo thwarted his foe and counterattacked. Xelvok dodged, unable to conceal his amused expression.

No longer inclined to find mitigating factors to justify acts of aggression, Kaimo thrust his sword at Xelvok several times. He veered to the side, evading an attack, and riposted again, aiming to amputate his opponent's arm. Evading the grand marshal by a hair, Kaimo pierced his armor with a precise strike but failed to wound him.

"Be warned, Xelvok. I have my wits about me."

"What is this poppycock?" he retorted. "You're nothing more than the rag, tag and bobtail in an abandoned alley. I am the Duke of Enbertum, Grand

Marshal of the Imperium, and Sword of the Emperor. Yet you dare challenge my limitless might? The gall of you!"

The swordsmen maneuvered steel, endeavoring to dismember each other. Courtesy of his optical eye, Kaimo parried and escaped death each time. Blades clanked and resonated, both warriors struggling for the upper hand. Kaimo's fencing skills were an intricate dance, frustrating Xelvok who grunted in defiance.

"Face the inevitability of your downfall, Sword of the Emperor!"

"Time shan't be reversed for you," Xelvok declared, blocking an attack. "Nay. You shall suffer my wrath a thousand-fold!"

Kaimo's remarkable skill kept him alive, but his blade snapped in two after parrying another swipe; the upper half punctured the soil beside him. He cursed and performed a roll to get out of harm's way. Making haste, he reloaded his gun. Xelvok repelled bullets from other insurgents, cutting them down while leisurely advancing on his primary target.

"Reverse this!" Kaimo bellowed, unloading his Grimtol's chamber.

The grand marshal blocked three bullets with his dented shield and cast the others aside by means of the Zenas Solma. The glowing tattoo on his hand dimmed, losing its radiance. Though his power needed to recharge, he strode toward Kaimo to slay him when a monstrous, bellowing roar stung his senses—the same earsplitting roar during the earthquake, when the mausoleum emerged.

"Impossible," the professor muttered, scanning the area. "Could it be a wyvinsaur?"

Everybody winced and ducked as a winged behemoth with purple slit eyes, ivory tusks, onyx horns, and black scales as tough as iron descended upon them. Enraged by the intruders fighting near its nest, the wyvinsaur lifted its razor-sharp talons. Good or bad mattered not. Like an avalanche with nihilistic, ferocious elements that lack a sense of morality, the vicious monstrosity randomly minced anyone in its path.

Undeterred by the emergence of such a creature, the grand marshal struck Kaimo with the hilt of his blade. Xelvok ignored Zylpha's scream at what had happened to her husband. He snatched the newly-discovered fragment, poised to deliver the *coup de grâce* to Kaimo when the incensed beast thudded in his direction. Gritting his teeth, Xelvok withdrew and punched Zylpha in the face, rendering her unconscious. Effortlessly, he laid her over his shoulders and retreated to his airship.

"Zelly!"

Having no choice, Kaimo assisted his fellow insurgents in attacking the roaring beast. Its hardened skin repelled most bullets, but some pierced its scales. The few imperialists still alive retreated with the grand marshal, leaving the rebels to fend for themselves. Using the trees as cover, they aimed for the creature's head and released salvo after salvo until the beast finally keeled over and perished.

CHAPTER TWELVE

Sword of the Emperor

I
Against Time

Despite their victory over the ghastly beast, the insurgents' morale was in tatters. They'd lost many comrades, Zylpha had been abducted, and the Etherstone's fragment stolen. To make matters worse, the *Iron Cloud* had already departed.

"Zelly!"

"Quick!" Marisa shouted. "To the ship!"

Rengis and the few survivors, along with the startled professor, obeyed and ran to the *Stormguard*.

"Time is not against us yet, Master Kaimo," Bartholomew said. "We can still catch the buggers and get your wife back."

He nodded at his noble companion, sprinting beside him.

The crew aboard, Marisa activated the steam engine and ascended to follow the *Iron Cloud*. Many of the rebels prepared cannons along the gunwale while Kaimo, Bartholomew, Rengis and a couple of his subordinates donned aviator helmets with goggles and got into biplanes.

"Let's blow those filthy curs out of the sky," Rengis said.

Zooming across the deck, one by one they flew off *Stormguard*. Despite the imperial dreadnaught being well ahead, the insurgents saw *Iron Cloud* in the distance. Pushing their engines to the limit, they edged nearer. While pursuing the imperials, the clouds changed, growing heavier.

Turbulence struck the planes, forcing them down a few feet. Both airships lost some balance and were thrown off course. Rain pummeled the vessels. Thunder crashed as if to split an escarpment. Lightning fizzed across the dark, gray heavens, all while the ships flew into the heart of the deadly storm.

"Should we retreat?" one of the insurgents asked.

"No," Marisa replied sternly. "This is too important. It may be too late, but I need you to use the last of our kogal to contact Mystwalker. I'm requesting reinforcements. Be sure to give them our coordinates so the flotilla can rendezvous with us."

"Yes, ma'am," he said, leaving the flight deck.

Despite the storm, the insurgents gained on the *Iron Cloud*. Crackling bolts of lightning flashed around them. Thrashing wind shook the planes. Ahead, a massive cloudburst erupted from sky to ocean. A torrent of rain and hail pounded the hulls of the steamships like needles and daggers.

"Shit," Rengis blurted. "This is insane."

Rengis hesitated to fly forward, eventually pulling back to rejoin *Stormguard*. Kaimo, desperate and reckless, accelerated his biplane, opening fire at *Iron Cloud*. Bullets grazed its aft. The vast airship maintained its course, ascending higher and deeper into the clouds. Kaimo pursued it, followed only by Bartholomew.

It pained Marisa, but she pulled out of the escalating hurricane before it tore her vessel apart. Tears of anger and frustration choked her, and she slammed her fist on a control panel. The risk was too great; she had to concede and accept that her engine would implode, killing everyone, were she to follow her son.

"What will we do now, Madam Marisa?" one of the insurgents asked.

"We wait for our reinforcements," she said, her eyes welling. "Hopefully, the storm will have waned by the time they arrive. Until then, it's up to my son."

II
Vengeance

Kaimo flew fast and hard against the battering winds. The voice of reason called out to him—stop this madness—but he rejected it. His ethical oath to do no harm had long been abandoned; the degradation of his tarnished soul no longer mattered.

Putting his newly acquired aeronautical skills to the test, he drowned out the deafening thunder and lightning bolts. He ignored the hammering rain. He ignored hail that threatened to crack his aviator goggles. And he shook away a sudden flash in his ruptured eye, the vitreous hemorrhage worsening and beginning to affect his macular. All he cared about was saving his wife, propelling through the frayed heavens like a rocket.

At maximum speed, shock waves twisted and warped around his shaking plane, at the brink of a sonic boom. Exactly as he'd intended, he approached the *Iron Cloud* from above and initiated a forced landing while opening fire. Soldiers scrambled for cover as Kaimo crashed on the dreadnaught's carrier-size deck. Bartholomew's plane collided with the upper rigid structure, exploding.

Kaimo would have panicked if his companion wasn't an automaton. He doffed his helmet and goggles, leaping onto the deck. Gun in hand, he shot approaching troops. His sophisticated telescope lent him clear vision through the hazy, crazed storm that would have otherwise blinded him.

Imperialists took cover, struggling to see their attacker. By chance, one of them caught a glimpse and took aim. Leaping down, Bartholomew blasted the soldier with his double-barreled shotgun in midair while his hat flew away. Landing hard on the deck, planks splintered beneath his metal feet.

The automaton stood up, pumping his shotgun.

"You made me lose my stovepipe," he announced to the regiment.

The surrounding soldiers opened fire at the automaton. He twitched and recoiled at the salvo of bullets, but he continued to decimate his enemies. Kaimo assisted his comrade from a distance, firing with precision. Moments later, three imperial automatons emerged with Xelvok from the rigid structure.

"These pests are anathema to the empire! Purge them!"

Kaimo's bullets, combined with Bartholomew's shotgun shells, severely damaged one of the advancing automatons. The other two encroached upon the butler and bashed his chest inward. Dropping his weapon, Bartholomew counterattacked with robust punches.

"Come at me, you pansies!"

The lens-maker attempted to help his companion but couldn't get a clear shot as the automatons wrestled. More soldiers emerged. Kaimo cursed, forced to take cover and defend himself against them. Bartholomew, meanwhile, grabbed a robot's arm as it reached out to punch him, whirled around, and flung it off the airship.

"Must destroy," the last one said without emotion, bashing the butler's back with all its strength, his frame denting inward.

"*Bart!*" Kaimo screamed in a tearful outrage.

"Oh, dear," Bartholomew muttered. "I think..."

Cogs and gearwheels spun out of control, gizmos jamming underneath the indentations within crushed metal. Again, the automaton bashed Bartholomew's back. Overpowering him, it dislocated his arms and smashed him until he collapsed, his mechanical innards spiraling madly. Then, the gears stopped altogether.

Roaring at the top of his lungs, Kaimo charged while unloading his chamber into the automaton. Sighting an officer from the side, he punched his helmet so hard that it dented—the gadgetry on the lens-maker's arm whirling—and crushed his teeth behind the visor. Reaching the humanoid construct, he stood toe-to-toe with it and delivered an uppercut with his enhanced arm; its head broke off. Still functioning, it gripped him. Before the metal being crushed him, Kaimo elbowed its body until his mechanical brace no longer worked.

The automaton's gears dislodged and ejected in

all directions. Filled with rage, Kaimo kicked its lifeless frame to the floor. Just when he'd defeated the robot, Xelvok and his imperial soldiers surrounded him. The grand marshal gestured for the soldiers to disarm him and remove his malfunctioned brace.

"It's over, *Doctor*," Xelvok said with a twisted smirk. "Oh, wait. You're not even medically licensed. You're nothing more than a fraud! How fodder for insects has managed to thwart me is another mystery. No matter. Such unheeded actions have consequences. You will observe what becomes of your precious Zylpha."

"Don't you *dare* lay a finger on her, fiend!"

Xelvok let out an amused laugh. "Fiend? That's a new one. Fear not, de Morté. Once the bloodline of Ma'vak Zaar flows within my veins, I'll need not touch your plaything again. Then you can both die together. Take him away!"

III
Coup D'état

The soldiers threw Kaimo into the ship's brig. No longer empowered by the brace, he gripped the bars of his cell and screamed in frustration. Tears escaped his eye. Thinking of Zylpha and her fate, he dropped to the floor in defeat. Hopelessness besieged him, edging him into despair and madness.

In the meantime, Xelvok transmitted a signal via a kogal machine to all imperialists loyal to him. Making haste, he returned to the flight deck and gestured for the captain to step aside. Taking control of the helm, Xelvok ascended *Iron Cloud* out of the severe storm. Above the swollen clouds, he flew his steam-powered zeppelin south.

Each hour that passed, an imperial ship emerged and joined him. By twilight, he had an armada of thirty warships. More than half the entire fleet of the empire drifted through the diffused, pinkish sky with him. Xelvok entered coordinates into the control dial and gave command of his vessel back to the captain. He left the flight deck and walked to the bow where smog embraced him.

Gazing up at the firmament, he waited until evening. In the dusk, he saw an odd distortion. The heavens appeared uneven, two skies overlapping each other. Drawing closer to the eerie phenomenon, Xelvok raised a fist in the air. His gesture notified the captain of *Iron Cloud*, along with the entire flotilla, to ascend toward the firmament.

Xelvok's dreadnaught collided with the twilight atmosphere, which shattered no different from a mirror, myriad pieces of glass falling into the ocean. Soldiers gasped at the sight, unaware of what had transpired. The esoteric location of the emperor's abode was known only to dignitaries in the upper echelons of the imperium, and even they had wondered many times if such a paradise was real—or a fanciful anecdote to strike fear into the hearts of their enemy.

Yet the truth stood before their eyes. Beyond the pseudo, shattered prism of a would-be sky was a grandiose castle hovering within the real heavens, suspended like a gleaming pearl. Crenelated turrets and stone ramparts glistened akin to quartz in the moonlight. The towering battlements soared as high as the central dome-shaped keep. Welkin was so vast, it compared with cities on Zykard's surface.

"Lord Cazar," one of the troops called out, approaching from behind. "His Imperial Majesty wishes to speak with you."

The grand marshal cast a malicious glance over his shoulder and swung his sword in an arc, splitting the soldier's body in half. Others ignored his fate, remaining at their mandated posts while Xelvok strode over to the exit. Before releasing a ramp, he waited for the *Iron Cloud* to align with the barbican's entrance.

When the vessel docked, the grand marshal disembarked. He reached the main gatehouse, where a decorated admiral saluted him. His warm reply was a sword to the chest. In response, guards closed the portcullis. Xelvok didn't even flinch; he simply raised a fist again. Cannonballs from his vessel obliterated the gate. Parts of the fortification crumbled and toppled over guards. Those who still lived in the vicinity stepped aside, letting Xelvok pass.

Scanning for royalists, the grand marshal marched into Welkin's courtyard and made his way toward the main dome. Midway across, a brigade of imperial generals and automatons emerged from the side towers. They met at the square's central fountain where an angelic statue discharged water.

"Lord Cazar," began one of the generals, "I am befuddled. What is the meaning of this attack? What are you doing?"

"Superseding the emperor," he said, thrusting his sword into him.

The grand marshal's crew from *Iron Cloud* sprinted into the courtyard, fully armed and shooting at the generals. As his loyalists battled, an automaton stomped toward him. Xelvok snorted, shooting off its face. It still moved, so he raised his chainsaw sword and cut through the robot's chest until it dropped to the ground, lifeless.

Warships encircled the floating castle, releasing a bombardment of cannonballs at the few drifting ships. Segments of the curtain wall collapsed from misfires, all the more exhilarating for Xelvok. Another wave of troops emerged, taking aim. He strode toward them as the Zenas Solma repelled their attacks.

Realizing bullets wouldn't do the job, a handful of commanders holstered their guns and unsheathed swords. Charging toward the grand marshal, they swung at him. Xelvok parried one attack while raising his shield to block another. Pirouetting, he maneuvered his blade and struck them both down.

With a single thrust, Xelvok pierced the heart of another decorated officer. Swerving to the side, he lacerated his nearest enemy and left him to bleed to death. The last imperialist attacked with caution, but

Xelvok deflected his attacks. Seeing an opening, the commander lunged at him for the kill. Reality distorted and, unbeknownst to him, he found himself three steps back. He stood still, unable to comprehend the surreal event as Xelvok abruptly carved the teeth of his reverberating blade through the commander's torso.

With no further obstacles, Xelvok let his loyalists finish the massacre. Reaching the large giltwood doors of Welkin's keep, he kicked them open and slayed two more guards at the foyer. Leisurely, he went through a carpeted hallway decorated with glittering chandeliers and oil canvases of the emperor's dynasty. Not to his surprise, more imperials emerged.

Xelvok taunted them, painting the walls with their blood. Cleaving every soldier in his path, he was an unstoppable force. The corridor filled to capacity with corpses, the grand marshal reached a portal at the end of the hall and entered the dome's inner sanctum that boasted oil-lit sconces and imperium tapestries. Xelvok ignored the gold-plated sentinels positioned at the upper balconies, sauntering directly toward Dalfein Af Ereganen.

"That is far enough, Cazar," the emperor commanded, seated on his throne atop a flight of marble steps.

When the grand marshal ignored him, Ereganen gestured for his bodyguards to dispose of him. The sentinels aimed their flintlock rifles and fired. His hand glowed, the Zenas Solma repelling every bullet. Lances in hand, the sentinels leapt over the balustrades and landed on the steps. Without fear, they thrust their silvery spears at Xelvok who merely waved his chainsaw sword, cutting off the pointed tips. Then, as with everyone else in his path, he slaughtered them.

"Betrayer!" bellowed the emperor. "I am sovereign! You are my pawn, Cazar! A means to an end under my rule!"

"I'm afraid you haven't been the puppet master for quite some time now," Xelvok said in defiance. "Your illusions of grandeur have come to an end. Pity that you won't be able to witness my ascension to godhood."

The emperor's wrinkled, coarse face contorted. "You wouldn't dare—"

Refusing to hear another word, Xelvok charged

up the staircase. Ereganen sat still, either paralyzed with absolute fear or beyond confident that some divine force in this existential crisis would prevent the grand marshal from his next act. Considering the emperor thought of himself as a god, Xelvok reasoned that it was the latter as he swung in a horizontal motion, beheading the emperor whose head flew off, tumbling down the stairs like a plaything.

At the grand marshal's command, an automaton entered the throne chamber and lifted Ereganen's bloodied body to dispose of it. Meanwhile, the grand marshal grabbed the emperor's head by a lock of hair and brought it over to the pinnacle of a tower, where he hurled it into the ocean.

"So much for being a god," Xelvok said with amusement.

For the remainder of the night, Xelvok's forces swept across Welkin, killing any guard loyal to the deceased emperor. More than half of them surrendered, prepared to support Xelvok's coup rather than die.

As dawn stirred, he gathered the Etherstone's shards together. Onne piece was missing. It had to be here, Xelvok rationalized. How else could there be a castle suspended in the sky? Hunting for the last fragment of the primordial gem, he rummaged through the deceased emperor's private chambers and then checked miscellaneous rooms throughout the ruined citadel. Yet the fragment was nowhere to be found.

Xelvok cursed, thinking hard. The last location to check, he thought to himself, was the throne room itself. He returned to the inner sanctum where he'd slain his former master when he abruptly heard an explosion. Turning around, he went into the courtyard, only to see another fleet of airships emerging. He squinted, his haughty expression replaced with contempt.

"So, you want to be executed today too?" he said aloud, ignoring the fact that every rebel airship in the world was upon him. "Your wish is my command. Let today be the last anyone resists my divine authority."

Returning to the throne chamber, he searched every nook and cranny for the missing shard. Again, the fragment was nowhere to be seen. Incensed, he kicked the throne. It shifted out of place. Raising an eyebrow, Xelvok examined a crevice. A trapdoor lay underneath, inspiring the grand marshal to crack a smile.

Exerting himself, he moved the throne and saw something flickering below. In great haste, Xelvok descended a ladder that led him down into a concealed treasure room. His eyes only fixed on one thing: at the center of the chamber, embedded in the mechanical floor, was the final shard.

"*At last!*"

He removed it from the conduit beneath his feet. Gears, cogs, and rotating wheels screeched. He did not falter at the reverberating dirge of failing engines. Instead, he abandoned Welkin altogether while imperials and insurgents fought for their lives.

Unfazed by bullets whizzing by him, swords clashing near him, or cannons going off, Xelvok returned to the *Iron Cloud*. Exhilaration gripped him as he summoned two automatons and rushed down to the gondola. Entering his private quarters, he seized Zylpha, who lay unconscious, while the automatons lifted the repaired transfusion machine.

They returned to the rumbling castle that struggled to remain suspended. Without delay, Xelvok went into the central tower and descended a spiral staircase. He and his minions entered an underground laboratory littered with instruments, empty vials, and ingredients for alchemy and chemistry. A master alchemist before the war, Xelvok laid out the Etherstone's shards and attempted to restore them while the automatons activated his aether-sucking contraption.

IV
End of the Line

Kaimo sprang to his feet and looked out of the cell. Instinctively, he gripped the bars to bend them but remembered he no longer had his brace. For hours, he'd been hearing gunshots, cannons, and explosions mixed with people screaming. It worsened as time went on, until this moment when the fighting ceased.

"Hello?" he yelled.

Footsteps within earshot, he withdrew from the gate. To his surprise, Marisa, Rengis, Oswald, and several others emerged.

"Kaimo!" his mother shouted with relief.

"Thank goodness," he said, approaching the barred door. "What the hell is going on out there?"

"Utter madness," the professor answered.

"Xelvok has initiated a coup d'état," Marisa explained. "We don't even know if the emperor lives."

"The grand marshal would be doing us a favor if he disposed of him," Rengis said.

"That's not the point," Marisa replied, attempting to pick the lock. "If we don't stop him, we'll have another tyrant ruling over us."

"Oh, is that why you're here?"

"*No*," she snapped, unlocking her son's prison door. "We also came for you and Zylpha. Now, where's Bartholomew?"

"He didn't..."

"Don't say it," Professor Briknoll intervened. "These fine folks have esteemed engineers back in Mystwalker. Myself included. Show me Gearstorm's body and I'll see to it that we get him repaired."

Kaimo failed to demonstrate any optimism.

"Here you go," Rengis said, handing him a new Grimtol.

Hope reemerging, Kaimo nodded and led the way. Reaching the deck littered with dead bodies, he found the disabled butler. Oswald and a few others took his clunky remains to the *Stormguard*. The others disembarked *Iron Cloud* with his mother and strode toward the rumbling castle.

The remaining army followed them, shooting imperial stragglers along the way. Kaimo gazed around the courtyard, stunned to see such an ornamented castle in shambles. Most of Welkin's curtain wall had been demolished, toppled stones on dead soldiers. Three of the four corner towers had collapsed. Worse, one of the imperium's warships had crashed, its splintered deck resting inside the barracks.

"I'll be damned," Kaimo blurted.

"You missed a lot," Rengis said.

"Apparently so. Well, there's no time like the present. We need to find Xelvok and put an end to his abhorrent scheme."

"You heard my son. Let's go, soldiers."

Most of Welkin in ruins, the only place left for them to explore was the keep. Facing fear head-on, the insurgents stormed the inner sanctum. Women and men poured in, guns akimbo. Again, the castle shook. People lost their footing but pressed onward, filling the throne chamber.

Rengis spotted blood stains along the blue cascading carpet. "I guess we don't need to worry about the emperor."

"I'm not sure I can truly believe it," Marisa said.

"But where is the grand marshal?" Kaimo wondered aloud when a woman screamed at the top of her lungs. "Zelly!"

He charged into an antechamber whose portal led to a staircase spiraling down. The insurgents strode into a dim labyrinth that led them to a hidden laboratory, finding Xelvok with two automatons that were ready to imprison Zylpha in the repaired transfusion machine. As everyone had feared, the grand marshal revealed the radiating Etherstone made whole.

"It's over, Xelvok," Kaimo declared, steadfast. "The rebels are victorious. Your empire and remaining loyalists have been crushed."

"You miscreants don't know when to surrender," Xelvok said, displaying a wicked grin on his masked face. "At long last, I have obtained the power of Ma'vak Zaar! Yield and bow before your true sovereign!"

"Nay," Marisa replied. "You're at a dead end. Come quietly and we will resolve your crimes in the court of law."

Xelvok burst into laughter, his intonation more than a little maniacal. "Court of law? Crimes? Such quaint, bourgeois morals from bohemian minds are irrelevant! I have achieved godhood! Behold!"

The gemstone glowed in a shade of emerald, unimaginable power emanating from it. Deep within, Kaimo felt another vibration. An impossible voice whispered to him in an unknown tongue. His chest burned, but not from antipathy. Yet before he could discern its origin, and the truth behind the inexplicable effervescence crackling within him, the Etherstone's hidden essence gripped Zylpha who screamed like a banshee.

Dread made Kaimo's skin crawl. He ran to her aid, but the automatons seized him. Insurmountable power from the reconstructed Etherstone pulsated like a beating heart, putting Xelvok into a trance. To the grand marshal's surprise, Zylpha seized it as if to destroy it while mist escaped its glittery elements and seeped into her skin and bloodstream. For the first time, Xelvok's concealed face creased with confusion; he turned to her, his once smug expression incredulous.

Everybody in the chamber, including the mystified grand marshal, witnessed the alchemical elements of the unnatural gemstone transmute from stone to mist. It lived and breathed with life, flowing into the descendent of Ma'vak Zaar. Her eyes gleamed dark green, and she levitated by means unknown to anyone.

"This cannot be," Xelvok muttered. "I have yet to begin the experiment. It's as if the stone has a mind of—"

Zylpha let out another agonizing screech, so terrifying several insurgents froze. A blast of unknown energy discharged from Ma'vak Zaar's descendent before Xelvok triggered the Zenas Solma. The imperial automatons malfunctioned, while Xelvok and the insurgents were knocked off their feet. Kaimo struggled to stand, the Etherstone's vaporous power holding him back.

"Zelly! You are not the past!" He stepped forward, resisting the gale of slashes from the whispering, menacing mist. "Ma'vak Zaar does not own you!" Taking another step, he added, "We do not wait for destiny. Destiny waits for us! You can fight this!" He roared in anguish, the whipping haze slitting his exposed skin. "Forge a new path!"

"I...can't!" she wailed, the coals in her eyes glistening.

"Don't do it for yourself," Kaimo rasped, straining to keep his foothold. "Don't do it for me, my love." He took one more step, ready to embrace her. "Do it for everybody! For the sake of all humanity! For the sake of the world!"

"Run!" she cried out. "Run, you fool!"

Before he could embrace her, the Etherstone finished its mutation and possessed her. Zylpha's skin crackled and discolored into twilight. She screamed again, alchemical power blasting outward. Kaimo fell and clutched his burning chest, watching his wife levitate and soar through the crumbling ceiling.

Zylpha rose into the sky, vanishing from Kaimo's telescopic vision. She reached the swollen heavens, where her discolored body exploded and morphed into pure aether. Its insidious, gelatinous form was a purple, viscous substance, able to take on any shape or form. It stretched and shrouded the clouds, engulfing them until replaced by miasma.

The atmosphere changed. Lethal elements mixed together to create a deadly concoction, the parasitical aether beginning to consume the world's natural resources. By devouring the natural gasses and chemical aspects of the air and everything in its path, it was only a matter of time before the world of Zykard, and all its denizens, would grow deathly ill.

Meanwhile, in the quaking castle, Kaimo coughed and wheezed. Despite breathing poisoned air, he lived. Xelvok remained on the floor, searching for his mask lost in the rubble. Though the grand marshal found it, the lens-maker had seen his severely burnt features—no doubt a result of failed alchemical experiments—and turned away in disgust. Everyone else lay on the floor, lifeless.

"Mother!" Kaimo shouted, gripping her body. "Wake up!" He checked her pulse but felt nothing. "Mother!" He shook her again and again. "*Mother!*"

Before he could even grasp the true fate of the world, Welkin finally lost its ability to sustain itself. Its mechanical foundations no longer generated a clanking dirge of struggling gears. Instead, the floating castle descended. The survivors, along with many of the dead bodies, flew up to the ceiling in rapid descent, bashing hard against it. They dropped back down as Welkin submerged into the icy waters of Faraheydein's ocean, and that was the last thing Kaimo remembered.

CHAPTER THIRTEEN

Last Epoch

I
Darkness Falls

After what might have been days, Kaimo woke. Although near a roaring fire in a cavern, he was freezing. He groaned, struggling to stand. Using the cave's jagged wall, he rose to his feet and readjusted his monocular telescope to a monocle with diopters. When his blurred vision came into focus, he saw the silhouette of a masked man entering the cavern. The man clad in a military uniform approached, and overwhelming fury filled Kaimo, drowning out the pain coursing through his battered body.

"I'll kill you!" he bellowed, pouncing on Xelvok like an animal.

The grand marshal barely resisted, falling to the rough ground. Kaimo wrapped his hands around Xelvok's neck, choking him. Despite all the inner rage and pent-up hatred within him, the grand marshal's lack of will to defend himself or fight back confounded him. Instead, he looked upon a broken warrior whose campaign lay in shambles. He released him and sprang to his feet.

"Pick up your weapon!" he yelled, his voice echoing. "I can't kill an unarmed man in cold blood. Unsheathe your sword: a duel to the death!"

"There's no point," Xelvok said. "We're already dead."

Kaimo scowled. "What the hell are you going on about? Be a man and own up to your crimes against humanity! The people you killed! Butchered! My father! Edgar lu Vogmorton! My... my wife!" He drew his Grimtol, the lower attachment of the mechanical barrel unfolding into a sword. "En garde!"

"Kill me if you wish. The empire is no longer mine. It's over. I'm done."

Shaken by such words, Kaimo holstered his gun and dared to walk toward the cave's entrance. His eye widened, and another flash momentarily blinded him—the macular in his ruptured eye beginning to tear. He blinked several times and gazed up, his face aghast as his vision partially returned. Horrorstruck by the ominous nightmare that supplanted reality, his emboldened countenance faltered. Gazing skyward, he saw vein-like stems weaving through the clouds where miasma filled the purple heavens.

"By all the gods!" he gasped, absolute terror gripping his mind.

"There are no gods or devils," Xelvok rebutted, joining him. "There is only man in this forlorn existence. But that thing in the sky? That is not manmade. I thought to seize the power of Ma'vak Zaar and claim the throne for myself. Yet the arcane legend has betrayed me. What we see...what we see is something unnatural. It is—"

"Not of this world?"

Xelvok nodded, grimness etched on his face.

"The atmosphere is terraforming. Alas, it is only a matter of time before extinction."

"No," Kaimo said, shaking his head. "The world cannot end. Not after everything we've been through." His nemesis remained silent, at which point he continued, "Something is wrong about this madness."

"What? That we still breathe? Some of the aether flows within me. Just not enough to have stirred the Etherstone. But you? The definitive answer evades me. Maybe because you slept with—"

Kaimo punched him in the face. "She was my wife, devil!"

"Then you tell me, *Doctor!*" he snapped, spitting blood. "It is most certainly *not* magic."

"Magic is unexplainable science for the superstitious mind. I refuse to believe that this is not of our world. It's the result of a demented, alchemical concoction."

"Surely alchemy has played a part in this insanity," Xelvok began, "but the true origin of the aether is not divine or even manmade. Impossible. Never has it been found anywhere in our epoch. Only in…"

Further irritated as his nemesis drifted off, Kaimo grunted. "Finish your stupendous assumption. Is there a solution to this lunacy?"

Xelvok hesitated but eventually responded, "If we are to survive, we'll need to put aside our differences. You want to kill me. I want to kill you. We both wanted to change Zykard with our own ideals. The emperor's substandard demagoguery failed. When his campaign ended monocracy to form the glorious imperium, he fell into a stupor. I was meant to redeem the empire and transcend."

"Redeem the empire? You paved every path with blood!"

"And the insurgents didn't? Both factions have blood on their hands. But enough with semantics. It's all the same. Bottom line: The only hope for our survival is a mere theory that may not even work. For us to consider such an option, we'll need an experimental ordnance on Iron Cloud, and that means trekking the frozen wasteland of Faraheydein."

"Why? Wasn't your ship—"

"Moored at Welkin? Iron Cloud crash landed in the snow. We fell from the sky. Remember? Or did you hit your head too many times?"

"How did I even survive that catastrophe? Don't tell me..."

"The citadel submerged and sank deep into the sea. As you were the only one alive, I swam us to shore."

"I'm going to be sick," Kaimo said, the urge to vomit acute.

II
Greater Evil

With no other choice, lest humanity face utter extinction, the duo left the cave without killing each other. Snow blanketed the arctic region. To the south, they saw hulky glaciers protruding from Faraheydein's frozen coastline. Just beyond it, debris from Welkin remained afloat. Ice-cold corpses bobbed in the freezing water. Believing one of them to be his mother, Kaimo no longer had the inner strength to hold back his nausea, puking on the snow.

"So arresting...this world of emptiness and death."

Xelvok remained silent, turning his attention east. Kaimo wiped his mouth, breathed heavily, and trudged forward with his nemesis. A vista of vast mountains with icy peaks roamed the north, cutting them off from civilization; but for the traveling pair, they had no need to reach Weneghen, Drenengarde, or Vel-Qatal.

Walking east, Kaimo used his telescopic vision and scrutinized the *Iron Cloud*, which had crashed into a mound of snow. Reaching a tundra, their buckled boots thumped against a permafrost terrain filled with lichen. They shivered through the freezing, treeless region caused them to shiver. Adrenaline pumping, they fought off the frost and strode onward.

Courtesy of the hybrid monocular, the lens-maker caught a glimpse of far-flung airships careening out of control. Two insurgent vessels collided into each other, an explosion blazing in the distorted heavens. Such a ghastly occurrence wasn't even because of an attack. Kaimo accepted the true culprit—not a single human could breathe the air because of the changing atmosphere. Galvanized by the horror, he fought off a metallic tang in his throat and maintained his pace.

One mile away from the *Iron Cloud*, the pair stopped as veiny stems in the firmament pulsed, flashed, and fizzed like lightning. Instead of ear-splitting thunder, a ubiquitous screech pierced the air. A bolt of gelatinous energy punctured the snow. The currents metamorphosed into a purplish black viscous of slime that hovered near them, swathed in miasma.

"Steel yourself!" Xelvok bellowed.

Fighting fear, Kaimo drew his gun and shot at the living, breathing aether. His bullets put holes in the eerie substance, but it mended in seconds. It reshaped into a gaunt entity whose elongated, slinky form resembled slimy, branched limbs. Sword in hand, Xelvok charged it and swung in an arc, splitting its lower half. The poisonous fumes choked him, but he roared in defiance, swinging his reverberating weapon, shredding it.

"This can't be real," Kaimo muttered.

The miasma dissipated, its corporeal substance staining the snow. Xelvok paused to catch his breath when forked bolts of energy descended. Striking the land like a web of lightning, purplish flame spewed out from its currents. The duo braced, raising their weapons as the aether split apart. Whether the eerie singularity duplicated itself, neither of them knew.

Defending themselves, the swordsmen boldly advanced toward the miasma and struck at the rematerializing slime. One of the elongated entities slithered around and seized Kaimo, who yelped, trying to break free. It tightened its grip on him. The aether was about to crack his bones when Xelvok shredded part of it, releasing him.

"Withdraw!"

Snatching the chance, the opposing duo broke into a run. Relentless, the aether's essence pursued them. A swelling tidal wave, it flowed over the snow, about to engulf them when something else emerged above—the *Stormguard*. In disbelief, Kaimo watched the steam-powered airship collide with it and explode, disrupting the aether's growing form; but not before Bartholomew swooped down with his shotgun.

"Miss me?" he announced, pumping his weapon and blasting the aether again.

"Bart!" Kaimo cried out, embracing the automaton. "You're all right! Where's the professor?"

"He did not survive," Bartholomew replied, a hint of sadness in his otherwise robotic voice. Hope ebbing away, he noted his companion's dismayed expression and patted him. "We must honor his memory and fight on." He then gazed at the grand marshal and twitched. "Stand back, Master Kaimo," he added, punching Xelvok so hard in the chest that he fell back several feet. "You should not be consorting with one of such dubious character."

"Believe me, I've wanted to do that myself. But we need him alive. The only reason this wretched fiend isn't dead yet is because he claims to have a weapon aboard Iron Cloud that can counter this catastrophic nightmare."

"We have quite the score to settle with this imperial bigot."

Kaimo lowered the automaton's gun. "We'll have our chance, Bart. I assure you. As for now, he stays alive."

"How thoughtful," Xelvok said, sneering despite his painful wheeze. Getting to his feet, he scanned the area and acknowledged miasma descending and encroaching upon them. "We mustn't tarry. If you insist on following me, then come!"

"After you, Master Kaimo."

III
Extinction

The trio left *Stormguard* behind, climbing where *Iron Cloud* had been nestled in the snowy mound. While scaling up, Kaimo heard the sounds of splintering wood and metal. He turned around, only to see the aether engulfing, deconstructing, and absorbing the remnants of his battleship into raw energy. Terror filled him as he struggled to ascend. Bartholomew reached a turbine and gave him a helping hand.

"Thanks, Bart."

The duo let Xelvok fend for himself, but he managed to grip a piece of the ruptured balustrade on the lower deck and lifted himself aboard. Together they sprinted across the wet deck, droplets from melting snow above falling on the planks. Reaching the upper deck, the grand marshal failed to open the iron door leading inside the rigid structure. Bartholomew pushed him aside, tearing off the door.

"Don't expect me to clap," Xelvok said caustically. "Now, why don't you make yourself useful again and activate the vessel on the flight deck while the good *doctor* and I examine the condition of my ordnance."

Bartholomew stared at him for a moment. If the automaton were capable of scowling or cursing, he would have done so. He complied, leaving them behind. Xelvok gestured Kaimo to follow him through the cold and darkened labyrinth of metal pipes, pistons, and gears. Hidden at the center of it all was the Zenas Solma—an enormous temporal engine beyond ingenuity. The duo stepped toward the bulky steel frame, mixed with crystal beams and innards similar to clockwork design.

"Could it truly be? Is this the—"

"Zenas Solma," Xelvok finished as the steam-powered warship activated. "Ah, perfect timing."

"Pun intended?" Bartholomew announced from above.

"What?" he barked, the butler's joke taking a moment to sink in. "Ugh, it seems your automaton is more of a jester than a thinking machine."

"Unlike you, that's what makes him human," Kaimo retorted, drawing his gun on the grand marshal. "Now stop wasting time. Your precious bullet-blocking gizmo is still intact. Show us the weapon that can stop the aether from terraforming our world."

"This is it."

Ire surged up Kaimo's burning chest, creasing his face. "I beg your very pardon?" he said, cocking his Grimtol. "Don't test my patience."

The automaton jumped down, landing beside them. "Shall I break his neck now?"

"Neanderthals," the grand marshal sputtered aloud. "Let me remind you that I made no guarantees coming here. This is a hypothesis. My greatest scientists constructed the temporal engine as an experiment. It reacts to the crystalized key embedded inside my hand." Removing his gauntlet, he revealed the tattoo-like widget embedded in his skin. "It distorts reality...my reality. Such manipulations of physics allow me to bend potential outcomes to my will."

Kaimo sighed with frustration. "Changing the direction of a bullet or placement of a lunging sword is one thing. But what you're insinuating is—"

"Impossible? Just as impossible as a sailing ship flying in the air? How about a walking, talking collection of cogs? Or an alchemical substance capable of obliterating everything on the planet?"

"Hmm...I think the cantankerous bastard's

got you there, Master Kaimo. I dare say even I am stumped."

The optometrist lowered his gun. "So what you're suggesting is, like an ophthalmologist looking through an oculus of lenses to bend light and see what the naked eye cannot reveal via refraction, one must peer deep into the past in order to bend the future?"

"Spoken like a true doctor. Suffice to say, that is the theory. Well, let me correct myself: it has already worked. Albeit, on a *much* smaller scale. I wouldn't be standing here otherwise, believe me. Now, we need only utilize the Zenas Solma on an astronomical level."

"This is getting rather peculiar," Bartholomew said.

Kaimo maintained a skeptical countenance. "How, pray tell, would you even know how far back to go through the looking glass? Because this sounds a lot like having binoculars with occluded lenses."

"Come now, did you think Professor Briknoll only assisted you? He served the empire long before you were born and aided my cause...at least until I attempted to have him killed by the mutilator upon discovering his betrayal."

"You have an insidious answer for everything. Fine. Let us see if such science is fictitious or fact."

"Are you sure about this, Master Kaimo? What if this is an elaborate trick?"

Kaimo shrugged. "To speak candidly, Bart, we're already dead. Let him test his precious theory."

"I knew you would oblige," Xelvok said, perfecting his twisted smile.

With great care, he activated the Zenas Solma's engine. It rumbled louder than the vessel's turbines, resonating with crystallized energy. On the keypad, he inputted a mathematical formula. The power gauge beside the dial was set to ten out of one hundred, but Xelvok flipped it to the maximum output. He then gripped the key embedded in his hand, pressing hard.

"Quick! We must seize one another as though our lives depend on it! And it may very well be so!"

In haste, they clutched each other's arms. Overcoming the repugnance he had toward the grand marshal, Kaimo gripped Xelvok's tattooed hand tighter than anything he'd ever held on to in his life. The engine's distorted vibrations were so powerful that it sounded like a bomb detonating.

"Gods help us," Kaimo blurted out.

"Only we can save ourselves."

"Sod off, you plonker! Master Kai—"

The temporal contraption abruptly bent inward, sucking the trio into what could only be described as a tear in space and time, a void-like aperture. High-voltage energy scrambled through their twitching bodies as their entire surroundings deformed and blurred in chromatic aberration.

Kaimo recalled the excruciating pain Xelvok had inflicted on him when slashing his face and eye. Yet that was nothing compared to the agonizing throbs that coursed through his frail body. He lost track of time and feared this was a trick—an eternal prison of suffering. The world around him shifted and regressed, but Kaimo did not change; through the looking-glass self, he remained in pure agony until the Zenas Solma imploded, vanishing altogether.

CHAPTER FOURTEEN

Bygone Era

I
Chrono-Field

Kaimo screamed in anguish, convinced his body would burst at any moment. Before fainting, he dropped from a rift in midair that immediately sealed and dissipated like smoke. The trio fell into a pool of warm water beside a geyser, its brilliant colors sparkling because of the thermophilic algae. Bartholomew lifted them out of the erupting springs. The swordsmen coughed, barely able to move.

After a moment, Kaimo opened his eye. The twin suns shone, and he squinted as he gazed up at the blue sky. Springing to his feet, he acknowledged Bartholomew's presence with a faint nod and scouted the dusty, humid environment absent of snow and ice. Xelvok eventually joined him, scanning around.

"Where the heck are we?"

Smug as ever, the imperialist pondered how to correct him. "The true question at hand is *when* are we?"

Kaimo dared not believe the grand marshal. In a strange way, he would've preferred to still be in his diabolical timeline; he would have preferred to find another way to destroy the Etherstone and its unbecoming effect on the aether. Bartholomew remained silent without any whimsical statements. Even he, a mere cog once trapped in a cosmic machine, needed to gather his wits.

"Bollocks!" the automaton blurted out. "I don't know about you, Master Kaimo, but that ingenious gizmo left me completely gobsmacked."

"What the hell is going on?" Kaimo demanded, still discombobulated.

Xelvok bent to the ground and clutched grains into his fist. "Akin to the sands of time, we have opened a rift...an arcane passage through time and space by means of the Zenas Solma. This is, beyond a shred of doubt, the very same tundra of Faraheydein, only thousands of years before the aether's descent. We have entered the fabled, renowned days of old."

"The epoch of the ancients?" Bartholomew said. "The time of heroic knights, gallant deeds, and damsels in distress?"

"One and the same," Xelvok answered limply.

"Where's the snow and ice? Why is it warm? If anything, we're in the northern continent of Horbentayle."

"It doesn't work that way," Xelvok snapped. "The Zenas Solma is not a teleportation device. What is this, science fantasy? We used an extremely complex mathematical formula to bend space and time."

"So, in other words, identical to the refractive index, we entered a dimensionless vacuum until the timelines of past and present aligned?"

"Your optometric analogies are amusing. However, this is more than optical frequencies or the phase velocity of light propagating in a medium.

But you do get the point, Doctor. Albeit, there *will* be distortions."

"Bloody hell!"

Kaimo glowered. "Explain."

"Distortions in reality," Xelvok said with a sigh. "Of what magnitude, that remains to be seen. All I know is it's no longer a theory. This is real."

"Can we ever go back?" Kaimo asked.

Irritation creased Xelvok's face. "How can one return to something that does not exist? What has not happened cannot be visited."

"But it *did* happen. We were *just* there."

"It does not exist any longer. That timeline collapsed...the Zenas Solma included. It is scientifically impossible to enter a timeline of prospect. Such a thing called *the future* shall only unfold from our actions today. We have but *one* chance to fix things. Make no mistake about it."

"Such confidence," Bartholomew replied. "Mayhap we have already done this and failed?"

"Bart, you're not helping."

The imperialist gave the butler a sharp look. "Temporal paradoxes are not something I want to dawdle over. We're here. Right now. This is the past.

The past is now the present. What happens in this very moment will determine the true fate of Zykard."

"*C'est la vie…*"

"I am quite inspired, Master Kaimo," Bartholomew replied. "Change the past. Seize the present. Control the future!"

Kaimo sighed.

"That would be exceptional propaganda for the empire if it existed. Alas, we have much to do before such a time. Let us go."

II
Knights of Old

Leaving the geothermal valley of geysers behind, the trio braved the peculiar yet somewhat familiar expanse while searching the gully for life. Hoping to find a village, they instead came across a pack of uy'kaja drinking from a creek. Knowing that such animals were tame, they approached without fear. Unthreatened by their calm approach, the uy'kaja remained in their habitat.

The trio swooped on them, and Kaimo gestured north to see if a town might exist where Weneghen had been erected in his original timeline. Like any uy'kaja, these steeds were as swift as the wind. Wings lifted, the wild animals increased their speed to a gallop. Reaching a gorge, they came across a savannah with paloki trees whose large, upturned mushroom-shaped crowns soared skyward. The captivating trees had multicolored foliage resembling clusters of daggers.

Attracted to the vibrant display, they traversed the expanse until the trees declined and vanished altogether, replaced by a prairie where golden wheat was interspersed with crimson botany. The blood-red flora swayed as the riders nudged their uy'kaja to gallop through it. Kaimo's nemesis and loyal companion followed him without rebuke, hoping to find some form of civilization.

The northern mountains were soon upon them. Despite such narrow paths, they cantered forth and trekked the ridges and cliffs. No matter how high the trio climbed, they encountered no snow or ice. The weather remained warm, cool breezes refreshing them. Greenery welcomed them all around, especially when they arrived on the other side.

In the foothills, farther north, the riders entered a dense forest. Though they had traversed through woodlands before, most regions in their original timeline suffered from deforestation. It was a welcome sight to Kaimo, yet he grew equally anxious when hearing howls that reminded him of veyra'nems.

Luck on their side, they did not encounter any of those violent, sadistic beasts. Though, he wouldn't have been upset if one emerged to eat Xelvok alive. Kaimo perished the thought right away, trying to be the better man. But he wasn't a machine like Bartholomew; anger still burned within him. Knowing his time for vengeance would come at the right time, he suppressed his urge to beat him to a pulp.

The mountains were far behind them, and the woods dwindled. To their surprise, when the steeds trotted out of the thicket, they came across the largest plantation they'd ever seen. Mountainous terraces swept across the verdant countryside. Fruits and vegetables grew in abundance, allowing Kaimo and Xelvok to eat to their hearts content. Before sated, a legion of thumps within earshot alerted them, accompanied by a tumult of voices that, at first listen, seemed foreign.

"*Les voleurs volent notre nourriture!*" one said.

"*Dépêchez-vous avant qu'ils ne s'échappent!*" said another, unsheathing his steel claymore.

It took a moment for Kaimo to realize they were speaking the ancient tongue, which was no longer archaic in this period. Despite his intrigue, the voices sounded enraged. He was about to draw his weapon when a dozen knights mounted on armored uy'kaja surrounded him and his two companions, swords pointed at their throats.

"Interlopers!" one of the armed knights shouted, the lens-maker translating the word in his mind.

Bartholomew cleared this mechanical larynx. "Do not be frightened," he said, speaking their language. "We come in peace." He whispered in Kaimo's ear, "That *is* what they want to hear, right?"

"What manner of beings are you?" another knight asked, staring wildly at not only their masks and clothes but especially the automaton.

"We are human like you. My name is Kaimo de Morté, and this is Xelvok Von Cazar. Oh and this... this is Bartholomew lu Vogmorton. Believe it or not, he was born near a volcano and has skin as strong as molten lava. He's...he's a golem!"

The knights glanced at each other skeptically.

"Where do you hail from?" the leader asked.

Kaimo began, "We come from um...from another continent."

"We have arrived by means of a ship," Xelvok stated. "Regrettably, storms of unnatural proportions wrecked my vessel. Worse, our army drowned."

"Army?" a warrior responded, alarmed.

"Not for conquest," Kaimo clarified. "Rather, to unite as allies against a common foe that threatens all existence."

"What is this hogwash?" the leader said, leaning the tip of his sword against Kaimo's neck, its blade so sharp that a drop of blood escaped. "Do you expect us to believe such rubbish?"

"Perhaps not," Xelvok responded. "But the fact remains we're on a quest to silence the evil at hand. My compatriot here has received a prophecy. The end times are upon us. As fellow knights of nobility and honor,"—Kaimo was never more tempted to shoot him when hearing that last word—"we seek an alliance to defeat the malevolent force."

"Is that so?" another warrior said rhetorically,

on the verge of guffawing. "And just how are we to deal with this...evil?"

"I have *great* power!" Bartholomew said, bending a gun.

"Indeed, and Kaimo de Morté is a grand wizard. Not only—" The knights interrupted Xelvok with a burst of laughter. He frowned but nevertheless went on, "Not only was he the one to receive such a vision, but his magic is our only chance of survival. Show them your sorcery."

Kaimo saw his eyes lower to the waist. Getting the message, he drew his Grimtol and shot a fruit off one of the shrubs. The sound alone frightened the steeds, let alone the knights. One of them was about to attack when Kaimo aimed at the épée and shot its steel. The upper blade blew off and spun into the irrigated soil. Bearing witness to his divine power, the knights dismounted their steeds and knelt before the trio.

"Behold!" the grand marshal said with enthusiasm. "Our savior!"

"I am not the sole protector. Fellow knights, I beseech you to hear me now. The world of Zykard will perish if we sit idle. We must endure. Please take us to your king so we may craft a strategy."

After witnessing the would-be mage's unfathomable power and hearing his words, the leader of the knights found it difficult to deny the potential threat. He complied, allowing the trio entry into their realm—the Kingdom of Weneghen. Making haste, the knights escorted their mysterious guests to a stone-strewed fortress beyond the plantations and village.

Within the castle walls, the heroes strode through a torch-lit corridor. In the regal throne chamber, Kaimo admired the carpet; the abstract patters matched the rounded banners and ornate décor. Elegant windows complemented the inner sanctum's pomp and heraldry, contoured curtains adorning them with embellished motifs and intricate embroidery.

A grand throne of marble sat under a canopy, where the king sat with the strongest of countenances. Everyone knelt with reverence, at which point the knights introduced Kaimo and his two companions to King Frénicle d'Orléans IX. He scrutinized the newcomers from head to toe with a critical eye, particularly their strange faces. After an uncomfortable wait, he gestured for the heroes to speak.

Erring on the side of caution, they maintained their dark tale while sugarcoating the truth with elaborate myths that portrayed them as extraordinary champions.

"We have seen his power, Sire," the leader of the knights said.

"He destroyed my blade with the mere wave of his metal scepter!" one of the others threw in. "He is a true wizard!"

"I, for one, believe his soothsaying," another said.

The king rubbed his charcoal beard, his dark blue eyes fixed on Kaimo. "It is a dreadful tale. More so, your perilous voyage across the infinite oceans." He took a deep breath and drank from his chalice. "Lord Cazar, is it?"

"Aye, Your Majesty," the grand marshal said. "I am king of my own nation. Alas, such evil already destroyed my fallen kingdom. The insidious force marches toward these beautiful lands. I've come seeking an alliance. My wizard and golem are at your disposal. Together with your incredible army, we may stand a chance."

"This does not bode well for the Kingdom of Man. How long do we have before the darkness comes for us?"

Kaimo took a step forward and knelt down. "Your Majesty, regrettably we do not have a definitive timeframe. It comes for us. That, I know and have foreseen. But until that day comes whether tonight, tomorrow, one week, or even a year...we must be ready."

"You can count on my brawns, King Frénicle," Bartholomew said. "Together we shall vanquish such villainy. Then we can drink to our hearts content."

The knights cheered, accepting his words.

King Frénicle, pensive, eventually gave a firm nod. "Very well. Preparations will commence at once, and an alliance shall be formed. In the meantime, Lord Cazar, you are an honored guest in my castle—as well as Magi Kaimo and Sir Bartholomew. Roux Le Sieur! Show them to their chambers."

"At once, Your Majesty."

"Respite is long overdue for such heroes," the king continued. "Tomorrow morning, we shall break bread in the great hall and parley to devise a strategy against the coming darkness so that we may triumph."

"Long live the king!" the knights shouted.

III
Memoir: Discerning Truth

I'm not sure where to begin. So much time has passed. It has beset me with emotions eating at my sanity. This timeline is just another penitentiary. One I cannot escape. Worse, I fear the king is already suspicious despite being more than cordial. Is it paranoia? The lies we told torment me. The truth has been twisted too many times. Yet it is also true that these good people would never believe where and when we are truly from.

It has been several months since our arrival in this timeline. With the exception of Bart, we've been given our own private bedchambers. But the mighty Gearstorm stays with me. Bart basically does not sleep. He keeps watch over everything. As incredible as he is, I fear what little kogal he has to sustain himself will eventually deplete.

Our friendship has been my only comfort in this madness. His presence makes me feel a small piece of my timeline still remains. He is a reminder that we truly did return to the past. One may say we have come from the future. Yet that fiendish imperialist claims one can never visit a timeline that does not exists. I dare say this nightmare is turning into a paradox that can easily make any rational person lose their soundness of mind.

Bartholomew serves the people throughout the Kingdom of Weneghen. Whether it be as a chef, farmer, herbalist, or even a blacksmith, he wields immeasurable skills and is a force to be reckoned with. The people here consider him an artisan. I say that is true in every way imaginable. Bart is not a golem. Nor is he an empty shell of gadgetry. He is not a machine, but rather a gentleman of honor and valor.

I stay away from Xelvok. Even writing his name nauseates me. Yet he is a part of this madness too. Now that the war is out of his hands, he has returned to his original roots as an alchemist. The king eventually provided him with a chamber ti use as a laboratory. He spends day and night in there. I prefer it that way. The less I see of him, the better. Xelvok still has a role to play, but his days are numbered.

But this is a digression. Perhaps this is what writing is all about? I was never one to gravitate toward pen and parchment. Drat, I meant to write quill and parchment. Not very literary of me. I digress again. Alas, during this troublesome time, it is all I can do. That, and reminisce on my old life. Each passing day, precious memories escape me in the way of dreams, as if they never occurred.

At times, I forget to honor the wonderful memory of Edgar. He was honestly the first genuine friend I ever had. Bart is a companion like no other, but he acts more on mathematical formulas incorporated by Edgar. In a strange way, having him is like having a part of Edgar's soul with us. He lives in Bart. Still, there are days when my mind betrays me and I forget my fallen friend. Even my mother.

The treasured moments I shared with Zylpha, however, will never leave me. We experienced a genuine bond of equanimity and trust. I won't forget my beloved wife. If such a day should ever occur, I would not be able to live with myself. I remember her clearly. Her beauty. Her charm and wits. Her strength of character. The friendship we developed. Our perilous journey together. Our growing love and beautiful wedding ceremony.

My wife is gone now. Was she possessed by that monstrous atrocity? Does such a force have a mind of its own? Is it a sentient entity or merely a parasitical force that sweeps across worlds like a mindless storm, eradicating everything in its path?

The ambiguity of the Etherstone and its connection to the aether continues to evade me. Originally, I thought they were separate entities, but now I suspect their origin is one and the same. Two sides of the same coin. The alchemical stone acted as an arcane key.

What if the fragments contained aspects of the aether itself? If it was a prison, Zylpha's bloodline triggered something akin to a proxy unlocking the aggregate. In view of what has transpired, I now realize the aether could have spread and infected others, not just Zylpha.

Surely my wife was not Xelvok's first target. Her mother was a victim too. I'm sure there were others unrelated to Zylpha, which would mean that her heritage is not necessarily tied to Ma'vak Zaar. That notion boggles my mind. Where is the legendary magus in all this madness? Am I too early or late for his arrival in history?

I'm rambling yet again. Somehow, the good people of Weneghen must have been poisoned eons ago. Correction…in this very timeline. Such a venomous substance could have spread like a plague, infecting more than one person. If this is, or rather, was the case, then we must ensure no one becomes tainted by the aggregate. Alas, my theory still does not explain the connection of the Etherstone and aether.

It is my hope to discover answers and prevent the calamity of my timeline. Most important, I live on for Zylpha. She did not deserve such a horrible fate. If we can change the past, perhaps there is a chance to save her. I once said that we do not wait for destiny; destiny waits for us. However, in these unnatural, abstract, and surreal events, we are at the mercy of fate. When will the catastrophic event of the aether begin?

As I wrote earlier, one of my concerns is the king's acuity. I'm fretful he has become suspicious of us during these uneventful months. I fear he is a naysayer and may one day cast aside our soothsaying prophecy. Should such a time come, I will not blame him. It is a miracle that we are still here, treated as nobility.

Conversely, my greatest fear is that Xelvok made a grave mistake when using the Zenas Solma. It was, after all, a simple theory. Back in our timeline, only a handful of people knew the authentic legend of the old world. The professor served the empire before us and undoubtedly aided Xelvok, but his mathematical algorithm was a farfetched venture of extreme risk.

For all I know, we may very well live out the rest of our deplorable existence before ever uncovering the events that led to the origin of the inexplicable aether, and especially the diabolical creation of the Etherstone. But for my beloved

Zylpha's sake, and for the sake of all beings in the past, present or future, I will maintain my resolve. Even if twenty or thirty years pass, I, Kaimo de Morté, shall remain steadfast until the end.

CHAPTER FIFTEEN

Eternal Recurrence

I
FATED TO SUFFER

Kaimo woke in his bedchamber and watched the arrival of dawn. To his surprise, he was beyond tired. Despite sleeping nine hours, he felt as though he'd only slept for two. The suns continued to rise, illuminating the verdant kingdom. Refusing to succumb to his extreme fatigue, he forced himself up from bed.

Approaching a porcelain tub that Bartholomew had filled for him, he splashed water to freshen himself. He donned clean trousers, a white ruffled shirt, and buckled boots before fixing his unkempt hair. Kaimo yawned, ready to join others downstairs for breakfast when knights burst into the chamber, seizing him. Though shocked, he did not resist as they forced him into the hall.

"Master Kaimo!" sputtered Bartholomew. "What in the devil is happening? Should we resist?"

"No!" he said curtly. "I fear we have overstayed our welcome. But—"

One of the knights hit Kaimo with the hilt of his sword, silencing him. As instructed, the automaton did not retaliate. The brigade dragged the duo into a dungeon below and hurled them into a cell where Xelvok already sat. One of the knights, his face distorted with rage, locked the cell.

"I will ask once more: what have we done to deserve such vile treatment?"

Roux tossed the imperialist a look of repugnance. "Your tales are humbug! The lot of you are nothing more than deceivers."

"Lazy thieves!" shouted another knight.

"Indeed," Roux said. "Neither of you performed an honest day's work. In lieu, you created an elaborate tale to sneak into our glorious kingdom and steal our hard-earned food. To make matters worse, you waltzed freely through our castle as if of noble birth. Only your golem proved useful throughout the seasons, but aiding criminals is unacceptable."

"This is a dreadful misunderstanding. Our tale is true, Monsieur."

The knights ignored the automaton, vacating the dungeon and leaving them to rot.

It took a full hour for Kaimo to regain consciousness. The sight of Xelvok turned his stomach. Alas, stuck with his nemesis, he had no choice but to accept his fate. The butler comforted him, indicating food and water that a guard had given them while he'd been unconscious.

"Thank you, Bart."

"I'm always glad to be of assistance."

Xelvok scoffed. "Perhaps you can do something more useful and break us out of this cage."

"No more violence, Xelvok. Your ways destroyed our world. I'll have no part in that. From now on we do things my way. It is evident the king no longer believes us. Nevertheless, we need to prove that we're not a threat."

"We don't need to be a threat. The king can choose to make us suffer indefinitely."

"Then so be it. Be grateful you have your head. King Frénicle could easily execute us. Patience is critical."

The imperialist grumbled. "Sooner or later, you will regret your blundering ineptitude."

II
Fourth Moon

Weeks passed. Kaimo wanted to honor the words in his memoir, but that was no longer possible as a prisoner. In time, he realized a grim truth—actions were always more difficult to execute than writing down fanciful thoughts.

Another month went by. Hope evaporated from his heart, replaced with gut-wrenching dread and crippling anxieties. He conjectured whether they should force their way out of the dungeon. It took all his remaining willpower and integrity to quell such a tempting notion. He was ready to scream in despair, only to be interrupted by the random shrieking of others.

In great haste, King Frénicle d'Orléans IX emerged with his knights. "Magi Kaimo! The darkness! It is upon us!" He glanced at one of his entourage and promptly continued, "Le Sieur, free them at once."

"Right away, Sire."

Roux unlocked the cell, but only Bartholomew moved with grace. The others lay still, lethargic expressions carved on their faces. After all the time that had passed, Kaimo looked as if he was paralyzed, unable to move a muscle. Somehow, he'd started to accept this new reality—an inescapable realm of anguish.

"Is this a joke?" Xelvok grumbled.

"No, Lord Cazar," the king said. "Your wizard was right all along. None of us wanted to believe. What I have done is unforgivable. Still, your allegiance is needed."

"At last, it is our moment to shine!" Bartholomew said, gleaming.

Kaimo shook off much of his torpor and vacated the cell, Xelvok following him. They both shambled like zombies out of the dungeon and went up the staircase. The sluggish pair, along with the invigorated automaton and fearful knights, assembled in the foyer. Upon reaching the giltwood entrance, they shuffled out of the fortress.

"Zykard be damned," Kaimo muttered.

To the lens-maker's knowledge, dawn had arrived one hour ago. Yet darkness swept over the land. Looking upon the black suns revived Kaimo quicker than a bucket of ice-cold water. The double eclipse was not the only nightmare within the darkening heavens. In the firmament, he acknowledged the fourth moon with his monocular.

He quickly reconsidered. It was not the hypothesized fourth moon. From a scientific perspective, he knew deep down inside it would be impossible for a celestial satellite to come into orbit so rapidly—even if he had been imprisoned for weeks. Adjusting the focus to optimize his objective lens, courtesy of the blood moons' crimson light, he saw an approaching asteroid of mass proportions.

"It is an omen among omens."

Before he confessed that the statement he'd just uttered was a lie, the king knelt before him. As he did so, the many knights and nearby noblemen prostrated themselves. They mumbled a phrase that was, at first, inaudible. But their chant-like mantra became clearer as they repeated it.

"Sent by the gods," they said in chorus. "He

is the chosen one. He is the messiah. He is the Ma'vak Zaar."

Xelvok gazed at him, his countenance shattered.

"Sent by the gods to become a god," Xelvok muttered, ignoring Kaimo's pale face. "It is impossible and yet I cannot deny what is happening. Ma'vak Zaar was never a person. It is a title. The messiah. The chosen one. You are the very being I have dedicated my entire life and campaign towards."

"Goodness gracious," Bartholomew said. "Let us dance to becoming a god!"

"Enough! I am *not* a god. I'm not a messiah or chosen one. I'm not a damn prophet, and I am certainly *not* the Ma'vak Zaar. I couldn't be farther from the divine."

"Your modesty is humbling, O wondrous Zaar," the king said.

"Stop. No. I never want to hear that name or title again. I am Kaimo de Morté. Listen to me. Now is not the time for fabricated legends or prophecies. That wretched thing you see in the firmament is very real and coming for us. It will annihilate *all* humanity. We must devise a plan immediately."

"Magi Kaimo," King Frénicle began, "I wanted

to believe your soothsaying words were an elaborate hoax. I had hoped you and your entourage were nothing more than clever thieves, here to steal our food and have a roof over your head without the need for artisanship. But it seems your prophecy bears merit."

Shaken by the omen, Roux approached the messiah. "Why do the gods seek to punish us when we have remained faithful?"

"Faithful?" Xelvok said with a look of scorn. "Such hypocrisy..."

Kaimo shot him a menacing glance. "The gods always test us. That is what true faith is about. We must retain our resolve. What we are witnessing in the heavens isn't just encroaching darkness but a divine message. Without such a warning, we would be ill prepared."

"The malevolent force comes for us," Xelvok said. "But now we know what must be done to preserve humanity."

"So, then the gods are with us?" the king reassessed.

"Indeed they are, my royal chap!" Bartholomew said. "United as brothers-in-arms, we shall do battle and prevail!"

As the knights cheered at his words, a meteor shower struck the entire kingdom. The warriors, along with distant noblemen and villagers, screamed. Kaimo's mind was spinning as he observed the bolides and smaller meteorites descend. Panic setting in, countless people scrambled to find sanctuary, including a few too many knights.

Kaimo remained stock-still, using his telescope. The meteorites were not the threat, he reasoned; rather, it was the massive asteroid entering Zykard's dark atmosphere. It loomed over the world like a raging fireball, zooming across the distorted heavens. Yet it did not land in their kingdom. Instead, it crashed on another far-off continent altogether.

"Jyu'Bakyi," he muttered. "Jyu'Bakyi!"

Cognizant of Faraheydein's fate in his original timeline, particularly the south, he did not need an astronomical telescope or even a wild imagination to determine the aftermath of such a cataclysmic event and its effects on Zykard.

The tropical island continent of Jyu'Bakyi burned as if a nuclear bomb had detonated. A gargantuan impact crater appeared in the heart of the region, and Mount Windom ignited into an active volcano, laying siege to the wasteland with lava, steaming geysers, and split mountains. Worst of all, tectonic plates shifted deep under the planet's crust. Tsunamis formed worldwide, and a crippling blast of gales swept across the ocean.

"This is beyond a nightmare," Kaimo said, losing his composure. "We need to reach Jyu'Bakyi as soon as possible."

"I beg your pardon?" the king replied.

Xelvok understood his former adversary. "Quick, Your Majesty! Rally your forces. We must journey to your kingdom's southern harbor and set sail at once."

"This is madness, Lord Cazar. We need to take shelter."

A tempest unlike any other forestalled replies to the king. It swept across the land, so intense that windmills toppled in the plantations. Knights and villagers lost their balance, falling to the ground. As they recovered their bearings, a cold front hit them.

"Your Majesty, I swear on my life and in the name of all the gods that *now* is the time to act. If we do not leave for the eastern continent, the world will be obliterated. This is our one and only chance."

"I concur with the messiah," Bartholomew threw

in. "And last I checked, gods send messiahs, so..."

He caught Kaimo shaking his head behind the group and left it at that.

The king's expression was grim. "Very well," he said, gloom dulling his rugged face. "Despite the dark magic at hand, we shall leave to find the insidious magus responsible for these wretched fireballs."

III
Origins

Preparations to leave were underway. They gathered emergency supplies for the long journey ahead. Kaimo assisted with the rations, while Bartholomew tended to heavier equipment such as weapons. Xelvok disregarded their plan of action and focused on his own provisions, ensuring he had an ample supply of alchemical materials for the coming battle.

By the next day, the legion was ready.

Mounted on steeds, King Frénicle and four hundred of his knights set out from the fortress. The army traveled south for days. They came across the same geyser springs where Kaimo and his two companions had first arrived in this timeline. Water no longer escaped from the spring, the residual water ice-cold.

The farther south they rode, the colder it was, a biting frost replacing the gentle wind that had once been refreshing. A hint of flurries peppered the legion and surrounding region, then the hint turned into a squall. The king and his knights found this bizarre, especially since their land was always warm.

With wide-eyed curiosity, the king seized one of the snowflakes. "The weather has been peculiar as of late," he said, the particle melting in his gauntlet. "Stories of this phenomenon have merely reached my ears. I dare say the gods are testing us to our very limits."

"Indeed," Xelvok said, the urge to grin acute.

Acknowledging the climate shift too, Kaimo concluded that the massive asteroid was responsible for such misfortune.

"Have you not experienced snowfall, Your Majesty?" he asked.

"Nay, it is a strange occurrence...these flakes."

"'Twas a jolly experience at first, Sire," Bartholomew said. "But now it is becoming rather nippy. The cold does not bode well for kogal."

Kaimo saw the king's perplexed features, no doubt after the robot's last word. "He means his heart, Your Majesty."

"I fear it is the malevolence," Xelvok said, trying harder to play along.

Struggling with the truth, Kaimo was unsure whether he should warn the king that his kingdom would soon succumb to an ice age. He made up his mind, however, when they reached the southern cape where the majestic harbor had transformed into detritus bobbing in a hoarfrost coast. The king halted his steed and dismounted it, gawking at the wrecked quay and swallowed village.

King Frénicle unexpectedly knelt on the permafrost ground as if in defeat. He scanned the remnants of his beloved oceanfront hamlet drift in the high tide, along with an armada of capsized vessels. Only three ships remained intact, one of them aground on the beach.

"What is happening to my Kingdom?"

"Please listen to me very carefully, Your Majesty," Kaimo said in a bleak tone while dismounting from his uy'kaja. Knowing he needed to speak their language in more ways than one, he went on, "I received another vision."

"I question whether I want to hear it..."

"It foretells forlorn changes in weather to all of Zykard, particularly Faraheydein. The Kingdom of Weneghen, that is. The evil will consume this land and turn it into an unreachable and unbearable arctic."

A great many knights gasped at the prediction.

"Master Kaimo," Bartholomew started in a whisper, "perhaps they need to hear some delightful news sprinkled into your, um, prophecy?"

"Yes," he added. "Fear not, valiant warriors of Weneghen. There is hope...for the land we set out to may be cursed now, but our battle will ensure its restoration. I promise you there will be a new paradise. Yet such a utopia will only manifest from victory."

Hope on his side, the king stood up with a stronger mien. "Claude du Blé! Jacques des Cutò! Étienne La Peyrère! Take your regiments back to the capital and inform them of this divination. The outer settlements must know the truth as well. Once you have completed your quest, return to the harbor with my people and rebuild ships to carry you to the eastern continent of this mysterious...Jyu'Bakyi."

"Aye, Milord," they said in unison, leaving with their battalions.

"Magi Kaimo and Lord Cazar," King Frénicle went on, "the rest of my army is at your disposal. Though, with only three vessels, it may be hard to determine our fate across the sea. May the gods guide us to safety."

The king and his forces of some two hundred knights embarked on the three remaining ships. Together with the time travelers, they set sail. Their destination: a once tropical island continent regarded as a hidden treasure of the world—now a volcanic wasteland filled with death.

It took them weeks to traverse the wild ocean. The eclipses ended and, fate dealt kindly, no further storms brewed during their journey. Before a full month out in the empty sea, they saw distant land. Just as they'd feared, the island continent was devoid of life. Mist engulfed the black sands that sizzled with basalt.

For a moment, Kaimo wondered if they had accidently sailed to the northern continent of Horbentayle; however, the split mountains and distinct rock spires farther ahead reassured him that this was Jyu'Bakyi from another epoch. Now, only one thing remained—to find the impact crater.

Reaching shore, the crew moored their vessels and disembarked. Laid out before them was an eerie spectacle. Burnt bones of wildlife littered the coast as far as they could see. Kaimo used his telescopic vision, unnerved to find no end to the devastation. The once wild, lush jungle lay in ashes.

"I want a fort established here immediately."

Listening to the king, his knights built a makeshift stronghold. Obsessed with alchemical decoctions, tinctures, and other miscellany for potions, Xelvok stayed behind to dabble in concoctions to provide greater mental clarity for the coming battle, while Kaimo and a brigade scouted the outer perimeters. Though much of the island was devastated, the outskirts remained intact, including a cave with mineral deposits. On the downside, Kaimo sighted miasma forming. After his reconnaissance, he returned with his group to report to the king.

"The evil hasn't spread yet, Sire. I surmise it is concentrated at the heart of the land. We must travel deeper."

The king's eyes remained downcast. "Very well, Magi Kaimo. We depart tomorrow."

For the remainder of the day, Bartholomew mined resources inside the cavern Kaimo had discovered. He was not an engineer, but as an automaton he understood the fundamental mechanics of his own being and intended to duplicate his physical design. By twilight, he had built a dozen makeshift, wireframed automatons.

"Very impressive, Bart."

"Thank you, Master Kaimo. "They are not as sturdy as I, but they are robust enough if I do say so myself."

"Excellent," the king said. "These golems shall surely bolster our forces."

"We will indeed need such...golems," Xelvok agreed. "They may very well be immune to the aeth—the blight."

The group retired to their tents and rested.

At the first sign of dawn, the army went northeast and trekked the sizzling valley, toward an ominous volcano none other than Mount Windom. An unnatural silence blanketed the region. Skeleton trees and sulfur ponds increased their unease. The stark vale shifted from a smokey gorge to one of miasma. Though not as dense as that in the future, Kaimo recognized it. In the upper crags of the infertile knolls, they came upon a gargantuan hole, comparable in size to the mountain before them.

It was the very impact crater they had been searching for. In the pit itself, aspects of a gelatinous substance took shape, resembling lightning that rose and fizzed fifteen feet high. Though the stifling heat seemed to slow it down, veiny stems manifested around it, expanding the viscous form.

"By all the moons," Kaimo said, his face aghast. "The aether!"

"This is the source, Your Majesty," Xelvok said. "We must vanquish all traces of this monstrosity!"

Bartholomew raised a robust arm. "Golems! Assemble!"

"Is it a demon?" one of the knights asked, horrorstruck.

"Nay," another warrior responded. "I fear it is the foulest of devils."

The king focused on his alarmed army. "Honorable knights of Weneghen, whether this be a demon, devil, or even a cursed god of darkness, the evil plagues our land. And like all evil, we must purge it!"

"Long live the king!" the knights shouted.

"Superstitious fools," Xelvok mumbled under his breath.

"We *ourselves* do not even know its true origin. So long as they fight beside us and vanquish it, they may name it whatever they want."

"Eloquent as always, Master Kaimo."

The knights and metal automatons charged forth, swords in hand. Together, they cut down the stems. Yet deeper within the crater, the toxic miasma choked and killed many of them. In great haste, Kaimo, Xelvok, Bartholomew, and the king made their way down to the central pit.

"Sire," the lens-maker called out, seeing him sway as if inebriated. "I fear the miasma is much stronger in these parts. We have, throughout our quest to slay this evil, acquired a certain immunity. Please inform your knights to avoid this zone at all costs."

"Be careful, Magi Kaimo," the king said, his eyes heavy. "May the gods be with you in this dark hour."

"And they with you," he said, bowing his head.

The trio broke away from the king. Kaimo approached the webbed patterns of purple lightning, and another eerie vibration stirred within his burning chest. An enigmatic voice called out to him; whispers of an unknown tongue surged and spiraled into his mind, mimicking madness. He struggled against it and fell into a stupor.

"Golems! To me!"

Hearing the call, Bartholomew's makeshift robots left the main army and rejoined their creator. A roaring wave of mist stormed toward them. Engulfed in a vicious dust devil of toxin and burning grit, they lifted their épées and struck the ethereal manifestation. Xelvok choked by the plumes of its churning essence, barely able to focus despite his rejuvenating potions. Curtesy of the automatons' resilience as they continuously struck the dispersing miasma, he regained his composure.

Kaimo finally snapped out of his trance, activating the Grimtol's built-in sword that swiveled outward. Rejoining his comrades, he swung his blade at expanding stem-like appendages that splattered and sizzled on the scorched land. They pressed on without respite, arriving at the base of the impact crater. At the heart of it dwelled a discolored puddle. If it weren't purple, they would have thought it the beginnings of a geothermal hot spring.

"What do you make of this insanity?" Xelvok said, his voice gruff. "Do you believe me now? Is it not extrater—"

"I comprehend the gravity of the situation. The parasitical substance cannot sustain itself in such torrid temperatures. Whether it has a will of its own, the fact remains it needs a host to persist like any parasite."

"Could such an organism be a contagion?"

Kaimo tilted his head, staring at the aether. "That's a rather interesting analysis, Bart. I'll put it to the test." Utilizing his monocular to act as a microscope, he switched through interchangeable lenses and homed in on its characteristics. "It is distilled. Weakened no doubt from the heat of the impact and active volcano."

"How do we destroy it, Zaar?"

"Do not call me that again," Kaimo said to the imperialist, his face wrath itself. "Though the temperature has sapped its dormant power, it can still regain itself. And like any parasite or contagion, it must be contained before it spreads as it has already in the future...our original timeline. I recommend—"

The whispering voice gripped him once again; he doubled over and reeled into the steaming puddle. It splashed him all over, a droplet seeping into his eye. Kaimo's hazel iris shifted to a purplish tinge. Frightening pain moved through him, a dark and indefinite wave tackling his soul. He screamed as the sclera around his eye reddened.

"Master Kaimo!" Bartholomew exclaimed, jumping down a molten crag and lifting him out of the lethal puddle.

"You're a clumsy fool."

"Shut your mouth, fiend. I have fewer traces of the aether within my body, leaving me more susceptible to the miasma. You have much more from those diabolical experiments of yours. Lucky for us, there's not enough in your body to stimulate the aether here."

Bartholomew rubbed his metal chin. "What do you propose we do now?"

"I recommend..."—he paused, an unexplainable sensation washing over him—"our presence here is not coincidence. Everything happens for a reason. The past has finally caught up to us."

"Speak candidly," Xelvok said.

Kaimo pressed against his irritated eye. "We have been stuck in an eternal loop that is yet unbroken. It's a paradox. But the key to ending it lies in the decisions we make at this very moment. To prevent the contagion from spreading, we must contain it. We can use wineskins, but they're only a temporary solution. Something else will need to be done."

"You're not possibly suggesting—"

"I am," he interjected. "You were here before, Xelvok. We all were. And now we know why the Etherstone existed. You must create it."

"That is preposterous!"

"You are the only expert in the field of alchemy. We cannot wait for a fantastical hero to appear. That is certainly not me. Whatever the Ma'vak Zaar was thought to be cannot come into fruition. Whether he was once you in an alternate timeline or I in another, the Ma'vak Zaar succumbed to the darkness. You must be the one to contain the parasite before it regains its power and uses our planet as a host to terraform."

"Good grief," the automaton blurted, only to catch himself a second later. "Oh, drat!"

It was difficult for them to accept Kaimo's revelation, but within such madness there was some measure of logic. The fact was that if the aether could not be contained, it would regenerate from the distilled puddle and consume everything in its path. And so, they gathered the aether's remnants in the crater, ready to repeat history despite their growing fear.

IV
Magnum Opus

Returning to the provisional stronghold, Xelvok stationed himself in his makeshift laboratory. Ill-equipped to handle the harrowing task at hand, his artisanship in alchemy compelled him to work. All he needed now was the primitive, formless base of matter to begin his experiment.

The others searched for natural caves throughout the island continent, mining whatever deposits they could unearth. With base metals of chromium, steel, and tungsten, along with the ultra-rare electrochemical kogal, they brought them to Xelvok who assayed them for quality.

Choosing those with the strongest properties, the imperial alchemist smelted them in a pot. As his alloying expanded, he hesitantly poured the aether into the constituents, embarking on the process to sublimate an amalgamation he'd spent his life searching for, only to now be frightened by it.

When twilight arrived, Xelvok stepped out of his tent. "It is done," he said, a lifeless expression on his smeared, pale face.

"Show it to me," Kaimo said anxiously.

Scowling at his former adversary, he revealed the prismatic jewel that glistened.

"Most terrifying," Bartholomew commented. "It is clear I have emotions of my own, lest my cogs would not feel as though they are about to reverse." He paused for a moment. "Master Kaimo, are we to destroy the solidified gem so that the aether remains hidden forever from all existence?"

"No!" Xelvok exclaimed, his voice shaky. "I may have successfully sealed the aether with diluted properties, but it still resonates with power."

"Agreed. As we know, shattering it failed. The empire sprawled like a plague, mining every nook and cranny for resources until the emperor discovered the shards in archeological dig sites."

"I'm going mental," Bartholomew said. "What is the solution?"

"There is no definitive solution. The damage has already been done. No matter how prepared we were, no one could've stopped an asteroid from colliding into our world. That being said..."

"It must be destroyed," Xelvok finished. "However, not as ineffectively as it has been done before. We cannot allow even fragments to remain."

"The volcano! The slimy bugger cannot sustain itself against such temperatures."

Kaimo pressed against his purple, throbbing eye and gave a faint nod. "Yes, we must scale Mount Windom and cast the solidified aether into its depths."

"What if that has been attempted before?" Xelvok posed.

"If we are in fact stuck within a paradoxical loop, such an idea certainly wasn't used last time."

Xelvok grimaced. "Fair enough, Doctor. Let us get this nightmare over with."

V
Fallacies of Grandeur

Aware that the path ahead was too dangerous for the king and his knights, Kaimo and his two companions waited until nightfall to move. When everyone fell asleep, the trio exited the camp on their steeds, leaving the remaining automatons to protect the army. They trekked beyond the crater—toward the looming mountain whose peak exhaled sulfur gasses, streams of magma, and charcoal-tinged smoke that soared into the hazy, midnight heavens.

The sweltering heat gripped them, making it hard for Kaimo and Xelvok to breathe. Even the automaton struggled, his little remaining kogal effervescing, his cogs and modus operandi unable to function as effectively. Still, they advanced as far as they could on their steeds until the animals resisted.

Forced to dismount them, lest they be thrown off, the three warriors pressed on by foot. Steam vents surrounded them. Geysers sporadically spewed magma. Lava cascaded down several ridges and crags. The trio often struggled to avoid volcanic emissions that randomly jutted out.

They would have normally never been able to climb farther because of the mountain's steep incline. Ironically, many of the molten rocks from dried lava created an unnatural path, offering columnar joints for them to clutch; yet they battled to maintain their grip. To fall would mean certain death, even for Bartholomew—the countless spotted pools of sulfuric acid below would rapidly dissolve his frame. When dawn broke, they reached a basalt summit where rocks had collapsed, nearly splitting the vast mountain.

Kaimo stopped, strange compulsions stirring. At first, Bartholomew thought he was catching his breath like the imperialist. But deep within his subconscious mind, a voice called out to him. The vibrations stirred again. Heart pounding and head throbbing, he pressed against his purple eye that leaked blood.

"Are you all right, Master Kaimo? I have noticed you gripping your eye as of late. I dare say it has even changed pigment."

"He is weak and should turn back," Xelvok said.

"No one leaves this mountain alive," Kaimo said, gritting his teeth.

Bartholomew twitched at his strangely aggressive words, particularly his tone. "I beg your pardon?"

"Can you hear it, Xelvok?"

The imperialist raised an eyebrow.

They do not hear me, the inner voice said. *No form of sentience can distinguish my presence lest it be parasitism.*

No longer able to contain the aether within him, Kaimo kicked Bartholomew down the columnar basalt. Xelvok took a step back, unsheathing his chainsaw sword, activating it. The opposing duo stood on the uneven jointed columns, enveloped in fuming smoke.

"At last. The truth is revealed. I must admit this has been lingering in the back of my mind, especially when you had me create the Etherstone. But make no mistake: I consented only because this volcano is humanity's salvation."

"Impart the stone to me," Kaimo said, his menacing voice more monstrous than human.

Xelvok scoffed at its demand. "The question is, when did Kaimo de Morté lose his will? Perhaps at the crater when he fell? Now everything connects. De Morté was not the fabled hero after all. It's actually you...whatever it is you are. You are the true mastermind. The legend itself. The magus. You are the real Ma'vak Zaar."

Baring a venomous smile that rivaled Xelvok's grin, he released the Grimtol's sword and charged forth with vehement swipes. The imperialist parried and riposted with his sophisticated weapon, its reverberating teeth dulling the Grimtol's sharp edge. Veering to the side, the Ma'vak Zaar struck without mercy.

The imperialist deflected his opponent's attacks but kept backing away, careful not to also lose his footing along the columned ridge. At the precipice, Xelvok let out a maniacal laugh: if he didn't fight with all his might, he'd succumb to death itself. Adrenaline pumping, he leapt forth and attacked like a feral animal. His wild assaults caught the Ma'vak Zaar off guard, giving him the upper hand.

Xelvok overpowered the Ma'vak Zaar with consecutive blows. He struck so hard that his sword, as before, shattered the possessed lens-maker's edge. Despite what happened, the Ma'vak Zaar was oddly smug. Raising his bladeless gun, he shot his nemesis. Hastening, the imperialist summoned his mechanical shield, blocking the salvo. Aware the metal shield could only deflect so many bullets, by impulse, he waved his hand in the air and gasped as the last bullet pierced his stomach.

"The Zenas Solma is no more," the Ma'vak Zaar said. "You are now nothing more than a fragile, pathetic human."

Gripping his wound, Xelvok hawked blood. "If we are so pathetic, why possess us?"

"You and your feeble species are a means to an end," the Ma'vak Zaar responded, its distorted voice ethereal. "This specimen, however weak it may be, is nonetheless a necessary pawn for me to amalgamate with the planet. In an amusing way, your ingenious creation of the Etherstone—the trapped essence of my immortal being—is how I intend to feed off the resources of your bountiful world."

"How are you still able to—" he coughed violently, spewing more blood. "How are you still able to control him if you're imprisoned?"

"Cut off a cockroach's head and it still lives."

Ending the exchange, he lifted Xelvok into the air as if by telekinesis and smashed him against the jagged mountain, cracking his bones and skull. He lay dead, the glittering Etherstone rolling several feet away. The Ma'vak Zaar turned to collect the alchemic gem when a synthetic voice shook him to his very foundations.

"Master Kaimo!" Bartholomew shouted, emerging from behind. "Remember what you told Zylpha! You are not controlled by destiny! *You* control destiny! I know you are still there. You are more than the Ma'vak Zaar. Do not let history repeat itself. Fight it!"

The lens-maker convulsed and dropped to the ground, his eye dilating and rolling back into his head as if from a seizure. A surreal vision came to him—the Ma'vak Zaar abandoned the mountain of death with his life—indubitably what had happened in the original timeline. Foam poured out of Kaimo's parched lips. His limbs twitched. His agonizing screams shifted into an earsplitting screech that was no longer human.

"Kill me!" he yelled, teary eyed.

"I cannot commit such a reprehensible act. This is a pivotal moment within the paradox. You must resis—"

"It's too late!" he interjected, his battered body

throbbing and ready to explode. "You are the...only one...Gearstorm!"

Bartholomew shook his head, defying logic for a moment. In that moment, he experienced the closest thing to a genuine emotion. He already lost a master. Losing another would not allow him to function further. Battling against his modus operandi, he defied protocol and let out a sonorous roar.

"*Master!* Remember what you told your wife! Everything we are doing now is for her and for the sake of all life! Fight it! Resist the bloody wanker!"

Kaimo screamed again, tears escaping him. He remembered his wife and saw her vividly in his mind; she sat in the armchair near his bed, smiling at him. He remembered her driving while he defended her for the first time. The perilous trek they had ventured on in Rezekos came to mind, as did the slinky gorges of Bogdar. He reminisced on their first kiss in the barn at Vinestead while stargazing. Like flicking between lenses, his memory of freeing her from the *Iron Cloud* flashed before him. He remembered their vows and wedding. The love they shared could never be broken.

Déjà vu flooded Kaimo as past-life experiences

washed over him. He'd been here myriad times, only to fail again and again. Yet something changed beyond his comprehension. Upon closer scrutiny inside his battling mind, he recognized the vibrations deep in his soul—an abstract strength within his churning blood that had followed him since Icdarus. Akin to a vaccine against a lethal virus, by sheer force of will from time unbound, his spirit had built immunity. Was it love itself? Or something else altogether?

"*Zelly!*" he thundered at the top of his voice, breaking free of the aether's grasp.

The human will is stronger than I thought. Very well, mortal. If you wish to perish, then perish you shall!

Reeling backwards, Kaimo regurgitated a portion of aether that slithered into Xelvok. The corpse twitched and sprang to its feet, a bloodied ghoul. He remembered the puppets in Enbertum and how aether could control inanimate objects—cadavers included. Rolling aside, he grabbed the former grand marshal's sword to defend himself.

"This is it, Gearstorm! Be ready!"

"Ready as can be!"

Kaimo was prepared to fight when the imperialist's corpse levitated. Dread consumed him, his grit ebbing as its purple eyes opened.

"Join your pseudo gods in oblivion!"

The Ma'vak Zaar conjured what could only be described as a fireball, hurling it toward the leaping pair. Flame missed them by a hair. Bartholomew lifted his shotgun, blasting the reanimated corpse while continuously pumping his gun. Seizing the chance, Kaimo primed his bladeless Grimtol and released a salvo of bullets.

"Wretched insects!"

Conjuring lightning, the demented magus unleashed multiple bolts at Bartholomew. The electricity stunned him. Kaimo, meanwhile, reloaded and fired again; the Ma'vak Zaar repelled the bullets with a frost barrier. The lens-maker flinched at such power and wondered how magic could exist.

Taking cover behind several pillars of basalt, he recalled the professor's concept of a superstitious mind. *There must always be a scientific explanation*, he thought. Kaimo assumed that the sentient, parasitical substance—the aether—must be manipulating the planet's elements in a metaphysical way, as an alchemist would with decoctions and tinctures.

Peeking out while shooting between columns, Kaimo noticed the Ma'vak Zaar continuing to hover high above ground and wondered how it was flying without an apparatus. Fear battled with logic. *Distortions within gravity are causing a flux that allows it to remain suspended,* he theorized. Steadfast, the lens-maker used his telescopic vision to see where he'd pierced the ice barrier and fired his gun until it shattered.

"Stop hiding, asshole!"

The fractured particles reformed into icicles and hurtled toward Kaimo. Out in the open with no cover, he winced when Bartholomew pushed him aside, taking the damage without much consequence. Together, the duo kept shooting at the corpse. It suddenly burst, splattering flesh and brains. Then, the same gelatinous energy that had roamed near *Iron Cloud* from the original timeline emerged.

Tossing his gun aside, Kaimo lifted the resonating chainsaw sword and struck its slimy form. Bartholomew repeated his master's actions, using his épée to thrust at the aether. With considerable strength, Kaimo swung his reverberating weapon across the aether's corporeal form, shredding it.

Despite his devastating assaults, globs slithered across the basalt ground, in search of its greater essence trapped in the gem.

"Master, the Etherstone!" Bartholomew shouted.

Conscious of their urgency, he seized it and darted toward the volcano's cave that opened up to a magma chamber. The automaton joined him. Sprinting to the precipice, Kaimo raised his hand over the lava pit. The alchemical stone glowed as a voice called out to him.

We are one and the same. Destroy me, and you destroy yourself.

Kaimo screamed again, his hand shaking as excruciating pain throbbed throughout his brutalized body. Bartholomew took a step back, displaying concern. His head ready to burst, Kaimo remembered everyone he loved and what was at stake: the fate of the entire world was literally in his hand.

"I am but a speck of dust in the eye of the universe! And you would consume it all. As for me, I'll see you in hell!"

His mien undefeated, he hurled the Etherstone into seething lava. As it plunged down, the aether let out a frightened screech that pierced their ears.

The ominous gem melted, its elemental constituents deforming. A bright flash blinded Kaimo, the macular in his ruptured eye separating from his retina. Though affected by this severe visual impairment, he switched to his strongest achromatic lens and rose to his feet.

Kaimo gazed at the lava, overpowering his blurry vision with the aid of his monocular and spotted the decomposing aether. It screeched again in its dimensionless shape. What was once form transitioned into formlessness. Transient like everything else in the universe, it bubbled and twitched within the lava, mingling until magma consumed it.

"Looks like you finally got the bugger, Master Kaimo."

"No," he said, wiping sweat from his grimy forehead. "We did it together." He patted Bartholomew and added, "You know something? You were right all along, Gearstorm. We *are* brothers."

The automaton stared at him, tilting his head as if touched. "Indeed, we are."

A burning pain gripped Kaimo, causing him to gasp. "It's happening. Without the heart of its essence, the remnant of the aether is dying. That means—"

"I understand," Bartholomew intervened, his robotic voice despondent.

"This is not the end, my brother. We shall see each other again. We'll meet once more in the present...the future."

The automaton acknowledged his words, replaying his entire life like a recording. His fondest memories, he conceded, were when he first met Kaimo, who'd convinced his former master to set out into the world. The adventure wasn't supposed to be a wild escapade. He never expected as much; but he was, all the same, grateful for it.

"As our dearest compatriot, Edgar lu Vogmorton would have once said with tremendous pride: *Au revoir!*"

Defying logic to find another master and keep functioning, Bartholomew remained beside his brother who fell unconscious. Moments later, the volcano fully erupted. Magma swallowed them both whole. While the automaton melted, he remembered his brother's words. The end was upon him, but he knew this was not death. Kaimo did not die, and neither did his former master. Where they may have failed in an alternate timeline, if such a paradox persisted or even existed, it had finally been broken. Bartholomew raised his fist in victory; it was the final action of an automaton one could easily argue had a soul.

EPILOGUE

RENAISSANCE

Horror flashing across their faces, the knights of old and their king witnessed Mount Windom erupting. Its magma engulfed the exterior crags, swallowing the columnar basalt. In time, the molten lava reformed into an upwarped mountain with arches on either side that resembled wings curving inward. Though alarmed by such a disaster, when the eruptions died down, the remaining legion returned to the crater and rejoiced that the evil plaguing their world had been vanquished.

Even though the king had heeded Lord Cazar's words, it was the Ma'vak Zaar whom he trusted and respected the most. After all, it was his "prophecy" that enabled them to achieve a glorious victory. And so, they honored him with a tomb. Bartholomew's knights rested there too, charged with forever guarding the temple that would symbolize an extraordinary hero who sacrificed himself to vanquish an unknown darkness.

Thousands of years passed. Zykard and its abundant landmasses changed drastically worldwide. The warm continent of Faraheydein shifted into an arctic region. The ancient Kingdom of Weneghen faded and receded to a backwater town with ancient ruins; but its history regarding the knights of old and their brave king endured.

Over millennia, the historical events gradually evolved into legends and myths. Exaggerated truths and epic retellings of the catastrophic events in the days of old steadily twisted, construed with whispers of magic and divinity. Then, forgotten altogether, the fable was remembered and studied only by academic scholars and professors alike.

The gods were forsaken. Science emerged.

Monarchy fell. An empire rose. A civil war ignited, lasting for decades. Thousands of soldiers lost their lives. One of those brave heroes was a rebel leader named Marisa; a memorial was dedicated to her in ancient Weneghen. Others were lucky enough to retire, such as Gabriel, an imperial veteran, only to pass away years later from old age.

After another decade, the war came to an end. The insurgents had finally defeated the emperor, imprisoning him and executing the Duke of Enbertum. At last, a new prosperous age was about to begin—a renaissance. One man who thrived in such an era went by the name of Kaimo de Morté. He lived a difficult but hard-working life as an optometrist, aiming to study ophthalmology and become an eye surgeon.

In the meantime, Rengis and the remaining insurgent leaders sought to bring political order to Zykard. The world of *man* fell. It was now a world of parity for humankind, men and women working together as equals to reshape the world. In time, with the war over, Kaimo gained enough courage to leave Icdarus and undergo his medical residency at the University of Krenanstein.

Six years later, he became an ophthalmologist. He even received a loan to open his own optometric clinic in the grand city of Enbertum, serving not only war veterans but all people suffering from low vision. As a well-respected doctor whose lenses and eye for catching obscurities was beyond compare, a sleuth by the name of Edgar lu Vogmorton requested his assistance with autopsies from grueling murders.

Naturally, the doctor was introduced to Bartholomew, who wasn't just a fine butler for the esteemed sleuth but also an accomplished automaton with expertise in optics. When the detective went missing after attending a performance at the opera house, Bartholomew sought out Kaimo for assistance to help find his master. The pair requested the aid of an ingenious scholar by the name of Oswald Briknoll to assist them.

Together they searched for clues and eventually put an end to a demented serial killer who'd been mutilating his victims. After rescuing Edgar, all four of them became the best of friends. In fact, Bartholomew connected with Kaimo so much, he volunteered during the day as an optician at the optical emporium; but the eccentric automaton always made it back home in time to prepare dinner for Edgar and tidy up the manor.

All seemed well, and the mundane eventually took hold of the adventurous doctor. Then, on an ordinary day, something unexpected happened. A young lady with blue eyes and curled brown hair that shone like autumn entered the clinic. The eyewear consultants were already assisting other customers, and Bartholomew was in the middle of creating custom lenses for another patient, so she needed to wait a while before being seen.

Doctor Kaimo, meanwhile, had just finished surgery on a veteran suffering from glaucoma. Wearing bioptic goggles with multiple convex and concave lenses attached to its bridge-like gears, he lifted it onto his forehead; by design, the extra apparatuses of monocles tucked themselves along the sides of both temples. Revealing his handsome face, he placed an eye shield on the veteran. After small talk, he saw his patient out.

He stood alone in the lobby, satisfied with the surgery's success. He turned, ready to return to his office when the same young lady who'd been waiting for assistance caught his attention. Her natural beauty and bohemian-style fashion enraptured him. He was unable to take his eyes off her, as if under a spell. No one else available to help her, Kaimo approached to assist his customer.

"Good day," the ophthalmologist said. "How may I help?"

The young lady curtsied. "Hello, Doctor. My name is Zylpha. I heard from several sources how exceptional you are and have a few questions regarding my mother. She's having trouble with her vision."

"Have no fear," the ophthalmologist replied warmly. "At my optometric center, there's a solution for just about everything. We can start with an exam to check for astigmatism. My new reading charts have an array of optotypes. We'll be able to determine her visual acuity right away, including how healthy her retinae are and whether she's affected by presbyopia, far or nearsightedness."

"That sounds like a great start for her. And I beg your pardon, Doctor, but are you an optometrist or ophthalmologist?"

"I'm a surgeon these days, but my partner Bart helps with refractive errors when he's not working in the lab. What you see here at the storefront is the optical shop itself, but we also have a clinic in the back for surgery. Even if she has an eye disease, I offer more than a few experimental—"

"Forgive me," she intervened. "But have we met before?"

Kaimo merely stared at her, lost for words. Yet strangely, he, too, felt something between them. Chemistry, with no pun intended, he thought. She smiled at him, amused by his shyness.

"It's possible, I suppose," he finally said. "But, um, perhaps...perhaps we can make it official over dinner?"

"I would love that, Kai. I mean, *Doctor.*"

About the Author

PAUL L. CENTENO is an award-winning author, born and raised in New York City. As a young adult, he studied at Herbert H. Lehman College where he earned a BA in Philosophy and Creative Writing. After graduation, he worked with Gabriel Packard, Associate Director of the Creative Writing MFA Program at Hunter College, to improve his craft. In 2014 and 2015, he won awards from Writers of the Future for his short stories, *Steamwalker* and *Celestial Heights.* As of 2020, he started receiving auditions from voice actors to adapt his novels into audiobooks. *Coup de Grâce* is his ninth novel.Visit his website at www.PaulCenteno.com.

Lightning Source UK Ltd.
Milton Keynes UK
UKHW020632071122
411784UK00015B/822

9 781644 565063